Also by Dion Baia

Blood in the Streets

MORRIS PI

THE MEN FROM ICE HOUSE FOUR

PI

DION BAIA

PERMUTED
PRESS

A PERMUTED PRESS BOOK

ISBN: 978-1-64293-898-2
ISBN (eBook): 978-1-64293-899-9

Morris PI:
The Men from Ice House Four
© 2021 by Dion Baia
All Rights Reserved

Cover art by Cody Corcoran

PERMUTED
PRESS

Permuted Press, LLC
New York • Nashville
permutedpress.com

Published in the United States of America
Printed in Canada
1 2 3 4 5 6 7 8 9 10

To Helen Grace—thank you.

PROLOGUE

On April 15, 1945, Edward R. Murrow's voice came through the wireless accompanied by an eerie, low-frequency hum that was married to the recording.

"Permit me to tell you what you would have seen and heard had you been with me on Thursday. It will not be pleasant listening. If you're at lunch or if you have no appetite to hear what Germans have done, now is a good time to switch off the radio, for I propose to tell you of Buchenwald. It's on a small hill about four miles outside Weimar, and it was one of the largest concentration camps in Germany, and it was built to last....

As we walked out into the courtyard, a man fell dead. Two others—they must have been over sixty—were crawling toward the latrine. I saw it, but will not describe it.

"In another part of the camp, they showed me the children, hundreds of them. Some were only six. One rolled up his sleeve, showed me his number. It was tattooed on his arm; D6030 it was. The others showed me their numbers. They will carry them till they die. An elderly man standing beside me said, 'The children, enemies of the state.' I could see their ribs through their thin shirts. The old man said, 'I am Professor Charles Risha of the Sorbonne.' The children clung to my hands and stared. We crossed to the courtyard. Men kept coming up to speak to me and touch me. Professors from Poland, doctors from Vienna, men from all of Europe, men from the countries that made America."

Emotion tittered in his voice.

"Murder had been done at Buchenwald. God alone knows how many men and boys have died there during the last twelve years. Thursday, I was told that there were more than twenty thousand in the camp. There had been as many as sixty thousand. Where are they now?

"And the country roundabout was pleasing to the eyes, and the Germans were well fed and well dressed. American trucks were rolling toward the rear filled with prisoners. Soon, they would be eating American rations, as much for a meal as the men at Buchenwald had received in four days…. I was there on Thursday, and many men in many tongues blessed the name of Roosevelt. For long years, his name had meant the full measure of their hope…. Back in '41, Mister Churchill said to me with tears in his eyes, 'One day the world and history will recognize and acknowledge what it holds to your president.' I saw and heard the first installment of that at Buchenwald on Thursday."

CHAPTER I

THE TOMBS

New York City, 1945, the early hours of May 11. The hundreds of brick, iron, and steel buildings that filled out the evening skyline with their many chimneys bellowed thick smoke into the atmosphere, one skyscraper seeming to climb over the other to reach the clouds and stars above. Some reached that height, disappearing into the smokescreen from the many chimneys piping out their own clouds over the isle of Manhattan. The glare from the tens of thousands of windows in the metropolis painted the night sky with a dreamy glow, creating a focused haze softening the brick-and-mortar stalagmites that shot upward as high as the human mind could design.

Past the steady drone of city life below, a faint police siren managed to break through the buzz of sound, getting increasingly louder. Down on the street level, an unmarked police sedan screamed down the streets heading downtown, haphazardly overtaking and passing slower-moving vehicles that pulled over to let the unmarked car pass. The car's siren squealed between the buildings of the avenue like a wailing banshee, blowing through traffic lights and intersections, with many other vehicles laying on their loud horns to make their feelings known. But the sedan persisted, picking up speed and taking more risky moves as it got closer to their downtown destination.

The vehicle took a hard corner, skimming the gutter, and screeched to a halt outside the New York City Tombs, the police department's detention complex. The four-year-old, fifteen-story Art Deco high-rise called the Tombs III or the Manhattan House of Detention had replaced the aging forty-year-old City Prison building that sat across the street. It was an entire complex of buildings connected by both above- and below-ground tunnels which sat on the same patch of land in which the former Five Points neighborhood previously resided.

With one tire up on the curb, the passenger's-side door swung open, and out jumped a man hidden under a black Stetson hat and matching long black trench coat. Two uniformed officers awaiting his arrival hastily saluted and led him into the building.

As they entered the empty lobby, the motley crew picked up two more officers, scooted around the massive security desk, and continued down the hall. The loud staccato clapping of their dress shoes on the marble floor reverberated inside the dark, quiet corridor. The man in black rounded the corner toward the elevator bank and came face-to-face with a waiting group centered round the chief of police, the commissioner, and the district attorney. The man flipped his high collar down and removed his hat, handing it to one of the accompanying officers. Hands flew out and the man in black shook them all. Without much more of a pause, the man in black led them toward a freight elevator. The group eagerly exchanged glances and hurried after their guest. They all crowded into the large lift and started to descend into the exposed elevator shaft, down in the subbasements, passing floor after floor. As they traveled further into the bowels of the building, the visible walls and brick got older and the paint continued to fade and peel. The group reached their destination, the lowest basement level of the facility.

They exited the lift and entered an old brick hallway illuminated only by a string of bulbs attached to the ceiling. The group passed by various-sized holding cells, some that still had the hundred-year-old grille-styled cell doors and peeling two-tone paint on the walls. They reached a tall, thick wooden desk with a guard stationed behind it who immediately stood to attention. He nervously handed a clipboard to the man dressed in black.

The man flashed a cold smile to the young guard and handed the clipboard over his shoulder to the commissioner behind him. The commissioner, not expecting this, awkwardly juggled it and pawned it off to the man behind him, the chief of police, who signed.

The man in black then dutifully started to unbutton his long black trench coat so the desk guard could see if he was armed. Underneath he revealed a slick but plain-looking three-piece black suit. Undoing those buttons, he opened his jacket and flashed a .45 automatic holstered under his arm to the guard, who acknowledged it. The man then plopped his foot up on the desk and hiked up his pant leg to show his backup .38 on his ankle. The desk guard nodded and turned to indicate they were now all allowed to pass.

The group continued past the desk, further down the hall toward the very last cell, which was guarded by two officers. The cell door they stood in front of only had an eye-level slit opening that offered a view inside. A third plain-clothed officer waited to greet the large party. His suit was stained, ripped, and torn. His name was Sergeant Ambrosio. He extended a hand to the man in black, who ignored it and peered past him through the peephole, into the cell.

"Is he conscious?" the man in black asked, his first words since he'd arrived at the Manhattan House of Detention.

"Uh…yes he is, sir," Ambrosio replied. "We just got back from the hospital. He needed patching up."

"How is he now?"

"He's been stabilized."

"Okay. How long has he been in custody?" the man asked.

"About an hour and a half. I was with him when this all happen—"

"Has anyone debriefed him?"

"I spoke to him. I've been working with him since the beginning, so I can appraise you on everything I know."

"I will certainly read your report once you submit it, Sergeant."

Ambrosio made eye contact with the brass standing behind their guest, who all glared right back at him. His eyes jumped back to the man in black. "Yes, sir."

The man looked at the two uniformed guards stationed on either side of the door. "Please open the door. I'm going to speak with him." He glanced back at the large group and addressed no one in particular. "Please inform me the minute the Secretary of Defense arrives."

Inside the dark, dingy cell, a lingering stench of bleach and mildew assaulted the senses. The room was lit by a single bare bulb that hung overhead, and this light allowed the four corners of the room to dip off into darkness. In the center of the small ten-by-ten room was a large wooden desk with a chair on either side. The sound of several locks unhinging broke the loud silence within the cell, and the huge metal door slowly swung open. The man in black stepped into the cell, and the door closed behind him. He shed the long overcoat, folded it, and placed it on the back of the chair.

Seated across the desk facing the door was a man with his head down, resting on his arms. He looked up to see who had entered. He was a black man in his late thirties, slender in build, with straightened, slicked-back hair wildly out of place. Both eyes were bruised black and blue, with his left almost swollen shut. His jaw was inflamed, and his entire face looked damaged. Dried blood was caked under his nose, and fresh bandages were visible underneath his shirt. His wrists were both handcuffed and attached to an old metal pole anchored to the floor.

His name was Walter Morris, a private detective by trade.

The man in black's suit was tight fitting, not as baggy as the common style, instead more streamlined, as if ready for action. He unbuttoned his jacket and took a seat across from the detainee. He removed his Stetson and placed it onto the table. "My name is Agent Graham. I'm here to debrief you on what occurred tonight and get an overall account on what led up to this evening. You think you can help me with that?"

Morris didn't respond.

"Would you like a drink? A coffee or a buttermilk? Something stronger, perhaps?"

Morris perked up. "I'll take a milkshake if you're asking. Chocolate, some whipped cream, and a couple of nice red Maraschino cherries on top."

After a pause, Graham continued, "Okay, we can do that. Would you care for a cigarette?"

The private detective looked up with his one good eye and for the first time made eye contact with the special agent. "Sure, that would be fucking fabulous right now."

Graham went into his breast pocket with one hand to grab his smokes and used his other to delve into another pocket for his Zippo. He gave Morris a cigarette, lit that, and another one for himself.

"We can get some pain medicine onboard as well to take the edge off…," he motioned to the facial bruising and Morris's battered body, "… how you are feeling?"

Morris took a drag from the cigarette, then exhaled. He looked the special agent up and down and had another drag. "What agency did you say you were from?"

Agent Graham politely smiled. "The DOD."

Morris nodded and looked down at his broken fingers that could barely hold the lit cigarette. "Department of Defense. Not connected to the Office of Strategic Services, are you, eh…the OSS?" Morris made himself smile.

Agent Graham smiled and shook his head.

Morris took another drag. "So you want me to lay the whole thing out, huh? Spread it and straighten it out, see if you can make heads or tails out of it all?"

Graham retrieved a notepad and pen from his other breast pocket, opened it, and settled in. "Roughly. Just spill it all out. Right now I'm just interested in your raw account of all this while it's still fresh. Everything, even as ancillary as it may be. Savvy?"

Morris had another drag and exhaled. He spat out a mixture of saliva and blood before he repositioned his body in the wooden chair. He took a minute to think and let out a long, deep, hearty laugh. "Alright, sure, what the hell." He shifted his weight once again because his position wasn't comfortable the way he was feeling. "From what I learned, this all started here in New York about a week ago...."

Graham removed the cap from his pen.

Morris brought his hands to between his legs under the table and leaned in. "Have you seen them yet? I mean, have you seen one of those freak shows up close?"

Graham looked into Morris's eyes and paused before he answered. "I have not yet been able to view what was recovered from the site."

That made the detective laugh. "Well, you should have gone there first, 'cause that would have saved us the bullshit of you asking me questions you could already know the answers to."

The special agent smiled. "Don't worry, Mister Morris. You will be very surprised how much I am willing to believe."

CHAPTER 2

TWO WEEKS PRIOR

The world was at war for the second time. Europe had been battling the Nazis along with Italy and Japan for nearly six years. With the Japanese bombing of Pearl Harbor in December of 1941, the United States *officially* joined the war. Italy declared an armistice in September of 1943, and two fronts then remained: the European and Pacific theaters. By early '45, Hitler's last attempt to keep a foothold on what he'd conquered in Europe became known as the Battle of the Bulge, which failed once the supply lines were cut off and the German army's precious Tiger tanks were starved of their petrol.

Now the Nazis were desperately trying to hold back the allied forces to the west and the Russians from the east. By April, the war in Europe was winding down. Allies had converged on Berlin and were going street to street, building to building, fighting the last of the German army. News could come any day now of victory and then the united forces could focus their energy on pushing the Japanese back in the Pacific and prepare for the inevitable, a ground invasion of the island of Japan.

In New York City, the population was still feeling the effects of the overseas war. Since early 1942, there had been strict curfews as well as blackout restrictions in place. After sunset every evening, Manhattan and its surrounding boroughs (along with every *other* city and town along the Eastern seaboard facing the Atlantic Ocean) were required to keep all lights off. Windows, bulbs, signs, and any other form of illumination was turned off or painted black so as to not be a potential target to any German U-boats or long-range bombers. Times Square, the entire Great White Way, skyscrapers like the Empire State and Chrysler buildings, and even the Statue of Liberty and her magnificent torch were all dark.

After sunset, vehicles had to use specially modified hoods attached to their headlights or slits called "eyelids" so their lights would only illuminate the street. Traffic lights wore similar coverings so only a small sliver of red or green could be seen. Streetlights had been turned off or their intensity lessened, and streetlamps had the tops of their globes painted black so their light would not be seen from above. Night games at Yankee Stadium or Ebbets Field were now prohibited, and even some observation areas atop skyscrapers like the Woolworth Building were closed due to their views of the Brooklyn Navy Yard.

The American public at large was more than happy to do their part, buying blackout curtains and keeping their shades drawn at night or their windows painted black. They enthusiastically stuck to the country's war rationing and restrictions on food, metal, rubber, and the like.

Air wardens patrolled the skies, and in New York City, searchlights were set up to look for any signs of a possible attack from the air. A steady lookout was kept along the waterfronts for fear of any possible covert submarine landings to smuggle spies and saboteurs ashore or any acts of overt sabotage on the New York area waterways and its ships. This potential threat became a reality in the public's psyche in 1942 when an ocean liner being converted into the troopship *USS Lafayette* spontaneously caught fire while docked on the West Side and capsized in the Hudson River.

Tensions were high. The public was on alert for any possible collusion with the enemy, and people were paranoid. As we would come to see, for good reason.

It was a foggy, overcast night in Manhattan. The dark skyscrapers that inhabited the garden of stone looked like colossal tombstones, massive monoliths that reached up and disappeared into the cloudy night sky.

Lanky chimneys pumped out endless plumes of smoke that connected like arteries to the foggy haze above.

A large postal service zeppelin appeared out of a bank of clouds and darkness, lumbering toward the Empire State Building's massive aerial mooring tower at the top of the tallest building in the world. Once the premiere docking station in the Western hemisphere for transatlantic flight traffic, commercial exchange had all but dried up with the Hindenburg disaster in 1937, and now the aerial mast that also doubled as a radio antenna at present only serviced government aircraft.

A smaller and stouter blimp was already anchored to the mooring station. It was a supply ship, awaiting the signal that it could commence with its embarking procedure to depart on its route north toward Bridgeport, New Haven, Hartford, and Boston. It was a tricky affair to monitor the wind speeds and directions for incoming and outgoing traffic, especially when more than one zeppelin was to be anchored at the mast. The aerial mooring station had originally been envisioned to dock up to four aircraft, but that soon proved to be impractical due to high winds, so it was determined only two should be secured at a time. What had also become an unforeseen complication of the zeppelin flight paths in the city were the region-wide blackout restrictions that had been put in place when the war began. Pilots had to rely on ambient and moonlight to navigate the city buildings, much like they did out over the Atlantic, keeping a high enough altitude to clear the majority of the tall skyscrapers, and rapidly ascend or descend on their flight path when navigating the Empire State Building station.

Air wardens on nearby rooftops stood next to enormous floodlights armed with binoculars, patrolling the skies, looking for anything that was out of place.

A large, sleek, and cylindrical gray postal zeppelin descended from above, righted itself, and floated lazily toward the building on approach, its engines already slowing down in preparation to dock. Searchlights on neighboring buildings clicked on and swung their beams of light like swords onto the airship so the serial numbers on the canvas fin could be checked. After cross-referencing with the expected night traffic of the evening, the wardens were satisfied, and the floodlights were extinguished like blown-out candles, making a notation in their logs.

The zeppelin's large engines changed sounds during its rate of deceleration, like a vessel in the water when approaching a dock. Various small infrared lights now turned on at the top of the building to help guide the airship to the station's berth. While the crew aboard the blimp and atop the mooring mast busied with the airship's approach, a creeping figure unclipped himself from the frame under the large rear lateral fin and began to crawl along the top of the blimp, making sure to stay low in the shadows of the massive vessel. The figure was dressed in all black with a matching ski mask over his face. The creeper was tall and very well built, his physique emphasized because of the snug outfit that could have almost been painted on.

The engine downshifted again as the zeppelin expertly pivoted into the correct orientation and ropes were thrown down from the nose section to pull it into dock. The airship's bow was carefully guided to the antenna and the nose cone was secured to the platform at the top of the mast. Workers on the mooring platform grabbed a gangplank that protruded from just below the vessel and attached it to a track that doubled as the railing. Wheels at the base of the gangway anchored it to the railing, which in high winds allowed the gigantic vessel to swing 360 degrees while connected. Once secured, the engines of the postal zeppelin were turned off.

The other stout dirigible shifted its engines into gear, was disconnected from its moor, and backed away from the building to embark on its journey south toward Atlantic City and Philadelphia.

Workers came down the gangway of the postal craft and began their duties of dropping various-sized sacks of mail down to the platform below, while staff on the station brought various parcel bags up to be loaded onto the floating vessel. Only once the workers were busy did the masked creeper scurry undetected along the top of the dirigible toward the nose. He got to the cone and gracefully jumped from the nose of the airship to the building's large radio antenna directly ahead and above, making hardly any sound.

Up in the Bronx, in a pre-war walk-up tenement way up in Woodlawn, a man dressed in a tank top, seated at his kitchen table, and reading the evening edition of the paper listened to his radio, while behind him in the kitchen, his wife fried a steak on a small stove. A policeman's cap was on the table next to his department-issued baton. The wireless on the dresser against the wall squawked out the news.

"The fiend who the New York newspapers have dubbed the 'New York Ripper' has struck yet again, ladies and gentlemen...."

Both their heads turned slightly in unison to better hear the radio reporter. A sudden jolt of static interrupted the broadcast, as though the signal was temporarily lost. Before either could acknowledge the interference, the station was back, sharp and clear as ever.

"...was on his regular milk route early this morning, when he unknowingly discovered the mutilated body of a woman in her twenties on the West Side...."

The man looked back to his paper and ashed his filterless cigarette.

The prowler secured his grip and footing on the antenna, careful not to damage anything. The Empire State Building workers continued their business of loading and unloading the day's mail, so the man's leap went unnoticed in the darkness. The creeper methodically scaled down the antenna to an access hatch cover at its base. With one sharp tug, he was easily able to break the strong iron hatch lock and, in seconds, silently disappeared into the building.

The engines on the stout zeppelin roared when shifted into gear, as the massive machine cleared the building's station and the other postal dirigible to begin its journey south.

Once inside, the masked man hit the stairs at an unnatural speed, the figure in black almost flying down the stairs, the loud sounds of the airship's engines fading away in the hollow shaft. The fast and loud staccato of his shoes racing down the stairs replaced any other sound in the narrow service stairwell.

Way down on street level, though it was late, the surrounding avenues and streets encircling the Empire State Building still had their share of vehicular and pedestrian foot traffic. A large touring car appeared and turned the corner, sped down the crosstown street, and pulled up outside a service entrance to the building. Before the car was shifted into park, three men exited from its suicide doors at the rear of the vehicle. Two of them huge, almost looking like twins to the masked prowler already inside. In their arms they held violin cases. The third individual, a very thin but tall man, carried a large briefcase and army duffel bag over his shoulder.

They all wore flesh-colored, plastic masks that were almost see-through, like the kind from the children's section of a store. The masks resembled those of the popular gangster movie stars of the era Edward G. Robinson, Humphrey Bogart, and James Cagney, but as exaggerated caricatures. The two large men wore Cagney and Robinson, while the thin man who carried the bags and led the pack wore the Bogart mask.

Inside the stairwell the prowler made it down to the ground level in a matter of minutes. He cracked open the door and carefully peered out to survey the lobby. The only part of his face that was visible behind his ski mask was the eye area, which was obscured underneath by black goggles.

At the security desk, a janitor rocked back in his chair, listening to the same news program, while an elderly guard made his rounds checking the doors of the lobby.

"...the sixth victim in the past two weeks. Authorities are baffled and young women in Manhattan, along with the other four boroughs, are frightened...."

As the guard turned a corner, the prowler made his move, creeping out and taking the seated janitor by surprise. He put a hand over his mouth and went for the key ring that was connected to the worker's waist. The janitor's eyes widened with terror as the prowler actually picked the man up and moved him to the side door that led outside.

Outside on the sidewalk, the service door opened, and the three masked men entered the lobby.

Their leader, Bogart, gave the large duffel bag to the masked prowler to carry, with not a word exchanged. They passed the front desk, and the elderly security guard turned the corner and put his hand up as if to indicate them to stop. In one fluid motion, Cagney pushed the man's arm aside, elbowed him in the face, snatched the guard's gun out of its holster, and pointed it at the janitor, who enthusiastically threw both hands up.

The other two continued to the elevators and pressed the call button. Bogart barked something out in German, and Cagney opened the cylinder of the service revolver, spilling the bullets to the floor before dropping the gun entirely.

Bogart put his finger up to his mouth as if to tell the janitor not to say a word. The guard was picked up off his feet, and they were both carried away.

Over on the other side of the lobby, a door creaked open and a younger janitor inched out, too afraid to move.

Inside the elevator the hostages were positioned in front of the group by the doors. Against the back wall the three goons stood like statues towering above, their heads almost touching the ceiling. The ski-masked prowler stood between Cagney and Robinson. In front of them was the slender ringleader with the Bogart mask, whose narrow, relaxed, and lifeless eyes could have burnt holes in the backs of the prisoners. One eye was somewhat fogged over with the appearance of being blind. He had a scar just above his brow dipping toward the cheek, though it was hard to see under the mask. The other eye was just as soulless and cold.

Not a word was said, the only noise coming from the elderly janitor and guard. Both pensioners, retired from their lifelong professions, tried their best to stay quiet. The black janitor, Gus Montana, worked this twelve-hour shift two nights a week after having retired from spending forty years as a porter on the New York Central Railroad. The white Polish guard, Bronislaw Potucek, or Ben as his friends called him, worked part-time after a twenty-five-year stint at the Brooklyn-Manhattan Transit Corporation, back when it was still called the Brooklyn Rapid Transit Company. The two retired civil servants were only in this situation because they had to take another job in their golden years to make ends meet. They now stood as quiet as they could and stared at the elevator floor; their breathing and occasional hyperventilating echoed within the small, confined space.

Bogart broke his stare and glanced down to the floor. Without hesitation he unsheathed a Luger P08 and shot both men point-blank in the back of their heads in quick succession. The sound was deafening within such a confined area. Gus and Ben collapsed to the floor, their lifeless bodies tangling with one another on the way down.

The echo of the report faded away within the compartment. Bogart holstered his Luger and stuck a pinkie in his own ear. Edward G. and Cagney opened their violin cases and retrieved stockless Thompson submachine guns, then, as if performing a synchronized timed routine, attached drum magazines and let the cases fall to the floor. They also connected the gun butts to shoulder straps so the weapons could be carried from the firing shoulder. The prowler in the middle connected to his shoulder strap a heavily modified sawed-off repeating shotgun.

Down in the lobby, Lamont, the young janitor, was urgently talking on the phone. "Operator, get me the police! Now!"

When the elevator came to a halt up on the seventy-ninth floor, the three exited and made their way down the carpeted hall. They came to a door with a sign that read OFFICE OF STRATEGIC SERVICES, NEW YORK BUREAU. Bogart gave his large briefcase to Edward G., who continued down the hall to the next office. The ski-masked prowler dropped the duffel bag he carried outside the OSS office door.

Cagney kicked down the OSS door and fired into the air.

"Everyone on the floor!" Bogart yelled with a thick German accent. A secretary was working late, and an older cleaning lady was also in the office. They screamed and dropped to the floor.

Down the hall, the figure dressed as Edward G. reached the last office on the floor, which had the words DEPARTMENT OF TRANSIT CLERICAL OFFICE stenciled on it. He methodically retrieved a locksmith toolset out of his bag, knelt, and started picking the lock.

In the other office, the ski-masked prowler positioned himself in the outer office area with the two women while Cagney fired at the doorknob of a locked door in the corner of the room that read CLOSET. He kicked it down and Bogart stepped in, followed closely by Cagney.

Hidden behind the unassuming door labeled CLOSET was a cavernous room lined with bookcases filled with files, books, and vast transit maps on the walls. A plain-clothed agent came out from behind a cabinet and rushed Bogart, but Cagney stepped forward and hit him in the face with the butt of his Thompson before he could do anything, sending him to the floor dazed with a bloody nose already beginning to swell. Cagney flipped the machine gun around, pointed it at the man, and pulled back the slide, putting a round in the chamber, but Bogart quickly intervened.

"*Nein! Verlasse ihn,*" he said in his native German. Cagney complied and swung the barrel toward another agent at the back of the office who had hesitated to act.

Bogart locked eyes on this man, who he sized up to be the senior agent in the field office compared to the younger man writhing on the floor. Bogart walked over to him, coming uncomfortably close to the man's face.

"Where are your files on Operation Overcast?"

The older agent unknowingly paused. He looked deep into the placid and vacant eyes of Bogart. They didn't betray any kind of feelings, let alone empathy. They weren't the eyes of a petty criminal, but the eyes of a war-weary killer, a man to whom death was a constant companion. There was an immediate recognition that these men were not to be trifled with and that the original question had been left unanswered for too long.

Bogart barked out an order in German and the towering Cagney approached with a quick but unusual measure of calm efficiency in his motions, his boots heavy with every step. The agent was thrown onto a desk, crushing the lamp and other items on top. The man attempted to put up a fight but was immediately made aware of the almost unnatural raw power of the man under the Cagney mask, almost like the unfailing energy within a hydraulic press. The older agent stopped putting up any defense.

Cagney let go, awaiting further instructions. The agent looked over to the tall, lanky Bogart, who queried again:

"Where are your files on Operation Overcast?"

There was no reply.

Bogart nodded to Cagney.

The agent turned back to the massive Cagney in preparation of what would be next. With one hand the henchman picked up a heavy metal desk chair like it was an empty shoebox and, with an effortless backhand, threw it through the window. There was an explosion of glass as the room depressurized and a gust of air blew through the window. Papers on other desks and anything else that was light enough flew up and were carried out the window following the shards of thick glass and the heavy, swiveling chair on their race down to the street seventy-nine floors below.

Bogart's eyes remained on the senior agent throughout this. "Show him where the files for Operation Overcast are or your last moments on Earth will be spent contemplating the aerodynamics of the human body as you hit the roofs of the many passing taxicabs below."

After a short moment, the terrified agent staggered to his feet under the watchful eye of Cagney and dejectedly made his way over to a large filing cabinet.

Down the hall, the masked Edward G. had carefully made his way inside the Department of Transit clerical office, taking care to pick the inner office door lock as he'd done with the first. He entered the room, which was full of large filing cabinets. Each had its own title written on the front: LONG ISLAND RAILROAD, NEW YORK CITY SUBWAY SYSTEM, and PORT AUTHORITY BUS SYSTEM.

Back in the Office of Strategic Services, the young secretary and middle-aged cleaning lady were brought into the inner office and made to stand by the wall, terrified as Cagney tore through the filing cabinet, searching.

Bogart's attention shifted, and he stared at the two females, his view becoming fixated on the older cleaning lady. Bogart's tall and thin frame was perverted even further by the abstract mask he wore over his face. He stood under a bright light overhead, which obscured any features behind the mask's eyeholes. Instead they were just empty black holes that looked endless and vast, like a demon's. Only the reflection from his retinas remained periodically visible, a reminder that there were actual eyes hidden within those sockets.

Down on street level, a dozen police cars arrived at the address. Uniformed officers secured the abandoned touring car left by the burglars and descended upon the building.

Cagney finally discovered in the filing cabinet what he'd been looking for: bundles of files labeled "Classified" and "Do Not Copy", with paperclips attached. He gathered everything from the folder and methodically placed the paperclipped documents into his large briefcase.

During all of this, the prowler in the ski mask remained motionless near the open window, waiting.

Bogart continued to stare at the cleaning lady, stepping forward until he was about a foot in front of her, looking deep into her sobbing, terrified face. He cocked his head to the left, as if in thought. Even the secretary was startled by his fixation, looking between the woman and the tall, sinister figure.

Down the hall the enormous burglar hidden behind the Edward G. mask stopped upon the cabinet marked PENN CENTRAL RAILROAD. In no time he had the lock on the cabinet open and searched through its contents. He paused upon the blueprints labeled GRAND CENTRAL TERMINAL. He carefully ripped them out of the book, put everything back how it had been found, and calmly left the room, locking the inner door just as he found it.

Bogart's gaze still hadn't wavered as his cohorts finished up gathering the files they had come for. He startled the office staff by speaking, moreover in German. *"Sprichst du Deutsch?"* then he repeated in English, "Do you speak German?"

The older woman began to shake with fright. Tears flowed, streaming down her face as she nodded. "I—*Jawohl*…." She was barely able to reply in the affirmative.

Bogart pressed on. "When did you come to America?"

"In thirty-nine, when Hitler invaded Poland…"

"In der massenflucht." Bogart continued once again in English. "You are from Bolshevik maybe? That region?"

The cleaning lady was astounded. "Why—that is right, I…I am Bolshevik…."

A smile could be detected by how his voice sounded from behind the mask. "*Ja*, I know my Jews."

The prowler in black who was standing like a sentinel sprang to life. He walked out of the office, through the outer area, and out into the hallway. He crossed over to the stairwell door and began to listen.

Down in the lobby seventy-nine floors below, the police, with the help of Lamont and now other building personnel, completed shutting down all the elevators, except for one which they had commandeered and, with the use of a fire marshal's key, programmed into emergency use. They packed in as many men as it would allow and started up.

The prowler walked back over to the office door and looked to his leader, as if silently conveying a message. The creeper behind the Cagney mask took the cue, secured his briefcase with stolen documents, and headed out into the hallway to join the ski-masked prowler.

Bogart looked from the woman to his men, sensing their departure. In one slick, fluid motion he drew his .22 and pointed it at the woman's face. She let out a loud yelp and the secretary screamed. The older agent on the other side of the room held out his hand as if to ask him to stop.

He held the barrel in her face, as if a jury were deliberating. After a long moment he relaxed his arm and lowed the weapon. "You are very lucky tonight, my little Bolshevik. Even acknowledging, though, your kind are the filthiest of the lot."

He stood there, gazing coldly with a deep pleasure into the souls of her eyes then exited the office.

Overcome with emotion, the cleaning lady collapsed to her knees and sobbed uncontrollably. The secretary threw her arms around her in an attempt to comfort her.

"My God…," she said through tears. "How do I know that voice?"

In the hall they were joined by Edward G., who had just finished locking the Department of Transit clerical office, being careful to leave it exactly as it had been. Bogart walked up to Cagney, nodded, and gestured with his head. He set down his briefcase and walked back into the office with his machine gun in hand.

Bogart said to the prowler in German, "The police are on their way up, then?"

The prowler nodded. There was a loud burst of machine gun fire from the office as Cagney unload a full magazine at the office staff inside. After he was satisfied, he returned to the others.

Bogart next commanded, "Then we are Code Pollen."

Upon hearing this, the group was on the move. The creeper behind the Edward G. mask handed the Grand Central blueprints to the masked Cagney man, who reloaded his gun then delicately put them in the same briefcase with the other looted files. They all proceeded down the hall to the far stairwell. When they opened the door, they headed up, not down.

They quickly climbed the flights of stairs and made it as high as that stairwell could take them, and the four exited by the enclosed office area on the lower observation deck.

The men rushed past the US Postal Office door and the employee inside noticed them running.

"What the fu—?"

The group entered another door that led to the final staircase that went to the very top of the building.

On the seventy-ninth floor, the police exited off the elevator and ran toward the Strategic Services Office.

At the very top of the building, a door was opened and a stream of hall light partly illuminated the observation deck where the airship access usually was. The four thieves ran out onto the deck. No zeppelins were currently tethered to the building.

The police exited the office on seventy-nine and quickly determined the robbers could have only gone up. Some jumped back into the elevator, while others took the stairs, and they all headed toward the roof.

On the observation deck, Edward G. went into the large duffel bag on his back and took out four backpacks.

They dropped their guns, secured the packs on their backs, and climbed over the tall, high fence that protected people from falling.

At the same time the police arrived on the lower observation deck and started up the final stairs to the very top. They cautiously burst out of the doorway and just caught a brief glance of the intruders before the four masked men jumped off the building. Shocked, the police rushed to the fence, thinking the men had committed suicide.

The robbers pulled their ripcords and the parachutes opened.

The police stood and watched the four men float down to freedom.

"Holy shit…," one cop said to no one in particular.

With the Empire State Building in the background, the four floated in virtual darkness toward the street. Floodlights on the surrounding buildings began to point their beams at the high observation deck to see why its bright lights were on.

Barely visible on the dark horizon of the abyss was the glow of the white navigation light on the nose cone of a Transit Authority Department blimp, blinking in regular intervals. Sluggishly making its way toward the aerial mooring station, it unintentionally caused the parachutists to flop and sway, rippling like pollen carried away in the breeze further and further away on the wind.

CHAPTER 3

WALTER EUGENE MORRIS, PI

During the daylight hours, New York City was pretty much the same during wartime as it had been before. Even with a war on against the Nazis in Europe and also with Japan out in the Pacific, not much of the city's day-to-day life was affected by the conflict. Of course, there were more soldiers around town—their existence was omnipresent—and more American flags were in the windows of residences and storefronts as a sign of solidarity with American boys overseas.

The area the average New Yorker felt affected day to day, like the rest of the country, was the rationing. Aluminum, rubber, and various other metals were in demand, and the country had to live under rationing. Even certain foods were restricted, going so far in the city as to suggest meatless Tuesdays and Fridays to help conserve meat. Victory gardens popped up wherever there was free space, in vacant lots and even in some of the city's parks. People grew all kinds of vegetables to compensate so fresh produce could be available to the public.

Up in Harlem, life was identical to that in Midtown. People went about their daily business, some even forgetting about the conflict that was happening literally a world away. For some, if it wasn't happening in the city—or more specifically on their block—it wasn't important. It was "outta sight, outta mind". For most people, aside from listening to the wireless and hearing the updates on the bulletins or in between their favorite shows, the newspaper provided the best glimpse into the war. The many daily editions would often sell out immediately, helping to curb that addiction of those wanting to say up to date with the latest news.

The morning turned out to be the making of a beautiful day with the fog and wet weather clearing out with the sunrise. The streets were crowded with folk going about their usual routines. On the newsstands the morning editions of the competing newspapers hung clothespinned across a line of rope so their headlines could easily be read.

A customer in mechanic's overalls picked up the latest edition of a paper, set it down on the counter, asked for a pack of Lucky Strikes, and went into his pocket for change to pay. The headline on the paper read:

RUMORS OF HITLER'S DEATH AS ALLIES
REACH OUTSKIRTS OF BERLIN!!

From the tall, long window of his corner office on the third floor overlooking the intersection of the old Lee Building on 125th and Park Avenue, Walter Morris watched with disinterest as the mechanic picked up his pack of smokes and newspaper and stepped off the curb, heading north on 125th toward the auto mechanic shop where he worked. You get to know the locals in your own neighborhood, the familiar faces you see day-to-day like clockwork.

Walter always watched. It seemed every waking hour of his existence he was watching. Not that it bothered him; he actually took an odd pleasure in taking an interest in other peoples' lives. So much so that he turned it into his vocation. He was a private detective.

He shared this office and was a junior agent in the practice with his partner and mentor, an Englishman named Jacob Roland. Back when Walter had run away from the demons of his past, or the one *demon*, he'd gotten work in the boiler room on the transatlantic luxury liner *RMS Olympic* and befriended the ship's detective, Jacob Roland. When Walter became homesick for the old neighborhood, Roland decided to leave the high seas and the extravagant floating hotel behind and open a practice in Walter's old neck of the woods, Harlem. Very forward thinking on Jacob's part, having an integrated detective agency, a Limey and a Negro, something Walter joked was like Al Jolson's "Me and My Shadow." They were able to get twice the business, moving between both worlds: the white middle- and upper-class clientele of cocktail parties, the suburbs and Central Park West, and the local black communities of Harlem and the other black neighborhoods Walter was able to work within. He thought he could give back to his community, help in any way he could.

Walter was in his late thirties with light skin, green eyes, and dark hair he kept long and had chemically treated to be straight, that he slicked back on his head. He was of average height, about 5'10", and had a sinewy, athletic frame.

His suit jacket was off and hung up, and his thumbs were inside the pockets of his vest as he listened to the story being recounted behind him by the lady seated at the front of his desk. He'd turned on his Zenith wireless when she first arrived to make it a more relaxed environment for his visitor, so the scene could be as comfy as an Errol Flynn Saturday matinee romance picture, and at the very moment, Glenn Miller and his gorgeous and seductive "Moonlight Serenade" was purring out of the speaker, filling in the rough edges of any uncomfortable silences or pregnant pauses a potential client might have. He and Roland realized that having calming music on in the background could really help put an anxious or nervous mind at ease.

Walter watched the man in the mechanic's overalls until he crossed out of view and refocused his eyes on the "ROLAND & MORRIS, PI" sign stenciled outward on the large window, making a minute readjustment to the blinds to ensure the day's sun wasn't making the room too bright for the young lady and killing the mood Walter was trying to create.

He turned when he heard her voice crack and she began to cry, attempting to muffle her sobs so she could continue with her story.

"And then on Tuesday, I was doing the laundry…and I found a train ticket stub in his pocket. It was a ticket to Bridgeport and back. Why…I mean, he has no business going on a train to Bridgeport. He would have told me if it was job-related…."

The young woman seated in front of his desk was beautiful, around twenty-five years of age and wearing an alluring red dress that was tailored to her figure. A matching large-brimmed hat was playfully cocked to the left. She glanced up at him when he turned back from the window, but only one eye was visible because of her brim. Tears began to fall down her cheek.

"Hey, hey…," Walter started in a calm, soothing, and almost seductive tone, "…I can't have a doll like you going to pieces on me, now. Calm down and take a breath." Walter picked up a box of tissues, crossed from the window around the desk with a drink in hand, and offered them to her. She took a tissue and attacked her tears before her eyeliner started to run. "Listen," he said in a warm, kind voice, "I think I know what the problem is." He sat down on the corner of his desk and put his cigarette out in his ashtray.

The woman immediately smiled. "Oh, I knew you'd be able to help…I just didn't know what I was gonna do."

"It'll be fine. You have nothing to worry about. I have the perfect man for the job. My partner, Mister Roland, would—"

"Who?"

"My partner, Jacob Roland."

"Your partner?" The smile left her face, and she angled her head so both eyes were now visible. "What do you mean?"

Walter stumbled, thrown off by her change in tone. He smiled before answering, like he were taking on the most serious and delicate of questions. "Um, yes my associate, Mister Roland." Walter raised his finger and pointed to the other desk in the room under the large window on the Park Avenue side of the office. "He would be exactly what you need for this sort of—"

"I don't understand. Why can't *you* help me?"

Oh boy. Walter hated this part. "I'm sorry, Missus Stodhart, but I don't do divorce work. My partner oversees that type of situation. I deal with insurance and criminal investigations, missing persons, or worse, say—"

"Who said anything about divorce?"

"I certainly don't want this to come off the wrong way, Missus Stodhart, but when you get right down to it, what you're asking me to do is go see what your husband is doing at night and report back to you. To me that falls under divorce work because, more often than not, divorce is where that kind of thing ends up."

"Why not, then?"

"Why don't I take on divorce work? Honestly?" Walt thought she had been sincere enough with him, so he tried his best with her. "It's all too messy for me. I'm not a very smart man, Missus Stodhart, in the grand scheme of things, and I can't begin to dive down the rabbit hole as to *why* a man—" Walter extended his hand palm up toward her, "—or a woman, may end up doing the things that nature, temptation, attraction, or whatever you want to call it, makes them do from time to time that may be termed as infidelity. I don't like to take a decisive role in situations like that if I can help it. All that comes with way too much judgement for me on people and their motivations in life. I try not to judge people too much. I like to keep an open mind about folks in general. So, that whole end of the business I do not deal in."

"Where is this other man now?"

Walter almost had to think about that before he answered, predicting how his response might go. "He's out on a case."

"You're telling me that the man I have to talk to is out running around for some other poor woman, and you are doing nothing but drinking and listening to Tom Mix and his *Ralston Straight Shooters* and won't get off your tail to help me?" Anger and outrage had replaced her sadness and crying.

This was exactly why Walter avoided this type of thing. "Well," he chuckled in embarrassment, "I wouldn't put it so hopelessly. I am always here to lend moral support, and I could most certainly get things started on this end to get the ball rolling. Jacob would just take over—"

"I don't believe this!" Mrs. Stodhart stood up and walked toward the door. "I sit here, waste my time pouring my heart out to you, and that's your answer?"

Walter raised his eyebrows and tried to make light of the situation. "Well—"

"I have no more words for such a fink like you. Good day, Mister Morris. I hope you have fun withering away in the bottom of that glass of gin."

"Whiskey, Missus Stodhart. I drink whiskey."

She hesitated for a brief moment then opened the office door that led to the small waiting area, and stormed through the outer office to the hall, and was gone. The echo of her high heels stomping on the linoleum faded as she made her way to the stairs. Walter stood there confused, not quite understanding what he had said or from what point the conversation went sour. He could only smile.

From the outer office, a brunette with milky skin stuck her head in the doorway. Her name was Tatum Marie Sullivan. "You really know how to sweet talk 'em, don't ya, Walter?" She smiled.

"I got you here, didn't I?" Walter threw his hands up and walked back toward the cabinet that had the Zenith on top. Tatum came out from behind the desk and entered the inner office. She stood about 5'5" now that she'd removed her heels to be more comfortable, with a tight dress that accentuated a petite body that could stop a clock. Walter changed the station from mood music to the news of the day.

"*…five days on, the country is feeling the shock over the sudden and tragic death of President Roosevelt, the father to us all who saw us through this horrible war. Even though the campaign in Europe may actually be over in weeks, it will not be as sweet a victory now that we have lost FDR. Let us pause for a moment and give you the other news of the day….*"

"Dames," Walter said, still shaking off what had just occurred.

"Well, you only got me for like another hour, then I have to relieve Dolores downstairs on the switchboard. Believe it or not, Walt, I do have a day job." Tatum placed a hand on her hip. "I'm an independent woman who makes her own living so she can pursue her dreams at night."

"I know, I know. Good for you, sister." Walt turned up the volume on the Zenith and headed toward his desk. "Just let me know if anyone shows up for the secretary position."

"I know, I know." She rolled her eyes and turned to leave.

"We're just getting information in regarding an amazing, puzzling feat perpetrated late last night at the Empire State Building." The announcer almost shouted out his copy as he read the news. *"Reports are still unclear about what exactly happened, but three to four men reportedly parachuted off the building in complete darkness, apparently to safety but leaving the police stumped. We'll bring more to you as details come in."*

"See, those are the jobs I will take."

The phone rang and Tatum headed back to the desk in the waiting room to answer it.

Walter sat down at his desk. Tatum's head popped sideways back into view around the doorframe. "Hey, sunshine! You got Roland on the line."

Walter nodded in thanks. He picked up the extension on his desk and held it to his ear, putting a finger to his other ear to cut out the loud volume of the Zenith. "Roland and Morris."

Morris's partner, Jacob Roland, stood in a phone booth in Grand Central Terminal. It was quite busy for the time of day there, and the cavernous space filled with marble and stone was loud with the sounds of daily commuters, sightseers, merrymakers, and troops coming and going. High up above, the reverse Scorpio chart on the ceiling was barely visible due to all the cigarette and cigar smoke that lingered over everyone, and the twinkling lights of the mural's lit stars gave a dreamlike quality to the whole scene, as if the stale smoke were passing clouds in a sort of night sky.

Jacob Roland was British of origin, in his late forties, with black hair and light blue eyes. He wasn't as svelte as Walter, but he definitely wasn't out of shape either. He covered his exposed ear from the room so he could hear. *"Walt, it's Jacob."*

Walter smiled, leaned back in his chair, and put his feet up on his desk. "Ah, Mister Roland, how is the fruitful marital end of our business doing? I hardly see you in the office. You're cheating on me, aren't you?"

Jacob grinned. *"I'm sorry, darling, but work calls. My end of the company is doing great. Who knew all these people were unhappy with their lives? And what about you? How's the hunt for a secretary going? I see you've enlisted the building switch operator to help us."*

Walter looked toward the outer office. "I did indeed. Tatum was kind enough to give up her morning to help us. She's a very busy woman, she tells me, of independent means. But remember, everyone must do their part for the war effort. Isn't that right, Tatum?"

Outside in the waiting room, Tatum's head twitched when she heard her name spoken on the call. She removed the receiver from her ear and quietly set it back down onto the cradle.

Once it was done, she yelled so he could hear in the other room. "What? What's that you say?"

"*Well, that's super,*" Roland said. "*Listen, I'm not going to make it back tonight. I've got this heel who's catching the 3:30 p.m. to New Haven and I need to tag along.*"

"I was just talking to a very outspoken young lady about travels to Pleasure Island in Connecticut."

"*Divorce work, eh?*" Roland turned to keep an eye on his mark who was in line to buy a ticket at the windows on the other side of the terminal.

Walter tried to make his answer sound as innocent as possible. "Nope."

"*When are you gonna learn that's where the money is?*" Jacob craned his neck to see around the large brand-new M26 Pershing tank that was on display there, so he could still see the husband he was tailing.

"So is the undertaker racket, but you don't see me running to do that," Walter was quick to point out.

"*I see your humor hasn't been affected. It's an interesting dilemma you impose on yourself because what if Negro clientele come to you needing help with a martial issue?*"

Walter looked up at the ceiling to think. He fancied another drink. "I guess I'd have to go on a case-by-case basis."

That made Jacob laugh. "*You have an answer for everything. Well listen, number one son, stick around there until about 6:00 p.m., okay? Maybe we'll get a girl answering the ad. Lord, I can't wait to not have to write my own reports up. Anyway, I must go, my boy's on the move. I'll call if anything changes.*"

Walter swung his legs down and looked for his glass. "Roger that, will do. I shall wave to you when you pass one twenty-fifth." Walter heard

Jacob's chuckle as he hung up the phone, which made him laugh too. He looked around then got up and walked over to Roland's desk. He retrieved a bottle of Jameson out of the bottom drawer and found an empty glass by the small sink in the corner of the room. He poured himself a large drink and walked over to view the world from his window, looking south over 125th Street.

"Here's to the war effort...." Walter threw back his head and the spicy liquid made its way down into his stomach. He hadn't noticed during his conversation with his partner that Tatum had closed his inner office door. There was a loud knock, and she opened it and stuck her head in.

"Someone here to see you, um, boss."

"Secretary position?"

She shook her head. "Business."

He paused. "Okay, give me a moment then send them in."

She shut the door and Walter gave his office a once-over.

He quickly fixed his tie, put his jacket on, made sure his straightened hair was properly combed back, and checked his cuff links.

A very proper and dignified-looking gentleman stepped through the door a moment later. He looked to be in his mid-sixties, was dressed in a fancy tailored black suit, and carried a cane which had a gargoyle face on its head. He wore a bowler hat, which he took off as he entered the room.

"Um...hello. I am looking for Mister Jacob Roland," the man inquired in a very learned English accent.

Walter recognized this since his partner was from the south of England. From the inflection on this fellow's words, one could infer he was from the northern region of England, perhaps Lancashire, or even higher than that. Hell, Walter felt lucky he could even discern the various accents in the first place. Pretty good for an uneducated New Yorker playing the role of Sherlock Holmes.

Walt bowed. "Mister Walter Morris, Esquire, at your service," he said, trying to inject some humor into the situation.

"Ah, just the man I wanted to see."

"Something I can do for you?" Walter asked with a grin.

"My name is Garland Crane. I represent a particular party that would like to engage your agency's services."

"An envoy?"

Crane's thin lips formed a pleasant smile, "My employer wishes to remain discreet. I have been asked to be a middleman in the primary stages and, after you have been properly satisfied, take you to him."

"I see." Walter offered the man a cigarette before lighting his own. "Well, Mister Crane, if your employer wishes to retain our services, it's twenty-five dollars a week, plus expenses."

"Oh, my employer was thinking along the lines of fifty dollars per week, plus expenses."

Walter frowned and pointed a finger. "Now see, that's the kind of thing that gets a person asking questions. What would someone be getting themselves into for fifty dollars a week?"

Crane paused but decided to answer honestly. "A person has gone missing north of One Hundred Tenth Street, and we'd like to find them as soon as possible. We were looking for you specifically, Mister Morris, because of your...," Crane gestured with his hat at Walter's appearance, "...experience with the area. Does that pique any interest?"

Walt took a drag from his cigarette and exhaled. "A missing person in our own backyard here in Harlem? Okay, turn the record over, let's hear the other side. Who do you work for, Mister Crane?"

Crane exhaled and said it slow for effect. "Mister Cuthbert Hayden. Esquire."

With that, Walter was speechless.

Minutes later Morris was shutting his inner office door and following Crane out. Tatum was seated behind the secretary's desk, doing her best to look the part.

"Got work," he said.

Tatum nodded and whispered, "Looks important and *expensive*." He moved his head away and she winked. "I'm gonna cut out soon because

Dolores refuses to work after dark with that New York Ripper lurking about."

"You can tell her she doesn't need to worry. The killer so far is only targeting blondes."

"I think she may be a natural blonde," she said then pulled her head back and raised a brow.

Walter matched it with a lift of his own eyebrow. "I'll come by the switchboard later then to see if the carpet matches the drapes."

Tatum didn't have a comeback for that.

CHAPTER 4

CUTHBERT HAYDEN

Walter stared out the back window of the 1942 Cadillac Series 75 limousine as they traveled along the West Side Elevated Highway, heading north. Technically the Caddy was the latest model because it was manufactured the last year cars rolled out before all of Detroit's plants converted over for war production, and Walter expected nothing less with the money Cuthbert Hayden possessed.

Crane sat in the seat facing him with both hands on the cane that was between his legs, staring at the detective while another employee drove them out of the city.

Walt looked down at the gargoyle on the cane's head that Crane twiddled within his hands and broke the silence. "Your boss anything like he's made out to be in the papers, Mister Crane?"

The Englishman smirked dismissively and shook his head. "You know how the tabloids like to single people out. You'd be pleasantly surprised. Since his accident, he's become quite the ambassador of goodwill, despite what those papers like to say about him."

Walter looked back out to the Hudson at an aging tugboat pushing a barge filled with ice from upstate down river toward lower Manhattan. "The press doesn't hinder his business success any, eh? Didn't his company just test a helio-copter with a Russian up in Connecticut?"

Crane smiled, genuinely impressed. "Yes, Igor Sikorsky. You surprise me, Mister Morris. For a regular Joe, you seem to possess your fair share of knowledge."

Walter looked back at Crane and smirked. "In my profession, a good amount of waiting is passed by reading. You read, don't you, Mister Crane?"

"Oh, of course, that's how we learned your father was a Pullman porter for the New York Central, as was his father before him." His smile faded and his face became serious. "What I am curious about, Mister Morris, if I may be so bold, is why you did not follow in their footsteps and right now be carrying some socialite like Mister Hayden's luggage on the Twentieth Century Limited or the Broadway Limited or, for that matter, stayed in the boiler room of the *RMS Olympic*, the last of the *Olympic*-class fleet, instead of setting your sights on a career as a gumshoe?" Crane looked intently at Walter. "And I mean no disrespect."

Walter smiled matter-of-factly with a look of understanding. "Of course, of course." He turned away from Crane and glanced out the window to the ice barge. "Divine intervention, so to speak. I mean, who wants to wait on someone their entire life, you know what I mean, Mister Crane?" Walter flashed a polite smile at Crane.

The large Cadillac limo crossed the Harlem River, leaving Manhattan Island, entering the Bronx and Riverdale, then headed up into Westchester County. The brick and mortar of the city was gradually replaced by the wood and stone of suburban homes, and before long, that gave way to trees and forests surrounding the curvy parkway. Walter didn't make it up into Westchester much, especially to the beautiful, rich, and wooded areas. Going to Yonkers didn't count.

It was twilight when they took the exit off the parkway outside of Sleepy Hollow, thirty minutes north of the city. They turned onto a secluded country road, shielded by trees on either side. Separating that from the motorway were two-foot-high rock walls that looked to be centuries old. They mimicked the hilly terrain and appeared to go on forever. At first there were long stretches of clear land which every so often had a large mansion situated upon it, far back from the main road, surrounded by expanses of green grass, accessible only by gated driveways.

The acres of land were abutted by long rows of trees of different sizes. Soon the open areas ended, and they were surrounded by a thick forest. Occasionally they'd pass a gate to a private driveway, which led up to an estate deep within, well hidden from the casual passerby. If you had the money to afford the homes around here, you were paying for the view and the seclusion.

After a couple of minutes they decelerated and turned into an impressive driveway flanked by a high stone wall shooting out in either direction from a stone gate. The lanterns that hung from either side of the large stone pillars beside the gate were shining bright as if visitors were expected. The limo stopped at the enclosed guard booth in front of a tall, closed silver gate. A plaque on the stone wall read HAYDEN MANOR. A guard opened the gate, and the limo disappeared into the small forest that obscured the Hayden estate from the road.

Across but down the street slightly from the gate, yet still in a position to have a good view of the driveway to see the vehicles that came and went, a black Packard was parked in the opposite direction along the tree line. Night was setting in fast, and dusk helped the flat black sedan blend into the darkening forest. A man sat hidden in the shadows behind the wheel, watching. Only the cherry on his cigarette gave away that someone was there when he brought it to his mouth and inhaled.

A delivery van came around the bend, a party rental company, and as it passed by, a strip of light from its headlights illuminated the top of the man's face in the driver's seat, highlighting his eyes. It was the ringleader of the Empire State Building robbery, who had one clouded pupil. Their intensity held a far-removed coldness for the world and its idle pleasures. They were eyes that had been conditioned by the horrors and atrocities of man, by the tragedy and darkness mankind was capable of. Some never came back after the evils they had seen and were never the same way again. "Shellshock" some called it. Then there are those who were perfectly comfortable with the darkness and horror, who even invited it in. People who enjoyed it. People like him.

They'd been driving for so long on this private road that Walter almost forgot it was only a driveway to this man's house. They continued up the windy lane toward the top of a hill.

"This must be hell to shovel in the winter, huh?" Walter remarked. Crane politely smiled.

Headlights appeared at the top of the driveway as another limo drove past them heading back down. Their vehicle slowed down as the woods ended, opening up and revealing another elegant, colossal, art-deco bronze gate that was already turning green from age, completely enclosing the vast green lawns that surrounded the house. Once they passed through the threshold at the summit, the large mansion came into view.

The house was enormous. Gothic and Victorian styles collided with a neoclassical structure, and it was covered in vines and brush. Where right angles of traditional corners would usually be on the building, instead were impressive and bold Corinthian columns framing out the structure. It was four stories, rising up in the center with a watchtower or turret at the very top reaching toward the sky. Each wing of the home stretched out in opposite directions like wide shoulders, resembling British Parliament under Big Ben more than it did a comfortable and inviting home.

A banquet was in progress. Other limos and touring cars lined up to drop off guests on a red carpet at the entrance. The mansion's walls, surrounding shrubbery, and the edges of the tree line were all covered in strings of white fairy lights, giving the entire vista the feel of a soft-focused, ghostly dream.

Their car pulled past the other vehicles and stopped ahead of the entrance. A valet ran up and opened the Cadillac's rear door for Walter and Crane to step out. "Maurice, please have her gassed up," said Crane. "I'll be needing her again shortly. Follow me, Mister Morris."

Walter followed Crane along the red carpet as they politely sidestepped the guests that were exiting their vehicles. He accompanied him inside and even in his three-piece suit, Walter felt very underdressed stepping into a large, formal dinner party.

The first room they entered after walking through the front door, where typically may have been a foyer or vestibule, Hayden instead had a massive front hall the size of a train station. Three stories high, the room was as long as the house itself was wide, the entire space lit only by candle-light. Chandeliers and immense candelabras with long, thick, white candles were everywhere. The intimate illumination of the flickering candles made Walter think of his youth in the tenements on the Lower East Side, where he ate his dinners by candlelight with his mother, father, and his younger brother…a memory Walt hadn't thought about in a long time.

Hors d'oeuvres and champagne were being served by an all-black staff, and a live classical music quartet was playing in the front hallway. It made Walter very aware of the class system around him, and even though there were famous black faces among the partygoers, because of his background, Walt felt a kinship with the people working this function.

"Please wait here a moment, Mister Morris," Crane said to his special guest. "I'll inform Mister Hayden of our arrival."

Walter remained as Crane disappeared into the crowd of partygoers, all impeccably dressed in ballroom attire, top hats, and coattails. A throw-back to fashion a decade before, prior to the war. Walter did what he always did, stepped back against the wall and watched the party around him. He recognized Carole Landis, who walked by with Fred Allen and Bob Crosby at her side. There were many other celebrities enjoying the festivities. He began to feel jovial and grabbed a glass of champagne off a passing tray.

He started to stroll through the people toward an adjoining smoky ballroom where he picked up the sounds of big band music reverberating in the air. The ballroom was luxurious and adorned with red garland. Walter estimated there to be well over a few hundred people within this room alone enjoying the festivities. At the far end, barely visible through the nicotine haze and dim candlelight, were what sounded like Kay Kyser and his big band on stage. Walter figured with all the famous attend-ees wining and dining, it probably was "The Ol' Perfessor" himself and his boys playing up there. He scanned the crowd for other famous faces, particularly for any brothers. Walt spotted Eddie "Rochester" Anderson chatting at the far end of the bar.

He was going to drift over toward them, but Crane appeared behind Walter and tapped him on the shoulder. Crane indicated with his head, and Walter followed him out of the large ballroom. He'd have to wait for another day to meet his matinee and radio idols.

After some skillful tangoing around the various levels of inebriation, they made their way out of the ballroom, down a long hall, and away from the noise and festivities. They passed many different areas that looked like wings of a museum. One was filled with medieval weapons and armor from both western and eastern civilizations, dressed up on faceless mannequins. One room Walt glanced into as they passed looked like a tribute to hunting. Hundreds of stuffed carcasses of almost every animal that walked the Earth were positioned inside dioramas suitable to their indigenous region. Elephants, bears, lions, giraffes, wolves, and dozens of other four-legged creatures, frozen in time forever. A taxidermist's dream but someone else's nightmare. The next exhibit hall apparently was reserved for various mediums of art. Paintings on the wall, statues, pottery, and other priceless items were everywhere. It wouldn't take an expert to recognize the untold fortunes gathered in this house.

Finally they came upon a doorway at the end of the long hall that led down a small flight of stairs, where they came out into another long, dimly lit passage, far away from the party. The bass of the swing music was still faintly heard in the distance, echoing toward them. Walt could barely make out the large dark objects of various sizes on either side of him, which in some cases extended from the floor to the high ceiling.

"Please make yourself at home." With that, Crane started to walk out, leaving Walter alone. When he crossed the threshold, Crane flipped a switch and the room became illuminated in a weird kind of fluorescent black light, spotlights overhead trained on the exhibits in the hall. Walter stood alone, deliberating exactly what these objects were.

He looked around, thoroughly scanning the area while waiting for his eyes to adjust. Walt wanted to make sure he was the only one in the room. Once his eyes adapted to the low light, he realized that these were exhibits. It was then he heard a loud, feral noise echo throughout the hall, a powerful, primal call that terrified him. His hand instinctively went to where his gun would be under his jacket, but he wasn't carrying it on this outing. He stayed still for a while, getting a feel for the room, making sure nothing was going to jump out at him. It suddenly became clear to Walter what all this was. At the nearest end, where he stood, there were sleek cages that had black steel bars with animals inside. It was an indoor menagerie. Walter began to inch closer, moving past the terrariums inside the various cages situated on either side, containing animals of who knew what species, to what lay beyond. He headed toward the far end of the hall, where huge tanks of water of varying sizes reached up like enormous monoliths into the high ceiling. Walter cautiously looked into a tank filled with water so dark he couldn't see through it. He tapped on the glass and realized it was extremely thick and had the texture of something other than the cold touch glass would normally have.

Walt lit a cigarette, turned around, and walked over to one of the cages to peer in. Within the cage was an odd-looking white tiger that was at least twice the size of what Walter thought the average tiger should be.

"I see you found Matilda."

Walter swung his head around toward the far end of the hallway, where a seated dark figure was gliding toward him, accompanied by an abnormal buzzing sound that got louder as it got closer. Traveling down the center of the hall, every ten feet or so the gliding man was illuminated by an overhead light as he passed underneath. It soon became apparent that the sound was a motorized wheelchair propelling the man toward Walter. The chair looked particularly modern, with flourishes of the popular Art Deco style and slick-looking aerodynamic skirts over the wheels.

Mr. Cuthbert Hayden was dressed in an extremely well-tailored tuxedo with a red woolen blanket covering his legs. He was slightly overweight, with dark gray slicked-back hair and a wrinkled face that didn't appear to smile often.

"Matilda?" Walter said curiously.

The wheelchair stopped right in front of Walter and the two sized each other up. Hayden pointed to the cage with the odd-looking animal inside. "She is a "liger". My pride and joy, a mix between a tiger and a lion. Only four are known to exist in all the world."

Walter studied the animal through the bars with a level of disdain and sadness. "And one of those four is locked up in a small cage in front of us, eh?"

Mr. Hayden laughed. "Ah, Mister Morris…. You must appreciate, when money no longer becomes a concern…well, we all have needs, but to not have wants? One does become mildly eccentric with such pleasures. Do you understand?"

"I believe I do."

"Forgive me. Please allow me to introduce himself. I am Cuthbert Hayden."

Walter nodded in recognition. "I kinda figured."

Hayden regarded the cage. "No need to worry about this poor creature's plight, Mister Morris. Matilda will have the best life she could ever possibly have, be provided with the greatest care available. Only the very best." He glanced from the animal up to Walter. "You must understand the context, Mister Morris. You see, all of this," Hayden gestured with his hands, "all these trophies, are a grim reminder of an extremely extravagant, dramatic, and overindulged previous life of mine. I am a far, far cry from the man I was even five years ago. This compound was at one time the East Coast's version of Hearst's San Simeon in every sense. We even have a manmade lake abutting the northwest end of the house that rivals Lake Hopatcong in New Jersey, just to be able to simulate a coastal view."

Walter continued to be pleasant. "Do you, now?"

"Indeed, Mister Morris. It was a very different world then. Wild parties filled with drugs, alcohol, orgies…you name it. Certain people care nothing about tomorrow as long as money is easy today."

"It seems a far cry from your public persona. Millionaire philanthropist, pioneering in technology and engineering, rivaling that of even Howard Hughes or Henry Ford. Developing various vehicles and aircraft, experimental weaponry and flying machines. Like that new helio-copter machine up in Connecticut. You must have been making a killing the past few years, since the war's been on."

"Yes, Crane told me how up to date you are on your knowledge. Surprising, I must say. And impressive."

"Well, I don't know a lot about anything, but I know a little about practically everything. Comes in handy in my profession."

"Ah, I see. But all this *excess*, the lifestyle and playboy living," Hayden patted the arms of his wheelchair, "all that changed on June thirteenth, 1938, when a bottle of JD and I decided to get behind the wheel of a Duesenberg and have some fun up on Mulholland Drive."

Walter glanced at Hayden's covered legs and slick wheelchair.

"God spared my life, but he took away my ambition and my mobility."

The wheelchair came to life and pivoted, and with Hayden leading the way, the two began to move down the hallway past the exhibits.

"It appears you've made the most for yourself, despite your ailments. Somehow, though, I doubt you brought me here to see your little mixed-race zoo and hear your biography," Walter ventured.

Hayden smiled. "You would be correct. To the point—I like that, Mister Morris. Speaking on the topic of mixed race, if I may be frank, I must admit it is very forward-thinking for you and your partner to have an interracial investigative firm."

Walter nodded. "Wave of the future. Getting to drink out of both fountains."

"It can definitely have its advantages, as evident now of a Negro gumshoe getting a crack at such a high-profile and sensitive case like this."

Walt curbed his reply and responded diplomatically. "With all due respect, you're the one who randomly summoned my firm to come over and take you away from this party of yours. I'm not an overly smart man, but like I said, as awfully inspiring as all this is, I don't think it was just to boast and discuss forward-thinking business models, unless you're looking to get into the private detective business and give the Pinkertons a run for their money."

Hayden answered with another chuckle. "You are bold and have a sense of humor. I like that in a man. You and your firm came highly recommended, particularly for your experience in the Negro neighborhoods."

Walking behind the automated wheelchair, Walter replied, "I am not a fan of that word, but in answer to your question, yes, we do a lot of work in various ethnic areas, black neighborhoods included. My partner and I, a Brit mind you, saw a corner of the market we could thrive in and a people we can help. We both possess certain talents from which we mutually benefit."

"What of the war prior to establishing your firm, Mister Morris? You don't feel so patriotic for your country that you will go fight for her?"

Walter flashed a smile. "I can't speak for my partner, but I myself can find enough trouble in Harlem and the Bronx. I don't need to cross the world to fight somebody else's."

Hayden took interest in his answer and pressed on. "Do you feel disenchanted with America? How the Negro is treated? Even though it's eighty-plus years after a war was fought and won in this country to free your people?"

Although Walter bit his tongue, he continued with his polite and professional demeanor. "I make it a policy not to mix personal politics with my job."

Hayden abruptly stopped his chair and turned to look up at the detective to make sure he saw exactly how his next comment would land. "What about the murder of your younger brother in 1930? He was supposedly under your care while your father was out working on the railroad? Do you blame yourself for that, or do you feel the government—your local police and by extension, your country—let you down?"

Walter's pulse quickened. This was uncomfortable subject matter for him, but he purposely attempted to remain calm.

"No, I don't think my baby brother being murdered by a sick pattern killer and it being ignored by the New York Police Department because, as they say, 'Who's gonna notice one less colored kid in the slums gone missing' is a letdown? Of course not. That doesn't put a bad taste in my mouth at all."

Walter finished with a pleasant smile, one that made his jaw muscles flex.

Seemingly satisfied, as if putting Walter through such unpleasantries was all part of the job, Hayden nodded. "You must understand, I like to screen all the people under my employ thoroughly, so please, Mister Morris, take no offense."

Walter put on his best pandering smile. "No offense taken. So, being frank myself, are we gonna dance around here all night, or are we gonna get down to business, whatever it maybe?"

This impressed Hayden further. "Ha! No sir, no indeed. Like you said, I have an event to get back to." Hayden gestured with his arm. "Shall we proceed?"

Walter nodded and they continued on toward the other exhibits on display.

"I had a head maid here at Hayden Manor, a beguiling Negress named Corrina Jones. It seems even now to be a lifetime ago. She had a daughter while she was with us, Caldonia. Such a beautiful girl. I kept an eye on her as she grew up and promised her mother on her deathbed that she would be taken care of."

"That's very generous of you. Did, God rest his soul, FDR's New Deal inspire you to help out someone less fortunate?"

Hayden grinned. "No, Detective."

The two stopped at one of the large tanks lit by fluorescent lights from above. It was made of a very thick glass. "This is a synthetic called acrylic glass, a revolutionary material discovered quite by accident in our laboratories. It is completely transforming our world, and *will* do so in every facet in the coming decades. The incredible strength allows us to simulate extreme conditions and pressures that you'd find leagues down at the bottom of the deepest oceans."

Walter nodded, impressed. "So, Corrina, her mother, you said she died then?"

"Tragically, yes. I am determined to keep my promise. I kept Caldonia by my side, trying by any means necessary to give her every chance she could have in this day and age, coming from, eh, class system."

"That's awfully gracious of you. Are you like that with everyone under your employ?"

Hayden glanced beyond, toward what was within the tank. "Corrina, she was an amazing woman. I…owed her this."

Unexpectedly, out of the darkness of the water, a very bizarre translucent creature appeared and swam past. It had a piranha's head with an elongated body, much like that of a snake.

Walter's eyes widened, betraying his fright while the creature slithered by them in the dark water. He didn't get startled very easily, so he tried to play off his unease with a timid smile.

Hayden responded with an emotionless smile of his own, not because of Walt's reaction but more toward the gravity and context of his story. He looked back toward his tank, the dim reflection casting a phosphorus glow on the millionaire's face. "In any event, Caldonia became wild in her teen years. She rebelled and started to frequent the underbelly of our society. You know how today's youth are. Wild swing bands, jazz, and that Negroid backwoods music, the wretched 'blues'…." He sighed. "Well, it caught up to her. The degenerates got ahold of her and she became a reefer addict. It all went downhill after that."

"What happened?"

Hayden made eye contact with Walter. "About a week ago, she phoned Garland to have someone pick her up on a Hundred Thirty-First and Broadway."

"Uh, that's Mister Crane?" Walt took out his notepad and began to make notations.

"Yes, she evidently had a confrontation with a few men, but by the time Mister Crane arrived, she was nowhere to be found."

Walter jotted more down. "You know what the argument was about or who it was with?"

"No, I do not."

"And you haven't seen her since?"

"No. No, word. Nothing." The genuine concern became apparent in Hayden's voice. "I just pray it has nothing to do with this 'New York Ripper' in the city."

"Well, so far from what I've heard, he's only been killing blonde white women, so we have that going for us. Have you contacted the police?"

"I thought it best to keep this a private affair."

"No police?" Walter frowned. Hayden revealed a lot by preferring to take this course of action. "And no other inquiries were made to locate her?"

"Mister Crane tried, to no avail. She has been absent from the estate before, but never for so long. This is why I decided it best to seek professional help. Your firm was recommended due to your absolute discretion and your experience in the Negr—uh, *ethnic* neighborhoods."

Walter nodded sympathetically. "Well, going at it on our own will complicate things to a degree. Without the police and all that manpower, it's gonna be a lot harder. No word on who she was arguing with?"

Hayden gazed down at the floor dejectedly. "No."

As Walter looked around the room, he couldn't help but be amazed at the absolutely strange and fantastical location he was in, straight out of a science fiction magazine, but he kept his astonishment to himself. "Anything else you can give me to work with?"

"Caldonia was an exceptionally close member of her church and the reverend there. That is, until her spiral into the abyss. She went to a popular house of worship down in Harlem. The irony there is going to worship God is how she was seduced by temptation."

"It's not something you can fault her for. Especially in this day and age."

Hayden stared up at the detective and crossed his hands in his lap. "Do you have any initial impressions?"

Walter was always blunt and saw no reason not to be. So far there wasn't anything that particularly made him like the old man. "Sounds like it could be a runaway case if she was unhappy here. Or…"

"Or?" Hayden raised an eyebrow.

"Do you have any enemies, Mister Hayden?"

"Aside from the Japs and the war in Europe? Ha, take your pick. Hearst, Howard Hughes, J. Edgar Hoover and his bureau, or…," Hayden pondered for a moment. "You think ransom? What would someone think they could gain?"

Walter closed his pad and stowed it back in his pocket. "Very good question. It's already gotten you to hire a shamus. Obviously if this was linked to you, they'd have to be keenly aware of your fondness for Caldonia and her mother. Just throwing around some healthy conjecture. Do you have a picture of her?"

"Yes, of course." This might have been the most honest yet betraying action by Hayden. He quickly pulled out his wallet from his inside breast pocket and removed a picture, then carefully handed Walter the photo. A beautiful young black woman was seated in a professional art studio, the photo was artificially colored, as the old-style portraits were once done. "Crane will provide you with whatever else you may need. List of friends, anything."

"I'd like to come back and talk to the staff if I may. Her friends and everyone she palled around with here on the estate. And I'll need access to the room where she slept."

"Done."

Walter paused a moment to contemplate and exhaled a long, slow breath. "Okay, I'll see what I can dig up."

"Remember, Mister Morris, please be discreet with this matter."

"Of course."

Hayden studied him with the conviction that only a ruthless cut-throat tycoon with years of experience like Cuthbert Hayden could pos-sess. "I would hate to see what would happen to an up-and-coming firm like yours if you were to foul up a tremendous chance like this."

Walter nodded solemnly. It was all he could do.

Hayden abruptly took a 180-degree turn with his chair and rolled away into the darkness.

"Thank you, Mister Morris. I trust you'll be in touch." It seemed as if the light in the huge space left with him as the buzz from his electric chair faded away from earshot. It was now back to being dimly lit and hard to see.

Once Hayden was gone and the sound from his chair had ceased, it was replaced with a loud silence and the far-off bass of swinging jazz. Walter suddenly felt very uneasy.

CHAPTER 5

OFFICE OF CHIEF MEDICAL EXAMINER OF THE CITY OF NEW YORK

The city morgue was a filthy place. It was filthy to visit and an even filthier place to work. The caked-on grime looked to go as far back as the nineteenth century. Walter could only begin to imagine the grotesque images these disgusting walls had been exposed to. The subway tiles, ancient and decrepit, had long ago lost their white sparkle veneer and assumed a nauseating yellowish-green or brown color, depending on the location and light. It was a place Walt never felt comfortable in. Death was all around.

The hallway was littered with gurneys with bodies atop covered by white sheets. Some of those sheets were stained with dried blood; others had bodily fluids soaking through. Walter rounded the corner with a freshly lit cigarette in his mouth. His eyes fixated on the man he was looking for, the assistant medical examiner, Tony Vincenzo. A stocky Italian with a short, military-style haircut, he was sucking on a lollipop and directing various assistants and staff.

"Larry, you can't leave him here. Take him over to the fridge 'cause the air is starting to make him fall apart. Popeye, stop acting like Mortimer Snerd and take her over to Phil so he can start that postmortem."

Walter glanced down at one of the bodies Tony was referring to but quickly looked away. "Whatdaya say, Tony?"

Tony removed the sucker from his mouth. "Walter."

Walt inhaled a large drag of his smoke and blew it out into the room. He was the only one in the office smoking. "Looks like business is popping. Speaking of popping, what's with the lollipop?"

A few of the various workers took notice of Walt's cigarette smoke. They snuck glances at their boss, Tony, and went on with their work.

Tony studied Walter with annoyance and waved his hand casually to dissipate the smelly smoke from around him. "How many people do you think come through here who smoked?"

"You mean who smoke?"

"No, they're dead. It's past tense."

"Wait. How's that now?"

Tony stopped what he was doing, put down the clipboard he had been looking at, and gave Walter his undivided attention. "I said, how many people do you think come through here that smoke? *Smoked.* Jesus, now you have me messing up."

Walt looked around, quickly realizing he was the only one smoking. "Well, I'd—"

"Do you know how many black and gray damaged lungs I see?"

Walter looked disappointingly at the cigarette in his hand.

"How much spaghetti-like fat we see that builds up, clogging veins, the arteries and valves?"

"So you quit?"

Tony laughed. "Yep, I quit, that's my point."

Feeling slightly disgusted, Walter threw his smoke to the floor and stepped on it with his shoe. "Well, good for you."

He followed Tony into the main examination room where several autopsies were currently underway.

"So, are you here to see the specials on tonight's menu?" Tony asked.

Walter chuckled. "Seeing if you have any female black Jane Does around the ages of sixteen to twenty-one. Would have come through in the last five days?"

"Negro, Jane. That all?"

Walter nodded. "That, and some advice on my victory garden."

Tony walked toward a collection of clipboards hung on the wall, filled with reports of those who had come in and gone out. "What's the weight and height?"

"About a hundred twenty to a hundred thirty-five pounds, around five-six."

Tony cross-referenced a sheet on a different clipboard then stepped into the adjoining refrigerator room. Walter, who had been staring at the bodies being dissected around him, hurried to catch up to Tony. In the next room the far wall had a dozen or so rectangular doors that hid coffin-sized refrigerated compartments.

Tony quickly scanned the small doors looking for the right number. A second later, after finding what he wanted, he opened a bulky door and pulled out the slab inside. He lifted the sheet and before them lay the body of a dead black female, roughly in her mid-twenties, her eyes glazed and her eyelids and lips eaten by the critters in the East River. Walter viewed his photo and compared the two. It was not Caldonia.

"Naw, not her, Vinn."

Vincenzo replaced the sheet and rolled the Jane Doe back into the freezer. He walked out of the room with Walter quickly following. Tony crossed over to his desk and checked his other logs.

Walter leaned against the counter, once again glancing at the various bodies being autopsied. One was an obese man, his chest was wide open in a hinge-door-like fashion, while another was that of a white blonde woman who was being cleaned with a trickling hose and a sponge. An electric saw sounded from the other end of the room, to which Walter shot a glance over. An attendant started the exploration of a cadaver's skull cavity.

Tony finished looking through his logs. "Nope, that's the last Negro female we got in that age range."

"Thanks for looking, Vinn." Walter sized up the busywork going on around them. "You got a proper Eli Whitney assembly line going on down here."

Tony exhaled loudly and gave a look of frustration. "With this Ripper character going, they got us working eighteen-hour days trying to make sense out of it all. It's up to six now."

"Yeah, heard that on the wireless."

Tony put the clipboard in his hand down and stepped closer so he could talk softer. "Walter, it's horrible. They're like grave robbers. You know, the robbers that used to dig up the English countryside to give med students fresh bodies to dissect? Eh? You know?"

Walter nodded. "We called 'em Night Doctors in our neighborhoods."

"Yeah, I heard of them down South. That's what this feels like. All these bodies are coming back with various organs perfectly removed. And you know what else? We've been finding dead skin, all around the victim's throat."

"Dead skin?"

"Yeah, all around the neck area. And the weird thing is I don't think it belongs to them. I think that if I—"

Tony's boss, the head New York City medical examiner, entered the morgue, and Vincenzo quickly silenced himself. "Erm, Sir."

Walter immediately spoke up, acting as though he didn't notice Tony's boss enter. "I guess next time watch out not to leave your wallet in a Parmelee cab. Luckily, I employ only honest drivers." Walter glanced over to the medical examiner then back at Tony. "And I'll take you up on those Dodger tickets, so let me know if anything comes in then."

"Okay, buddy, and thank you again."

Tony walked away in the direction of the medical examiner. Walter turned to leave, but he paused.

The blonde-haired female body was just being moved from a table by two attendants and it caught Walter's eye. Rigor mortis had set in and the left hand was caught, almost holding onto the side of the metal table before being pulled free with an unpleasant dragging sound. Like it was the last desperate inanimate action of a brutalized victim.

It brought Walter back to unpleasant memories he'd rather not have dancing around in his head.

❖

Walter held up the small picture of Caldonia closer than necessary to the tiny man's face.

It was particularly loud in the seedy pool hall and thick with a haze of cigarette and cigar smoke. The clacking of cue balls being smashed together and the chatter of the many groups hanging out in the dimly lit establishment was all around them. It was more crowded than would be expected for a weekday afternoon, but for a lot of these patrons, this was their livelihood. The weathered clientele resembled men out of the Depression era, with gaunt faces of all sizes and styles, wearing all manners of facial hair—clean shaven to mustaches to stumpy beards. They barked back and forth bets, side bets, and side action; it was like the floor of the stock exchange, in a massive hypnosis as they watched the events of the many games happening on the tables.

Walter stood next to the owner's desk. It was slightly raised against the wall, like a judge's podium. Below the front counter, a large aging sign hung with the hourly rates and rules of the establishment. The lanky poolroom owner, "Small Change," was sat up high behind the tall counter and was dressed in an old, stained shirt, dusty cardigan, and wrinkled hat. His round glasses were about an inch from Caldonia's picture.

A waft of thick gray smoke escaped Small Change's nose and mouth while he spoke through stained yellow teeth, engulfing the detective. "Nope, never seen her before. I would have remembered a beauty like that. Sorry, Walt."

Walter lowered his arm and put the photo away. He peered around at the groups of men huddled around tables and seated up on the wooden pews that were built in below the dado rail on the outer walls. "You've always got your ear to the pavement. You hear about any extortions or ransoming of wealthy Westchester tycoons?"

Small Change followed Walter's eyes out toward his congregation and felt a sense of pride looking out on his flock. "Nothing like that since the war's been on. All the big-time confidence games have been halted. Sure, there's some petty pickpocketing or maybe an obituary-page con, but that's it. Nothing as high profile as a kidnapping or extortion, not with the war. We've all come together to help Uncle Sam and our boys." Small Change grinned as he looked back down at his old pal who stood below him. "I got ration cards if you need them." Walter winked at Small Change. "You looking for anything—gas, meat, alcohol?"

"Naw, Small Change, I'm okay with ration cards. Can you do me a favor and check the flophouses and shelters? Here's her info." Walter tore off a sheet of paper from his notepad, handed it to him, then asked, "What's the latest you hear about this New York Ripper thing?"

Small Change took a long drag before the journey. "I've heard the bodies are having organs removed…." His calm eyes accentuated the last words spoken.

"That's why they're calling him the New York Ripper."

Small Change nodded. "That's not the only goings-on." He exhaled the smoke, which poured out like an exhaust pipe into the detective's face. "The police are holding back some details that the papers haven't reported either."

There was a pause. Walter regarded Small Change and the latter slowly nodded, with a coy smirk that revealed the pride he felt in knowing that he had a piece of information no one else knew. It was one of the reasons why Small Change was such a wealth of information and a great source for a private investigator. This particular private detective always knew exactly the right way of getting it out of him.

Walter realized Small Change was waiting for an acknowledgment. "Really?" he said with an elongated reply.

Small Change removed his glasses and used the bottom of his cardigan to clean microscopic splashes of coffee off the lens. "Well, from what I've learned, the bodies have had all their blood drained right out of them. They're bone-dry." He looked through each lens to inspect the job he had done.

"Really?" Walter said again.

"Yep." Small Change did a final polish and held his glasses up to the desk lamp light for inspection. "Like a vampire." His eyes widened as he went on. "They got two puncture wounds in the jugular. And no blood. So where is it?" His eyes locked on Walter's. "It ain't at the crime scene. Savvy? It's taken. Someone's stealing their blood, along with their organs."

Around the corner at the closest bench seat, out of the view of Walter, a small, almost emaciated Japanese man sat puffing on a long, thin pipe. His eyes had a cloudy, fogged appearance as if he were blind, and he was wearing a large-brimmed hat, partially obscuring his face. His head was cocked slightly toward them so his ears could pick up what was being said by the billiard room's proprietor and the private detective.

Small Change put his glasses back on, taking the time to hook the thin wire tips around the back of his ears. "Now we gotta worry about goddamn Bela Lugosi creeping around the back alleys of this decaying berg. Who the hell knows? Maybe it's the Nazis' secret weapon for a New York invasion."

Walter looked back out toward the crowd. "The war will be over any day now in Europe," he said to the small man lurking behind the desk. "So, they'd be a little late for that."

A loud *crack* that sounded like a pistol shot reverberated in the smoky hall as the clay billiard balls smacked together on a nearby table.

❖

Walter spent most of the next day scouring every inch of his home turf, Harlem. Pounding the beat, he showed the people he passed Caldonia's picture but got nowhere. He tried almost every business applicable, but still, nothing.

At one point he stopped to view a long procession coming down the street. The spiritual guru and demigod himself, Father Divine, sat atop a float that was being carried, surrounded by white-robed disciples. He claimed to be God, and his followers believed him. And when he had a parade, everyone knew about it. The procession sluggishly made their way along the road singing old spirituals, backed by a brass band taking up the rear.

Walter took a break and had a quick bite to eat at the nearest soapy saucer. He ate in silence, contemplating his case thus far while watching Father Divine's parade pass. When he was done refueling, he stepped back outside and walked across a side street, stopping in front of Caldonia's church called the Divine Grace. He heard singing inside. He quickly checked his notepad and walked up the stairs.

As he opened the large double doors, he immediately felt like he wasn't "in Kansas anymore". The packed congregation swayed to a large, boisterous, all-female choir that sang up front next to the pulpit. They were singing a lively rendition of the traditional spiritual song "I'm On My Way to Canaan's Land." It reminded Walter of the fevered energy he used to encounter going to church as a child with his little brother and mother before she died; the joy and excitement was intoxicating. The congregation were all on their feet, stomping, clapping, and moving in time with the music.

"Had a mighty hard time, but I'm on my way. Had a mighty hard time, but I'm on my way."

The atmosphere was contagious, and before he knew it, Walt found himself unconsciously mouthing along too. *"It's a mighty hard climb, but I'm on my way; On my way-hey! Glory Hallelujah, I'm on my way."*

As the song and its lyrics came flooding back to him, a broad smile appeared on his face. He gradually lost his demure insecurity and sang along with the next verse.

"Along the way, Satan lies a-waiting; Every night and day, Satan lies a-waiting."

Walter sang louder in sync with the congregation and began to sing with the same heart, soul, and feelings as everyone else in there.

"Hear me shout and say! Get behind me Satan! *I'm on my way, Glory Hallelujah, I'm on my way."*

At the front of the church on the stage next to the large choir, the reverend sang along. He was an elderly, round-bellied, dignified gentleman whose scant gray hair encircled the top of his head like a halo. He watched

Walter since he'd entered, nodding with a smile of satisfaction, seeing a newcomer off the street joining right in.

Walt continued singing happily along with the congregation.

"Fight the devil and pray, take another step higher; Fight the devil and pray, Lord, I wanna climb higher.

"Chase the Devil away, Lord, I'm caught in his fire; I'm on my way, Glory Hallelujah, I'm on my way."

The song ended and everyone applauded, including Walter.

When the services were over, the parishioners exited the church and passed the reverend, who stood on the top step just outside the large doors, saying goodbye and shaking hands with each churchgoer. Walter waited patiently, remaining last in line, and only after every member was gone did Walter walk out to chat with the reverend.

"Reverend? Might I have a word with you?"

"Of course. I saw you in the back there. What can I do for you, son?"

"I'd like to ask you a few questions about one of your flock."

The reverend smiled and looked Walter directly in the eye. "You a police officer?"

"Not exactly. My name is Walter Morris. I'm a private investigator and working on a case." Walter already had his wallet out and opened it to show him his identification, discreetly keeping it low by his hip to not make it look like the reverend was talking to the cops. "I thought maybe you could help."

"Private investigator, eh? Well, Mister Walter Morris, my name, like it says on that sign there, is Reverend Percy Clarence. How can I be of assistance?"

Walter didn't get the impression the reverend was being insincere or pandering, which could be the case with some in Mr. Clarence's profession, so he jumped right in at the deep end. "You know a girl by the name of Caldonia Jones? She commutes down on the train from Westchester. I was told she's a member of your congregation?"

The reverend's smile immediately faded, and he glanced down at his feet then back up at Walter. "Is this about her disappearance?"

"Yes. I'd love to know anything at all you could tell me about her that may help me track her down. How many people know?"

"It's gotten around town. And the police haven't gotten involved. Did her father hire you?"

"I'm sorry, but I'm not at liberty to say." Walter quickly changed direction. "Do you know who her father might be, Reverend?"

The reverend nodded at an elderly parishioner who yelled his named from the other side of the street and waved back at her with a warm and sincere smile as he answered Walter, "Someone who would be publicly ashamed if it ever got out that he had a child out of wedlock. A colored child, at that. It would be scandalous. Someone whose status in the public eye might be forever tarnished by such news becoming public."

Walter didn't respond. Reverend Clarence looked back at Walt. "We seem to be talking about the same person here, my son?"

The private detective smiled. "I believe we're on the same page, Reverend. My client is worried about her safety first, which has now become my concern as well."

The reverend turned his back to the street and held his bible close with both hands down by his belly. "She stopped coming to church and bible study 'bout four months ago. She used to be real close to the church until her mama passed away some years back. That's why she came here. Her mama was from this area after she'd originally moved here from Holden, Louisiana. Once her mother passed on, I think the devil got a hold on her and introduced her to the wickedness of the world that, sadly, our surrounding community has to offer."

"Know anyone who was close to her, anyone who could help me locate her?"

The reverend squinted his eyes to block out the sun. "Maybe Mister Howard, the groundskeeper at the Hayden Mansion, he might know. She considered him the grandfather she never had, if I remember correctly."

"That a fact?" Walter took the name down in his notepad. "Mister Howard?"

"Yes, Howard Crothers I believe his name is."

"Anything else you might be able to tell me about her?"

"Well, that I hope for her sake she hasn't followed in the path of her father. The Lord saw fit to punish that man for his sins before he'd even left this Earth. Mister Hayden is an evil man who deserves all that was dealt out to him, believe me."

Walter frowned. "Excuse my frankness, but that doesn't sound a very 'godly' judgment coming from you, Reverend."

"It's not coming from a place of God, Mister Morris. It's coming from a member of the community, someone who knows a little too much more than he should know from personal experience."

CHAPTER 6

HAYDEN MANOR

Early the next morning Walter drove up to Hayden's Westchester estate in his '39 Mercury Town Sedan. He was allowed onto the estate after he flashed his identification and gave his name, leaving his Merc in the roundabout right in front of the mansion. He told the first footman he saw that he was looking for a fellow by the name of Howard Crothers and was pointed in the right direction.

They told him Crothers was at the zoo, and at first Walter thought they were messing with him. So, when he was taken to an actual zoo that abutted the house and probably the indoor hall from the other night, Walt had no words. Along with Hayden's museum menagerie of exotic animal rarities, he also had an entire zoo on the grounds with all the animals you'd see at the circus or in your everyday box of animal crackers. The private zoo had all the architectural flair of Central Park Zoo, with its habitats patterned with the same stone and rock style, and the more Walter thought about it, with Hayden's wealth, it was probably designed by the same guy.

Eat your heart out, San Simeon.

An enormous black panther paced around a huge cage, staring out through the bars, looking bored and waiting to be fed. Walter walked over, fascinated by the animal. In the back of the enclosed area, a small metal door opened and a metal cookie sheet with raw meat on it slid out. The animal hurried over.

After a few moments of watching the panther feast, Mr. Howard Crothers, the head groundskeeper, headed over to Walter. The bowlegged, elderly, dark-skinned gentlemen introduced himself. Chatting, the two walked throughout the zoo's path, passing various animal exhibits.

"So you take care of all these animals, Mister Crothers?" Walter asked with a respectful demeanor.

"That's right, sir. Fo 'bout twelve years, since Mista Hayden been keepin' a zoo here, I've been tendin' to 'em."

"You take care of all those wild animals out there—the lions, tigers, and bears—all by yourself?"

Howard nodded.

"Oh my."

"A lot better than plowin' behind a mule down in Clarksdale...."

Walter nodded. "I hear that. Seems to be a tough job, taking care of these exotic creatures. I mean, how'd you come about learning how to care for each one?"

The question made Mr. Crothers stand a little taller and prouder as he replied. "Yes, sir. Basically, you soon gonna learn what you can and can't do with these critters. Gotta respect them and treat 'em like people. People who got personalities and different moods." He lifted up his right trouser leg to show Walter while they walked. He revealed a disfigured leg with a good-sized piece of his calf missing. Walter stopped in his tracks. In place of what was missing was a fancy metal plate, which had skin partially grown over the edges.

"This is from when I got careless wit' a gator we had here back in thirty-eight. Hahaha...Mista Hayden had his rich doctor friends who were over visitin' from Europe fix me right up. I don't know what I woulda done without them."

Howard rolled his pant leg back down and they began to walk again. Howard headed over to a railing overlooking a silverback gorilla exhibit. "They only discovered these guys in the wild at the turn of the century."

He gestured toward the primates who were sitting comfortably and eating fruit and leaves.

"Amazing," Walt observed in awe. "And this motha has got them in a cage in his backyard," he added in with a shake of his head.

Howard paused, thinking for a long minute, and looked over toward the detective. "I get the feelin' you ain't come to talk about no zoo, Mista Morris man."

Walter smiled. "You're right, I'm sorry to say, Mister Howard. I wanted to ask you about Caldonia Jones."

Howard's face dropped. "Such a shame. I knew her motha Corrina too. Such a sweet woman, I tell yah." He took a stained rag out of his back pocket that substituted for a handkerchief and rubbed the sweat away from his forehead and the back of his neck. "Real close to Mista Hayden. Was even talk that they bed togetha, but you know how sewin' circles be, Mista Morris, 'specially in our line of work."

Walt nodded. "Mama passed away a few years ago?"

The elderly man frowned. "The big *C* got her."

Walter took off his hat and fanned his face. "Did you know Caldonia well, Mister Howard?"

Howard laughed and put both his hands into his back trouser pockets. "Wha—shit…. I helped raise her. We all did. She wanted to be a singer, like Bessie Smith, Ethel Waters- you heard of Ma Rainey, right? Cause they don't make her discs no more." Walter nodded. "You never know with you young kids. Or that…," Howard's eyes detoured to the left to remember the other name, and a twinkle hit his eye when it popped into his head. "…Edith Piaf, the French crooner, as she liked to say." He looked back at Walter. "Then when her Mama got sick and Caldonia took care of her until the end. She just stopped smiling then. That was so sad. Lost all her drive to be that singer she once wanted to be. And, since her ma passed away, she just ain't around here as much as she used-ta be."

"You have any idea what happened to her?"

"I don't know, sir, seems she disappeared. We all is as worried as Mista Hayden is. It ain't like her." Howard shot him a serious glare to convey the fear and concern he and the others had.

Walter nodded in understanding. "Do you know who she ran around with? Where they would go?"

"Not really." Howard turned away. "Used to hang out in Harlem, in the clubs there. There's talk she dated a musician. I think a white fella, but nobody's supposed to know that, especially Mista Hayden." Howard smiled as his mind wandered. "I used to go down there during 'a early Depression. Last time I was there was the night Louis knocked out that German Schmeling in thirty-six. It was like New Year's Day, Christmas Day, and the Fourth of Ju-ly, all wrapped into one."

"I can only imagine." Walt paused before asking one of his biggest questions. "Do you like Mister Hayden?"

Howard stared down at the silverbacks and thought long and hard. "Look, he's a tough man. He has a way 'bout how he wants things. But he takes care of us all and certainly spares no expense when it comes to makin' sure we all looked after. Yeah, he be a hard man, but he's okay." Howard pointed down to his leg. "I wouldn't be walking on two legs right now if he ain't got his rich European friends to fix me."

Walter nodded in understanding, and looked down at the gorillas, who were peaceful and serene.

❖

A maid unlocked and opened a wooden door, and Walter walked into Caldonia's room. The room was plain but spacious, and it was shared with another maid. There was little on the walls, or any personal items for that matter, on Caldonia's side. A window between the two beds at the far end gave a beautiful view of the grounds behind the house and the woods beyond that. Two lonely gray single beds were separated by a bare night-stand under the window, and about the only other thing that could fit in the room was a bureau for the clothes they both shared. This entire wing of the house was for the servants' quarters, with the females on this floor and the men below. Crothers brought him up, escorted by a maid so they had a chaperone on the female floor.

Walter stepped in and cautiously looked around. "This was her side?" Walter said to the maid, indicating to the right side by the window. The maid nodded.

The only picture on the huge wall was a small framed photograph of a young girl, which Walter assumed was Caldonia, seated on the lap of an older woman in a maid's uniform outside by a rope swing. Walter gave the room a polite once-over.

Stuck up on the dresser mirror on her side was a more recent photo of Caldonia and her mother, both noticeably older.

"Can you tell me any more about her fella?"

Howard turned back to the maid, who was standing in the doorway, and nodded to indicate it was okay answer to Walter's question.

"She never really talked about him," the shy maid shared. "All she used to say was that he was a musician. A professional one." She shot a glance to Howard, and he nodded again for her to continue. "We're pretty sure he's white. He was helping her with her singing, practicing. Teaching her stuff."

Walter looked around on the dresser and opened the drawers, checking to see if anything was taped to the underside or stuck to the back of them, hidden. He looked back at her with a warm smile. "Go on."

The maid slightly blushed and returned his smile. "A piano player, I think she said. I hear he's a foreigner, friends of Mister Hayden's friends."

"If Mista Hayden knew about that, my gosh." Howard shook his head and sighed.

Walter crossed and sat down on Caldonia's bed next to the nightstand. He opened the top drawer and discovered a bible. "A musician, eh? You ever hear his name mentioned?"

The maid shook her head. "No, only that. I think maybe she met him up there, where she used to go to church, at a place in Harlem."

While examining the nightstand, he saw something was on the floor against the wall, down between the bed and the piece of furniture. He bent down, picked it up, and brought it into the light in front of the window. It was a half-spent matchbook. The advertisement on the cover read:

THE CREO ROOM

"Swell as Hell"

131ST AND BROADWAY

"Harlem."

Walter recognized the address. The Creo Room, the last place Caldonia had been heard from and where she told Crane to pick her up before she vanished.

CHAPTER 7

THE CREO ROOM

If Walter led an exciting and thrilling life, he'd take the night off. But he didn't, so he decided he'd make a night out of it anyway and knew the exact place to go.

He went home, cleaned up, and changed his shirt before heading back out. He took a cab over and could hear the bass notes emanating from the nightclub even before he laid eyes on the place. People were everywhere, coming and going from the club. Walt paid the cabbie, took out the matchbook once more to confirm the name and address, and crossed the street toward The Creo Room.

He nodded at a rather large bouncer at the front door who looked him up and down. Walt smiled a broad, happy smile and entered the establishment.

His eyes had to gradually adjust in the smoky and dimly lit club. It was a huge space, half-moon in shape, with an enormous bar on the left side that curved around toward the back of the venue. There was a long partition about five feet high that separated a section of booths that overlooked the main sunken area of the club. After that was the general seating space, and past that the large dance floor and expansive stage against the far back wall.

The Creo Room was a black-owned club, catering almost exclusively to a black clientele. The surrounding neighborhood and community were very proud of this, and for good reason. It did occasionally attract white patrons coming in to hear good music and also had regular white jazz musicians playing the latest swing or bourgeoning bebop music that first appeared on Swing Street. Unlike other clubs that had Negro workers and musicians playing to white-only audiences, The Creo Room took pride in being pro-black. They almost encouraged a black-only customer base, with, of course, several exceptions.

Walter had never been here before and could instantly see why people loved it. The club had a Haitian and Jamaican island theme to it, and the lighting made the space feel like it was continuously twilight on a beach. Fast jazz was flowing through the air from Charlie Parker and Dizzy Gillespie and their band onstage. People mingled about, while others had a good time trying to keep up with the music on the dance floor.

After taking the scene in, Walter gravitated toward the bar. "Well, you have good taste, Caldonia," he muttered, almost feeling embarrassed that it took a case for him to check out a hip and swinging place like this in his own neighborhood.

The bartender made his way to him. "Drink?"

"Please. Wild Turkey. On the rocks."

The bartender reached for a glass. Walter leaned against the bar, making note of all the entrances and exits and where the office and backstage doors were located. It was an entire operation they had going on here, with hostesses, waitresses serving food, busboys, and cigarette girls; then there were the dancing girls dressed to match the island theme of the club. They walked around and mingled with the patrons, dancing in synchronization with some of the larger musical numbers.

Walter got his drink and lit a smoke.

"Can I help you with anything else?" the bartender asked.

"Not at the moment, thanks."

The man politely nodded and went over to serve someone else.

Walter sipped his drink while taking in the scene and swinging music. A very attractive dark-skinned woman wearing a sarong walked up and put her arm around him.

"You looking for a date tonight, Mister?"

He winked at her. "Already got one. Thanks." She shrugged and walked away.

On the stool next to Walter was a man with a pair of nasty scars on both his cheeks, starting from the corners of his mouth, as if his cheeks had been ripped apart. When he and Walter made eye contact, the brother's stare was like ice, so Walt manufactured a courteous smile and looked elsewhere.

Up onstage, the band finished and a bald, middle-aged, dark-skinned man emceeing appeared onstage in a single spotlight, filling the time as the musical acts behind him switched out.

"Let's have another round of applause for Bird himself, Charlie Parker! Or back when I knew 'im, *Yardbird*—" he shared a loud laugh with the saxophonist, then raised his arm, pointing at the musician, "—just before he heads out for a tour of California."

The crowd answered with applause.

Once the stage was clear, he repositioned himself. Now with the single spotlight cast upon him, Scatman the emcee was an oasis in the empty darkness on the stage.

"Hello again, ladies and gentlemen. Tonight, we welcome back to The Creo Room our old friend, the incomparable, remarkable, irrepressible— Hell, he's the funkiest brother I've ever met who tickles the ivory…. Ladies and gentlemen, Mister Laszlo Strozek and the Improvisations!"

From the wings, Laszlo Strozek walked out onstage. He was a short European, with prominent blue eyes that were emphasized by dark bags underneath. His dark greased-back hair was parted off center and shined, appearing glossy and wet under the harsh lights above. He wore a pencil-thin mustache above his lip. His demeanor was sedated and relaxed, and all eyes unconsciously appeared drawn to him. And it wasn't because at this point Strozek might have been the only white man in the club.

Laszlo walked over to the microphone, shook the announcer's hand, and took a drag from his long, thin cigarette. "Thank you, thank you. You're all too kind, thank you." A very slight German accent could be detected. "I feel like I'm about to give a sermon…. Go buy some war bonds!"

The crowd laughed hysterically.

Walter had a thought and looked down at his pad, checking the notes about Caldonia's supposed "boyfriend." His scribbled ink read: *BF White - possible foreign / possible musician ~*

Laszlo went on. "I thank you all again for lending us your ear."

He signaled with his hand, and the spotlight trained on him was replaced with a soft, fluorescent kind of glow lighting the entire stage. It revealed the other members of his band, behind their instruments.

"Shall we begin?"

Laszlo turned to his boys and counted off. They started a very fast-paced version of Ray Noble's "Cherokee." The crowd immediately went nuts and began to tear up the dance floor.

Laszlo took his time moving over to the piano, letting the other members of the band jam out to the intro. Once he took a seat, he waited a few bars before joining in.

The musicians were at the top of their game, but it was Laszlo now who had all the attention. It was like the crowd was witnessing magic right before their eyes. Laszlo's tremendous piano skills were otherworldly, hypnotizing. His hands were a blur. At times it was like two sets playing some of the solos. Walter couldn't begin to describe what he was seeing, a virtuoso on display. He was speechless, and not just because of the musical performance but also because of the excitement, the entire atmosphere.

Something he didn't expect on a Wednesday night in The Creo Room.

When the last number of the set ended, thunderous applause met Laszlo and his band. He got up from behind the piano and walked over to the microphone on center stage. He was covered in sweat.

"Thank you, we'll be right back."

Laszlo walked off the stage, shook a few hands, and exchanged some kisses on the dance floor before making his way over to the bar.

Walter made room for Laszlo as he crept in, waved the bartender over, and ordered a drink.

"Let me get that," Walter offered.

Laszlo did not make eye contact at first, then acquiesced and looked at him. "Thank you, you are very kind."

They received their drinks and both raised their glasses.

"You put on an amazing show. I've never quite heard or seen anything like it."

Laszlo smiled. "That's our music. They call it bebop."

"It was incredible. Everyone loved it."

"Wave of the future." Laszlo smiled and took the last shot of his drink. "All about swingin'."

Walter finished his also. "Well, I tell you I'm impressed. A lot of people recommended this place, but I'm glad I finally listened to them. Just yesterday a girlfriend of mine told me to come check your band out."

Laszlo glanced around the club to see who else was in the audience, beginning to become disinterested in pursuing a conversation with a stranger at the bar. "You don't say…."

Walter placed his glass back down on the bar. "Yeah, she said I'd have a swell time up here." He looked straight at Laszlo to see how he'd react to what he said next. "She comes here all the time and loves this place. Hell, maybe you know her. Girl named Caldonia Jones?"

There was an immediate reaction from Laszlo. It was slight, but Walt saw it.

"What, you know her?"

Laszlo raised his glass for a refill. "Never heard of her." The bartender refilled his drink. "Thanks, Jerome."

"I could swear it looked like you knew her," Walter pressed on. "Was supposed to meet her here tonight, actually. Sure you don't know her?"

Laszlo's eyes regarded Walter with a cold rage. "What's your game, mister?"

"I don't understand."

Laszlo slammed his glass down. "What do you want? Who are you?"

Walter gave him a studied, innocent look that even his mother would believe. "Who am I? Just a musician, like you." Well, maybe not his mother.

Laszlo appeared genuinely shocked. "A musician?" He looked him up and down as if to infer it was laughable that Walter Morris would know how to do anything, except maybe be a stand-in for Manton Moreland. "What do you play?"

Walter narrowed his eyes to seem more convincing, baiting him. "The horn."

"The horn?" Laszlo passed that notion around in his head for a moment. "Why don't you come up and sit in on a tune or two? Where is your instrument?"

Walter chuckled and feigned embarrassment. "No thanks, I'll pass."

Laszlo smirked. "Don't worry, we won't embarrass you."

That made Walter smile. "Naw, I ain't worried about that. I only play mine when I get paid." Walter winked at him.

After a brief pause, Laszlo blinked first and looked away. "Well, as exciting as this chat is, I have to get back. It's been a pleasure, mister…?"

"Morris. Walter Morris."

"Thank you for the drink."

Walter didn't hesitate. "Likewise. I'm sure we'll speak again real soon."

Laszlo seemed to understand the implication. "Excuse me." He turned abruptly and walked down the aisle toward the far wall and into a door leading to the back with a sign on it that read *PRIVATE—Band Only.*

A very large man probably the width of an oak tree was positioned as a sentry outside the doorway. His complexion gave the impression that he'd died about a month ago, and he wore a huge pair of dark black glasses that obscured any view of his eyes. Not someone Walt thought he could have a productive conversation with. Getting access to the backstage area through that door would be a challenge, sizing up the employee that looked bigger and wider than the actual doorframe. Walter put out his cigarette.

Walt exited The Creo Room and stepped down onto the sidewalk. He meandered away from the front entrance, acting as though he was searching the storefronts for a pharmacy or newsstand. Once he was confident the doorman was busy with other new arrivals, he ducked down into the side alley that separated The Creo Room from its closest neighbor. The narrow side street was the old cobblestoned variety and curved to the right behind the neighboring building, obscuring the dead end.

Walter made sure no one was watching, staying low and moving further inward while sizing up his options. Steam spewed from the middle holes of a sewer cover, obstructing from view what lay around the corner at the back of the alley. He hoped to see some windows to the rooms backstage, but there weren't any windows along The Creo Room's side wall.

There was a door by some trash cans and a dumpster. It must have been the stage door for everyone except the public. Walter didn't want to stay too close; who knew how frequently that door opened or who he might see go in or out. To buy himself a little time to survey the situation, he dropped to one knee to fix one of his spats, concealing himself behind a dumpster, which he peered around.

To his left below the club was an illuminated cellar window. He shifted to his other knee and inched a little nearer to the wall, now playing with his other spat, attempting to get a closer look in the basement window below. He cleared a couple of crumpled newspaper pages that were blocking his view and peered in.

Inside, from what Walter could tell, there were two gentlemen, both white. They were standing in what looked to be a dressing room. Both were extremely well dressed, like they'd just stepped out from a night downtown at the opera. The older of the two closest to the door was in his early sixties, very lanky, and had a top hat in his hand. He impatiently tapped his hat against his hip.

The other man behind him and closest to the window was hidden under a wide-brimmed Stetson hat. He wore a large overcoat with his collar up, completely concealing his face from view. At about six foot seven or eight, he had a very commanding physique hidden under his long overcoat. Unlike his lanky partner, this one was clearly the muscle because of his beefy shape. He stood like a statue, completely motionless.

The dressing room door flew wide open and Laszlo burst in, slamming it shut behind him. The piano player was hyped up as he spoke with the tall lanky man who was waiting for him. Laszlo's hands waved frantically and accentuated every word. He grew angrier and was beginning to yell, waving his arms around, spit flying from his mouth. From Walter's narrow vantage point, he couldn't see the tall man's reaction. Laszlo snatched a copy of the late edition of the newspaper from his dressing table and pointed furiously at the front-page headline, which was the Empire State Building parachute jump. Laszlo then pointed upward to the club level, gesturing back and forth, as if throwing something in the older man's face.

Walt did his best to understand what was being said, closely watching Laszlo's mouth to see his lips moving. He'd learned a very handy trick years ago, lip reading. In his line of work, a rare talent like that was invaluable. Just like Superman, Walter had his super power too. But he couldn't understand a darn thing Laszlo was shouting. And for the life of him, he couldn't figure out why he was having such a problem understanding. Then it hit him, like a falling piano, what the problem was. It was another language. Finally Laszlo stopped speaking, and breathing heavily, he waited for a reply.

The old man turned to gaze at his taller colleague behind him and Walter was able to catch a glimpse of his face. What struck Walt immediately were his eyes. One was cloudy with a scar above reaching far below the socket, but moreover they were evil. Black, empty pools of eternity that contained a calmness, a death.

Walter wanted to look away before those eyes met his.

But he knew from his experience that at nighttime, if someone was inside with the lights on, they couldn't usually see something outside in the darkness. It was next to impossible. So Walter stood his ground and continued watching the little vignette play out.

A smile appeared on the lanky man's face and he turned back toward Laszlo. He acknowledged the bigger man, pointing his thumb up to his friend. The piano player's anger fell away and his skin paled. His face became horrified and he stumbled backward, knocking into the dressing table and dropping the paper.

Laszlo spoke one word that Walter was able to read and he repeated it out loud. "*Totten core*? Is that what he said?"

Without warning, a large black hand gripped Walter by the shoulder and all at once Walt was in the air and slammed against the wall on the opposite side alley. He fell like a sack of potatoes onto the ground.

The detective was lifted up again, this time by the throat, into the air by the mountainous Oak Tree from inside the club. At the angle he was being held, he could see down behind the dark glasses and into the man's eyes. They had a milky, foggy quality to them, like the pupils of a corpse. It was quite the contrast to his dry, ashy, cracked pale black skin, which made the startling eyes stand out all the more.

Great, he thought, *another new friend to play with.*

Oak Tree held Walter above him by the neck like he was a ragdoll. Dangling there in the air, his large hand looked like an adult's around a child's little teddy bear.

Behind the mountain stood the club's head of security, a slimy zoot-suit-wearing fellow by the name of Luther. He was a shorter, light-skinned man that may have had Spanish blood in him judging by his looks. He had light brown hair that matched his skin; it was relaxed and perfectly straight, parted right down the middle and matted to his head. A gold chain ran from his suit pocket up to a button on the jacket.

Walter gathered his bearings and accessed his situation, his eyes moving between Oak and Luther. He found his voice to be a tad hoarse when he said to Oak Tree, "Uh…hi there, big fella…," which fell on deaf ears. Hell, looking into those vague eyes, Walt thought there might be nothing much going on upstairs.

Luther popped his head into view from behind Oak Tree. "What ya doin' here, fool?!"

Walt took a deep breath and cautiously went on. In his best Jack Benny, he started with a slick and confident, soothing tone. "Well! I was *trying* to correct my spat, you see, which had started to bunch up to the left because they're cheap spats. Got 'em from my ex-secretary who really didn't like me. Anyway, I was adjusting my spat, when your man here, uh, um…," he looked at Oak, "hi there," then back at Luther, "…all of a sudden the son of Kong here started messin' with my equilibrium. And then I was on the other side, against this wall here, looking at the brick decay in the gutter."

Luther wasn't impressed by Walter's explanation. "What's your spats gots to do with that window right there?"

Walter played dumb. "What window?"

"What window?" Luther repeated in a mocking tone.

Walter's face reddened and it got harder to breathe when Oak raised him even higher, like a marionette whose strings had been cut.

"Do it."

Oak Tree drove his fist hard into Walter's stomach then dropped him. Walter collapsed to the ground in a daze, coughing, trying to suck the air back into his collapsed chest.

Luther stepped in and snatched Walter's wallet from his pocket and placed his shoe on Morris' forehead. He scanned through the contents. "Walter Morris? You...wait..." Luther kept looking. "You got all kinds of IDs up in here. You a private investigator? Whatcha doing here at The Creo Room, brucka?"

Walter tried to speak but was still coughing and unable.

"What's that?" said Luther. "I asked you a question, fool."

Walter cleared his throat and made sure his head was still connected to his body before he spoke. "I—I just came up to hear...to hear this new *bebop* everybody is talkin' about...."

"What!"

Walter again pled ignorance. "And what you talkin' about? And *who* the hell is you?" Walt's mustered his most convincing outraged voice his throat could manage under the circumstances, even executing an authentic falsetto to convey his unwitting shock.

Luther stepped back and made a click with his teeth. On cue, Oak put his foot on Walter's chest and applied pressure like a vice, pressing his back into the uneven bricks below.

"You lyin' to us, boy?" Luther's eyes narrowed at Walter.

Barely able to speak, Walt countered, "Now, why would I do that?"

Oak applied even more pressure.

Luther took the cigarette out of his mouth and used the Pall Mall between his fingers to punctuate his next point as he wagged it at Walter. "Let's get something straight. You come around here again and start askin' about shit that's none of your business, my man here is gonna experiment on your bone structure. Got it?"

The pressure at this point was all he could bear, so Walter nodded.

Luther responded with a huge, gold-toothed grin. "Good, you're getting it." He motioned to Oak.

Walter saw black as he was thrown one-handed at least ten feet. He flopped, unconscious, onto the sidewalk at the mouth of the alley.

CHAPTER 7.5

BAD DREAMS

A hazy series of images played through his head in a blurred vision of a dream.

A little boy that Walter struggled to recognize sat playing jacks on the dirty floor of an uneven and cracked hallway in an old apartment building.

Out of the darkness a man emerged and ambled up to the small boy, and they began to converse. The boy's face came into focus and Walter recognized his little brother from so very long ago. The boy nodded and the older white man extended his hand, which the boy accepted in his small one.

The child was helped off the ground, and together the two headed down the dimly lit hall hand in hand toward the basement.

Walter heard an omnipresent voice, asking him questions, wanting to pry. "What happened to your brother, Walter?"

He heard his teenage voice answer with an uncertain resonance. "The boogey man got him, sir."

Before they disappeared down the stairs, the older man turned his head and Walt saw the terrifying face of child-killer Albert Fish.

Walter remembered shouting for his brother to stop, to come back, but the harsh shrills of the prepubescent teenager didn't stop his little brother from walking away with that demon of a man. His head turned and, looking toward a young Walter, Fish smirked at him and waved goodbye. It was this sneer that shaped young Morris's life. That single image locked inside Walter's young brain. The events after that were to fuel the next eighteen years of Walter Eugene Morris's life on up to his present circumstances.

Instantly Walter heard the voice, the one that haunted his thoughts, his dreams, and his nightmares. The sound he could never forget. That calm and soothing voice that haunted him forever.

"First I stripped him naked. My, how he did kick, bite, and scratch. I didn't fuck him, though, I could have, had I wished. He died a virgin."

Young Walter's eyes welled up.

CHAPTER 8

DRUNK DUMP

Walter very slowly opened his eyes. It took him a couple of minutes to fully come around and realize where he was. He was laying on his back on an uncomfortable metal cot, staring up at a dank stone ceiling that was covered in a layer of peeling, century-old paint. He recognized his surroundings at once.

He was in jail.

Walter grimaced in pain when he attempted to sit up, but his cranium wasn't having it. His world began to spin. Walt put his hands to his face and felt his bruised cheek and a lump on his head. He winced from the pain, and the cut on his lip that he hadn't known existed reopened.

It took a couple of minutes to fully gain consciousness.

Out in the hall the guard out on duty walked over to his desk and picked up the telephone receiver. "Sarge," he said quietly into the phone. "Yeah, he's coming around now."

Walter swung his legs onto the floor, his arm held tight around his side to shore up his bruised ribs. His hand again found the swelling on his head and he gently probed the area with his fingers. "Jesus."

A loud clanging startled Walter as his cell door was unlocked. In walked Sergeant Ambrosio, a well-seasoned, plain-clothed police officer in his mid-forties who came from a long line of cops. The spitting image of his father and grandfather before him, with chiseled features and short brown hair that was graying on the sides. He was followed by his younger partner, an energetic plain-clothed officer named Davies. Life on the job hadn't burnt out the spark inside of the young man yet; he still had the drive to change the world. That drive needed just a few more years on the force for it to be brutally stamped out. That came naturally with time and age.

"Walter," Ambrosio said with a kind smile.

The detective took his time fully sitting up. "Wha—oh, hey, Sergeant...."

Ambrosio watched him struggle to get his balance back. "What's going on, Morris? Went on a bender last night?"

Walt's eyes settled on the sergeant. "I feel like I have...." He smelled his shirt and jacket. "Jeez, and I smell like I did too. Where'd you find me?"

Young Davies answered that one. "In the gutter, on a side street off of Riverside Drive by the Westside Highway construction. You were soaked in gin."

"Wow, that far out?"

Sergeant Ambrosio fished into his pocket for a smoke. "What place exactly were you putting a new coat of paint on?"

Walter checked out his pockets to see what he still had on him. "Certainly not with the fishermen way out there." He laboriously got to his feet. "Last I knew, I was outside The Creo Room off Lexington."

Ambrosio rolled his eyes but said with genuine concern, "Walt, what the hell you doing up at The Creo Room? That's no place for a guy like you. What, d'ya think you're in a Warner Brothers gangster picture?"

Walter's wallet, notepad, and smokes were gone. "Out on a case. Must've done a 'drunk dump' on me. He didn't miss anything. Do you by chance have my stuff?"

Ambrosio nodded. That was a relief.

"No money, though."

Walter rolled his eyes and even that hurt. "Jesus." It was becoming his new favorite word. He examined the rest of his face then his teeth, checking to see if any were loose.

Ambrosio continued to watch Walter with interest. "You should consider yourself real lucky. You coulda ended up in a barrel at the bottom of the Harlem River. What's this case you're working on?"

"Nothing I can talk about at present. Patient-doctor confidentiality, you know that." Walter cautiously took a few steps.

"Alright, Morris, I'm not gonna lean on you, just take care of yourself. I don't want to be finding parts of you in a train canal up in Woodlawn Heights."

Walter grinned. "Thanks, Ambrosio."

He followed them out. At the desk in the hall, they handed him his belongings. Davies was called over to another officer who'd just arrived, and they conversed in low tones. Walter's wallet and his notepad containing several pages of the Caldonia Jones case had been ripped out. While Walter continued to examine his possessions, Davies finished being briefed by the uniformed officer. He walked back over to Ambrosio and whispered into his ear. It was quiet, but Walter still could make it out.

"They got another one. We gotta roll."

"Shit," was the Sergeant's response.

"Work?" Walter said rhetorically, to get his mind off what was stolen.

Ambrosio nodded solemnly. "Yeah. Another victim of that Ripper, we think. You heading uptown, Walter?"

The three shared a police car uptown, sirens blaring. Even at this early hour, the streets in the city were filled with people less than happy to have to make way for the racing Plymouth police cruiser.

"You guys got any leads on this guy?" Walter asked loud enough from the back seat to be heard over the siren.

There was a slight hesitation as the officers looked at each other before contemplating whether to answer or not. Ambrosio made the decision and started the conversation rolling.

"Whoever he is, he's smart. He goes after the fringes of society, the ones who don't know they're dead yet. The ones that John Q. Public won't notice or care about, the throwaways."

Walter understood what that meant. "Prostitutes?"

Ambrosio nodded. "A victim with no witnesses. We have no informa-tion; we can't even identify the body half the time, except by the way she's dressed. We surmise that they're street-walkers."

There was a pause in the conversation and Davies jumped in. "The only reason the public is paying any mind to it is because of the areas where the bodies are being left. Washing up on the Westside docks by the transatlantic passenger liners or left in Eastside alleyways."

"Or by the piers where the neighborhood kids swim," Ambrosio inter-jected, making eye contact with Walter through the rearview mirror.

"All young, blonde, white women," Davies went on. "Wasn't for that, no one would care."

They arrived at the scene and exited the cruiser. Ambrosio finished up Davies's point. "Sadly, in this world, there are the haves and the have-nots, and these victims are the have-nots. Plain and simple."

Walter sighed. He could only agree. "I know that world. So sad."

A crowd was gathering in the mouth of an alley. Even this early in the morning, a body could create a horde of gawkers.

Ambrosio glanced over at the gathering crowd. "Sorry, Walt. This is our stop."

Walter understood. "Thanks, I can walk the rest of the way."

Ambrosio glanced at Davies, then back to Walter. "You wanna come have a quick look? See what a different set of eyes could lend?"

Ambrosio and Davies made their way through the crowd with Walter following behind. They passed a uniformed officer who was holding back the masses. The head of his baton went into Walter's chest. "Where d'ya think you're going, Bojangles?"

Ambrosio abruptly walked right up to the uniformed officer, getting in his face. "He's with us, officer." The young cop's sneer morphed into indignation and resentment.

Walter squeezed past and entered the crime scene while Ambrosio lingered over the beat cop, pissed and ready to crack him in the face before Davies hurried over and intervened.

Walt examined the scene before him. The harrowing remains of a gutted blonde woman lay at the end of the alley on a pile of garbage. The detectives conferred with an on-scene officer, and Davies took a knee to inspect the violence more closely.

Walter moved over to Davies. "Mind if I have a look?"

Davies glanced behind Walt's shoulder to Ambrosio, who stepped over and nodded. The young cop looked back at the detective. "Have at it."

Walt took a step around Davies and bent down. He noticed first that no blood was present anywhere at the scene, despite the fact she had been horrifically dissected—tissue, organs, and even bone had been removed. Walter beckoned with his finger for the two men to come closer. Ambrosio bent down, and Davies shuffled his feet closer.

"What you got for us, Mister Moto?" Ambrosio asked.

"No blood." Frowning, Walter pointed around the alley floor. "There's no blood anywhere near or around the body, despite the massive injuries. You know what that means, number one son?" he asked Davies.

"She wasn't killed here," Ambrosio answered before his partner could. "Just dumped."

"That was for him," Walter said, gesturing toward Davies before turning back to the body. He pulled back a piece of the victim's clothing using his pencil and whistled. "Now that's interesting."

That got Davies's further attention and he moved even closer. "How's that?"

Walter pointed to the dissected chest cavity of the victim. "Here, the insides." Walter pointed to the grisly exposed part of the woman's stomach. "They look to be frozen."

Ambrosio scooted Davies aside to look closer. Walter pointed with his pencil. "See where the kidneys used to be? Doesn't it look as if the insides are cold and almost frozen? Peculiar to see in the month of June."

Davies whispered under his breath to Walter, "Yeah, it's the same MO as other crime scenes."

Walt carefully got to his feet. "Well, thanks again for the ride and look-see. I got my own case to deal with, so I'd best be on my way."

Ambrosio also stood. "Okay, Walt. Just remember to keep this info close to your chest, my friend. I'm trusting you, Morris."

"I know, I know, and thank you for that. Truly. Take it slow." With that Walter turned around and headed out of the alley into the crowd.

Davies directed his gaze at his partner. "Interesting, but curious fella. He used to be a cop?"

Ambrosio shook his head. "No."

Davies frowned. "So does he have some kind of morbid fascination or what? Aside from professional interest?"

Ambrosio thought for a moment on how to respond to his young partner's questions. "His little brother was murdered by the pattern-killer Albert Fish back in 1927. You know the name Albert Fish?"

"Of course. The Boogey Man, Vampire of Brooklyn...he used to eat children."

Ambrosio gazed out in the direction Walter had disappeared, a look of revulsion on his face. "Yes, yes he did. That maniac cooked and ate Walt's brother over the course of an entire week. Then told Walter all about it in every precise and disgusting fucking detail."

"Shit."

CHAPTER 9

HOTEL CLARIDGE

Walter shot back up to the office, washed, and quickly changed his clothes. Downstairs, two men sat parked across the street in a blue sedan. They clocked Morris as he headed out. They were large gentlemen, bruisers in matching black suits with Stetson hats. They both chain-smoked and their narrow eyes never once left the detective's face as he crossed the road and got into his '39 Merc.

The driver started the car and the two men waited until Walt pulled his vehicle out into the traffic. They let a car pass by before pulling away from the curb. They stayed on him as he drove downtown, keeping a safe distance so as to not be spotted.

Walter lucked out and found a parking spot a block away from Times Square near his destination, the Hotel Claridge. He was meeting with Hayden to check in and discuss his progress on the case thus far. One of Walt's "new friends" stayed with his car, circling the block while the other chose to hike the cement trail, keeping a peripheral distance from his subject.

The receptionist at the front desk of the Claridge made a call, and once he was approved, Walter was instructed to take the private elevator at the back of the lobby up to the penthouse. An employee was already expecting Walt and opened the elevator doors for him.

During the ascent he found himself trying to pop his ears due to the change in pressure. The doors opened at the penthouse level, and Walter headed down a private hall until he came to a large and very luxurious waiting room decorated in varying shades of crimson. Steps the width of the room led down to a couch and seating area, where a young female secretary was seated behind a modern oversized and aerodynamic desk. There was a lot of hustle and bustle in the office. Walter got the impression the commotion was perhaps because the man in charge was actually gracing the workplace with his presence today. It quickly muted with the appearance of Walter. The employees scattered, disappearing into other rooms.

Hayden's secretary waved him over toward her massive desk. "Mister Hayden will see you now."

Walter smiled at her. She appeared even smaller up close, behind such a display of masculinity made of stone and wood, like a ventriloquist's dummy behind an oversized dinner table.

A job is a job, he thought.

As if on cue, the wall cracked open and a door appeared where seconds before there had been nothing but wood paneling. It opened up to an enormous office that was double the size of the first room.

"Can I bring you anything to drink, some tea perhaps?" the demure secretary inquired.

"No, but thank you."

Walt walked into the office, where couches lined the walls and matched the modern décor of the space perfectly. Toward the center of the room was a huge boardroom table and chairs. Beyond that, at the far end, was an enormous Dalbergia desk positioned in front of a wall of windows, providing an absolutely incomparable view of lower Manhattan south of Forty-Second Street. Square footage was obviously not a concern this high up in the sky.

In very dramatic fashion, Mr. Hayden swiveled his leather high-backed chair around from the window, behind the impressive desk. "Mister Morris, it's very good to see you. Please, shut the door so we can have some privacy."

Walter shut the door, which disappeared into the wall.

Hayden gave him a once-over and chuckled. "Have you been in a fight, Detective?"

"No, just training a little too hard down at the gym."

"I see. So, do you have anything to report?"

"Maybe. Have you heard of a nightclub in Harlem called The Creo Room?"

Hayden didn't even pause to consider the question before answering. "The Creo Room? I think I have not. What kind of a place is it, a dance hall or something?"

"It's a Negro club, pretty much caters to a black-only crowd."

"Doesn't sound like a place I'd much want to visit," Hayden shot back. "A darkie-exclusive club."

Walter had learned a long time ago that in his line of work he had to leave his temper at the door and tolerate remarks which may offend or infuriate others. So unless a big bag of money was going to be the next thing coming over the horizon, Walt carried on, deciding to hit the ball back just as quick. "How about a piano player named Laszlo Strozek? White, Eastern European, he's quite possibly German or Czech?"

Hayden paused. "Laszlo Strozek? Do I know that name…?" Hayden repeated it out loud, so he could process the words. He turned his chair back toward the window. The Empire State Building was within view and had a zeppelin docked at its antenna tower. "It does not immediately bring anyone to mind."

"He might just be the best piano player I have ever heard. Caldonia possibly frequented this particular club, and I think this Strozek might know her. I was told she was dating a musician who might be white and foreign, a piano player to be more specific. He does fit the bill."

Hayden cocked his head to the side. "Then the two might be one and the same?"

"Perhaps. He was pretty unconvincing when I questioned him about her, and I got the brush-off shortly afterward from the management…so I wonder if there's something there too."

Hayden continued to stare out of the window at the zeppelin and the city beyond.

"He was socializing with some serious-looking gentlemen. White Eastern European, I think, meeting under the club. Speaking German from what I could make out before I was…interrupted."

Hayden looked genuinely perplexed. "At a predominantly Negro establishment?"

"Yes, that's why I found it too disconcerting not to be connected. It could be nothing, but things got strange. Not what you'd except to see at a black-owned club. I still have to properly look into the place; maybe it's a white-owned front, catering to the black neighborhood and music scene."

"What of the men he was meeting? Who were they? Could they have been music agents, financial backers? Or what about fans?"

Walter shrugged. "Don't know yet. Honestly, one looked like Frankenstein in a trench coat, and the other looked like Conrad Veidt-straight out of a Universal horror movie."

Hayden still hadn't bothered to make eye contact with Walter. "Laszlo Strozek…"

"You know, the bad guy opposite Bogart in *All Through the Night* and *Casablanca*?" Walt laughed, to no response from Hayden. "I'll take that as a no?"

Hayden was deep in thought, "Laszlo Strozek…" He said the name again, this time slower. His eyes narrowed, his facial expression changing slightly, as if he had a spark of recollection.

Walter remained silent for longer than he wanted, only because he was trying to be gracious to his current employer. "You sure you never heard of him? Laszlo Strozek?"

Hayden finally met Walter's questioning green eyes and his response was immediate. "No, no, Mister Morris. It doesn't ring a bell." The old man returned to his thoughts.

CHAPTER 10

LASZLO STROZEK

Walter crossed the faded marble floor of his office building, absently staring at the pattern the tiny tiles made below his feet. As he passed the tiny room that housed the building's switchboard operator, a woman's voice called out from inside the small nook.

"Hey, Walter!"

The detective stopped in the doorway and grinned at the young black-haired woman wearing a headset. "Hey, Dolores."

She held her hand up for him to wait until she had finished transferring a call. When she inserted the phone plug into the appropriate jack, she covered her headset microphone and pushed it away from her mouth so she could talk to Walter. "Oh gosh, Walt, what happened to you?"

Walter touched his still-tender face. "Oh, just cut myself shaving is all."

She leaned closer, possibly for effect. "Hmm, well you got a visitor up in your office. Real suave fella, I think he's foreign." She made a snooty face and pursed her lips.

Walter laughed. "Thanks for the heads up, Dolores. Keep up the good work." He winked at her and walked away.

Laszlo Strozek's gentle, soothing voice was as calm and accommodating as he could muster. He sat in the center of Walter's inner office, right in front of the detective's desk. The piano player lit a cigarette, and his tranquil eyes wandered around the room before settling on Walter.

"So then, you do understand why I was hesitant to interact with you regarding this emotional situation. You could have been anyone trying to pick a fight or looking for a scoop. As you can imagine, we are all extremely concerned about Caldonia, and we all want to find out where she is."

"You ever read Dashiell Hammett, Mister Strozek?"

"Who?" Laszlo looked a little confused.

Walter smirked. "No matter. I got to meet your overprotective friends from the club. The slick-looking, zoot-suit-wearing *souteneur* and that side-show freak he has for muscle."

Laszlo smiled, maintaining his sugar-laced demeanor. "Mister Morris, The Creo Room likes to make sure their entertainers are comfortable. We need to feel safe and at ease in order to perform." He purposefully made direct eye contact with Walter before saying, "It is Harlem, Mister Morris."

He stared right back. "It *is* Harlem."

Walter subconsciously chewed on the cut on his lip. "So neither you nor anyone at the club have any idea where she could be or her condition?"

"We fear she simply has gotten fed up with her provincial life and jumped on a bus or hitchhiked out of the city."

Walter raised an eyebrow. That was a new one. "So when did you last seen her, then?"

Laszlo gazed up to the ceiling before carefully replying, "I can vaguely recall, maybe three, four weeks ago?"

"Almost a month, huh?" That information completely contradicted what Hayden's people had told Walt—that Caldonia vanished in front of The Creo Room only a week and a half ago.

Laszlo grinned, his smile very self-assured. "We were not an item; we were free to see other people. I didn't have a hold on her, and she hung out with a lot of other men, you know."

The more suave the piano player attempted to be, the more repulsed Walter felt. "Did you know much about her background? You said you met her at the club?"

"Yes," Laszlo adjusted in his seat. "We met there and became acquainted with each other."

"Do you know where she lived?"

"You mean the estate with Cuthbert Hayden up in Westchester?"

"And you know who he is?"

Laszlo appeared perplexed. "Of course I have heard of him. I read the papers."

"That was my next question. Cuthbert Hayden."

"Yes, I know him from the society pages."

"You two ever m—"

"Nope," the piano player answered before Walter was even finished asking the question.

"You've never met him?"

Laszlo shook his head. "I have never met him."

Walt lit another cigarette, offering his visitor a fresh one in the process. "So, you honestly think she just up and left due to some kind of rebellious streak within her?"

The piano player politely waved away the cigarette. "Mister Morris, most girls at that age are confused and uncertain about life. All they need is a little guidance, and with some persuasion, you can usually get them to do anything," he said almost seductively.

Directly across the street from the Roland and Morris office, in a small run-down room at the Park Avenue Hotel, Walter and Laszlo's conversation came crackling through on a short-wave radio frequency, hissing through the extremely narrow space. A long German K98 Mauser sniper rifle with scope and sound suppressor leaned against one of the grimy walls, its steel tip starting to dig into the plaster. The window's yellow drapes were drawn closed with only a small gap remaining, just enough for a pair of tripod-mounted binoculars to peek out. Connected to their small portable radio was a reel-to-reel machine, recording the conversation that was taking place right across the street.

One man lay on the small single bed against the wall, its faded sheets untouched. His tie was loose and his top button undone. He listened with his eyes closed and his hands clasped together around his stomach, all focus on the conversation across the street. His partner had just enough room between the bed and far wall to fit a small folding chair. He hunched over the tripod so he could look through the binoculars. The air in the room was stale from cigar and cigarette smoke. The man watching by the window had taken his suit jacket off and was eating Chinese takeout with chopsticks. He stared past the "Roland and Morris" sign on the window at the men seated at the desk. Walter stood and walked around the desk toward Laszlo, they both shook hands, and the detective began to show the piano player out.

The man looking through the binoculars took a break from inhaling his meal long enough to breathe and let out a belch.

"I'm getting sick of chink food. A guy can only eat so much of this crap before—"

"Ed, shut up," the man on the bed barked.

Across the street Laszlo left the office and headed out.

Walter pulled down the blinds, and from the side of the window, he watched as Laszlo left the building and walked across the street. Laszlo got into the back of a large Studebaker that was double-parked in front of a bus stop. The door shut, and the car attempted to speed off before getting stuck in the heavy 125th Street crosstown traffic.

Walter stepped back, turned the radio off, grabbed his hat and coat and dashed out of the office.

The man watching across the street turned with a mouthful of food and picked up the receiver to the telephone extension they had set up in the room. "Yeah, call that same number, please." There was a slight pause while he waited for the front desk to dial out. The receiver clicked over. "Hey, he's on the move."

He hung up the phone and looked over at his partner, who had finally opened his eyes. He swallowed the remainder of his food. "You know, we should be following him wherever he goes. If he's following the piano man, we should be there to see what develops."

The guy on the bed nodded. "You're preaching to the choir, Ed. Look at the upside, at least you get to listen to your stories."

Seated at the window, Ed glanced at his partner and agreed. "I do wanna hear how King Fish and Andy get outta this one tonight."

The man on the bed lowered his brow and angled his head in question.

"They've put a down payment on a place up in the Catskills," Ed said. "Ahhhh."

❖

In the heavy afternoon traffic, Walter quickly caught up with the Studebaker and tailed the black car downtown. Walt's '39 Mercury Town Sedan had been modified and reconfigured all to holy hell by Del Ray Goines, his old friend and mechanic who owned the garage two blocks north of his office. Walt and Del Ray had grown up in the same tenements and, despite the heinous odds, had both achieved the American Dream. Now, along with the bank, they both owned businesses within mere blocks of one another.

Having a mechanic's garage so close made it possible for Walter and Jacob to have an automobile and a place to store it. It also let Del Ray tinker around, turning Walt's car into a sort of inconspicuous vehicle like The Shadow and his taxicab. Walt loved *The Shadow* and never missed listening to the weekly show. Their Merc certainly wasn't a yellow cab, but it was painted in such a way that it would blend into midtown traffic, looking like it belonged rather than sticking out like an unmarked police car. Del Ray had even installed a taxi sign on the roof that could be turned on while in traffic or double-parked, helping the Merc blend in even further. When the sign was off, it melded into the roof and wasn't even noticeable, looking decorative or perhaps like a kind of Art Deco-inspired fin. That was just the tip of the iceberg. There were police sirens hidden within to use when needed, among a few other surprises. The Mercury was a pretty neat piece of modern engineering, a Frankenstein monster of a car.

Walter zigzagged through traffic at a steady pace, all the while tracking the limo that Laszlo was in. The Studebaker made an abrupt stop
around Seventy-Second Street. Walt passed the car and parked about a half
a block away, turning his taxi sign on to illuminate "on duty." He watched
through the car's sideview mirror as Laszlo jumped out and ducked into
a nearby pharmacy. Walter was parked in a no-standing zone and clicked
on the parking lights so the car would look like a taxi that was occupied.

Walter quickly made his way over to the pharmacy window, carefully
making sure he was also staying out of the view of whoever was in the
Studebaker. He caught a glimpse of Laszlo walking to the back of the
apothecary, where he ducked into a phone booth.

Inside, Laszlo made a call and recited the pharmacy's number from
the circular center of the rotor to the party on the other end. He hung up
and waited inside the booth. Walt grabbed the late edition from a nearby
paperboy and held it up to his face as if he was reading, but peeking over
the top of the paper and through the window, keeping an eye on the enig-
matic piano player.

Some minutes later Laszlo picked up the phone to answer it. He spoke
excitedly for a couple of moments, then hung up and exited the phone
booth. Walt hurried back to his own car as Laszlo left the pharmacy and
jogged across the street to the large sedan. The Studebaker didn't even wait
for him to shut the door completely and pulled out into traffic. Walter
was back behind them at a measured distance. The black sedan continued
south, navigating the dense city traffic as it arrived in Midtown. It pulled
up to the corner of Forty-Second and Fifth Avenue in front of the library.
A man with a cane walked toward the car, and the door was opened from
the inside. The gentleman unconsciously flipped back his overcoat and
removed his hat when he bent down to enter the car, and before he was
obscured by the suicide door, Walter caught a glimpse of his face. It was
Garland Crane, Cuthbert Hayden's manservant.

The door shut, and the Studebaker drove off.

"Ain't that a fuck?" Walter said to the empty vehicle.

They continued south on Fifth Avenue. Walter opened the glovebox,
where he removed a camera from among the gear secured inside. Some

of Del Ray's modifications, like his glovebox, were right out of a Dick Tracy comic strip. He anchored the base of the camera into a special screw mounted on the dashboard.

Walter got as close to the limo as he possibly could to try and see through the large back window. It looked like Crane and Laszlo were in a heated argument or a very animated discussion.

This day was full of surprises. He clicked the button on top of the camera, and it started to snap away on a crude timer.

The black sedan next stopped at Herald Square, and Crane exited the vehicle. As he switched his cane to his other hand, the pair had one last exchange. Laszlo threw Crane's bowler hat out at him, and it fell to the ground.

The back door shut, and the Studebaker drove away. Crane grabbed his hat, swore out loud, and shot his arm into the air to hail a cab.

Walter made sure his lights were off and sped up to keep after Laszlo.

The Studebaker headed west and crossed the Avenues until it hit Eighth, where it turned right to head back uptown. It got to Penn Station and the car signaled left, crossing the lanes on the Avenue. It stopped right past Thirty-Fourth Street in front of the New Yorker Hotel. The back door opened, and Laszlo jumped out. By some miracle, Walter found a parking spot across the street. The Merc's engine purred like a beast in hiding as Walt tapped the gas to inch into the narrow space.

From under his bench seat, he produced a large first aid tin. Stowed within were an assortment of basic disguises and other items to throw off the curious or suspicious eye. Walter found these tricks to be very helpful when he and Jacob did surveillance. If they changed maybe two things while following a mark, like add a mustache or sideburns or per-haps switching up their hat or jacket, people didn't expect it, and they, in some instances, could go virtually undetectable throughout the day. Sherlock Holmes employed the same technique, and after seeing his idol Lon Chaney do it, why couldn't a modest-yet-enterprising Harlem private detective firm do the same? Lon Chaney served as a lot of inspirations for

Walter, who learned that he shared many things in common with the late screen star.

Walter unfolded a small piece of wax paper and removed a false thick-haired mustache. He lightly dotted some spirit gum to his upper lip and, using the mirror on the inside of the metal tin to get the angle right, he held it down with a couple of fingers and started to count the Mississippis to twenty. He let go and instantly had a hip bohemian/bebop-jazz-scene 'stache. He finished his new look off with a pair of thick glasses and jumped out of the car.

While crossing Eighth Avenue, he adjusted his fedora and flipped his overcoat inside out so it looked like a different jacket. He turned his collar up and used it to block his face when he passed the idling Studebaker.

He entered the vast Art Deco lobby of the New Yorker Hotel and scanned the massive hall, looking for Laszlo. He spotted him by the check-in desk with his elbow resting on the counter. Walter pulled out the evening paper from his jacket, adjusted the thick pair of glasses on his nose, and sat down on one of the lush, red circular couches that surrounded the huge lobby columns. He opened the paper and acted like he was reading while focused on the front desk.

Laszlo asked the hotel clerk to ring a room. Focusing in on their lips, Walter easily read what they said to each other. He jotted down in his notepad the room number, *1213*.

The clerk retrieved the house phone, dialed a four-digit number, and spoke to someone on the other end. After a moment Laszlo nodded in thanks and headed toward the elevator bank at the back of the lobby. After a short wait he entered an elevator. Walter checked the time on his wristwatch and logged it in his tiny notepad.

An hour later Walter was reading the evening paper for the third time. He took off his glasses and carefully cleaned them with his handkerchief. He put them back on, carefully folded the material, and replaced it in his pocket. He tapped his mustache to make sure it wasn't starting to peel off, then took out his notepad. He paused for a moment, then removed his wallet from his inside breast pocket where an old, faded black-and-white photo fell out onto his lap. He grabbed it before it could fall all the way to the floor. He carefully turned it over in his fingers. It was a picture of his brother Stevland, sitting on a young Walter's lap outside on their tenement stoop on a sunny day. Walter was in his late teens, and his brother was maybe seven or eight. Walt stared at the old picture intently, his eyes focused on his brother's smiling face. The boy was filled with joy and excitement.

Walter smiled. He was tickling Stevland's sides that day to make him pose for the camera. The happiness and laughter on his little face was infectious. This picture always made him smile. As long as he didn't think too hard or too much about his brother, he could always smile.

He couldn't think too hard about his poor, innocent little brother, or Walter's thoughts always took him to the same place. Back to what the final hours must have been like for that sweet little child.

Laszlo exited an elevator with two men in tow. Walter put his photograph and wallet away. One of the men was the older gentleman Laszlo had been arguing with the night before in the basement of The Creo Room. The other appeared to be their muscle. Walter picked up his paper with one hand, and with the other he went into his inside overcoat pocket and removed a small camera. He quickly adjusted the aperture so it was wide open and discreetly snapped a few pictures as they crossed the lobby.

Even though Walter hadn't been able to clearly see the face of the man Laszlo was having words with the night before, he recognized the slender figure, high cheekbones, and haircut of the man. Laszlo's friend was dressed in an elegant tuxedo and topcoat. Walt's stare immediately went to the man's eyes and his scarred face. The same soulless, empty eyes from last night. Behind them was the tall man from the basement. He was like a gorilla in a black overcoat bulging at the seams, dressed in all black with an unusually long collar on his jacket, his black fedora hat and large brim obscured any of the features underneath the almost seven-foot-tall mountain of a man. As they walked by, the lobby's lights caught the reflection of the sunglasses the man wore beneath his large hat.

The group headed for the front doors.

As they walked out, Walt stood up and tucked the paper under his arm. He kept his distance but made his way to the revolving doors while the men stepped outside and waited for the doorman to hail a cab.

A checkered cab pulled up and the men separated. Laszlo went solo in the taxicab, and the other two men got into the waiting Studebaker, which had been idling outside and out of sight this whole time.

"Interesting," Walter mumbled to himself. He exited the hotel, nodded to the doorman, and quickly headed back to his Merc. He took off his jacket, snagged the first aid kit from under his seat, and started the car. He pulled out and decided to tail the two gentlemen in the Studebaker. He wanted to see where his new friends might take him.

He sped up and kept a comfortable distance, using the spirit gum remover to take the mustache off his face with one hand. He put the thick glasses in the tin and put the 'stache back in the wax paper.

CHAPTER II

PIER 72, ICEHOUSE #4

Walter tailed the cab out to the elevated West Side Highway and headed south toward the dockyards and the tip of lower Manhattan. On the highway he passed by a series of billboards in succession that were part of an ad campaign, starting with the first that read, "Angels," the second, "Who Guard You," the third, "When You Drive," the fourth, "Usually," and the last, "Retire At 65." The punchline made Walter smile, and he simultaneously read aloud as the last billboard came into view, "Next stop, Burma-Shave." He always got a kick out of those advertisements.

They took an exit off the motorway at the bottom of Manhattan, where many of the turn-of-the-century factories, warehouses, and antique slaughterhouses still stood. These vast industrial neighborhoods made of iron, brick, and cobblestone were isolated and dimly lit in the evenings because the most of the establishments closed after dark. The long, wet streets were empty, with only the occasional heavy-duty truck shattering the stillness, coming or going from various businesses.

Being somewhat a ghost town, it forced Walter to keep the Merc at a distance behind so he wouldn't be detected, especially with no other vehicles moving around the neighborhood. The Studebaker made its way to the last street that ran parallel to the Hudson, a beat-up dirt maintenance road where massive warehouses lined either side. Some were built so half of the building extended over the water, big enough so even smaller-sized freighters could dock within the hangars.

Tall wooden fences separated the buildings from the road, obstructing the view for anyone who might want to snoop. The limo eventually came to a stop alongside a large gate with a guardhouse next to it. A night watchman came out to meet them. He tipped his cap at the driver and opened the gate for the Studebaker to drive through.

Walter rushed to park the Merc around the corner, keeping it out of sight. He reached under his dash and pulled out a hidden drawer that contained a blackjack, stiletto, and .22 and .45 caliber semi-automatic handguns. He chose the stiletto but bypassed the others, choosing instead to take a .38 caliber revolver, which he sheathed under his arm. He checked how many pictures he had left on his camera and opened up the glove compartment for a pair of binoculars and another roll of film. Leaving his hat on the front seat, he got out of the car.

Walt hurried over to the corner and peered around, hoping to quickly size up the situation. He didn't want to waste any time and lose track of where their Studebaker was headed. He was just in time to see a large Cadillac drive up from the far end of the street and turn into the driveway by the gate and guard booth.

The detective took advantage and swiftly crossed the street, keeping close to the high wooden fence and out of sight. He stayed down low as he got closer, masked by the darkness.

The guard left his booth again but stopped abruptly after recognizing the approaching vehicle. The overweight, elderly man spun around and opened the gate as fast as he could. The gate opened, and the shiny Cadillac continued down the same gravel road the Studebaker had just traveled.

Walter took out his binoculars and found a place in the fence that had a big enough gap between the wooden planks to view below. The Caddy stopped in front of a large old wooden warehouse, right across from the parked limo. Two figures exited the Studebaker and were greeted by the people who were waiting in front of the building.

The Cadillac flashed its headlights at the two men, bathing them in bright light. Through his tiny binoculars Walt recognized one of the guys from The Creo Room- the slender one with the huge scar over his eye. He was a lot paler than he had been before; it was eerie. Away from the public, he resembled a demon in the form of man.

A figure exited the Cadillac and stood in front of the car's hood, silhouetting itself from Walter's vantage point. The guy standing next to the warehouse's huge sliding doors flipped a lever, turning the building's loading lights on, and clearly showing the man in front of the Cadillac.

He was dressed in a pure, angel-white trench coat. Underneath he wore a matching white double-breasted suit and tie, and matching large-brimmed Stetson. His collar was turned up and the man's face was cast in a shadow, a small beam of light dancing off a pair of round wire-rimmed eyeglasses.

The man with the scar approached the figure in white eagerly, his face lit up into a broad-toothed grin. He greeted the mystery man with a warm embrace. Walter captured all of this with his camera and, using his binoculars, saw that the warehouse was "Icehouse #4." He quickly jotted the information down in his notes. After the embrace, the scarred man pointed up at the warehouse excitedly. The man in white nodded. A few others had exited the Cadillac, and the group shared greetings, shaking hands and smiling. They all made their way into the warehouse.

Walter double-checked his surroundings before carefully and quietly pulling himself up and over the fence. He got a good footing on one of the planks and he went over a lot easier than he expected. He was careful to land on the dirt rather than cement, which muted his shoes when coming down. He stayed low in the shadows and crept toward the warehouse.

He climbed on top of a large dumpster on the far side of the building, which got him to the warehouse's lower roof. He crawled along until he reached a large upper window which was partly open. He carefully opened the window just enough to get himself inside, jumped down onto some large wooden boxes, then lowered himself quietly to the ground. He crouched down on the floor as low as he could.

Walter looked around and was surprised to see it was a giant icehouse, a depot connected to the Hudson River that received boats from upstate carrying blocks of ice of all sizes to be cutdown and sold for refrigeration in the city. The enormous warehouse was like being inside Penn Station. Certainly, large enough to fit a ship or a train inside. Stacked high to the ceiling in every direction were massive blocks of ice. Towering, sleek semi-translucent obelisks.

He realized how lucky he was to have found an open window because the place appeared completely closed off and specially insulated for the low temperatures, like a meat locker in a gigantic slaughterhouse. There was a heavy mist swirling over the floor, moving up and around the thick rows of ice. Walter saw the vapor of his breath. He buttoned his jacket and pulled his collar up.

A string of lights hung high between the floor and the ceiling but did little to illuminate the narrow passageways down below. The bright white of the ice made the huge slabs radiate with an eerie phosphorescent glow.

Walter lit his Zippo to see the floor clearly through the fog and moved on.

Once he started to get a little deeper within the ice maze and turned many frozen corners, it dawned on him how claustrophobic it was getting. Eventually some of the blocks began to shorten in height, and he came upon a clearing, a kind of large cavern shielded on four sides by the walls of ice. This area would have been invisible to anyone looking in from the outside, the room hidden from prying eyes like his. Walt could just about make out some large wooden boxes and crates wrapped in cargo netting. They looked so out of place, hidden away here in the back of an ice factory.

He ventured closer to see under the netting. In a prior life had, Walter worked on a transatlantic ocean liner, so he instantly recognized that the battered appearance of the large heavy-duty crates was from being on the move, the multitude of dents and scratches from being transported and loaded in and out of hundreds of cargo holds. Walt searched high and low but couldn't find a label on any of them. The area he was in was vast, the size of a high school gymnasium. He estimated that all the wooden crates could fill the cargo hold of the average tramp steamer.

Keeping out of sight, Walter bent down low on the ground, took out his stiletto, and tried to pry a board loose from one of the smallest crates, which was still pretty large in comparison. It took a lot of elbow grease and patience, but Walt was eventually able to quietly remove two nails from one end of a board and make enough space so he could peek in. Using his Zippo for a light, all he could see was the straw stuffing that was spilling out.

Holding the stiletto, he carefully stuck one hand in through the crate to feel what was in there. It didn't feel like anything solid was hidden inside all that stuffing, so Walt switched the blade to his other hand and cautiously reached in. He felt something small enough to extract. A large solid gold cigarette case.

Very puzzling, he thought.

He put his arm back through and this time pulled out a gold pocket watch, circled on the face by diamonds. He stuck his hand in a third time, felt around, and closed his fist around something small and plentiful. It felt almost like Cracker Jacks. He pulled them out to take a look.

Walter couldn't see properly in the darkness, but it felt like a handful of gold nuggets. He jiggled them around in his palm curiously then took the lighter out of his pocket and carefully lit it again, bringing his hand closer to the lighter's blue and yellow flame. Even when the contents were in the light, he was unsure what he was actually looking at.

His eyes widened. He realized he was holding actual gold teeth and fillings in his hand. He looked back and forth between the items in front of him and the mammoth number of scattered wooden boxes and crates of various sizes, which were hidden in between the mountains of ice. Who knew what the others were filled with. Some of them were as big as automobiles, some even larger.

Walter's brows furrowed as a thought flashed through his mind. Horrified, he plunged his arm back into the box, hurrying to put everything back in.

The reason he was in the warehouse to begin with rushed back to him when he heard the sound of voices. He put his knife away and put the board back into its slot. Walter moved on his knees like a baseball catcher and navigated through the boxes, toward the sound. He continued among the shadows, down and around the cold slabs and wet corners.

Down below, at the farthest end of the factory, a group of men were standing together where the warehouse reached out over the water. One was leaning against the large machine used to cut the ice into smaller, sizes depending on the customer's specifications.

Walt stayed low and managed to get as close as he could without being spotted.

He listened intently and strained to see the faces of the men speaking. He was still seventy feet away and the words were barely intelligible. He hastily determined they were speaking another language entirely, probably German, like the other night at The Creo Room.

Suddenly he was Humphrey Bogart in *All Through the Night*. That almost made him chuckle. *That'll be the day*, he thought, *a black man in a starring role*. It made him remember how hard it was to even see *Cabin in the Sky* when it came out a couple years back.

Anyway, the only thing he was sure he heard was the English phrase, "Operation Overcast." But then that term "totten core" came up again. Walter had forgotten he'd seen them say that in the basement of The Creo Room before he was drunk-dumped. Walt removed his notepad from his pocket and jotted both down in the dark. He put the pad away and took out the small camera from his breast pocket and tried to get eyes on who was speaking. He inched along the ice and found a corner where he could twist his head out to see the situation slightly below him but still have good cover.

The men were down by the inside dock area, next to the long slip where a vessel would wait to be loaded. Scattered about the floor of the warehouse were guards in dark suits on patrol. The man in white stood perfectly still with his hands clasped behind his back, nodding and listening to a report from the two men who were waiting for him here at Icehouse Number Four.

Behind Walter was an colossal chunk of ice, at least fifteen feet high and eight feet wide. Walt knelt around the corner and turned toward the frozen wall so he could light his Zippo underneath his coat and check his watch. The block he was crouching against lit up because of the flame, and unseen by Walt, was the outline of a lower leg and torso became partially visible encased within. The cadaver it belonged to was over six feet tall with an athletic frame and bald head. Black goggles were strapped around the face and covered the eye sockets. The complexion had a yellow/green hue, and the body was laid as if positioned in a coffin, with the hands and arms crossed over the chest.

Walter heard a noise. Someone was approaching. Walt quickly tried to find a place to hide, but it was too late; the individual turned the icy corner and saw him. The man was just able to reach for his gun before Walt was on him, his hands reaching for the man's throat so he couldn't scream. They tumbled to the floor and wrestled on the ground. Walter glanced down at the gun he was trying to fight for, and his jaw dropped open in an almost comical fashion.

In the darkness it looked like a Colt 1911 .45 automatic handgun, but heavily modified. Its barrel had been extended by several inches, and it had a Thompson submachine gun's foregrip attached past the finger guard and by the muzzle for better control. It also had a long banana magazine where the regular would normally be, descending from the grip, which alone would double the weapon's capacity.

"What the hell is tha—"

Walter was kicked in the groin and suppressed a moan as he was thrown hard against two ice blocks. The top one slid forward and jutted out. He ducked a blow but was pushed onto his back. The guard was on him quickly. The large block of ice on top rocked a bit more and stuck farther out as their legs kicked at the lower block for footing. The barrel of the gun was just inches away from Walter's face, and he struggled to hold it back. With all his might and using the strength in his legs, Walt threw the man off and slammed him to the ground. Walt jumped to his feet, but the guard retrieved the gun and pointed it at the detective. Walter reached up and pulled down the large block of ice, squashing the man below him.

He screamed. It startled the other men in the warehouse, alerting them to their location.

Walt grabbed the man's gun. Just as he gripped the handle, Walter's eyes discerned one of the cadavers encased in the ice. He looked around and saw they were everywhere.

Horrified, he stopped himself before he could yell. "Wha—?!"

Guards scattered, pulling out weapons like to the one Walter held in his hand. Walt saw more nearby ice blocks, and realized they too had these giant men frozen inside of them.

"Jesus."

The men pointed and hurried toward his location. The tall, scarred man took charge, placing himself in front of the man in the white suit.

"Apple? Apple?" was one of the closer man's call near where Walter was hiding. Walter ducked behind a block of ice and spied on the guards who were closing in from all directions.

"Apple?" the scarred man said.

Walter didn't know what the hell to make of it and figured if he answered right, it could maybe get him out of this whole situation. After a brief pause, Walter responded, "Pie?" There was silence.

Maybe he'd guessed right?

Everyone in the warehouse opened fire at Walt's location. The modified weapons fired like small submachine guns.

Walter dropped as low as he could go for cover. "Shiiitttt!"

The incoming bullets shredded the ice around him, sending shavings flying into the air. It looked like it was inexplicably snowing on the detective. The scarred man and others around him shielded the man in white and rushed him toward the far door.

Walter decided to head back the way he had come and darted for cover behind some of the wooden crates. He chambered a round in his new toy, jumped up, and fired back at the advancing guards. He hit a few and the others ducked for cover. Walt was amazed at the power and speed of this tiny automatic.

"Now we're cooking with gas," he thought.

Past the crates, toward the end row of even more ice blocks, he saw a huge window, the panes of which had been painted over.

He aimed his weapon up at the overhead lights and fired. Shattered glass cascaded through the darkness. The men stopped firing and took cover from the falling debris. Walter ran as fast as he could. He slid across the ice shavings toward the window, slammed against a slab of ice and took cover behind it.

Outside, all seemed peaceful, the gunfire inside muffled by the walls. That changed when Walter came crashing out of the painted window at full speed and rolled onto the adjoining roof, then quickly made his way down to the ground below.

He raced away from the warehouse toward the tall fence. He scaled that fence like he was an Olympic pole vaulter, hitting the top in one jump then twisting his body legs over first in one fluid motion. The night watchman at the gate awoken by all the commotion caught a glimpse of Walter's silhouetted body on top of the fence against the city skyline. The old man ran into his booth and came back out with a flashlight and a bolt-action rifle, running toward the intruder.

Walter hit the concrete hard, the shock reverberating from his heels all the way to the top of his head, making his teeth click together. He almost lost his balance but caught himself with his hands before he completely fell to the ground.

"This is why I should have a partner on these gigs," he muttered.

He jumped to his feet and loped around the corner toward his car. A loud shot rang out behind him; it sounded like it a rifle, most probably the night watchman. Walter dove into his Merc and sped off.

CHAPTER 12

M1911A1 .45 PISTOL FULL AUTO CONVERSION

It was a busy night at Small Change's pool hall. There was a tournament in the back-left corner that had attracted a good-sized crowd, though it was barely visible through the nicotine-colored haze. The local youths (the neighborhood's very own version of the Dead End Kids) made up a good portion of the spectators despite the late hour. The regulars and old-timers up front played straight eight-ball, while a mark was getting hustled by a traveling pro. When the call came in from Walter, Small Change could barely hear him.

"How's that? ...Yeah. His name is Elisha Cook. He's *the* best guy to talk to about that, Walt." He put his index figure in his other ear so he could concentrate on what was being said. "Yep. Guns are his hobby. He'll be there now. Yeah, I'll call ahead. Right. Okay."

Small Change put down the receiver, then pressed it a couple of times to clear the line for a new connection. "Yeah, Operator?" He smiled and his voice became soothing and soulful. "Hey, Grace. Naw, I told ya baby, I can get whatever you want. Sure, even if you don't have the ration cards. All you gotta do is let me take you out to a picture show. Sure. You can call me Rags Ragland, baby...." His smile faded and changed into a scowl. "Well, how the hell am I supposed to know you're with Bobby the Rack now! Naw, forget I even asked! No—never mind, I don't want to talk about it anymore. Just please connect me to AC2-4444. Naw, I'm done talking, just connect me."

❖

City Hall was massive. An entire day could easily be spent navigating the winding corridors that led to every municipal department, bureau, agency, and organization that governed New York City. Many an afternoon Walter had found himself meandering his way around the labyrinthine hallways, going from an office the size of a bingo hall, to retrieve copies of files, only to need a treasure map to find another office the size of a broom closet for the signature or stamp needed for release. One area seldom seen by the average New Yorker was the basement of the enormous marble headquarters. Below all the hustle and bustle, half of the entire basement was dedicated to storing all the city's records. Forms studiously filed away for future reference.

Despite the late hour, there was one lone gentleman working in between the tall stacks who felt it was a great charge placed on him by the almighty powers that be of the city of New York to comb through, read, absorb, and properly catalogue the records. Gotham's very own bookworm, Elisha Cook, who virtually lived down there, acting as an overseer and guardian of knowledge. To him his job was never done. There was no other vocation he could imagine himself doing or that he was better suited for, and the more time he spent among the shelves, the more satisfied he was.

Smack in the middle of the never-ending file cabinets and bookcases that spanned in every direction was a large old wooden desk the size of a car, lighted only by a lone pendant hanging far down from above. It had a single bulb encased in a metal bell-shaped shade. Beyond the fixture's circle of light were shadows and darkness.

Hunched over the enormous desk, Walter hovered over Elisha's shoulders, trying to see while making absolutely sure he didn't cast a shadow over the weapon Elisha examined in his small, pale, and nervous hands.

The petite man wore large, thick glasses and Walter noticed that his chestnut hair was thinning on top. He was dressed in a bulky shirt that puffed out around the tight suspenders he had strapped onto his small frame, accentuating his frail and timid demeanor. Elisha's chair was rolled over to the far end of the old desk where there was a drafting table. He looked intently through a huge magnifying lens connected to a metal armature on his head, squinting his eyes so he could read the inscription on the weapon. Elisha's other hobby, aside from his underground dwelling, was studying firearms, old and new. If this was the person Small Change recommended he discuss theoretical firearms with, Walt knew he was in good hands.

The heavily modified Colt 1911 .45 automatic handgun looked even more sleek and impressive in the low light.

"I've never seen anything like it. I mean, in theory, it's always possible, but wow. You say its full auto?"

One side of Walter's mouth grimaced, producing a half frown, and he nodded while leaning slightly to move away from the wafts of Elisha's Lucky Strike smoke. "Fast as a Chicago typewriter."

"Fast as a Thompson?" Elisha studied the weapon up close. "Brings a whole new meaning to the term 'submachine gun.'"

"You never seen anything like this before?"

Elisha's eyes didn't stray from the gun as he turned it over in his hands. "Well, I've heard of it being possible, yes, but it's very dangerous if someone is not a skilled gunsmith. The gangsters from a decade ago had *similar*—" he slowed and emphasized the word, "—modifications made to out shoot G-Men and such, but never anything like this. The problem was always the reliability of the augmentation on the classic .45 caliber design while keeping accuracy and durability on the battlefield, or on the streets. I mean, what's the point of going through all this darn trouble if the barrel is gonna heat and warp after only a couple hundred rounds are passed down through? Makes the whole contraption kind of pointless." He chuckled at his own words. "You should see the innovations in machine gun design that are coming out of Russia to see where the future of the weapon's capacity…and how the hell are you supposed to control this damn thing here, when you got practically a rock missile in your hand? By the time you're on your target, you'll be outta ammo…" Elisha said the last sentence to himself, barely audible. He trailed off into silence and continued to study the weapon, which didn't bother Walter. He'd lost him back at G-Men.

Elisha pulled the slide back on the weapon to get a look inside the chamber. He beheld it with as much reverence a teenage boy watching a young girl's skirt rise up her leg for the first time would have. "The sixty-four-dollar question is where'd you find it?"

"Where'd I find it?" Walter repeated, irritated by the question. "I found it on a picnic is where I found it."

Elisha's eyes remained focused on the weapon as he nodded with a professional understanding and let the slide click back into place. "I'll tell you something, this is right out of Dick Tracy, down to the type of steel the barrels are made of. The muzzle suppressors so it won't overheat." He smiled with an unconscious satisfaction. "The forward pistol grip for control and accuracy. Wherever you got it, I can tell you one thing, it's American-made. Not a single part is foreign. Good to see this isn't some Kraut design on a Luger. Is this the only one?"

Walt rubbed the back of his neck and exhaled a deep sigh. "From what I saw, it was one of many."

"Wow, I think it has to be secret government stuff. They're the only ones who could come up with something like this and mass-produce it. See here?" Elisha pointed to the banana mag and Thompson foregrip at the front. "Doesn't look like someone made it in their basement. This is industrial." He put the gun down. "Would really come in handy for our boys overseas, eh?"

That was a very good point, Walter agreed. "Yeah, you wonder why our guys don't have this…or maybe they do?"

CHAPTER 13

OUCH

Walt arrived back to his workplace later than usual. He was sore, and by now his entire body ached. He entered his outer office and even though the couch looked inviting, he walked by without stopping. What he really needed to do was wash up and relax a little. Maybe he should have gone straight home, but this was closer. He felt for the wall switch to his inner office and turned on the overhead light.

Two large men who had been lurking in the shadows now became fully visible. They were the same ones who had been surveilling him, Ed and his partner. Both were tall, beefy-looking men—definite bruisers. They wore black suits that were wrinkled, like they hadn't been pressed in days.

Walter froze when he saw them out of the corner of his eye. They positioned themselves on either side of him. It was the oldest trick in the book, and Walter Morris, PI, had fallen for it. He stayed still for a second then took his hand off the light switch and held it in the air to indicate no sudden moves.

After getting an eyeful of both heavyweight contenders, Walter wished that he should have just gone straight home.

Hopefully they weren't killers. If they were, chances were Walter would already be dead.

"Hi, fellas. You guys here to fix my noisy toilet?"

They silently observed Walter with looks that could give Superman's X-ray vision a run for its money.

The one farther away spoke. "Hello, Mister Morris."

Ed, who was closest, commenced patting him down, and Walt thanked his lucky stars that he was so tired because he'd forgotten his newly acquired toy and left it down in the hidden compartment of the Merc. The one he liked to call the "strong box," under the driver's seat. That spared it from being discovered. For now. Ed wasn't using kid gloves in searching Walter either. He found the camera inside Walt's jacket and took it from him.

"Hey now, that's private proper—"

"Shaddup," Ed replied. The other man still did not move nor take his eyes off Walter.

Walt was getting irritated. "Listen, guys, I'm tired. I've had a real shitty day, and I'm not in the mood for whatever this is. If you wanna play, please just flip the record over so we can get to the point."

Ed finished up his search and smiled politely at Walter. "Where were you tonight?" He handed the camera over to the second man.

Walter looked closely at them, sizing them up. He didn't think they looked like thugs for hire; their nondescript suits didn't scream lavish or even expensive. Instead the symmetry of their identical attire indicated more salaried employees, usually found behind the desk of a government organization.

Walter attempted to play along. "Me? Where was I tonight?"

"That's right," said the other man with a warm smile, his face strangely radiating the same kind of pleasantness one would see coming from a neighbor who might ask to borrow a cup of sugar.

"Oh, I was out and about. Had appointments to keep. On the clock, you know how it is."

The man leaned against the wall. "Dancing at The Creo Room?"

Walter grinned. "There's a multitude of perks one has in my line of work."

"So that's your answer?" Ed asked. "Who are you working for, dick?"

"Well, you're rather direct." Walter smirked and turned to look at the other gentleman. "Isn't he?"

"It's a fair question," the man against the wall replied. "So why don't you do us all a favor and answer it honestly?"

"Listen," Walt said, turning back to Ed, "thank you for dropping by tonight, fellas. I don't know what your angle is yet. All I'm at liberty to tell you both is that I'm working on a case. Official, organizational, and union-bound business that I cannot discuss."

"Why are you taking such an interest in Laszlo Strozek?"

Walter glanced over at Ed's partner. "Whoa, buy me a drink first, why don't ya? I'm easy but not *that* easy."

The one against the wall was beginning to lose his patience. "Cut the shit and answer the question."

"Why don't you guys answer *my* questions? You can start by telling me who in the hell you are. This is my office you broke into. Who you mothas working for?"

Ed swung his head back and forth in disappointment and like a bolt of lightning, shot out his massive fist into the detective's gut.

Walter doubled over in pain; the wind knocked out of him for the third time in as many days.

Yep, he thought, *these guys are definitely professionals.* Walt saw the second man still over against the wall. He opened up the camera, exposing the undeveloped film, and started pulling it out, destroyed it.

Walter mustered up what energy he could to protest. "C'mon! You can't do that! Jesus."

Ed, who could easily pass as a professional boxer at the Garden, crouched down and peered directly into Walter's grimacing face. "Listen, Dumbo. We ain't playing. Where were you tonight?"

Walt let out a heavy sigh, as if he was about to give in and reveal a top secret to his two new friends. "I was eating at the Automat down on Forty-Second Street. You know the one, they got the new pudding flavors at that location only?"

The other man let the exposed film drop to the floor, slammed the camera shut, and tossed it back to his partner who didn't need take his eyes off Walter to catch it.

Yeah, these guys were pros. Ed grinned when his partner snapped the camera in half like it was a toy, his jaw muscles flexing as he crumbled the camera like an empty cigar box and tossed it over his shoulder.

The man against the wall spoke. "Who are you working for?"

Walt cocked his head slightly to one side. "You're rather to the point."

"One more time- Why are you taking such in interest in the German piano player Strozek? We're not stupid, Mister Morris."

Walter raised his brows innocently, "Laszlo who?"

The fellow in the back sneered. "Don't play games with us, Morris. We've seen you tailing him, and they don't seem to like you very much at The Creo Room. What's your angle?"

"Well, first off, I wanna thank you for all your moral support, fellas."

"That's all you got?" Ed angrily shot back. "That's all you got, you little shit? A punchline for everything?"

"Who are you," said the one near the wall, "Amos Jones?"

"I was waiting to see how long it would take you to start calling me *boy*, *shine*, or something else. You gonna have me sing 'Old Man River' next?"

That seriously infuriated Ed. He dropped the forced smile from his face and pointed a stumpy finger toward the detective. "Of all the cotton-picking nerve—where do *you* get off accusing us of something like that?! We wholeheartedly support the Negro cause, and don't you ever say different, goddamn you!"

Walter was taken aback and looked dumbfounded at Ed, who was inches away from his face and ready to bite his nose off. Before he had time to formulate an intelligent response, the man in the back got testy as well.

"Morris! I don't mean to burst your bubble, but whatever petty bullshit marital spat you might be investigating, it probably doesn't compare to real life. So why not level with us and do your part to defend your country, okay?"

"What's next? You gonna strongarm me into buying war bonds?"

Ed turned his head and shot his partner a look of impending rage. The other man answered with a nod.

Ed gripped Walt by the throat and with one arm, stood back up, lifting Walter as he rose. He slammed Walt against the office door, holding him so high he could feel the draft from the open transom. Ed pointed a finger in the private detective's face. "Listen to me, you little fink, I'm done giving you the benefit of the doubt, so let me give you a heartfelt word of advice. Stay away from Laszlo Strozek. Do you understand? You don't go near him, you don't talk to him. Got us? Don't interfere with shit that's none of your business."

A slight sigh was Walt's only reply, and he calmly stared down at the thug who had him suspended in the midair. There was a pause while they waited for Walter to say something, and when their patience ran out, Ed curled his hand up into a fist and punched Walter hard in the gut. He let go and Walter fell the three feet down to the floor where Ed then decided to give him a sharp kick in his side.

"Ed, enough!" said his partner.

Ed took a step back. Walter coughed and stayed curled up in the fetal position. "That's right, Ed. This tough guy thing really isn't you, my man."

The other man sprang into action and in two large strides was bent over Walter. He grabbed him by the collar and spat down at him, "Listen and listen good! If we find out that you're still tailing Laszlo Strozek and sticking your nose where it doesn't belong, you're gonna end up behind a tin cup outside the Hippodrome, and that's a promise."

He let Walter go with a hand shove.

"You know," Walter said, holding his stomach and struggling to breathe, "if you bums came in here and asked properly instead of coming across like two of assholes, maybe we could have exchanged some information. They obviously don't let you G-men out enough to learn how to communicate."

Ed looked at his partner. "Oh please, let me?"

His partner stepped back and grinned. "Be my guest."

Ed bent down and punched him hard one last time, and Walter's world once again went black.

CHAPTER 14

GROWING A TAIL

Once he eventually came around, Walter had a splitting headache and scratches on top of his already-bruised face. Oddly enough, the room hadn't been ransacked, but when he checked his breast pocket, he realized his notepad was gone. He scanned the office and found it over by the corner of his desk. None of the pages were missing. However, he quickly surmised that the men were had read everything he had written down.

He propped himself up over the tiny sink in the corner of his office, letting the water run cold. He examined his sore face in the mirror and groaned in pain when his hands explored his stomach and sides, realizing as he bent down to splash water over his face that he might have a bruised rib.

He picked up the iodine. "Well," he said out loud, "Looks like I gotta have a nice long chat with Laszlo Strozek."

❖

Walter left his building and headed down the street. Behind him, about a half a block away and on cue, a man exited out of the passenger side of a parked DeSoto sedan and began to follow, mixing in with the other pedestrian traffic. Walter didn't notice him.

They both continued down the street and Walter turned the corner onto Park Avenue heading toward the elevated train. He walked through a small crowd toward a newsstand. His tail hung back and tried to blend in.

Walt reached the newsstand and dug into his pocket for some money. "What'dya say, Squirt?"

"Hey Walter, how they hangin'?" replied the elderly man inside the wooden newsstand. His name was Vincent Tellasna, but his friends called him Squirt.

"To the left, Squirt, always to the left." Walter placed his change down on the counter, his eyes scanning over the many front page headlines exclaiming, *THE PROGRESS OF THE ALLIED FORCES PUSH INTO BERLIN* displayed for sale on the many strings below the tiny window. Without being asked, Squirt put down Walter's usual pack of Lucky Strikes. The newsman noticed Walt's shadow then; he was lingering awkwardly and trying to look busy, while at the same time keeping an eye on his mark. He stuck out like a sore thumb.

Squirt looked directly at Walter, who wasn't paying attention. "You got any numbers you wanna play tonight?"

"No thanks, Squirt." Walt continued to skim through the news headlines and still didn't look up at him.

"Looks like you got something in your eye, Walt."

Walter glanced up, and Squirt nonchalantly gestured with his eyes over the detective's shoulder. "You should check in the mirror." Squirt removed his round eyeglasses and inspected them for smudges. "You got a piece of fuzz in your eye the size of Johnny Weissmuller over your left shoulder."

Walt nodded and rubbed his eye as if there was something in it. Squirt put his glasses back on, collected the change from the counter, and went about his business in the little enclosure. Walter used the small rectangular mirror that was tacked to the side of the newsstand window to examine his eye. He glanced at the reflection over his shoulder and identified the individual tailing him. He was a young man in his mid-twenties, white, average height, with the physique of an all-American college boy, and wore the same style suit that his last visitors who sent him to dreamland wore.

This all but confirmed that those men, and now this guy, had to work for a government agency, quite possibly the FBI.

That's just great, Walter thought. It also made him wonder how his partner Jacob was doing up in Connecticut on his marital case. Just maybe Roland had the right idea with creeping around in the bushes.

"Got it, Squirt. You are a lifesaver, thank you." Walter picked up a newspaper. "I'll come back later and play some numbers for the week."

Squirt grinned. "Remember what my favorite philosopher, Charlie Chan, once said: 'One grain of luck sometimes worth more than whole rice field of wisdom.'"

Walter laughed and nodded in recognition of the advice. "Take it easy."

Walter put the smokes in his pocket and the paper under his arm. He crossed the Park Avenue traffic heading north along 125th and past the train station. He headed west and crossed the southbound lane of traffic. His shadow followed close behind, the traffic lights working in his favor. Walt entered the Yorkshireman Building on the corner of 125th and Park, going through its revolving door exactly as the lights turned green for the southbound avenue.

The tail quickly rushed to cross the lanes of Park Avenue, trying to beat the drivers who were stepping down on the gas. He threw his hands up in the air to stop the traffic while crossing and received multiple honks from the vehicles in return.

Walter walked through the massive lobby of the creepy Yorkshireman Building and immediately veered left to hide beside the doors. He nodded in acknowledgment to the doorman sitting behind the small desk at the other side of the entrance.

"Ernie, my brotha."

Ernie gave a quick nod of his head back at the detective but remained looking down at the funny papers. "How goes it, Walt?" he said rhetorically.

Walter's eyes wandered up to the focal point of the lobby, way up high on the far-end wall by the stairs and steel-cage elevator. There was a huge, forty-year-old mural commemorating the sinking of the *PS General Slocum* in the middle of the East River back in 1904. The horrendous disaster was depicted in all its brutal, atrocious, and fiery glory, and Walt could only imagine what looking at that grisly painting every day would do to a man's mind. Most people couldn't come together to decide what was actually happening in the faded mural for some reason, even though it was just an ordinary, simple, two-dimensional painting. It was as if each individual saw a different picture when they looked at it.

"Must be *horrible* having to look at that every day, Ernie," Walt said, gazing up into it.

Ernie didn't look up as he responded, "It'll drive a fella mad, Walt."

"Yep."

The revolving door began to turn.

Walter nodded goodbye to the man. "Well, then."

Ernie turned his paper, his eyes focused down. "Thanks for stopping by."

Walter ducked back into the revolving door, passing his tail who was just stepping out into the lobby. The man registered and did a double take. He quickly jumped back in, right behind Walter. As the detective stepped outside, he pushed the newspaper from under his arm right into the door, jamming and preventing it turning, and trapping the tail within.

As Walter hurried away, the tail yelled and banged on the heavy glass to try to get the door to move, but it didn't budge. He began to yell even louder. The more he tried to push his way out, the more the door fought back.

Ernie sighed and closed his funny papers. He very slowly got up from behind his desk. "Alright, alright, just give me a minute, fella…I'm an old man, for Christ's sake."

Walter ran back across the avenue, down the street, and out of view away from his shadow. He rushed up the steps to the 125th Street train station and headed for the platforms. The train to Grand Central Terminal was just pulling in. When the doors opened, he jumped in. His head was throbbing, and his entire body was sore.

So much for taking it easier, Walt thought.

The train pulled away from the station as the young man was still shouting, stuck in the revolving doorway of the Yorkshireman below.

Ernie was up against the door yelling back so the man could hear him. Walter's tail wasn't listening.

"I can't help ya from this side, buddy!" Ernie shouted. "Yeah! You gotta get someone outside to pull the paper loose!"

CHAPTER 15

MOTTERMAN'S SALT & PRESERVATIVES PRESENT: JOHNNY FLASH, INTERGALACTIC SPACE MARSHAL

The doorman's palm needed greasing, and he told Walt to tiptoe as he opened the sarcophagus-like door that led to the cavernous, sealed soundstage. The high walls were lined with a plush crimson-colored tufted material used for luxurious soundproofing. Long and elegant barrel-shaped leko lighting units hung from the ceiling, shooting narrowly focused beams down to the floor that widened as they descended into puddles of spherical yellow light illuminating the room through the thick cigarette smog that hung near the ceiling.

It was a full house with almost a hundred people in the audience, fans who'd mailed away for tickets weeks in advance for tonight's performance. Behind the audience and in the aisle along the back wall were a few studio executives giving a tour to a large group of network sponsors, vying for the best view to watch tonight's performance.

Up front to the right of the audience area was a two-foot riser, and on that stage, this week's live performance episode of the *Johnny Flash, Intergalactic Space Marshal* radio program was in progress. To the left of the stage a full orchestra was seated slightly higher on their own platform. In the center of the main stage the host and seven other actors gathered holding wrinkled, marked-up copies of tonight's script. They stood in pairs in front of three tall steel stands with gold cardioid microphones on top, suspended by delicate springs within a large metallic ring.

The male actors were dressed in regular everyday suits, a couple of them had their jackets off, and the two female players were in smart dresses.

Between the stage and the audience on the far wall were the sound effects and Foley artists. Spread out around them on top of two tables were an assortment of eclectic items for making all kinds of sounds. The technicians stood at the ready, following their own scripts, positioned in front of an assortment of kinds of microphones.

Walter gestured to the usher inside to indicate the direction he was headed. He turned to his immediate right and opened a door leading to the control room.

The first door opened, and he entered into a tiny, padded vestibule; Walter waited until the door behind him on its delayed hinge shut completely. Only then did he carefully push open the control room door, making sure no one was standing on the other side. He entered the sound-proofed studio control room where the producers, radio technicians, and the director sat behind their consoles, producing the show.

Walter nodded to a producer who glanced over and smiled at the young, attractive script runner waiting to be called into action. He shut the door behind him and positioned himself in the corner out of the way. When he looked through the control room window out at the stage, his eyes focused on his friend and fill-in secretary, Tatum Marie Sullivan. She stepped up to the microphone in a controlled motion and cocked her head awkwardly to the side to produce a kind of vacuous speech, adding an inflection onto her tone.

"Johnny...the ropes are too tight!" she said with more force than her body and demeanor would suggest. Her voice had the stereotypical New York accent. Tatum rocked her head back and forth near the microphone. *"I can't wiggle loose!"*

Sharing the mic with Tatum was a large, burly gentleman who pulled a cigarette from his mouth and said, *"Try harder, Zallerilla!"* All the actors onstage flipped to the next page in unison. Tatum and her costar twisted their body away enough to cautiously turn their pages away from the sensitive microphone. He seamlessly continued, *"We have to escape evil Von Baron Rothchild's castle. He must be stopped from turning the Earth into mindless zombies!"* He remonstrated enthusiastically, in a voice from deep within his chest.

"I'm trying!" Tatum yelled back, her body arching toward the ceiling.

Walter approached and knelt down next to an audio technician, named Russell Chamberlain, who was sitting in front of a large electronic soundboard with numerous dials, switches, and knobs. He was monitoring the different microphone levels and tweaking the final show mix being piped out over the airwaves. He noticed Walt out of the corner of his eye but kept his gaze firmly focused on the actors and musicians onstage, following the script while simultaneously listening to the director seated next to him in the booth. Russell slid his headphone earmuff off so he could hear the detective.

"My man." Russell smirked with one side of his mouth. "Whadda ya hear, whadda ya say? I haven't seen you since that night at Small's Paradise with Bugs Morganfield playing. Here to flirt with Tatum?"

Walter raised an eyebrow and smiled. "No, Russell, my man. I'm just livin' and loafin', livin' and loafin'. Actually, I'm on the clock." He paused while Russell tracked up a microphone that was positioned over by the Foley guys. The sound of a ray gun was being produced by a small electrical current arching between two steel rods that were being held close to the microphone then taken abruptly away, creating an electric, pulsating sound.

Russell brought the fader back down, cutting the microphone. He checked a few other knobs then shot a brief look at Walter to continue.

"Let me ask you a question," Walt began. "You're pretty familiar with most of the musicians that play in the city? I'm looking to see if you know an ivory player—name's Laszlo Strozek."

"Who *doesn't* know him would be a much better question. Foreign guy, right?" Russell stole a glance at Walt while keeping a steady eye on the performance onstage.

"Yep, that's the one. He got a yarn?"

Russell turned the page of the script over in unison with everyone else and nodded at Walter. "German, I think. One hell of a player."

The director turned to Russell and said into his headset microphone for all to hear, "Cue sound effect."

Russell repeated, "Cue effect," and faded up a microphone.

A sound effects man offstage fiddled with a doorknob next to a microphone then quickly replaced it with a squeaky hinge that he creaked open next to the microphone.

Tatum frantically shouted, "*Johnny, the door's opening!*"

Russell looked at Walt. "I've worked with him on a few other shows here, and at CBS and NBC. He's a session guy for gigs like this and the big ballroom stuff, but he also plays uptown in Harlem at the colored clubs. He's so good."

Walter nodded.

Tatum moved her head back and Johnny Flash leaned into the microphone. "*Ahhh!*"

The director raised his hand and said into his headset mic, "Okay… cue Vinny!"

A suave-looking gentleman with a pencil-thin mustache playing the role of Doctor Von Baron Rothchild strode up to his microphone and spoke with a thick German accent. "*Not so fast, Herr Flash!*" He threw a finger up with his free hand. "*My hydrogen ray gun will stop you in your tracks!*"

Russell leaned back so Walt could hear him, and they both watched the stage. "I *think* the story is that he was a classically trained guy and was forced to come to the States before the war broke out, with that wave who came over in '37 and '38. Then he got into jazz." Russ shrugged. "It's a living. One hell of a piano player."

Tatum screamed, *"Johnny, look out!"*

The director said, "Cue Larry."

Johnny Flash put his free hand up to his forehead. *"Ahhh!"*

The cast all turned to the next page.

Russell turned up a knob on the board in front of him and there was another kind of ray gun sound. The director raised his voice and lifted an arm, "Cue orchestra." The music swelled into a crescendo then abrupt silence.

Walter's gaze shifted back to Russell. "Do you or anyone in the band know where I might find him play here in Midtown?"

The director pointed toward the stage, "Cue Don!"

The master of ceremonies, a rotund gentleman with a kind face who also doubled as the show's announcer, passed by the performers and headed up to a microphone to read from his script, injecting a dramatic inflection to heighten the suspense. "Will Johnny Flash and Zallerilla get away from the eeevil, sinister, and insidious Von Baron Rothchild in time to stop him from turning the Earth into mindless voodoo zombies? Will the courageous Sergeant Blaze and his GIs find the Von Barren Castle in time?" The music steadily rose to underscore the peril.

Russell shifted in the chair and moved his head closer to Walter. "Yeah, Rudy might. He plays the circuit. I can bring you over to him and to Tatum when we're off air."

The music swelled.

Don Wilson, the MC, continued, "Tune in next week for another electrifying episode of…*Johnny Flash, Intergalactic Space Marshal* with special guest Sergeant Blaze. Also, joining the show next week will be our special guests Vincent Price on loan from Twentieth Century Fox and RKO's very own Joseph Cotten."

Russell, who was a little more at ease now that the show was wrapping up, looked over at Walter for the first time and smiled. "People pay top dollar to see your man Laszlo chase the devil's tail."

The music reached its climax then a soft, heavenly melody started to play. The acting troupe put their scripts down on the music stands and began to quietly exit the platform. Don continued while a lone man walked onto the stage and approached him. "But first, here's Bob Stark, spokesman for Motterman's Salt and Preservatives."

Bob Stark stepped up to Don's microphone and began his pitch. "Hello, fellow Space Marshals. Have you gotten your de-coder rings yet out of your mother's Motterman's Preservatives XL Soapbox? Well, here we go. Get ready to decode the newest message."

Everyone in the control room began to take off their headsets, light up cigarettes, and exchange farewells.

❖

While the audience was filing out, Russell walked Walter over to the orchestra area to Rudy Spears, a light-skinned vibraphone player who occasionally performed out at Jones Beach with Russell in Guy Lombardo's orchestra. After introductions, Walter questioned Rudy about Laszlo.

He was packing up his equipment along with the rest of the band. Walt got right to the point.

"You know how I can find him?"

"Well, he plays in the big band at Whalley's on Saturday nights. Fancy joint."

"Whalley's? On Fifty-Second Street? That's a top-hat-and-tails place."

Rudy nodded. "He's there tonight, I believe. That's when he's not up in Harlem, or at the Gramatan Hotel up in Westchester."

"Let me ask, you know all these guys…did you ever hear of a girl by the name of Caldonia that went with him? From Westchester?"

Rudy finished boxing his vibes. "Yeah, he might have dated a girl from Westchester, colored girl, if I remember right. Don't know her name. I only recall 'cause she was a real fine sister."

Walter pulled out Caldonia's photo and showed it to him. Rudy nodded. "That's her."

"Thank you, Rudy."

Tatum made her way over to Walter. They shook hands and she stood on her toes so Walter could kiss her cheek. "It's a shame you missed the beginning."

"Well, from the sounds of it, as per usual, Johnny was in a hell of a pickle with Zersinda." Walter grinned.

Tatum rolled her eyes. "Zallerilla, Mister Morris." She smirked, took a sip of water, then cleared her throat. "So, are you here to decode the secret message?"

Walter led her away from Rudy and Russell. The audience had cleared out and the band and technicians were wrapped up. "What are ya doin' tonight?"

"Well Sebastian and I just made up, and he asked me if—"

Walter's grin faded, and it was replaced by a look of disapproval. "Sebastian? Jeez.... Okay, pick out a swell dress. I'm gonna take you to a real fancy place."

"Oh yeah? Where?"

Walter winked. "Whalley's."

The smile on Tatum's face was quickly replaced with a frown. She put a hand on her hip with the realization. "Whalley's, really? This a case?"

Walter hesitated then nodded, trying to look as innocent as he could. "Maybe...."

CHAPTER 16

THE WHALLEY ROOM

Walter, escorting Tatum, climbed the long and elegant flight of stairs and entered Whalley's ballroom off of Broadway. It was an enormous room and had a large stage at one end where a big band was playing mellow dance music. Atmospheric string and track lighting outlined the dance floor, the dining area, the stylish trim along the walls, casting the ballroom in a soft and radiant glow. Cigarette and cigar smoke added to the fantasy-like setting, rendering it magical. The far end of the ballroom had large windows that showcased a commanding view looking south over Times Square. They were fitted with navy blue velvet drapes on either side that could be drawn in case a more intimate setting was desired.

Walt and Tatum checked their coats and Walter turned his hat in with the cloak room attendant. With her hand gripped firmly around his forearm, they strolled over to the maître d' stand.

Tatum smiled up at her date. "You sure know how to court a girl, Walt."

He smiled. "Luckily I have my good friends Mister Washington and Mister Lincoln backing me up."

"Mister Washington and Mister Lincoln?" Tatum looked puzzled

One of the hosts approached Walter and they shook hands. Walt palmed him a five-spot and whispered, "Something nice, please, with a good view of the stage and the band. My boss here...," Walter gestured to Tatum behind him, "...she likes to be able to see the fellas as they play."

"Well," the smug gentleman looked down at his tip and back up, "I have the perfect table then, sir, for you and your *boss*." He winked. They followed after him.

Walt smiled "You know the greens, young Tatum...."

Tatum laughed. "Ah yes, that Lincoln."

Couples danced, swaying the music, while others dined at the many tables and booths lining the rear, elevated sections encircling the center of the hall. Walt and Tatum were seated at a table next to the dance floor.

Eyes wide, Tatum gazed around her at the high-end clientele socializing. "Look, it's Robert Moses over there," Tatum leaned in close and spoke softly so only Walter could hear her. "And there's no guff about a white woman and black man sitting together in a club like this?"

Walt looked around. "With any high-class place, if you can actually get in and *look* like you belong, they don't care if you're black. Or if you're black and white and sitting together, or even if you're a homosexual. With friends like Jackson, Grant, and Franklin, the world is your oyster."

"What a bunch of hypocritical..." She smirked. "You got to be pretty connected to know the Franklins—or the Grants, for that matter."

Walter grinned. "Yep."

His looked toward the stage where Laszlo was playing with the big band. The piano player had his back to the couple and performed a much more sedate and slow accompaniment, in stark contrast to what Walter had seen him do at The Creo Room.

Walter scanned the many faces bopping up and down in the crowd.

A waiter approached them. "Good evening, can I start you off with a drink tonight?"

"Sure." Walter smiled. "Dewar's, on the rocks."

"A glass of champagne for me please, Moët perhaps?" Tatum asked softly.

The waiter nodded and walked away.

"This night is gonna cost, yeah." Tatum winced. "I can tell already."

Walter removed the silverware from his napkin and placed the cloth across his lap. "Well," he chuckled, "luckily, this falls under what we in the business like to call 'expenses.'"

Walt took notice of a large booth on the other side of the dance floor. Seated there were three sinewy gentlemen, who all looked rather out of place. The two at the ends didn't give the impression that they belonged at such a toney establishment, even though their luxurious tuxedos said otherwise. Their faces displayed the wear and tear of life, as though they'd been paid to play the role of a punching bag at the local gym. In the center of the booth was a man in his late fifties, to whom the others listened intently.

"Well, look what we got here," Walter muttered.

"What?"

"Red booth, at the far end over by the bar, the fella in the middle of the two guys who look like they haven't had a woman since the war broke out."

Tatum laughed and surreptitiously glanced around. "Who is it?"

"That's Rory Caven. He's the top man running the Irish mob in Hell's Kitchen. The Cavens are the only syndicate to give the Italians a run for their money. They have a reputation for being a little crazy. The guy next to him, I'm pretty sure that's his right-hand man, Seamus O'Shaughney. They call him Fingernails, and it's not because he likes to paint them."

Tatum pouted in confusion.

"He likes to use bolt clippers for fun." Tatum's eyes widened. "Merciless, that guy," Walt whispered.

When the song ended, Laszlo stood and bowed along with the rest of the band. They walked offstage, passing a smaller group who had arrived to give them a break. The new band started with a slow waltz. Laszlo made his way offstage and shook the hands of a few admirers, then made his way over to Rory Caven's table.

The waiter put their drinks down on the table. Walt waited until he left then said to Tatum, "This could be getting interesting. Let's check it out. Would you care to dance?"

"I just got my drink…."

Walt practically dragged her out of the booth. "I bet it'll be a slow one."

They walked onto the dance floor together and drifted toward the other side, placing themselves as close as possible to the Caven table without being noticed.

"Do you think they're friends?" Tatum asked, with her back to the table so Walter could observe over her shoulder.

"Don't know."

Without getting up, they had all shaken Laszlo's hand, only Rory making eye contact with him as he did so. Laszlo moved a nearby chair and sat down. He put his hand up to flag down the waiter.

Walter and Tatum danced together smoothly. They moved in and around the other couples with ease, not making it obvious what they were up to. A mixed couple dancing on a Saturday night would always attract attention. At least in a high-end ballroom like Whalley's where some of the biggest stars of stage, screen, and radio could be seen, Walt was betting they wouldn't cause much more than the occasional double take. This was the only venue that it *would* be deemed appropriate because for all anyone else knew, he and Tate could be the latest couple from Gay Pareé or the newest hot pairing from Tinseltown. They could be the next Nick and Nora Charles in their own Republic serial. As long as they remained low-key, they could go unnoticed. Luckily, no one seemed to care.

They moved a little closer and Walter got another vantage point of the table from over Tatum's shoulder to try to "read" what was being said.

Tatum saw the look of concentration on his face, his lips moving slightly, mouthing the conversation. "How did you learn that little trick of yours?" she asked, her eyes diverting to the bruise on his cheek.

"Well, I was always very nosy growing up. I wanted to know what the girls were saying about me across the room."

"So that's the line you feed to everyone who asks you then, yeah?" She was half kidding. Half not.

Walter smiled and really looked at her for a moment. He had never been comfortable divulging personal information. But he liked Tatum, and more importantly, he knew her question was sincere.

He looked up to the ceiling then back at his quarry across the floor. "Okay...growing up, my little brother was deaf and mute, so while my mom was out working in some hellfire factory all the way out in Brooklyn, killing herself to keep us fed, it was up to me to take care of him, to watch him."

Walter paused after saying that last part, absorbing his own words.

He hadn't spoken about his mother or his brother since the first conversation he'd had with his future business partner, Jacob Roland the night Walt saved his life on the *RMS Olympic*. Then Hayden mentioned it the other evening. Walt didn't like being pushed to speak about his brother.

"Dad wasn't around?" Tate queried.

"Yes and no. He was around, but almost never home because of work. He was a Pullman porter and then a brakeman on the *New York Central*. So, he was always away, riding those iron horses all over Oshkosh B'gosh." Images of his hardworking father came into his mind, but Walt shook them out.

He held her tightly during a slower and more intimate dance number, "…I learned the best I could how to communicate with my brother in order to keep him safe from the bullies in the neighborhood. Sister Janice at Saint Stephens—when Sister Marilyn-Paul wasn't beating us with the back of her yardstick—taught us sign language, which was a tremendous help. A breakthrough for me." Tatum smiled warmly at Walt, who reciprocated. "I guess I just picked up reading lips like he did. Like riding a bike; you never forget. But it takes constant practice."

Tatum didn't respond. Walt was too busy watching the events taking place over her shoulder. She gazed up at his face, lost in her own thoughts.

"I like this," she said quietly.

"What," said Walt, "coming on this job with me as my cover?"

"I don't mean that, I mean…," Tatum flushed demurely.

"What? Are the bubbles getting to you already?" Walter grinned and raised an eyebrow and smiled.

She didn't reply or look up, just continued to smile, her head resting on his shoulder. Walter watched as a waiter approached the booth and placed a drink in front of Laszlo, who lit a cigarette.

The one in the middle was speaking, the boss, Rory Caven.

"Fair play to ya, Laz. You certainly can carry a tune. I hear you give those jungle bunnies in Harlem a run for their money as well, eh?" He grinned.

"'Course, why you'd even play up there with them is anyone's guess," Seamus added, trying to get a rise out of Laszlo, who ignored him.

"I couldn't say," Laszlo said, ashing his cigarette. He brought the lit end up to his lips and shaped the cherry at the end into a little red glowing ball with his smooth blowing, giving more attention to the head of his smoke than the conversation he was in. "It's great work if you can get it, my pale friend, and gives a guy like me a good cover."

"Let me ask you a question…they pay you in bananas or do you gotta take a cut out of the jungle pussy they throw at you?" Seamus had a huge grin on his face, again daring to poke the piano player.

Laszlo turned his head sharply and his eyes narrowed when they found Seamus and his taunting smirk. "You know," Laszlo said, turning back to Rory, "it's not true what they say about the Irish. That the habitual drinking ruins your brains. Look how intuitive you can be when you just apply yourselves."

"What?" Seamus cut in with a fury, his smirk gone.

"I just gave you a compliment, Mr. O'Shaughney. That being a drunkard you are still luckily able to form coherent sentences."

Seamus's face turned red, and he reached into his coat, placing his hand on the gat under his arm.

The smile dropped from Rory's face. He put his hand out toward Seamus, a single finger pointing low against the top of the table, causing the hothead to immediately back off. Rory's warm demeanor was now gone. "I've killed men for less than that, you fucking little bottom-feeder."

Laszlo winked at a female onlooker that passed by then lit another cigarette. He waved over another waiter who was waiting in the aisle. The young man hurried over and brought his tray to Laszlo. On it was a thin cardboard tube a little over a foot long. Laszlo carefully picked it up and in its place, put two folded bills on the tray. "Thank you, Jonathan."

The waiter smiled and walked away. Laszlo handed the tube over to Rory. Without looking at it, he passed it to Ernie, a heavyset, red-haired man seated immediately to his right. Ernie took his reading glasses from out of his pocket and put them on. He discreetly placed the tube low between himself and Seamus so prying eyes couldn't see what they were doing.

Walter swayed and shifted positions on the dance floor to avoid detection.

Ernie opened the tube and very carefully pulled out and examined what looked to be mechanized schematics. The man checked them over, verifying their authenticity, then nodded to Rory.

Laszlo smiled. "I told you I'd deliver. The blueprints to practically every Grisham Company vault across the fruited plain of this country. They're like the Ford or Packard of the vault makers."

Ernie nodded. "They're everywhere."

Rory wasn't buying it. "You trying to impress us here, Laz? Your lot try to out-do Dillinger and throw in a touch of Howard Hughes for theatrical flair. Just so every single Joe Q. Public takes notice? I'm glad you've all figured out the angle on good public relations."

"I don't follow," Laszlo responded, his demeanor suggesting he was bored by this chitchat.

"You think we're stupid? That we don't know how you got your hands on these? A simple bloody burglary would have sufficed, not the goddamn Normandy invasion." Rory pointed a finger at the piano man. "You got your men parachuting off the tallest skyscraper in the world during a dim-out? You know the heat that's on these schematics now? Why don't you just pull a fucking Hindenburg and burn one of them zeppelins up there too, 'cause I don't think you got enough attention. You want the ones overseas fighting the war to put down their guns and swastikas to take note?"

"Fuckin' hell," Seamus piped in, "You were even able to push the goddamn New York Ripper off the front page."

Laszlo narrowed his eyes. "When the adults are talking, little boy, I suggest you keep your mouth shut and go back to polishing your tree trimmer or whatever the hell it is you like to use."

Rory had his hand on Seamus's arm even before the latter had time to rise. The table moved as Seamus knocked against it, but he restrained himself at his boss's behest. Rory looked over at Laszlo, who seemed unaffected. "What in the fuck is wrong with you? If you've got a death wish you should have stayed in Germany."

"Don't lecture me about geopolitical shit. We're all *still* in Europe. You got the blueprints you wanted, who cares how we got them?"

"Because we don't appreciate the attention. That kinda heat went outta style in the twenties, along with shooting it out with the cops in the streets for a bag of money with dollar signs on it. Now every copper and G-man in the country knows. They are all busy contacting the owners of Grisham vaults."

"That is not our concern." Laszlo shrugged. "The people I do business with fulfilled their end of the bargain. We want payment." There was silence at the table as the men sized each other up.

Finally Rory relented and nodded to his friend who had the blueprints. Ernie reached under the table and pushed a briefcase over to Laszlo. He took it and placed it under his chair, between his legs.

A couple whirled into Walter's field of view, blocking his eyeline. The lady was dancing with a shorter partner and he had his back to Walter, his head on her shoulder. She opened her eyes and saw Walter was looking her way. She threw him a flirtatious, inviting smile, but Walt was looking beyond the lady, trying to keep up with what was happening at the table.

"Damn it."

"What?" Tatum said with concern.

"Hard to read them in this crowd. Too many people and distractions."

His line of sight cleared, and he moved Tatum a little closer so fewer people could pass through. In this low light he was happy that his eyes were still good, but it wasn't enough. "I'm only kinda getting pieces."

Laszlo rolled his eyes. "You're lucky you're still even being considered for our next venture."

The Irish men all laughed. The slow song ended and a faster, more foot-pounding beat commenced.

Seamus put both his elbows on the table and leaned in. "Considered for your next venture? Are you balmy?"

Rory was having a hard time through his laughter figuring out if Laszlo was serious. "What, are you serious? This is on the level?"

"Serious as a heart attack, Mister Caven. And we'd like to cut you and your leprechauns in, fifty/fifty."

Rory grinned. "Oh really? Who else do you think you're gonna get? You think the wops or Jews are gonna drop everything and help you and your—" Rory made air quotes, "—*mysterious friends* in the shadows and won't even take a meeting? You may not have noticed while you've been living it up in your windowless bars and juke joints, but there's a war on. It's not a freelancer's market. Especially dealing with partners you don't even get to meet. Having to go through a slimy piano player. Very dodgy times, mate."

"It ensures security and anonymity for my employers. Something that working with you seems to be hard to keep in check." Laszlo's spoke in a monotone.

"This coming from the guy whose crew kills two workers and jumps off a ledge?! Hell, the air wardens thought we were being invaded! We should really cut ties with you, permanently."

Seamus interjected. "You're about two seconds away from being dismembered in a bathtub and sold to feed them off the boat down in Chinatown."

Laszlo smirked. "Mister Caven, must every road lead back to impotent intimidation? I have been instructed to make you privy to a plan that would make the Empire State job look like mere chump change. You see—"

A visibly drunk couple accidentally bumped into Walter and Tatum, momentarily distracting Walt.

"Sorry, fella," the man said. "She's a wild one." They stumbled on, dancing and laughing.

Walter looked back at the table of men and tried to pick up on what he'd missed. Laszlo was mid-sentence.

"—these are my employer's wishes."

Rory leaned back, lit a cigar, and narrowed his eyes at Laszlo. "Tell me more about this scheme, and I'll tell you if we go forward on the little problem of yours that we currently got on ice."

Laszlo exhaled unhappily. "It's nothing that we can go into great detail about here." He looked around him and back at Rory. "All I'm at liberty to say is it will be in the immediate future, and your cut will be around a hundred large."

"A hundred large?" Seamus's eyes were wide. "What d'ya want us to do, ransom the Queen Mary?!"

"Or the whole Cunard Line, eh?" said Ernie.

"I assure you, my simple friends, it really isn't that complicated," continued Laszlo. "But it will certainly be the most *flashy* job yet. So if you don't like the proverbial heat, then get out of the kitchen. Remember the old slogan, 'Freedom through Work.'"

"But one hundred large?" Seamus asked again.

Rory puffed on his cigar. "Well, you have my attention, Mister Strozek."

"You see, Mister Caven, you are in a unique position as freelancers to be included—"

Another couple stepped in front of Walter and his view was again temporarily blocked. "Goddammit," he uttered. He quickly moved with Tatum so they could find a clear sight line.

Tatum was restless. "Hey, the very least you can do is keep me involved here. Talk to me. What are they saying?"

"Extortion maybe, or another robbery."

"Extortion, eh?" Tatum wanted to get a glimpse now. She smoothly spun them around to get a good look at the players seated across at the booth. This all happened before Walter realized what she was doing and because they were already committed, he had to let her spin so they could go back to their first position.

"It sounds like my guy there, the piano player, is a middleman for some syndicate." Walter said softly into her ear. "He's involved with the gang behind that Empire State building caper from the other night."

"That was a big deal, front page stuff." Tatum closed her eyes as they swayed.

"Yeah, and I don't think the public knows the half of it. It's all very baffling." Walt looked away so it wouldn't seem obvious he was staring at the table. "Maybe Caven's West Side boys are muscle on this potential kidnapping I'm working?"

"Kidnapping?" Tatum opened her eyes. "It's a kidnapping?"

"Ssshh! Well, it might not be a kidnapping. Still trying to figure that out. It's a missing person that I am starting to get very worried about."

Laszlo's impatience overtook him. He looked back at the stage. "That's all I can say at this time. I have to get back to the show. Please excuse me."

Rory reached across the table and grabbed Laszlo's arm before he could walk away. "This partnership stays together as long as we're keeping our whistles wet. That dries up, especially with the heat you and your crew seem to have no problem attracting, then you and I are gonna have some problems. So let's make sure we keep it all on the level, eh?"

"Of course, my friend," Laszlo proclaimed, wearily. "Anything else would be bad for business and bad for the both of us. The results of our last enterprise should be an example of our integrity, eh? Let's just hope you can play with us big boys now."

Everyone at the table remained silent. It was clear that Seamus was biting his tongue.

"Good evening, gentlemen. Enjoy your whiskey." Laszlo got up and headed toward the bathroom.

Walter continued to watch him closely. Once Laszlo was past the bar, two men who Walt instantly recognized got up and followed the musicians down the hall toward the bathroom. It was Walter's stalkers, Ed and his hard-nosed partner.

"We got company watching Laszlo."

"What?" Tatum said.

"Two fellas who were waiting for me in the office last night told me to lay off this piano player. They just followed my man to the can."

The song ended, and the band announced they were taking a break.

"Who are they?"

"I think they're the law, but I'm gonna find out. Excuse me for a minute, Tate." Walter and Tatum stopped dancing, and she headed back to their table while he hurried toward the bathroom as fast as he could without being conspicuous.

The two men behind Laszlo were careful to keep an eye out, and as soon as Laszlo entered the men's room, they followed him in and shut the door behind them.

Inside the lavish restroom, Ed flashed a badge and silently gave the attendant the boot while his partner made sure no one else was in any of the toilet stalls. Laszlo was at a urinal, so when he was finished and turned around, the surprise was evident on his face when he realized the bathroom door was now locked.

Walter came around the corner in time to see the bathroom attendant being pushed out and the door shut and locked behind him.

"Shit."

"What's the matter?" asked the washroom attendant with a level of concern as if this type of situation happened every day.

"I'm on a job, and I really need to hear what's being said."

"You a cop?"

"Private detective."

"No shit? You putting me on, brotha?" the attendant said with a sly grin.

"I'm not, and I need to hear what they're saying." Walter sighed in defeat.

The older, bowlegged bathroom attendant stroked his thin mustache and gazed at Walter like he was sizing him up. He smiled. "How much is it worth to you, my young, overzealous friend?"

Without hesitation, Walter dug into his pocket and produced a crisp five-dollar bill. "It's worth a whole lot to me, brotha."

The washroom attendant's eyes lit up when he saw the fiver, and he snatched it as fast as a magician palming a card in a magic trick. "Shit, Negro, all you have to do is ask, and the world shall be *yours*." Coinciding with his last word, the man reached over to a large device on the wall and clicked on a dial, turning it to a number that lit up. It was an intercom system. At the desired number, the attendant held the button down. Immediately Walter could hear the echo and hollow-sounding voices of the three men speaking inside the lavatory.

He rushed over and pressed his ear against the small speaker mounted in the wall. The older man continued to hold the button down that enabled them to hear inside.

"This fancy contraption was put in so I can talk to the maître d' or he can talk to me, so we can look after the big names that perform here. Any of the employees can stay in contact and be able to give a heads up to where the VIPs are in the club. They can also tell me when it's time to get the VIP back onstage. Ya dig me?"

"Oh, I get you completely." Walter angled his head in such a way that his whole ear covered the small speaker inside the wall.

"And," the attendant continued with a smile, "anybody who knows anything knows all you got to do is flip the switch the other way round and the speaker inside becomes the microphone, you dig?"

Walter nodded in excitement. "Oh, I dig you, my brotha."

The lavish, mahogany-colored and art-deco-styled speaker wasn't the best microphone amplification system as was currently purported to be, but aside from making the three sound like they were in church, it got the job done. Walter listened intently, straining to distinguish the three different voices through the echoing of porcelain.

Inside, the partner stood in front of the locked bathroom door smiling at Laszlo. He leaned against the large counter that was next to the sink, knocking over the bottles of colognes and other tonics the attendant had laid out on the counter for patrons to use, ignoring the clinking sound the bottles made as they slid off into the sink.

"Pretty fancy place here, even for you, Strozek." Ed had his back against the full-length mirror.

Laszlo shot back a condescending smirk in response. "I never thought you'd be admitted in a place like this on a salary like yours, Mister Helms."

The other man, now behind Laszlo against the bathroom door, cut to the chase. "We want an update on Overcast, music man."

Laszlo turned so he was able to see both men on either side of the palatial lavatory. "It is an extremely delicate situation, and I don't think pulling something this dramatic will do anything except blow the whole operation wide open. I mean, in the middle of everything else going on here, just to burst in so I can give you an 'update' could jeopardize it all." This was the first time he was really showing his temper apart from the blowup Walter saw below The Creo Room. He could detect more of

Laszlo's German accent sneaking out, something Walter figured he probably strove to conceal, while the country was at war.

"Well, you're such a hard man to get a hold of, Laszlo," the man by the door said. "Why are you ducking us? Why, when this thing has gone live and we're so close?"

Laszlo shook off his anger with a snap of his shoulders and straightened his tuxedo jacket. "I am not ducking you. Just trying to keep everyone happy." Laszlo smiled, with a look of annoyance more than warmth. "Sometimes juggling these dogs in the air can be uncomfortable to the poodles involved."

"What about Grand Central?"

Laszlo lit a cigarette, affecting a relaxed and cordial manner. "What about it?"

"Don't screw with us, Strozek," Ed Helms jumped in. "You know as well as I do that the OSS office wasn't the only agency your boys hit the other night, and we wanna know why."

"I don't know what you're talking about." Lazlo looked at the cherry on the tip of his cigarette. "One could only surmise, Agent Helms—mind you, this is merely unsubstantiated speculation on my part—that maybe they wanted some sort of additional collateral while they were there. Maybe they thought having a file like that would keep everyone from dashing out onto the playing field and blowing the game."

Walter leaned in as close as he could, but it was getting harder to hear. He jotted down the name "AGT. HELMS" into his tiny notepad. A group of ladies chatted with each other on the way to the powder room, drowning out what was said next. Walt strained to follow the conversation.

The man next to the door was irritated, and it came out in the tone of his voice. "—is not enough, Strozek. Okay? You start pulling this kind of shit and the stipulations of our mutual agreement are gonna start disappearing. We can promise you that."

Laszlo exhaled, beginning to get angry again. "Don't threaten me. You want to start playing those games, I'll start forgetting where people are hiding out and you'll have nothing to—"

Someone from down the hallway shrieked with excitement, and Walter was again prevented from hearing the voices coming from the small intercom speaker.

He quickly turned his head, exchanging ears so he could keep a view down the hall of the club, and plugged his other ear with his finger so he could continue to eavesdrop.

"They are taking about an overcast day?" he said while scribbling it down into his pad.

"*Overcast?* Like it's gonna rain?" the bathroom attendant echoed.

Walter made eye contact with the attendant. "Maybe a code name for something. You know, top secret stuff?"

The attendant shrugged.

"Maybe my guy is playing both sides?" Walter thought aloud.

"Could be," the attendant agreed, which made Walter look at him again and pause. The bathroom attendant continued, "I always thought he looked like he could go both ways, that he straddled the fence, as they say."

"No, no, that's not what I meant." Walter grinned. "I mean I think he may be playing everyone like a fiddle, not…never mind." He trailed off realizing he was having an in-depth conversation with a total stranger.

"Gentlemen," Laszlo said, dropping his cigarette and clapping his hands together, "as exciting as this chat is, I must get back to entertaining. I'm sure they're looking for me onstage."

The agent who was blocking the door didn't budge. "You just remember our timetable. You are to deliver him and Overcast's contents directly to us by the week's end. That was the deal."

Laszlo raised his hands palm up, giving the most innocent look he could muster. "Gentlemen, I am doing my best with what I have to work with. You want amateur hour, go hire Charlie Chan and his number one son. So, again, excuse me, please."

"You just remember where your loyalties lie," Helms said. "You double-cross us and I swear to God I will personally make sure you'll be back playing bingo halls and bombed-out buildings in Berlin when the war is over, buster."

Laszlo leveled a cold look of disgust at the two agents, then went to the door and got in the man's face. "Excuse me, Agent Mathers."

The attendant let go of the button 'and Walter quickly ducked into the ladies's bathroom.

Mathers didn't break his stare but stepped to the side and unlocked the door. Laszlo swiftly exited the bathroom, passed the washroom attendant, and headed back out toward the stage.

Moments later, Agent Helms and his partner Agent Mathers left the bathroom. They dug into their pockets to give the attendant a tip.

"Sorry, fella, here's a little something for your trouble." They each slapped a dollar into the man's hand and walked back into the ballroom.

A few more seconds went by before the ladies' room door inched open and Walter peeped out.

"You're in the clear," said the washroom attendant.

Walter nodded, added the name "AGT. MATHERS??" to his notepad, and left the women's bathroom. "Thanks for all your help, my friend."

He took the long way around the ballroom, staying close to the back wall. Tatum was waiting for him.

"There you are. Those gorillas you were scoping out paid their bill and left."

Laszlo Strozek made his way back onto the stage and was met with applause. He waved at the crowd then sat down and started another set. A relaxed, romantic instrumental.

Walter sat down and tossed back his shot of whiskey. A thought popped into his head and he jumped back up. "I'll be right back," he said. "I gotta to check my messages. Sorry, Tatum. I usually work solo, you know."

"I can see why." Tatum sighed, settling back in her seat.

Walter waited for the phone booth near the bar to empty and dialed his answering service. "Any messages for Walter Morris, please?" He waited a few moments, and hearing the response, his eyes widened.

"Okay, um, thank you." He slammed down the receiver, picked it up again, and rapidly tapped the switchhook to clear the line and get the operator. "Operator? The Hotel Claridge two-four-two-four." He waited as the connection was made. "Yeah, connect me to the Hayden suite, please. Yes, yes, thank you." He waited, tapping his foot.

Someone answered on the other end of the line. "Yeah, this is Walter Morris. I need to talk to Mister Hayden right away." Walter cleared his throat and decided to stand up in the booth.

"Who is this? *Crane?*" His brow furrowed. "What the hell is going on? Where's Hayden? Yeah, I got your message. So someone made contact with you? *No!*" Walter lost his cool and yelled, "Let me ask *you* a question. Why, for *fuck's sake*, would you pay a ransom without consulting me first, the expert you hired?!"

Walter now looked as perplexed as he did worried. "But herein lies the problem. Verification, Crane. What incentive do they have to give her *back* to the fam… They're going to leave her *where?* Okay, I'm going to drive out there now. But—Wha…? *Crane,* don't hang up, you ignorant—"

The line went dead, the connection lost. Walter exhaled in disgust and slammed the receiver down on the hook.

On the other end of the call, at the Hotel Claridge, a black-gloved hand took the receiver away from Hayden's trembling manservant. Crane was seated, paralyzed with fear. Beads of sweat poured down his temples, the color drained from his face.

His wide eyes followed the other gloved hand by his neck. It held a large syringe filled with a glowing yellow liquid, its giant needle pointed into Crane's jugular vein. The tip pierced the skin and a drop of blood appeared. He attempted to keep as still possible so it wouldn't go in any deeper. The gloved hand placed the elegant telephone receiver back down on its cradle.

Walter rushed out and bounded down the long staircase, passing the many couples climbing up the other side of the center railing to The

Whalley Room. Tatum attempted to keep up with Walt, but it was difficult in her heels, and she also had to dodge the people coming up the wrong side of the stairs. Walt was focused and had completely forgotten all about her.

"Goddamn it, Walter Morris, if I take a header down these stairs chasing *your* tail, I'm gonna be so mad!" Tatum belted out as she followed closely behind. This caught a lot of people's attention and they turned their heads in her direction as she hurried past. They let her through. She caught up to him when they hit the sidewalk.

"This is just not fair, Walter," she said, trying to slow him down so they could speak.

Behind them, crowds were flooding out of Madison Square Garden Arena looming over Eighth Avenue and Forty-Ninth streets after a night of boxing.

Walter didn't want to be dismissive of Tatum, but he was worried. He got the impression the Cuthbert Hayden party was veering into bad territory. The really bad sort. Deep inside, Walt was fearful for the safety of his missing victim, Miss Caldonia Jones. She had her whole life ahead of her. He found it extremely odd that after almost *two weeks* of silence from whoever had snatched her, this was now a kidnapping. Why now a ransom? And from what he could get out of Crane, who himself sounded very strange over the line, no one had even attempted to talk to Caldonia to verify she was alive. In the short time he'd been out of the office and away from his phone, kidnappers had been in contact, demanded a ransom, *and* had already received payment from Hayden's personal Mortimer Snerd, Garland Crane.

And now, the kidnappers were giving them an address where supposedly Caldonia could be picked up from? They weren't even going to include Walter; he'd only gotten lucky because he called within minutes of it actually happening and, despite the stonewalling, got the address out of Crane.

At the curb he paused. "I'm sorry, Tate to rush outta there. Thank you so much for coming with me tonight, but I have to go. Here's a twenty. You can still make a night of it." He gave her hand a gentle squeeze.

Walt crossed Broadway, heading toward the Garden and the parking lot his car was in. He was happy he'd told the guy not to put his Merc too high up in the automobile hotel because he didn't want to have to wait long for it to be brought down to him.

Tatum started after him. "What? That's not part of the deal! What happened?"

"I can't explain now, but I'll call you tomorrow." Walter reached the Kent Automatic Garage and gave his ticket to the attendant. The young man disappeared into the vast elevator banks of the Art Deco skyscraper. Somewhere inside the twenty-five-story building, among a thousand other autos, was Walter's Merc.

"I'm not staying there alone!" Tatum almost screamed at him in an attempt to get his attention.

Walter pressed his lips and turned around. "Then I'll call you a cab, Tate." He walked out toward the avenue and put his hand up to hail a cab.

"To hell with that." Tatum stormed past him and headed into the garage, where she sat down on a nearby bench to wait for Walter's sedan. "You ain't shaking me that easily."

Flustered, Walter took a deep breath, walked back over to her, and tried to protest. "Tatum, I—"

"Walter, I agreed to come out with you tonight as a favor, and you just drop me because things are starting to heat up?"

"Because it's getting dangerous," he hoped might shake her off.

She shook her head like a small child, crossing her arms. "You got me for the long haul tonight, pal!"

"Pal? What the heck have you been listening to lately?"

A freight elevator door at the opposite end of the lot opened and Walter's Merc came out on the electric parker, a carousel-like conveyer belt that moved cars around. Walt's car was delivered to its designated point and the valet got in. The Merc purred to life and was driven off the platform over to where they waited.

Not waiting for an invitation, Tatum walked right over like it was her own car, opened the door, and sat down in the passenger seat.

"Tatum! Jesus Christ!" Walt said, frustrated. But she wouldn't budge, and more importantly, he didn't have the time to stand on Fifty-First Street and argue like an old married couple, especially if this case really was a kidnapping and Caldonia's time was running out.

Walter realized it might actually not be a bad idea to have a woman along to deal with any kind of situation that may present itself with the victim, especially when Walt would be doing all the driving to who the hell knew where in the sticks. At least that was how the detective tried to rationalize taking a civilian, a woman for that matter, on a call like this.

Walter gave up. He tipped the attendant and got into his Merc, slammed the door shut, and turned to her. He raised a finger up and pointed it toward Tatum. "You're only coming for the ride. That is it. You do not get out of the car no matter what, understand?" He paused. "Understand?"

Tatum nodded once, beaming from ear to ear. "Perfectly."

Walter scowled at her. "Plus, I figure having a woman along might be a help if there's anything immediate that needs doing like consoling or first aid while I drive."

"Absolutely."

He knew he was saying it more to convince himself rather than Tatum. He glared at her. "But you listen to whatever I say."

She nodded again.

"Shut your door."

CHAPTER 17

OUT, PAST LONG BEACH

Walter and Tatum traveled over the long suspension bridge on their way out to Long Island. To their right, on the other side of the East River, New York City's dark skyline flickered in the distance.

Tatum spoke up. "So, are you going to tell me what the hell's going on?"

Walter reached over and turned down the radio. "My client got a call tonight. He was told to put two hundred thousand dollars in a bag and drop it off. My missing persons case has just exploded into a kidnap and ransom."

"Wow. You could buy Rockefeller Center with that kind of dough. Was that the idea, to ask for an impossible amount of money so the victim's family couldn't pay? I mean, who has that kind of money?"

"Yeah, well, my client does. He's got so much money he could make King Creosus blush. And what do these people do? Make rash decisions without consulting the supposed 'expert' they hired to do that for them in the first place." Walter exhaled a long, deep breath he hadn't realized he'd been holding. "They dropped the money off without a plan and without me, hoping that the bad guys will keep up their end of the bargain and release the victim."

Once they were over the bridge, Walter turned the radio off completely to concentrate on the signs and figure out where to go on all the new winding parkways. "The kidnappers called my client back and told them where to find her, this young girl Caldonia."

"Wow," said Tatum. "That's pretty lucky they rang back."

"Yeah. Now we just gotta take it slow. They said she's in an old flat out on the South Shore of Long Island. They gave an address and that's all I got."

They sat in silence as Walt followed the signs carefully on the interchanges and transferred to the parkway heading east.

"That seems a little too cut and dried, no?" Tatum suggested.

"Exactly," Walter answered. "And I think some of my employer's people are playing for the other side."

"They're queer?"

That made Walter smile. "No, Tatum, not *that* other side."

"Just make sure you're going the right way. If it's out in Long Beach, I know how to get there from going to Jones Beach. I went to see Guy Lombardo with my ex in his Plymouth."

"Okay then, Tate, keep your eyes peeled and just keep pointing me in the right direction."

They drove for just over another half hour on the parkway. They saw one of Walter's favorite billboard campaigns for Burma-Shave, then passed a huge billboard sign erected high up in the sky on a steel arm that read "Stanley Levi Development Project: Levittown." Just off the highway, acres upon acres of forest were being leveled and the land dug up and paved. They passed entire neighborhoods under construction. Miles and miles of suburbia, each house a duplicate of the next, stood in various stages of development. The future of America.

"I guess all the soldiers returning are gonna need a place to call home too now, once the war is over," he remarked, more to himself than to anyone.

Tatum nodded in agreement.

After stopping for directions at an all-night greasy spoon, they bought a local map and made their way out into rural Long Beach. They drove through flatland wooded areas, in and out of view of the ocean, past secluded bungalows, fisherman cottages, and hermit shacks. The air was filled with the smell of salt water, and when they put the windows down, they heard through the darkness the sounds of the Atlantic.

After much searching, Tatum spotted the street that the house was on. It was a long, overgrown gravel road with a few scattered homes toward the end. From what they could make out in the darkness, they looked to be quite old and dilapidated. Each house was on its own good chunk of land, perhaps a half-acre or less, and hidden from view by thick trees, bushes, and forest.

They found a mailbox post with no mailbox on it next to a long driveway leading into darkness. Cross-referencing the other addresses on the street, this had to be it. Walt passed the driveway, and once they were a distance away, he jumped out and Tatum slid over behind the wheel. With the fancy flashlight he'd insisted the Merc have, he crept over by the post and quickly discovered the rotted mailbox in the thick grass. He kicked it onto its side and saw the fading address they were looking for.

Walt got back in the car and had Tatum turn the Merc around and park facing the driveway, some distance away down the road. She killed the lights and cut off the engine.

The house couldn't be seen from the road because of the thick trees and bushes. It had to be right up on the water though, judging by the distance they were from the ocean. However, he had to admit that the lack of streetlights could throw anyone's bearings off.

"Which way is it?" Tatum whispered.

Walter pointed into the night where he thought the place was. "I think it's down that driveway there."

Once their eyes had adjusted to the darkness, they both thought they could see some sort of faint glow in the woods. It was just too obscured by the trees to clearly make out what the light source was exactly. Walter guessed that it had to be where the house was. Somewhere toward that light.

"Listen, Tatum. You to stay here and do not, under any circumstances, get out of the car. Understand? Just sit here with the doors locked and keep a lookout. If you sense any kinda trouble, lay on the horn. Okay?"

"Okay."

"I don't know what condition the victim might be in, so be ready for anything. And I may need your woman-type help here, depending on her situation, you get me?"

She smiled reassuringly at her friend. "I understand, Walter."

"If need be, I got a first aid kit in the trunk." He placed his hand over hers and looked directly at her. "If comes to it, you get the hell outta here and go back to that old truck stop on Groversville Road and bring back the state troopers, okay?"

She grinned. "We both know I won't be doing that!"

Walter slid out one of the hidden trays underneath the glove box, quickly going over in his mind the requirements ahead. Tatum's eyebrows raised with a nervous energy, her eyes glancing down at all the weaponry available.

"Probably not the best time to tell you I'm a pacifist, Walter?"

He grabbed the stiletto, a long, slim flashlight, and handed Tatum the smaller one he had in his hand. He skipped over the .38 revolver and the .22 automatic. "I might need something with a bit more stopping power than normal, something where if I shoot, I would only have to hit them once. That would keep 'em down and give me time to get outta there."

Tatum nodded at his lesson. "Sure."

Walt picked up the Colt 1911 .45 automatic and two magazines from the tray. He checked that the mag inside the gun was full, then got the spare.

"Okay, Tate. Lay low and stay safe. I'll be right back. Be ready to go if we need to get outta here in a hurry, and open that back door for me if I'm carrying her." Walter took a deep breath. "Alright...."

The surrounding woodland had already started to reclaim the property that the rotting colonial-style house sat on. An odd design close to the ocean. The place was once nicer than the other shacks and one-story cottages scattered around. It was maybe once an old farmhouse. Now it was the worst looking house they'd seen in the area, due to wear and tear of the erosion from the salty sea air.

Out of the darkness came Walter, hunched over low with his .45 in hand, crept cautiously toward the house.

Everything was wild and overgrown around the house. The grass was at least three feet high, full of thick brushes and weeds. The paint on the wooden siding was falling off, and the overall state of disrepair made the house look uninhabitable. Once there was a clear view of the house, a faint light was visible deep inside. Walter thoroughly examined the front of the property. He kept low and made his way around to the backyard.

The screen door was hanging by one hinge, and the screen itself had long since been torn out. Walter tried his best to get the screen door open without making any noise, and he then tried the back door. It was locked. He took out the stiletto and dug at the jamb where the deadbolt connected to the door, and within seconds he was able to pry open the door with minimal noise.

He clicked on his flashlight and crept into what had been, at one time, the kitchen. Gun drawn, he surveyed the room with his light, always keeping the beam pointed straight at the floor so it was diffused, the ambient spillage his source.

Walter crossed into an adjoining room and peered in. The floor in this room was completely warped and on the verge of collapsing. At the other side of the room was a closed door which seemed to lead to the room where the light was coming from. He headed back into the kitchen to find another way around.

He moved through the kitchen and entered what looked to be the parlor. An old rusty stool was on its side next to the remains of a stand-up piano. Trash and empty cans of food littered the floor. Walter crossed the room and entered the main hallway with his gun raised. Although he hadn't heard any noises coming from within the house, he took his time being careful. But as always, the quieter he tried to be, the louder he was. At the other end of the hall, Walter found the closed door that concealed the lit room.

He passed the staircase that led up to the second floor, quickly scanning it with his flashlight, but from the looks of it, they hadn't been used in years. Next to the stairs was a half-open door. When he peeked in, he saw some rickety steps leading down to an oh-so-creepy-looking basement flooded with a foot or so of water. Walt continued down the hall toward the closed door, which presumably led to the room where the light was. He turned off his flashlight as he got closer to the door. He pushed it open, keeping tight against the wall. It creaked noisily, taking its time before swinging back and hitting the wall. Then silence. Walter stuck his head around the corner to get a peek into the room.

Inside was a single bulb dangling from the ceiling by a long cloth-covered wire, and a candlestick phone on the floor next to a wooden chair. A yellow-stained mattress was strewn across the floor on the far side of the room. There were numerous metal tins on the floor which had recently been eaten from. Maggots wriggled inside the steel cylinder containers. Walter lowered his weapon and took a second look around the room. He stood for a minute before walking over and picking up the receiver. He heard the clicking of an open, working telephone line. He replaced the brass receiver on the hook and sighed. He was going to have to search the entire house just to be safe.

Thoughts of his little brother sprang up in his mind. He'd spent the last moments of his life being lured to a house just like this, a deserted, rotting shell of a house in the middle of nowhere. The thought repulsed and frightened Walter. Exhaling, he forced the memory out of his head as quickly as it had come, the same way he usually did.

He clicked his flashlight back on, but before he could move, he heard a slight creak from out in the hallway. He turned his head in that direction and realized someone was definitely out there. He placed his flashlight on the floor next to the chair and ducked behind the door in two long but silent strides. Keeping his breathing steady, he waited patiently, ready for anything. The door started to open, and he leveled his gun at where he estimated the head of the person entering the room on the other side would be.

A very elderly man wearing thick glasses and suspenders walked into the room and looked around. He was carrying a lantern in one hand and in the other, a double-barreled shotgun under his arm, his hand in his pocket. When he turned his head toward the door, he saw Walter aiming his .45 directly at him. Eyes wide, the man instinctually dropped his shotgun on the floor and threw his hand up in the air, his focus on the muzzle of Walter's automatic.

"Whoa there, fella! Don't shoot me, take whatever you want!"

Walt exhaled a breath in relief. What else did he expect from a redneck farmer coming across a strange black man hidden in an abandoned house in the middle of the night? The situation was almost comical. Walt lowered his gun.

"I'm not gonna shoot you."

"Don't shoot me!" the man screamed back.

"I said I'm not gonna shoot you!" Walter said a little louder. "Who are you?"

"Me? Who in the Sam Hill are *you*?"

Walter smiled. "One question at a time, and I asked first. Who are you?"

"I live down the road and take care of these properties." He paused while Walter sheathed his automatic. "Now, who the hell are *you*?"

"Phillip Marlowe with the zoning department."

The man looked confused. "Zoning department? At this hour?"

"Uh, surprise inspection."

"Lots of people have been showing up around here, holing up in these condemned houses. I thought you might be a robber." He rubbed the silver stubble on his chin, looking intently at Walter, obviously sizing him up.

"You've been getting traffic around here recently?"

The watchman lowered his lantern. "At all hours of the night and day, that's why I'm here. Since I live down the road, I told them I'd start to keep an eye on all these places, to keep the riffraff out."

"Who do you work for?"

"I told you, I'm the caretaker."

"I mean who owns this property?"

"Used to be the Mitchell clan until they were forced out by the highway department. They were gonna turn the land into luxury homes and private beaches, so the Mitchells were the last ones to be foreclosed upon and—"

"Who owns it all now?"

"Astitate Incorporated," the old man said.

"Astitate Incorporated?" Walter's brows furrowed. "That rings a bell."

"Hold on a minute, fella. I think I wanna see some identification. If the zoning department is sending coloreds to come check their land in the middle of the night, that's fair enough, but you should have some identification to back that up."

There was another noise out in the hall that got both their attention. The old man instantly shut up and his face completely paled. Walter drew his weapon and motioned with his head for the man to get behind him. They simultaneously stepped behind the door. Walter leveled his gun to the estimation of where the head of the other person coming through the doorway would be. He looked down at the double-barreled shotgun on the floor then back up at the watchman questioningly, who answered the look with a shrug.

Tatum entered the room with the revolver in her hand. Her head was much lower than Walt had anticipated. When she saw them behind the door, she didn't scream but she certainly jumped. Breathing a sigh of relief, Walter grabbed the revolver out of her hand and lowered his gun.

"Jesus, Tatum, didn't I tell you to stay in the goddamn car?"

She had placed a hand over her heart as if she was trying to calm down. "Jesus Christ on the cross, Walter! You scared me half to death. You're lucky I didn't shoot you and your new friend here."

He replaced his gun in its holster and looked at her in astonishment.

"You know this guy?" the caretaker said to Tatum.

"Wha—? You would shoot me?" Walter stared at the revolver he took away from her, her words sinking in. "What the hell are you doing outta the car?"

"Hellfire," the elderly watchman jumped in. "What the heck are you *both* doing here?" Walter put his hand up and the man rolled his eyes. "I know, I know, one question at a time."

They both looked at Tatum, who suddenly felt all eyes were on her. "Well, I uh, I went into the woods cause I had to, you know… Nature called. I did have a bit to drink tonight." The old man nodded understanding. Then it clicked with him.

"Wait, you mean booze? You both have been drinking on the job?"

Walter ignored him and kept his attention firmly on Tatum, who continued. "Anyway, while I was in there, a car pulled up, a big old sedan, with three heavy-looking guys in it. One got out and started to check out the Merc. Then another car pulled up behind theirs, with more torpedoes in it. And I tell ya, they didn't look like the law. So that's when I hurried over here. It was hard to stay quiet in the dark and in heels, Walt!"

The caretaker looked down at her feet.

"Three guys? What guys?" Walter asked.

"Now look," the old man said, shaking his head and walking over to pick up his shotgun from the floor, "I don't know what's going on or who you work for, but I wanna see some identification. And a good reason why a colored and a white woman, who are both dressed like they're putting on the Ritz, are out here at this time of night, or I'm gonna call the state troopers, so—"

"Two cars showed up, eh?" Walter frowned.

Car engines roared outside, and Walter dashed toward the window.

"Yep, those guys," Tatum said.

Two four-door sedans were making their way down the overgrown driveway.

Walter took Tatum by the hand and darted toward the window, where they both dropped to the floor to stay out of sight.

"Ah, more of your friends, I suspect!" the elderly man said.

"Not our friends, old-timer, now get down and turn that damn lantern out!"

"Hey, that's private property and someone is gonna have to clean that up! I'm going to get to the bottom of this right now," the caretaker protested, his lantern still on.

From what Walter could make out, neither vehicle had any emblems, hood ornaments, or anything else that would allow him to denote their make or model. Both touring cars had three men within. The first screeched to a halt on the tall, muddy grass parallel to the front of the house. The other car picked up speed and headed around the back, plowing over the high bushes and weeds.

"Shit!" Walter yelled. "This is *why* I don't bring civilians on a job."

"Don't shout at me!" Tatum said, her grip on Walter tightening.

The elderly caretaker raised his lantern and headed for the front door. "I'm calling the state troopers. I'm tired of you young people not respecting private property!"

"Hey, wait a second!" Walter yelled but the watchman had already opened the front door and was heading out onto the front stoop.

"Damn it! Get back in here!" Walter's warning went unheeded.

The old man hobbled down the front steps. "What the hell is going on here?! This ain't the parkway, you know, this is private property! You guys from the bank? They still trying to get us farmers to sell our land, eh?"

Walter smashed the bulb swinging in the air, extinguishing the overhead light. He looked on, crouching down low behind the window while pushing Tatum's head down and out of sight.

The back suicide door opened and a man exited the first car. He had a Thompson submachine gun in his hand. The driver slid over to the passenger window and produced what Walter thought was a Browning Automatic Rifle, commonly known as a BAR. He pointed it out of the window toward the house.

The other car was stopped by the back door of the house. Two men got out carrying the same Thompson submachine guns.

A third man exited the sedan parked in front of the house. The fiend was huge, built like a mountain, and *it* didn't look like the others. It had a deliberate way of moving, almost mechanical. While the others wore suits with long black overcoats, it wore fatigues. The skin was gray and wrinkly, the hair blond stubble on its head. It also had black goggles on that concealed its eyes.

Walter had a realization that the ghoul resembled one of the things he'd seen frozen inside the blocks at Icehouse Four *and* similar to the man Laszlo had met with.

The monster leveled his Browning Automatic Rifle at the house.

Simultaneously in the backyard, another almost identical-looking giant wearing black goggles, but with short black hair, got out of the rear car. Its movements were also stiff and awkward. Emotionless, that ghoul pulled a Browning from the back seat and took aim at the back of the house. The other men clicked back the bolts on their weapons.

It was dawning on the terrified watchman that these men were not the good guys. He lifted a trembling arm. "Now—now, please just hold on just a minute, uh—"

Everyone fired at once, thirty-ought-six and forty-five-caliber rounds.

The old man's lantern imploded with a flash of flying metal and glass.

The interior of the house shook from the deafening gunfire. Bullets ricocheted throughout the rooms, splintering wood and plaster, turning the residence into Swiss cheese. Dust and debris filled the air, visibility inside now was next to none. The piano rang out two notes which reverberated before it disintegrated altogether.

"Holy *fucking shit*!" Walt screamed.

At the rear of the house, the back door and kitchen walls erupted from the massive projectiles, rocketing through the rotting walls. The elderly watchman looked like a chunk of raw meat on a slaughterhouse floor. His body was blown to pieces, turning the stoop, front door, and its surroundings into a Rorschach test. The thick pieces of gory torso, limbs, and part of his head still spraying out blood came to rest on the stoop and dirt below.

Walter kept his hand and forearm placed firmly on Tatum's head and upper back to keep her down. He looked toward the kitchen and pulled her with him as he slid for the hallway. In the backyard, the driver stuck a Thompson out of the window and joined in with his large, tall friend in their efforts to destroy the house. Walter stuck his head into the hallway just long enough to get a fleeting glimpse at the kitchen cabinets exploding into tiny pieces. Bullets flew through the kitchen and into the hallway, embedding themselves into the walls by the stairs.

"Shit!" Walter shouted above all the noise and destruction. "We gotta go back, go the other way!"

They crawled back into the parlor where they had just been, heading toward that other closed door. Walter remembered in the room that connected this room to the kitchen, the floor had looked too spongy and too soft to walk on. The long flashlight in his hand was hit. Everything went black, causing Tatum to scream. Her flashlight spun around on the floor, sending an eerie beam of low-angled light up at the unfamiliar room.

Walter and Tatum's hands and shins were being sliced open from glass and other flying debris as they slid along the floor. Walt grabbed the small flashlight and placed his hand on her shoulders. He spoke as loud as he could so she could hear him over the carnage. "Okay, darlin', you're gonna have to really trust me here." He got them both to their feet. "On three!" he screamed.

"What? On three what?!" she frantically screamed back.

"One-two-*three*!" Walter swung his body and leapt up, Tatum blindly followed. They charged and with all their might, they smashed into the door, breaking it open. Bullets zinged through her long trench coat, missing her body by inches. The two came flying through the door into the adjoining room with the spongy floor. They both made air momentarily before crashing down and through the warped and weak floor.

Walter cradled Tatum, angling his shoulder, and his body went through first, shielding her as they went through the ceiling, and down onto trash and cluttered boxes that floated in the musty, flooded basement. They fell onto pieces of wood and glass, coming down hard in the three feet of stagnant water. The flashlight hit the water but surprisingly did not go out. It illuminated the basement just enough before it sank for Walter to get his bearings.

The awning above the front door crumbled, and parts of the roof partially collapsed. The shooting outside gradually came to a stop as the weapons ran out of ammunition. The men began to reload their weapons, and the two giants on either side of the house simultaneously moved toward the entrances, their big boots smashing down on the debris and shattered glass, getting louder as they got closer.

In the basement, Walter realized he was still alive when the murky water up his nose forcefully spluttered out. Tatum rustled in the water beside him and tried to get to her feet. Walter felt a sharp, shooting pain. He put his hand to his side and it came back covered in blood. He scanned the room and saw a pair of wooden storm doors leading to the outside.

"Hey, you okay?" he said softly, inches from her ear.

"I think so…"

"Okay, just bear with me."

The ogre with the blond stubble kicked through what was left of the front door. The headlights of the car silhouetted the massive figure against the doorway and gave even more emphasis to its abnormal physique. It stepped inside and unloaded another magazine of the BAR at the interior walls, spraying left to right, creating a deafening sound within the small space.

When the BAR was empty, Walter made his move. "Okay, c'mon." He got to his feet and pulled Tatum up with him. They trudged through the knee-high water, trying not to imagine how loud they must sound. Walt tried to open the wooden storm doors, but they were locked.

With the .38 in one hand, Walter threw up his .45 and fired it at the storm door's lock. He held his arm firmly around Tatum and used his other shoulder to crash painfully through the rotted storm doors out of the basement and into the backyard. Walter let go of Tatum, rolled away from her, and came up firing both guns.

Before the big one with the black hair in the backyard could even swing around, Walter unloaded his .38 into the center of its back. It staggered a bit but did not go down. Seeing this, Walter reconfigured his aim before emptying the pistol, sending the last few bullets right into the giant's face, which got a reaction. Walt swung his .45 at the sedan and sprayed the car, killing the driver and the other man who were both still reloading. Luckily, he was a good shot. The giant staggered, holding its free hand up to its face. Walter took that moment to reload his last magazine into the .45 and ran over to the cowering Tate. He grabbed her hand and fired at the large ogre. It still didn't go down but did drop the Browning.

Walter pulled Tatum to her feet and rushed her over to the driver's side of the idling black sedan. He emptied the rest of his Colt 1911 into the Frankenstein monster in front of him, insuring it kept its distance, and swung open the side door. He pushed Tatum onto the front seat, kicking the dead driver out of the way. He jumped onto the running board and threw his empty guns onto the back seat.

"Drive!" he screamed. Tatum fumbled to get the car into gear, and the sedan jerked forward as it started to move. Walter was still climbing into the back when the car sped off like a rocket, and because of the angle of the car's sliding back end, the centrifugal force slammed the back door shut. Walter hung on, leaning over into the front seat, and snatched the discarded machine gun from the floor next to the dead driver. Luckily for Walt, the gun was completely reloaded before he had expired. Walter chambered the first round and stuck the barrel out of the window.

Tatum leaned into the car's spin, pointing the front end in the right direction, and hit the gas. The car spun around and caught the large giant who was staggering between their headlights. It glared at them, the face filled with a demonic rage. Tatum and Walter both saw it had two bullet holes in the face, one in the cheek and the other that had broken the jaw, but by the expression, it didn't seem to be bothering the fiend.

Walter put his free hand on Tatum's shoulder and squeezed. She understood and put the pedal to the floor, and a moment later they plowed right into it. The goon was somehow able to get ahold of the top of the hood, its feet jockeying for a position on the bumper.

The touring car came speeding around the front of the house with the ghoul clinging onto the front end, spitting up grass and dirt behind it, taking the other gunmen by surprise. Walter squeezed the Thompson's trigger, and the barrel began to dance on the windowsill.

He took out the one shooter who was standing on the lawn; he stumbled over and fell to the ground dead. Walter then directed the remainder of the full drum magazine at the idling car out front, and the vehicle began to erupt from the impacts. The other driver, still inside, ducked down for cover.

The other ghoul came crashing through the front window of the house and stood up firing his Browning Automatic Rifle. The rear fender and trunk of their fleeing car exploded under the close-range heavy gunfire, causing the taillight to disintegrate and the small number plate to fly off into the darkness.

Tatum didn't brake, in fact, she sped up, T-boning the other idling sedan squarely in its center post, bending the frame and propelling it clear out of their way. The collision crushed their new friend hanging onto their hood, squeezing and pulverizing its body and twisting it unrecognizably into the steel and iron of their car's front end.

So understandably, Tatum and Walter were both dumbstruck to see the figure still holding on, a demonic look of rage plastered onto its face, staring right at them. The giant held on for a few more moments trying desperately to get to them. Finally, the weight of its own broken body tore off the car's entire front end, and the bumper, left fender, headlamp, and front grill ripped completely off. Along with it, the touring car bounced savagely over the mangled body that went underneath the whitewall tires.

The blond goon still gave chase, as the battered sedan they had commandeered barreled toward the street ahead. It threw down its empty rifle and miraculously caught up to their car when it came screeching out of the overgrown driveway and onto the gravel road. Tatum braked so the car wouldn't overshoot and slide into the woods, and at that very instant the blond giant leapt forward and grabbed hold of the back bumper of their fleeing sedan. It was dragged along the road until Tatum straightened the car out and hit the gas.

The sedan sped away, careening past Walter's Mercury and almost sideswiping it. Walt saw all four tires had been punctured. He'd have to deal with that later; right now they needed to get the hell out of there.

Walter was in a state of shock and was amazed that Tatum was still able to drive after what they'd just witnessed. He didn't really snap out of his astonishment until she started screaming.

In the rearview mirror, the black silhouette of the blond ghoul's figure rose up from out of the darkness, blocking her view as it climbed. Her screaming was so frantic it took Walter a few moments to register what was happening. Walt looked in every direction and only figured it out when he saw the direction of her gaze. He swung his head around to the back window and was astounded as the large fiend rose and climbed up and over the rounded hump of the trunk. But the sleek design of the aerodynamic vehicle made it impossible for the intruder to grab onto anything solid to hold, since the roof was one smooth piece of curved metal.

Walt checked the weapons, quickly figuring out his options. In the meantime, the giant somehow stood and cocked his fist back, and sent it crashing down with such a force that it punctured a hole in the metal roof just large enough that it could secure a firm grip.

The Thompson was empty, and Walter looked for something else to help him stop the advancing juggernaut, who was now sticking his free arm into the broken back window. Walt stayed low, and the ghoul started to punch away at the hole it had created, widening it. Walter searched along the floor of the back seat and in the darkness he found a double-barreled sawed-off shotgun. Once he realized what it was, he picked it up and swung the business end of it around.

The goon punched the roof again, this time making a big enough hole that it could start clawing at Tatum. She screamed when part of her dress ripped off. The giant adjusted his grip and swung over and down onto the car's left sideboard, causing the whole car to cant to one side. It fumbled to open the car's back suicide door.

Walter pointed the double-barrel toward the door and pulled the trigger, but the first barrel was empty or it was a misfire.

"Sssshit!" he yelled. He clicked the other hammer back on the double-barreled shotgun.

With its free hand, the goon ripped the back door completely off the hinges and threw it onto the road. It leaned in and Walter pointed the gun directly at the ghoul's face, but it moved as Walt fired. The buckshot landed in the shoulder of the arm that gripped the roof. At such close range the arm was completely severed from the body. The goon lost its balance and fell back onto the ground, tumbling down the street and disappearing into the darkness.

Walter stayed with his head out of the doorway of the car and his foot on the running board longer than he should have, making sure nothing else was going to creep up and surprise them. Soon they were back on the main roads and starting to see other drivers. It was only then that Walter exhaled a huge sigh of relief.

He sat down on the back seat and tried to gather his thoughts. His side was on fire. He snatched a discarded jacket from the seat, rolled it up, and put it under his suit. He pressed it against his side and held it in place with his elbow. He hoped he didn't need immediate first aid because he didn't have his...*shit!* The Merc. He'd have to go back for it at some point.

Then he thought about that poor caretaker. Walter hadn't seen what had happened when the man stepped out on the front stoop, but he knew enough to know that the poor man was no longer alive.

"Are you okay?" Walter yelled to Tatum. She didn't reply. He could see how tight her knuckles were gripping the wheel. "Tatum!"

She looked up at him with teary eyes through the mirror.

"Are you okay?" he asked her more softly this time. She slowly nodded without speaking.

Walter checked his side again. It was still bleeding profusely. He closed his jacket and elected not to tell his companion about his injury. "Turn onto the next side street you see, then pull over."

Tatum slowed the battered sedan and turned a corner, where it clanged to a stop several yards down a dark, tree-lined street off of the main road. When it came to a stop, smoke started to come up from around the edges of the bent hood.

"We may have to keep moving to keep the engine cool. I'll drive."

Walter exited the now doorless side of the car and carefully helped Tatum out. She was shaking. They embraced, and he held her tight against him.

"You okay, kid?" he asked.

She clung to him and nodded into his chest. Walter ran his hand through her hair a few times, before resting it on her shoulder. "I've never, ever seen someone take all that lead and not go down."

"What?" Tatum said.

Walter glanced at the dead man crunched up on the passenger side floor.

"The ox with the BAR, the one you ran over. I unloaded my .45 into his chest and he didn't go down."

He glanced around at their wooded surroundings. They had to move, or the car would never make it back to the mainland and the five boroughs.

"You had to have missed him...."

Walt knew he hadn't missed. She knew it too. He climbed in to take a look at the corpse. He gripped a handful of the dead man's hair and pulled the head up to see his face.

"What do you think, Irish? Or…German, maybe?"

Tatum raised an eyebrow and stared at Walter for a long moment. Finally she sighed and looked down at the corpse. She tilted her head and shrugged. "I have no idea."

Walter shook his head, laughing on the inside that he'd actually asked her to look at a killer's face and guess the nationality.

"What do we do now?" she asked.

"We drive and pray this jalopy makes it." He checked the dead man's pockets but there was no identification. "Well, you certainly don't look like your friend the Golem back there," he muttered, studying the corpse's face.

Walter got out and walked around the car, sizing up the damage and the vehicle's condition. He opened the passenger door and dragged out the body, sending it tumbling like a broken marionette into the darkness down the wooded hill they were parked along. He slammed that door shut and hurried back around to Tatum.

"Alright, let's get this show on the road, we need to get back to the city as fast we can and ditch this car."

Walter pushed her into the sedan. After a couple of false starts, the engine turned over and came to life, coughing out black smoke from the vibrating exhaust pipe. He put it into drive, pointed the smoking wreck toward New York City, and gunned it.

CHAPTER 18

THE ORIENT

They made good time and got back into the city within thirty-five minutes. And considering the car was missing one of its headlamps, front fender, grill, bumper, had no license plate, no brake lights, had a bullet-riddled back end, a ripped-open roof, and the back passenger suicide door was missing, they didn't actually attract much attention other than the wandering eye from their fellow drivers and the toll booth collector who was stunned into silence. Luckily the vehicle stayed operational. Go Detroit.

Walter drove into the tenement neighborhoods of the Lower East Side and parked the car in the first spot he saw. Carrying the weapons, they both exited the beat-up sedan. Walt was sweating and starting to feel faint, but he had to press on. Once outside of the car, his eyes focused in on the giant's severed arm, which was still attached and holding onto the roof.

After a lot of effort, Walter pried it off of the car. He studied the severed shoulder. Around the joint area he saw what looked to be metal attachments, perhaps gears or pistons, mixed into the flesh and muscle. While he was under a streetlight, it was difficult to see properly in the dark, but he'd never seen anything like it. Walt found a trench coat in the back seat, wrapped it up and tucked it under his arm, careful to favor his wounded side, in which pain was now becoming unbearable.

He took Tatum by the hand and led her up the street. "Are you okay?"

She shrugged. "I think so."

Tatum was a tough kid. If anyone could get through a night like this, it was her. Walt's old radio actress, part-time switchboard operator, and good friend, Tatum Marie Sullivan. They got to the corner and Walter raised his hand to hail a cab.

He attempted to lighten the mood. "Well, thanks for the exciting night."

A couple of unoccupied taxis went by but didn't stop.

Tatum laughed. "You sure know how to show a girl a good time, Walter Morris."

Another cab passed by but didn't pull over. Tatum put her arm up, and within seconds, a taxi stopped. Walter exhaled in frustration.

He opened the back door for Tatum, who got in, and looked over at the hack in a dubious manner. "Thanks for stopping, my man." He winked at Tatum, while the cabbie tried to decipher what Walter had meant by his remark.

Walter was about to tell her to use the cash he'd given her back at The Whalley Room but realized she didn't have it.

Tatum must have sensed what he was thinking, and at the same time said, "Oh no, I left my bag in your car."

"Shit."

Walter dug into his pocket and handed the cabbie some cash. He stepped back and closed the back door of the taxi. "We'll go for it in the next day or two, with the law backing us up."

Tatum put her arm out on the window frame and rested her head against her forearm. "Are you okay, Walt? You didn't get too hurt back there, did you?"

"Naw, I'm fine."

He pressed his elbow against the rolled-up jacket that was wedged at his side; it was a warm, wet glob at this point. A sharp, shooting pain told him he needed to get whatever was wrong sorted immediately. "I'll be fine."

He kissed her lightly on her forehead. The cabbie's eyes bulged, watching in the rearview mirror.

"You're swell, kid. This whole darn thing just burst wide open, and I gotta go after it before it all goes down the drain."

Tatum smiled. "Let me know if you need anything else, okay?"

"I will. And good work tonight. Shall I tell Jacob we may be getting a new partner?" She laughed and he winked at her. "Now get outta here."

He tapped twice on the roof of the sedan and the taxi drove off.

Walter stood there for a moment longer, thinking about what he had tucked under his arm. "Love you too, Tate."

❖

It was well after midnight when Walter made his way to Chinatown, but you wouldn't know it by the crowds. It was like Chinese New Year, a parade on the sidewalks. There was a surreal, carnival-like atmosphere, akin to some far-off exotic port of call. Walter maneuvered his way through the busy masses, tourists on his left and plenty of sleazy market dealers on his right. It *was* Chinatown.

By now Walt was unconsciously showing the physical pain he was in, favoring his side and holding it with his free hand. He was hunched over with his new knickknack under his arm. He wiped the sweat from his brow and carefully made his way through the streets, passing the various bakers, frozen fish stands, and trinkets for sale.

He walked by a circle of men betting on a praying mantis fight in a side alley. There was a crowd of shouting onlookers and a couple of men took notice of Walter and stared at him in bewilderment as he walked by. At the mouth of the alley, he made room for a large cage that was being wheeled down the street; it contained a pacing tiger which was growling at the people nearby.

Just another night in Chinatown.

Walter staggered over to a building's entrance, to a set of stairs that led down and under the structure. He nodded to an elderly man who was sitting next to the steps.

"*Ni hao,*" he said before descending into the darkness.

Walt walked through the old damp passageway of the building's dimly lit basement, ducking to clear a low threshold. Abruptly, the darkness faded and the room opened up into a maze of enormous tunnels and walkways. He headed down a catacomb, moving on a downward incline for what surely was the length of a city block.

He finally came out in a large, manmade space built of brick, mortar, stone, concrete, and who knew what else. It stretched high up into the darkness. Above, the room was filled with cast-iron pipes and conduits that had steam pouring down them, spanning every direction as far as the eye could see.

He continued on, occasionally stumbling over the uneven floor. He passed giant vats of cloudy water where Chinese men in traditional suits and hats were tending to the contents. There must have been hundreds of entrances and exits to this place, but this was the only way Walt knew. He walked through multiple work areas; laundry was hung up in all directions and there was a large room with endless troughs of exotic plants growing under bright, artificial lights. He passed Titanic-sized machines, boilers, and engines, outlined by thousands of rivets, that rose high up into the darkness of the labyrinth on either side of his path. Sweaty equipment was busy working away at tremendously loud decibels. Steam and fog surrounded the area, and the sound of loud machinists working in the distance could be heard all around.

Walter was in a totally foreign world to the one that existed above the streets, one completely hidden from the average New Yorker. Occasionally the odd laborer would glance up from the job they were doing and notice Walter, and the unanimous reaction was to stare at him with a mixture of shock and curiosity, as though he was the first black man who'd ever set foot in their hidden world. He didn't want to cause too much alarm, so he soldiered on, going deeper and deeper underground.

His path narrowed and he was once again walking through tight brick-lined catacombs that eventually opened up to a vast space a couple of stories high. Directly ahead was a type of shanty-town, full of Chinese, Korean, and Vietnam immigrants. Some took notice of Walter and

stopped what they were doing, staring at the private detective in bewilderment. He truly was in another world.

Walt stumbled along, persevering through the labyrinth of underground dwellings and encampments toward the other end. The passageway narrowed even more, lit from above by single bulbs spaced twenty feet
apart. Walter started to feel more isolated. The area around him unoccupied, becoming more akin to what one would normally see underground
the further he traveled. He was determined to find a quicker route to his
destination next time.

Eventually the narrow corridor widened out, and ahead of him stood
two very large Japanese men the size of sumo wrestlers. They were dressed
in formal but old, black Japanese gi. Their complexion was graying and
their skin dried and cracked. Their faces were like white Kabuki masks,
frozen in an unspeakable terrifying expression, and their eyes…their empty
eyes were like those of Haitian zombies, wide and black, with pupils as
tiny as pinheads, as bottomless as an abandoned well. They towered over
Walter like statues.

In between them they guarded a rusty iron door with a porthole-styled
window in the center that would have been more at home on a submarine
than it would have down in this crazy seventy-five-year-old space under
New York City. The entire scene was an extremely odd sight, right out of
a pulp magazine. The men looked like supernatural entities straight out
of the Orient, that would be more suited to guarding an ancient temple or tomb.

When Walter was close enough, they came to life and moved forward,
blocking his way. Walt stopped and leaned up against the brick wall to
rest. He was pretty sure the blood was leaking down into his loafers.

"I need to see Gray Matter." Sweat was now pouring down the side
of his face.

Behind the towering underlings, a raspy, high-pitched voice called out
from the darkness. "Walter Morris? Is that you, Walter Morris?"

The sentinels separated, and a small, emaciated, blind Japanese man
came into view, the same frail man who'd been eavesdropping the other
night on Walter's conversation with Small Change at the pool hall. He

was sitting on a tall stool, looking as ancient as the two giants standing guard, smoking that long, thin, curved pipe of his. Walter had immediately recognized the voice. How could he ever forget the man who had once stabbed him in his shoulder blade?

"Mao Lo, I need to see Gray Matter."

The thin man's reply mimicked that of the current Charlie Chan cinema parlance. "*Forgive please, forgive please...so sorry...*" He couldn't even finish the sentence without sniggering in his shrill snicker. "He is with Zipper."

Fatigue was setting in and the pain was almost unbearable. "Can you tell me when he's not with Zipper?"

Mao Lo laughed and gestured with his pipe. "You should really watch out walking around the catacombs without being escorted. You may lose your way." He let out another snicker. "You may even yield to temptation."

Walter ignored the joust. "Thanks for caring, Mao. You never did tell me how a Japanese man acquires a Chinese surname. That some sort of insult or cultural downgrade? Mama-san musta really hated you."

"You won't be the first to go missing down here. It would be very unfortunate for your partner to lose his boy."

"I really need to see Gray Matter and Zipper, and I need to see them now."

Another giggle escaped Mao's mouth. "Then you should always mind the path you walk on, Mister Morris, not to step out of the light."

Walt was beginning to see double, and he'd had enough. "I don't have all goddamn night for your fortune cookies, you necrophiliac. Now screw!"

Mao Lo glanced toward Walter with a fierce rage. The muscle under his right eye pulsated with anger and a loud, quick giggle unconsciously escaped his throat.

The large metal door creaked open, disappearing on a sliding track into the wall, and Walter staggered in.

The cavernous chamber resembled a traditional nineteenth-century circular operating theater, complete with dramatic lighting from above that illuminated the lecturing section. White sheets hung below and around the presentation space to act as a barrier and provide contrast to the lit area. Walter found himself at the top of the theater looking down to the circular space below. He collapsed into a chair on the last row. Another two extremely large bodyguards, who looked like the lobotomized twins to the two outside, stood like statues on either side of the operating theater's presentation area.

Almost as if it had been switched on, one of the guards became alerted to Walter's presence and started up toward him. Down on the third row, at eye level to the lecture area, sat a man in the shadows that Walter wanted to see, Gray Matter.

A gentleman named Zipper worked on a man who was laying on the operating table. The patient's chest was wide open, and the surgeon's hands were deep inside. Zipper had black hair down to his ears, parted to either side, and it was drenched in sweat. He wore a huge bloodstained white apron which concealed most of his slender frame. Along with his patient, he had an IV coming from his arm leading to his own drip; it was hanging from a hook next to the others. His was filled with a clear liquid to keep him hydrated and awake long enough to endure the many hours their surgeries usually took.

Numerous tubes and wires were attached to the body on the table, each leading to surrounding machines which monitored different life functions, keeping the patient alive. A large RCA television camera was mounted right above the surgical table, pointing down at the patient, and directly across the room from the shadowed man in the third row, hung a fifteen-foot-high projection screen that displayed the live zoomed-in camera shot of the patient's operation.

In the middle row of the theater sat two Italian gentlemen dressed in three-piece suits, covered with blood. They stared at the man on the table, anguishing over the surgery below.

Closer to Walter in the back row sat a skinnier man dressed in a light blue suit with a loosened tie and an unbuttoned vest. He had blondish hair, which was wet and combed to one side, five large, awkward bandages on all fingertips of his left hand, and one on the thumb and pointer finger of his right hand. Walt couldn't decide if the man's hair was blond or in fact brown; it appeared to change depending on the angle of the light.

The large guard made his way up to Walter.

"Tell 'em it's Walter Morris."

The sentry turned around and headed back down. Walter looked over to the blond/brown-haired man with the bandaged fingers. "What did I miss in the first reel here?"

The skinny man didn't look over at Walt as he lit another cigarette and pointed with the fingers holding his smoke. "They brought him in about two and a half hours ago." His accent was minimalized but still present, what sounded to the trained ear of something from maybe an Eastern European region.

"Gunshot wound?"

Without taking his eyes off the show below, the skinny man nodded. "In the chest. Large-caliber round."

Walter was starting to get interested. "Is he gonna survive?"

The skinny man tipped his head slightly so the lazy smoke that burnt off the cigarette hanging in his mouth didn't get into his eyes when he inhaled. "Well, with the magic Zipper can perform nowadays and Gray Matter's knowledge of the body, be it human *or* animal," he winked at Walter before turning back to the show, "if you've got the cash, I'd say there's a one in two chance of beating any affliction a piece of red-hot lead or cold hard steel could inflict on you…bearing in mind you'd need the connections and a wheelman to get you here fast enough." The man had certainly been working on dropping the accent; now only a very slight inflection put on certain sounds and syllables, but his foreign speech pattern was still apparent. Walt figured a prop like this would have it completely Americanized in weeks if not a month.

He inhaled a drag and took a long, hard look at Walter. "You a *polite boy?*"

Walter was beginning to drift into his own little world, extremely lightheaded due to the pain, and was sure he had a fever. "No, I ain't no cop. How 'bout you, my friend?"

The skinny man smiled. He blew lazy smoke rings out through his mouth and watched the scene below like he was a spectator at a college football game. "Far from it. I had the foresight to schedule something months in advance while I was in town on business. I was penned in for a procedure to erase my shadow…" He winced while waving his seven bandaged fingers in the air, "…and I was midway through when these wops brought this guy in." The skinny man finally took notice of Walter's tormented body language. "Care for a cigarette?"

"Not right this second, thank you," Walter said through gritted teeth. He took note of the man's face. Someone like this might be worth putting in the old card-catalogue in the back of his head.

The guard finished speaking with Gray Matter and returned to his original position.

The man in the shadows known as Gray Matter wore a black Stetson hat with a large brim that concealed most of his face. He addressed Walter in a raised voice, one that suggested a slight Japanese accent. "I don't care for your timing, Mister Morris. You must stop with this sense of entitlement. Next you'll be wanting to vote."

"Gray," Walter replied in a loud voice, "I don't have time for jokes right now. I need a favor."

Gray Matter carefully eyed the image on the projector screen. Under his hat, the only noticeable feature through the shadows was the projector light reflecting off the dark circular glasses he wore that were closer to being thick goggles.

He addressed his partner, Zipper. "Zoom in five degrees to the right, the arterial cavity."

Zipper put down his tools and pulled off his face mask. He looked into the specially modified viewfinder and readjusted the long focal lens that pointed down at the body. The view on the projection screen changed dramatically and refocused. It was a microscopic view of the wound. Gray Matter pointed to the upper right area of the picture. "Use that capillary as your dominant blood supply, Zipper, and rework it over to the muscle."

Gray's arm had become visible from the elbow down, lit by one of the overhead spotlights. It was metallic, a bright, shiny silver arm like a knight's gauntlet. The apparatus he wore always reminded Walter of the female robot's bodysuit from the silent film *Metropolis*, which was probably done on purpose. As Gray Matter gestured with his hand, it was evident that three of his fingers were absent. Not only that, there wasn't even a position allotted for two of the digits on the metal glove he was wearing. His pinky and thumb were average size, but the pointer finger was a stub and barely moveable.

Zipper stepped away from the viewfinder and narrowed his eyes to get a better look at the projected image, his hands coming to rest on his hips. "Shouldn't I try to save the pulmonary valve?" He gestured in exhaustion at the image in front of him.

Gray Matter cocked his head to the side and his gaze shifted from the screen to his partner. "If you attempt that, my darling, we will lose the bipolar membrane and we will lose the muscle, therefore losing the entire duct and valve. Do not question right now, Zipper, only perform."

Zipper groaned and rolled his eyes like a frustrated child. He put his mask back on and got right back to work. Around him, the machines continued to buzz, beep, and pump blood, inhaling and exhaling for the man in a rhythmic, monotonous fashion. Zipper performed the next stage of the procedure, and blood spurted out all over his mask and neck.

"As you can see," Gray said without turning his head to look at Walter, "it is not the most optimal time for conversation, Mister Morris."

An alarm sounded on one of the large machines. Multiple dials lit up and fluctuated on the control panel. "We're gonna lose this guy's kidney...." Zipper methodically toiled in the exposed chest cavity.

"Pull back the membrane and control the bleeding by the bone," Gray directed.

Walter took a slow and measured step down toward Gray Matter. The room was spinning, but he tried to hold on. "I'll be out of your hair in ninety seconds flat. I just need a quick word."

One of the two men seated in the middle section sprang up at Walter's interruption. He looked over at Walt and threw his arms out. "Are you fucking serious right now? Is he fucking serious?" he said to his companion, who seemed just as irritated. Both men's pained expressions betrayed how fried their nerves were.

Gray Matter looked in their direction, his Stetson hat hiding most of his face from view. "Gentlemen," he said in a deep, resonating tone, "I'm so sorry for the intrusion, but you must remember, as you came and took priority over a matter, something or someone may also take priority over you, albeit only for a very brief moment."

The two Italians glanced at each other with clear frustration, but the second quietly persuaded his friend to sit back down and continue to watch the screen.

Walter stopped when he got to the row behind Gray Matter. Gray was watching the surgery and spoke without looking at him. "Mister Morris, one truly wonders why we tolerate your idle interruptions." He glanced at Zipper with a look of concern. "Zipper, start on his valve."

Zipper made a face and mimicked him silently, muttering under his breath, "Wouldn't be doing that if I were me...."

More of Gray Matter became visible. His body stood erect, supported by a large metal frame. His back was arched, reinforced by pistons, and his neck was stretched by a metal brace that propped his head up straight.

"Gray, I need...I think, ah shit...."

Walter lost consciousness and fell lifelessly to the stairs, along with the package he was carrying wrapped in the overcoat. His world went black and he plunged into the abyss.

CHAPTER 19

MORE BAD DREAMS

Out of the shadows of his mind, child murderer and cannibal Albert Fish gradually came into focus underneath a bright single bulb in a visitor's cell. He didn't exude any bravado when he spoke, only a cold, hard, matter-of-factness.

He sneered. "Do you want to know what became of your little brother?"

A young Walter Morris strolled down a long cellblock hallway toward an open door. Inside that room, Albert Fish waited, seated behind a simple wooden table.

He looked up as Walter entered the doorway. "Do you want to know?" he said to a teenage Walter. "Come, I shall tell you every beautiful and exquisite detail."

"I want to know…." Walter sat down, but he was being pulled away, dragged back to consciousness.

He came around with a shock. "*I want to know!*"

Walt was lying on the operating table, his body in restraints. A sense of calm came over him once he realized where he was. Zipper was standing directly above him, busy sewing Walter up.

"What do you want to know, Mister Morris?" Gray asked.

Walter closed his eyes for a brief moment to shake off the bad dream replaying in his head. Gray Matter was in his usual spot, and aside from the underlings, the theater was now empty. The Italians, and the lone mystery man who was removing his fingerprints, all were now all gone. A strange emptiness, like he was in a limbo, far below the hustle and bustle of the city, here in this secret underground world, alone with this symbiotic pair.

"How long have I been out?"

"Long enough for us to have finished our last two clients and send them on their way," Gray answered.

"The dago with the gunshot...," Walter said aloud as he remembered. "And what was the other?"

"Just a shadow erasing his identity before he exacts a revenge onto the world," Gray Matter answered.

"Have you heard of the man they call *The Trouble*?" Zipper's tone was one of admiration.

"*The Trouble*, yeah I know that name."

"The details of our clients are no one's business but their own, and that is why they come to us, isn't it, my darling Zipper?"

Zipper scowled at Gray but continued sewing Walter up.

The detective let out a long sigh and closed his eyes to block out some of the artificial light shining down. "How bad was it?" he asked as Zipper finished up.

Walter tried to raise an arm but forgot he was strapped down. Zipper saw this and began to unfasten the restraints. With his chest and left arm now free, Walter carefully attempted to sit up, but a stabbing pain in his side abruptly stopped him. "Holy shit!"

"He needed a kidney," said Gray. "Luckily enough, you were both the same blood type."

It took Walter a good few seconds to process what was being said before his eyes widened and he jerked his head up to look at his stomach and the projector screen. He saw a close-up shot of his exposed chest and a freshly stitched incision where the injury in his side had been, along with another recently stitched, long, angular area on his other side.

Walt's eyes bulged. "*Gray...!*" He glared at Zipper. "What have you done?"

Zipper smiled, an embarrassed and playful smile, like he'd just been caught with his hand in the cookie jar.

Gray Matter shifted in his seat. "Mister Morris, two functions were served. Your life was saved—and for that you are very welcome, by the way—and you saved a life. Which, knowing you, I think your code of morality would appreciate."

Walter couldn't believe it. A goddamn kidney….

"How the hell am I supposed to work without a kidney?" He glared up at Gray Matter, trying to focus in on where he was up in the shadows. Gray was much more visible from this angle, probably so Zipper could have a clear line of sight to him. His upper body was erect, supported entirely by the large metal frame it was securely fastened into.

"You'd be surprised at what medical advancements have been made, and the recovery time for these things have vastly improved. Plus, we used a revolutionary method internally, utilizing dissolvable stitches, and each incision was coated with a medical glue that we ourselves have personally pioneered." Gray smiled proudly. "It will keep that wound closed no matter what, and it's a substance that will eventually dissolve over time."

"Glue?" Walter wasn't sure if he was still dreaming.

"Do not worry, Mister Morris," Gray responded with a rare chuckle. "You could take on a herd of elephants and I promise you, with our substance coating your incisions, they will not reopen. Why do you think Zipper and I are the biggest game in town?"

With that, Zipper held his head up high, and a proud smile spread wide across his face. Walt regarded him and tried to offer the same enthusiastic smile in return, but he just didn't have the energy.

Walter propped himself up on his elbow and tried to rise, grimacing at the amount of pain on both sides of his abdomen. "Jeeeesus."

"Don't worry, you have pain meds onboard."

"This is *with* something for the pain?" Walter asked.

Zipper removed his thin rubber gloves. "It'll kick in soon enough. You may get a little extra out of them too. You'd be surprised at what you're able to do while you're recovering." He winked at Walter, a smirk coming to his face. "Within reason though, Mister Morris. With the aid of modern medicine, we can keep you going and help with your pain. But at some point you will need to rest and let your body convalesce."

"Well, I would think so, for someone who's just had their kidney forcibly removed!"

"You came to us, Mister Morris." Gray pointed down at him. "And in the condition, you were in, needing the medical attention you needed, we helped you, and you in return helped us keep our impeccable standards at an exemplary level. But don't worry, we will find you a replacement, whenever it is convenient for your schedule, for no charge, compliments of the house." Walter did not react to that. Gray made notations in a ledger. "Now, we can certainly help keep your body going for a limited time, but it will crash eventually. How much time do you need? Realistically?"

"Realistically?" Walter used an arm to shelter his eyes from the bright lights hanging above. "Probably between twenty-four to forty-eight hours."

"Hmm, that's pushing it, Mister Morris." Gray hit a button and the lights above Walter dimmed in their intensity. "Afterward you're going to need to rest and sleep, preferably get off your feet for a while, in a bed, under observation. Zipper, we will have to increase his Pervitin and give him a high dose of our special proprietary blend." He regarded Walter. "This is a highly potent cocktail we developed ourselves. It will keep you going and completely eradicate any pain you may feel." He turned back to his partner. "Make sure you wrap him tight around the waist, the outer coat will need to be insulated as well."

Zipper nodded and set about his work.

"This is a material we've been using in Japan for centuries," Gray expounded. "Traditionally, it is used by samurai and other swordsmen because it is extremely flexible and tough to slice through. It won't stop a direct knife or bullet puncture, but it will offer you enough protection and abdominal support."

Walter nodded and slowly sat up. "Much obliged, Gray."

Zipper began to pile up the supplies he needed on a nearby table.

"Now, to the million-dollar question, Mister Morris. Where on earth did you get this?" Gray clicked on a light that illuminated a desk immediately in front of him and gestured to the severed arm.

Walter, a bit confused from the anesthesia, shook his head vigorously and looked up to where Gray was sitting in the shadows. Gray picked up the robotic arm and examined it. It was only then that the memory of the night's events came flooding back to Walter.

"Oh, that…I forgot all about that. That's a little souvenir from some freakshow hit squad I met out on Long Island."

Walter carefully laid back down. Zipper adjusted him to a semi-seated position and Walter was propped up.

"I'm pretty sure I was set up," he said, "and instead of my missing person being handed over at the meet and greet, I had Frankenstein monsters coming at me, both the Boris Karloff *and* Glenn Strange versions."

Gray had a small pair of pliers in his hand with which he was prodding the arm, fascinated by the mechanics and design. "You may not know how true that statement might actually be. And this came from one of them?"

"It did."

"Then you are an extremely lucky man, Mister Morris."

Zipper stabbed a hypodermic needle into Walter's tricep. Walter looked up at him. "I still can't believe you took out my kidney."

Zipper shrugged slightly and started to carefully wrap his abdomen, then whispered, "I'll put you at the top of the list for a new one." He playfully winked at Walt and smiled.

"You have two, Mister Morris. And we could always use another," Gray said as he inspected the arm.

Walter placed his hand on the injection area to massage out the sting and he instantly began to feel a whole lot better.

"Do you understand the magnitude of what you have here?" Gray asked. "This technology is decades ahead of its time. Someone has fused robotics with organic matter."

Zipper promptly stopped what he was doing and walked over to take a look. He stood on his tiptoes to see what Gray was examining.

"Yeah, that was gonna be your payment." Walter winced, when his fingers found the raw areas on his body. "Not my goddamn kidney."

"Are you still going on about that?" Gray said without looking up.

"Hell yeah, I feel violated."

Gray stopped what he was doing and briefly scowled at Walter, then continued examining the arm. "Who can even fathom how something like this can function. How is it not biologically rejected by the body?"

Zipper nodded at his partner's fascination.

"It's *that* complex?" Walter asked.

"That's an understatement," Zipper replied, turning his head to answer Walter.

"This was taken off from a man you came in contact with?" Gray Matter surveyed the rotting flesh that was fused to circuits and different mechanics. "Judging by the size of this arm, he must have been, six foot five, maybe six foot six?"

"Sounds about right, possibly taller. Like I said, Frankenstein."

Zipper walked back over to help Walter, who sat up and threw his legs over the side of table. "You mean Frankenstein's monster," he corrected. "Frankenstein was the doctor. Played by Colin Clive, God rest his soul."

"Yeah, I know that Dwight Frye."

"That's not funny." Zipper frowned. "But I guess I'd rather be compared to Fritz than to Igor."

"Touché."

"You'll feel a little dizzy at first, but we've stocked you with enough pain meds that you can go about your normal daily tasks without too much discomfort. You must rest soon."

"He can rest when he dies, isn't that right, Mister Morris?" Gray brandished a large scalpel from his coat and began to dissect the forearm area of the limb. "Tell me more about these scary monsters you encountered."

Walter probed his chest and shoulders for other signs of pain. "I shot one of them in the face twice. And those shots landed."

"What? Are you sure?" Zipper demanded.

Walter looked directly at Zipper. "Yes, I'm sure. He looked squarely at my companion and I, with black holes the size of a quarter in his face. He was none too happy about it either."

"Did they show any signs of pain?"

"No, none whatsoever. Maybe they were hopped up on bennies too, eh?" Walter laughed, but instantly regretted it after a sharp stab of pain in his side.

"I don't think even Pervitin could have helped with that," Gray Matter volunteered. "What sort of intellect did you witness? Any articulation? What about motion? Were they lumbering around or swift?"

The detective's brows wrinkled in concentration as he tried to remember. "I didn't have enough contact to make a judgment call on their intellect. They were extremely quick on their feet. In that respect they weren't at all like…" his eyes darted to Zipper, "…Frankenstein's *monster*. More like the Wolfman with their speed and leaping abilities."

"And you said there was more than one of these spectacular creatures?"

"Actually, a whole warehouse full of them, I think. Frozen, in blocks of ice."

"Fascinating, absolutely fascinating. Zipper, we must examine the arm immediately."

Walter cautiously stepped to his feet. "I was gonna say keep it." He was still quite dazed.

"Slowly, Mister Morris," Gray Matter said. "Though your mind is starting to feel no pain, your body still needs you to take it easy."

"Like you said, Gray, I can rest when I die." Walter grinned and moved very tentatively to the outskirts of the operating area.

Zipper took the arm and placed it onto a large metal tray that was lined with a clean linen cloth. He placed the tray on the table, clicked the lights to their full power, and adjusted the camera. "Incredible!" Zipper exclaimed. "What do you think powers it?"

"*It?*" Walter repeated. "You keep calling it *it?*"

Gray Matter leaned forward to get a better look at the intricacies on the projector screen. "Mr. Morris, you're telling me this man took a .45 to the face and continued coming at you?"

Walter nodded. "As well as a shotgun blast at point blank range."

"You really think this was just a man under the influence of drugs?" Walter studied the arm on the screen as Gray continued. "His body would have clearly failed him even if his mind was still able to function. Come now, Mister Morris, this man, these *men,* they are different. They are not what we would know as *human.* This is something that has been created. A future warrior, if you will. Made to withstand extreme trauma, possibly sustained on the battlefield."

Gray glanced over at Walter. "Do you have any clues as to where they may have come from?"

Walt thought for a moment before asking. "Have you ever heard the name Laszlo Strozek before?"

Gray Matter's head tilted slightly to one side. "What makes you think I know every man in this city?"

Walter raised an eyebrow at Gray.

"He's a German exile who happens to be an exceptional piano player," Gray answered. "Next you'll ask me if I know Vito Genovese."

Walter chuckled. Gray always seemed to have detailed knowledge on the city's masses. "Well, I think he's the link to all of this. There's an ice-house on the west side where his friends are keeping those human-sized popsicles on ice."

Zipper pulled back a piece of muscle that was attached to a silver, metal-lic piece of steel skeleton. "What is it you said you think powers them?"

"Exactly," Gray replied.

Walter turned because Gray Matter's voice was closer than usual. He was leaning so far forward while studying the projector screen that his hat had lifted and Walter, for the first time, was able to fully view him in the light, something that no one with the exception of Zipper ever got to see. He had a full metal chest plate that was connected to neck supports holding his head. Half of his face had completely lost its Japanese features due to severe burns on the right side. Much of his cheek had been burnt away, exposing the teeth. It resembled the wicked grin of a skull. Below his Stetson hat, his round jet-black glasses that fit his head more like goggles, covering his eyes. His nose was a stump with an insufficient amount of a bridge. It wouldn't support a regular pair of spectacles anyway.

"It's an organic creation, so fossil fuels like oils or petrol wouldn't work. Something alive, preferably oxygenated, perhaps a kind of synthetic substance that could replenish the tissue and deliver nutrition directly to the muscle and cells. The foreign objects implanted are only there for reinforcement, for protection and strength. They could be powered by a byproduct of that."

Walter really thought about what Gray was saying. "Blood."

"And a lot of it, especially at the rate this thing would be burning energy," Gray observed.

"The New York Ripper?" Zipper whispered, emphasizing the words with his eyes.

"I've heard rumors floating around the medical community that the perpetrator's been using a Liston knife, just like the original Ripper in London sixty years ago. It was created for battlefield surgeons who had to remove a limb quickly and without anesthesia." Gray looked down at Walter and visibly became embarrassed that the detective could see his appearance. The latter stayed silent for a moment, then continued, "More to the point, I've heard from that very same community that there wasn't a single drop of blood left in the victims' bodies when they were found."

Walter thought for a long moment before asking, "Tell me, what do you know about Cuthbert Hayden?"

"Hayden?" Gray frowned, "Nothing, aside from being a very active supporter of the Bund Party on this side of the Atlantic, leading up to the war."

"Wasn't that the name of the American wing of the Nazi party before the war broke out?"

Gray Matter nodded. "Yes. Back when the Nazi party was still fashionable over here. You'd be surprised at their size. They even had summer camps you could send your children out to in New Jersey and Long Island. Men like Charles Lindbergh, Henry Ford, and Cuthbert Hayden were all members. You must remember the rally in Madison Square Garden in 1939. Of course, before Hitler went into Poland."

"Was Laszlo a Bund member as well?" Walter asked.

"Who knows? A lot of Germans, as well as regular hardworking Americans, were. Part of the Prime Minister Chamberlain's way of thinking, or even sympathizing with the plight of the German people with the aftermath of the Treaty of Versailles, before the Third Reich's true intentions were revealed to the world. But many also fled Europe when war was on the horizon. Laszlo could have been very connected when he came to America."

"Maybe he didn't flee, maybe he just wanted it to look that way," Walter said to himself.

He continued to get dressed, replacing his holster before shrugging on his coat. "I gotta go. Keep the arm and have fun. If you learn anything new, give me a call. I'm on a clock and I think it's starting to run out."

Gray pointed at the side table. "Stay safe, Walter Morris. Zipper has prepared a medical kit for you to take home. You must be diligent and take the medicine within if you want to keep standing for as long as you need to. Take the tablets as needed, they will give you energy and keep you feeling upbeat. They're not just for pain management, but also to stop any infections so you don't drop dead. Keep your abdomen wrapped and drink lots of water. Hydration. That's very important."

Gray Matter smiled the best way he could with the working side of his face. "We don't want to be seeing you again anytime soon."

Walter grinned back. "Don't worry, you won't."

Gray grinned at the detective, "Good because who knows what organs we may need to borrow off you next time?"

CHAPTER 20

VE DAY

Hayden's midtown office was located at the Claridge Hotel, just off of Times Square. Since that was the last place Garland Crane was when he sent Walter out to Long Beach, Walter figured that was the first place to go to start looking for answers.

But tonight its lobby and the sidewalks outside, from as high up as Yonkers to all the way back down in Coney Island, were packed to the gills.

It must have happened while Walter was down in Chinatown because by the time he had taken the subway up to Forty-Second Street, everyone had stopped what they were doing and spilled out into the streets to celebrate. They would always remember where they were and who they were with when they heard that the war in Europe had ended.

Times Square was packed with thousands of people rejoicing, and cars were parked in the middle of the streets or abandoned in between intersections. People from the surrounding buildings were running down the sidewalks, laughing and celebrating, many crying from happiness that the war—in Europe at least—was over. Some were stumbling around drinking beer, liquor, or wine, grabbing the closest person they could find to hug or to kiss, even if that person was a complete stranger, all to celebrate and thank the Lord above that Hitler was dead and victory was imminent.

Walter dodged the growing crowds, bouncing around in his own little world—somewhere far beyond the Milky Way due to the powerful medicine coursing through his veins, courtesy of Gray Matter.

He glanced up and began to read the headlines on the front of the New York Times building, keeping up with the words that rocketed by and around the corner. He stopped in his tracks, just realizing the lights were on. All of them. For the first time in *four years*, the nationwide brownout had been lifted and Times Square's bright, glowing, neon lights were finally back on. Walt stared in awe at the huge spectacle before him.

New York City *looked* like New York City again, lit up and ready for action.

"The war's over. Thank you, God." He exhaled and closed his eyes.

Walter only exited the subway station at Broadway, but it took him longer to travel a block than it had to come all the way up from Chinatown. It took another ten minutes just to cross Seventh Avenue and arrive at the hotel entrance on West Forty-Fourth.

The Claridge Hotel had temporarily closed its doors to deal with the massive influx of pedestrian foot traffic. Luckily Walter was able to gain entry by flashing his PI license to the hotel detective, whom he knew.

He stepped off the private elevator of Hayden's penthouse suite and headed down the hall, where the first of the carnage was apparent. The security guard who was normally stationed outside the suite when Hayden was visiting was laying on the floor with two bullet holes in his face. His eyes were no longer present, replaced by pools of dark, crimson blood and ivory-white bone. The door of the office he usually guarded was ajar.

Walter unsheathed his .45 and realized the Colt was empty from being out on Long Island. He didn't need to check the guard's pulse to know he was dead, so Walt knelt down and, skipping the formality, put his .45 back in its holster and borrowed the dead man's revolver and spare cylinder of ammo. A .38 Detective's Special they were called, and as luck would have it, the same caliber as the other empty .38 he had on him. He aimed the snub-nose and pushed open the door.

He cautiously peered around the corner. The large, luxurious waiting room was in shambles. He gradually stepped in, taking two long steps down to the seating area, where many of the plush red chairs were overturned. There, Walter spotted another victim. Sprawled out along a crimson sofa was a black man in a servant's uniform, a brother working his shift at the wrong time and wrong place. The majority of his face was missing, due to the high-caliber gunshot to his head.

Walt focused his attention on a heavily blood-stained surgical apron discarded on a nearby waiting room chair.

"Oh boy."

Past that, the oversized aerodynamic desk made of wood and stone was upside down against the far corner of the room, like a discarded cardboard box. He saw a leg peeking out from underneath, a bare leg with a high-heeled shoe. Then Walter remembered the mousy little secretary. He knew she was dead before he even checked.

He clicked the hammer back on the .38 and walked through into the inner office, where he was shaken by what he saw.

The shades were fully open and that incomparable view of lower Manhattan and the Empire State Building and a moored RCA dirigible were visible despite the passing gray clouds.

Down in the sunken area, the couches that had once lined the walls were thrown throughout the room, their fabric tattered. Toward the center of the office, the large boardroom-style table had been smashed, its chairs hurled out of the way like dollhouse furniture.

Hayden's manservant, Garland Crane, was tied up to Hayden's high-backed leather chair at the end of the room. Above him on his left, a nearly empty bag of plasma hung from a nearby lamp. It was connected by an IV to his arm.

To say there was blood everywhere, Walter thought, would be an understatement. Crane was slumped over in the chair, not moving. His body and the area around him were glistening with splashes of the deep red liquid, and below him, a large puddle of blood coagulated on the floor.

Next to Crane on Hayden's enormous Dalbergia desk, thanks to lack of blood splatter, there was a clear outline of where an object once stood, something the size of a toolbox. And piled up all around that outline were blood-stained bathroom towels. Beside the towels, on a small white facecloth, was a piece of red meat about three inches in diameter. Curious, Walter leaned in to get a closer look. A wave of disgust rolled over him upon realizing the piece of meat actually had flesh on it…white human flesh. And upon closer inspection, he could see that the piece of human flesh had muscle still attached to it from when it had been surgically removed with delicate precision. It was a piece of Crane.

It was around this time, while Walter was studying the mess on the desk, that Crane wearily raised his head. Walter looked over his shoulder and almost climbed onto the desk from fright. Crane's eyes had been turned a milky blue, and the right side of his face, from his hairline down to his chin, had been removed down to the bone.

Walter glared down at the piece of bloody meat on the towel.

Crane tried to talk but was only able to moan.

"Jesus, Crane!" Walter didn't know what to say to the man. He didn't deserve…this. "Here, let me untie you." He quickly began untying the ropes.

Crane's eyes strained to look at him, but he eventually found Walter's frame. He began mouthing words and gradually found the strength and the resilience to form sentences.

"Morris…Walter…" he croaked, barely above a whisper, "…is that you? Am I hallucinating? I can't see…everything is blurry…."

"Yep, it's me, Garland. What the hell happened here?"

"He…he kept giving me transfusions…so I wouldn't pass."

Walter glanced at the IV bag attached haphazardly to the freestanding lamp. "Why?"

Crane attempted a smile, but with only the left side of his face remaining, his pain turned the gesture into a grimace. "You—you, Morris, did your job and fouled it all up."

Walter had a sudden realization as he looked at the bag hanging above Crane. It was empty.

Crane had been tied up with a phone cord, not a rope, meaning they must have ripped it out of the wall. Walt searched around the desk and the office, but he couldn't see another phone anywhere.

"Garland, what the hell is going on? Where's Hayden?"

Crane closed his eyes, his breathing becoming shallow. "They…they took him. They're done with their little parlor games. They didn't count on someone as elementary as you turning the stones over and doing some actual detective work. They thought he'd fold like a…a cheap suit."

"But *who*, Garland? Who did this to you? Where's Caldonia and Hayden?"

"Caldonia?" The exposed muscle on Crane's face started to pulsate from the lack of blood. "Hayden's gone."

"What? Why were you meeting with Laszlo Strozek?!"

"They couldn't keep playing these games, they need to leave. They couldn't lose their window out of the coun—" Crane started to cough, drops of blood spattering from his mouth. "They need to get away to succeed."

"To succeed in doing *what*, Garland? Damn it, man!"

Crane's free arm shot up and he put his hand on Walter's shoulder, scaring Walt half to death. "Further the cause!" After his sudden burst of energy, Crane closed his eyes and his body went limp.

Panic swept over Walter. He gripped Crane's shoulders and shook him repeatedly to keep him conscious. "Crane! Who did this to you?"

Crane's eyes shot open and his new blue pupils appeared ghostly in the lamp's lighting. "Herr Doctor! He did this. Von Stroheim was assigned to him…in the event that operation Westward Expansion went into effect. For these men, the war was already lost months ago…" Crane started to spasm. "…they need Hayden to get their cargo out of…"

"Crane? What about the war?! C'mon, Crane! Please, where's Hayden and Caldonia?"

His muscles tensed and his body convulsed. He slowed, and a deep breath escaped his mouth. His eyes relaxed. Garland Crane was dead.

The suite door crashed open and Special Agent Helms and Agent Mathers rushed in, both men simultaneously taking in the carnage before them. They automatically aimed their handguns at Walter and began barking out orders.

"Hands in the air!" Helms screamed as loud as humanly possible.

"Don't you fucking move, you fucking piece of shit!"

Walter threw his hands in the air.

Helms hurried over to Crane and checked his pulse, then began clearing the rooms.

Mathers grabbed the .38 in Walter's hand, tossed it to the floor, and frisked him at gunpoint, turning him around and discovering the empty Colt .45 under his arm and the other empty .38 in his waistband Walt still had on him from the car. He threw both onto the carpet. Mathers shoved him to his knees and put his new automatic to the back of Walt's head.

"So what now?" Walter asked over his shoulder. "Is a bullet to the back of the head gonna be my final exit?"

There was no response from either agent.

Finally, Helms spoke. "Okay. Let's roll."

Mathers holstered his gun, took out a long switchblade, and finished cutting Crane loose from the rest of his restraints. His body fell to the floor. Mathers took hold of Crane's shoulders and started to drag him toward the adjoining bathroom.

"So are you guys the FBI?"

Helms holstered his shiny automatic and lit up a cigarette. "We're not FBI, but close enough."

He pulled over one of the overturned office chairs and sat down in front of Walter, who was still down on his knees. He took a deep breath and exhaled out. The plume of smoke engulfed the detective's face. He jabbed his cigarette at Walter. "How much do you know about what's going on? Really know?"

"I'm getting there. Kinda. Still finishing the four corners of the jigsaw," Walter confessed in a slightly defeated tone.

"Well..." Helms took another drag and exhaled it as he went on, "...we're under a time constraint now that victory has been declared in Europe. I'm Agent Ed Helms, and officially meet my partner, Agent Gene Mathers."

Agent Mathers didn't acknowledge the introduction, only continued his laborious task, sluggishly pulling Crane's body into the enormous claw-foot tub in the bathroom near the staff's small kitchen and dry bar. Once most of the body was physically in the tub, Mathers retrieved a small bottle from inside his suit jacket.

Helms pulled out a black-and-white photo from the inside of his single-breasted suit and held it out for Walter to see. It was a magnified picture of the man with the scarred eye, dressed in a Nazi SS uniform, photographed with a long telephoto lens somewhere in a forest. "You ever see this guy?"

Walter took a moment to figure out his response.

He heard a sizzle, like bacon going onto a hot grill, and glanced over at the bathroom. Mathers carefully finished pouring the bottle's contents all over Crane's face. Walter saw vapor from the acid escape and float into the air. Mathers delicately placed the bottle down onto the sink then methodically raised both of Crane's hands so the fingers would touch the face, singeing the fingerprints.

Helms followed Walter's gaze to the sounds of flesh burning and acid eating away at the skin. He looked back at Walter, who was still processing what he was seeing. "Okay, I'm done playing games. You ever see this guy?"

Walter looked at the photo in the agent's hand. "I've seen him." This was the mystery fella Walt last seen in The Creo Room basement and at the Icehouse, with the dead eyes.

Helms nodded and put the photo away. "His name is Oberscharführer Hans Von Stroheim, Nazi SS high command. For the past three years he's been the behind-the-scenes overseer of the Auschwitz concentration camp. Which leads us to our next man."

Helms pulled out a second photo and showed it to Walter. "Have you seen this man?"

There was a pause.

Walter's brows furrowed. "I don't think so."

Helms took another long drag, held it deep in his lungs, then exhaled it out toward Walter. "You sure?"

"I've seen the backs of some people. But I reckon they were important people, sure. By how that Obermeister or whatever you just said, that Von Sto—"

"Stroheim."

"Stroheim," Walter continued. "Well, by how they all acted together, especially your man there, and how I saw him greet one guy in particular the other night."

Helms appeared more interested than ever. "How about this guy? Are you sure you haven't seen him?" The picture in his hand was a black-and-white photo of a dark-haired white man, probably in his early forties. "Does he look familiar?"

"He does not."

Helms put the picture back into his pocket. "Have you ever heard anyone refer to someone as the 'Angel of Death,' Mister Morris?"

Mathers exited the bathroom carrying a large, sleek art-deco trash canister, and placed it in the middle of the floor. He pulled a handkerchief from his pocket and began to systematically wipe down various areas with one hand, spraying a substance from a spray bottle in his other hand on fabric and plastic surfaces, which instantly began breaking down the topical area of the material it landed on. Mathers scanned the room, and anything that could be classified as evidence, he threw into the trash can.

Walt watched Mathers tending to his various tasks with a curious fascination. All the while, Helms didn't break eye contact with Walter.

"I have not," Walt said.

"The man in that last photo is Doctor Josef Mengele, head doctor of the Auschwitz concentration camp. These are the men we have to find before it's too late."

That made Walter break his concentration and look back at Helms. "What do you mean 'before it's too late'?"

Helms stared at Walter intently. "Mister Morris, what hasn't been released to the public *yet* is what the Krauts have been doing at these camps. It's only beginning to be disseminated in the public square."

Mathers threw papers from Crane's briefcase into the canister then tossed in some liquor from the dry bar, lit a match, and everything went up in a flash.

"What do you mean?" Walter asked.

Helms was contemplating if he should continue when Mathers walked up to them. "We can't stay here."

Agent Helms took his eyes off Walter and looked over at where Agent Mathers was standing. "Agreed."

They both stared at Walter.

He looked between the two. "Can I get up now?"

CHAPTER 21

LAYING IT ALL OUT

Helms drove uptown at an incredible rate of speed, using the car's deafening siren to deter the crowds and move the stagnant vehicles out of their way. Walter rode shotgun, while Mathers sat in the back seat. They quickly made some much-needed distance between themselves and the throngs of revelers in Times Square.

Once traffic had eased, Helms continued on with the discussion from Hayden's office. "They organized a mass deportation of the Jewish population, sending them to the concentration and work camps they set up in Dachau, in the hills of Mauthausen, and Buchenwald. But what about the Jews who couldn't be used as workers?"

Helms glanced in the rearview mirror at Mathers, who picked up the conversation. "At first they would put a bullet in the base of the neck and throw them in a ditch. But soon this became a waste of a much-needed bullet."

Helms looked at the private detective.

"Jesus Christ," Walter muttered.

Mathers nodded. "The deportees were coming in from all over Europe. They arrived in groups by train, up to six hundred at a time. Sometimes they'd get up to a dozen transports a day." Mathers dug a photo of Von Stroheim from his inside breast pocket and handed it to Walter, whose expression was betraying his interest in the agent's information.

Mathers pointed at the picture. "This Von Stroheim that we're looking for, he spearheaded the next step." Mathers exhaled deeply. "Large buildings were specially developed; they housed several gas chambers and were connected to crematoriums."

Helms jumped in. "They told them they were cleaning and disinfecting them for lice or fleas after their long journey. Sometimes, while they waited to enter the buildings, they would play music to keep the atmosphere relaxed."

Helms took his eyes off the road and looked directly at Walter.

"Once they undressed, the prisoners were locked in the chamber and gassed with Zyklon B, a cyanide-based pesticide. Afterward, the bodies were cremated in a furnace. We're told they averaged," the agent took a breath to make sure any level of emotion he felt didn't unconsciously make his voice alter or crack, "…around three hundred at a time. Their best day was nine thousand, from one single furnace."

About ten seconds of silence followed with the vehicle's cabin. He then continued. "Herr Stroheim ran the entire show flawlessly. His very own assembly line."

Mathers picked up where Helms left off. "Those chimneys," he looked over to Walt to make sure they made eye contact, "…they burned bright in the Birkenau sky for three whole years, Mister Morris." He emphasized the syllables in the words. "Twenty-four hours a day, seven days a week." He placed the photo back inside his pocket, a bitterness and wave of frustration passed over his face.

Walter looked out at the night sky. "My God." It was too much for him to process. If everything they were saying was true, all on the level…it was just too much to even comprehend. This whole conversation disturbed Walter on a guttural level that made him dizzy in the head and emotional.

Helms handed him another picture. "Doctor Josef Mengele there, he would force those he deemed healthy enough to work in appalling conditions manufacturing supplies for the war. He also picked the ones he deemed to be unworthy of life, like the old and the frail, the sick, even women with young children, the people who wouldn't separate…he was the one that sent them to the chamber." Helms tapped the photograph. "He was the crematorium's chief provider."

Walter looked away from the photo in disgust, nausea weighing heavily in his stomach.

"We have it on good authority that he's hiding out here in the city," Mathers went on. "We need to get this guy. This lunatic did medical experiments on the mentally ill, on women, children, and babies, all without any kind of anesthetic. He chose who would live and who would die."

"That's why they refer to him as The Angel of Death," Helms chimed in. "Always dressed in white, he personally chose from the tens of thousands getting off the trains who would be sent to the chamber and gassed."

Dressed in white… Walter frowned. The man Stroheim had greeted so eagerly at Icehouse #4 was dressed impeccably in white.

"The ones who made it through the initial selection, the average prisoner," said Helms, "we're told they only lasted about twelve weeks."

There was a long, reflective silence within the sedan. Walter decided to keep the knowledge of the doctor to himself for now; after all, these were the same men who'd roughed him up just a few nights ago. But there *was* something he was curious about. "What are the *totten core?*"

Helms slammed on the brakes. Mathers and Walter rushed to brace themselves, both holding out their hands to grab the nearest surface. The cars behind them honked their horns and Helms pulled the vehicle over to the side. He turned to Walt. "Where did you hear that?"

Walter wasn't sure what to say. Should he trust them and lay all his cards out on the table?

After a short moment of Helms not getting an answer, he started the car and drove off in a different direction than the one they had been traveling.

"Wait, where are we going?" Walter asked.

Mathers looked at Helms through the rearview mirror and raised an eyebrow.

"We're taking you to the tombs," Helms replied. "Central booking. We need to find these guys and we need to find them tonight."

That got Walter's attention. "How is putting me in there gonna help you find them?"

"One less prick we need to worry about poking the barrel." Helms shrugged without looking over at Walt. "No offense."

Walter twisted around to see Mathers, who nodded. "And we need to debrief you as soon as possible."

Feeling defeated, Walt turned to gaze out of the passenger window hoping to come up with some kind of plan. He sighed. "I guess I'm sorry, then."

Helms didn't take his eyes off the road when he asked, "Sorry for what?"

With a confident smirk on his face, Walter beckoned with his finger for Mathers to come closer and indicated down at his shoe. Mathers, looking bewildered, unconsciously moved closer, peering over the front seat to see what Walter was pointing at. Walt leaned forward as though he was grabbing something from his foot, which didn't alarm the agents as they knew he wasn't packing a heater since they'd already patted him down back at the hotel.

He crouched down as low as he could then shot up like a spring, smashing his head hard into Mathers' face, while simultaneously slamming his left elbow into Helms' temple. The car swerved abruptly and skidded along the street. It clipped a double-parked delivery truck before bouncing off of a Packard's fender and darting to the right, where it started to slow down. Walter turned around just as Mathers was reaching for him and punched him square in his already swelling face, sending the agent flying back against the seat.

Helms cranked the wheel hard after clipping a Ford cab-over-engine truck, but he overcompensated and the sedan came to a stop in between two parked cars. Walter immediately kicked the door open and leapt out. He hurried down the street as fast as he could and disappeared around the corner. Helms and Mathers exited the car and tried to give chase. They turned the street just in time to see Walter stepping up on a park bench to jump up to and leap over the stone wall into Central Park.

Mathers drew his service revolver and took aim at Walter while he was mid-air over the wall.

Helms quickly pulled his arm down, stopping him. "What! Are you crazy?! We're on a crowded city street!" he screamed at his younger, hot-headed partner.

Mathers sneered at Helms and threw his arms up in defeat. "I'm sorry…I guess I'm not thinking clearly, seeing how I was just hit in the god-damn head. Twice."

The two glared at each other in frustration.

❖

Walter came upon a trail in the park and followed it as far as he could before it closed due to playground construction. He leaped over the fence and cut through the center of the construction site before getting back out onto the street. He ducked into the first "five and dime" he could find, a Schwab's Pharmacy. He passed the counter and hurried down the main aisle to get to the back, where luckily the telephone booth stood empty. He closed the door, leaving a small gap so the light overhead wouldn't engage and he could have a moment alone in the dark, where he was safe enough to think.

When a stab of pain lanced his side, Walt took out a small bottle of pills from his inside pocket marked "Pervitin," swallowing a couple dry, praying Zipper and Gray Matter's magical glue lived up to its expectations. He settled back in the small seat and closed his eyes. He needed to clear his mind, to relax and get thoughts of his little brother and a million other things out of his head. He already felt the medicine coursing through his veins; it was beginning to work. And now that his head was starting to clear, he needed to formulate a plan.

Laszlo.

Walt needed to get to Laszlo. He knew he could break him; he just needed to apply the right amount of pressure and do it now before it became too late. He'd be performing at The Creo Room tonight. And Walt knew exactly how to get in there to see him.

He picked up the receiver, pressing his finger down on the cradle a few times to get an open line. "Operator? Yes, Alexander, 4444. Thank you...." A long pause of silence passed and Walt kept his fingers crossed. "C'mon, Bugs...be in New York," he muttered.

He listened to the soda jerk up front in the pharmacy flirt with a young girl over a banana split. He closed his eyes and saw Crane's face and his shiny white cheekbone, looking back at him in the darkness. Walter's eyes shot open and he exhaled with disgust.

A connection was made and a voice came across the other end of the line.

"Hello?"

"Bugs? It's Walter!" A huge smile spread across his face. "Yeah, I'm good, listen, I need a *huge* freakin' favor...."

CHAPTER 22

THE CREO ROOM TAKE II

Harlem was bursting tonight. The nightclubs and restaurants were popping, practically jam-packed with crowds and lovesick couples out looking to have a good time celebrating the end of the war in Europe.

Walter stepped out of a 1942 Cadillac touring car with his friend from the old neighborhood, Bugs Morganfield, one of bebop's premiere saxophone players. The detective adjusted the silver Colt 1911 .45 automatic holstered under his shoulder and straightened his tie. He had stopped by his office to change and borrow a handgun from Jacob's desk. Bugs retrieved his horn case and locked the car, and the two crossed the street, headed for The Creo Room.

Walter buttoned up his suit jacket and said to his friend, "Thanks again for meeting me on such short notice, and for driving."

Bugs grinned. "No problem, you're lucky I wasn't going to Louisville. I wanted to stay and celebrate VE day in the city of my birth." He gestured to the bruises on Walter's cheek. "So, your last visit to this place musta really been fun."

"This?" Walter laughed. "Naw, a friend of mine wants to break into the field of facial reconstruction."

"Ah…," Bugs responded with a slight smirk.

As they neared the club, the bass vibrations from the live band inside came blasting out of the door. It was hopping.

Walter stopped them before they got any closer. "Okay, as soon as you can, sneak to the back of the club," he pointed down into the alley, "and open that side door there."

Bugs snickered. "Oh, that's all? Would you like season tickets to the Dodgers too, nigga?"

"Just take your time, and maybe while you're on your way to the bathroom, accidentally get lost or something. No one is gonna care; you're Bugs Morganfield, for Christ's sake." He smiled warmly at his old friend.

Bugs rolled his eyes. "Yeah, yeah, I'm Bugs Morganfield. I know that, you motha—"

"After that, feel free to jam and then take as many girls home with you as possible," Walter interrupted. "Thanks, Bugs, I owe you"

"No, I owed *you*, my friend. So we're even after this. Slate is clean."

"Absolutely, completely agreed." Walter said.

Bugs banged loudly on the oversized, prohibition-style front door. After a moment, a sliding peephole opened up and a pair of curious hazel eyes stared back at him.

"How now, brown cow!" Bugs laughed.

It took a minute for the man to realize who was standing at the club's entrance. The peephole slammed shut, the door simultaneously flew open, and Bugs was ushered in.

The club was standing room only and at full capacity. Onstage, Scatman Crothers joined a grinning Cab Calloway and his band to do a special rendition of the song "Exactly Like You." The entire crowd was entranced with the musical brilliance unfolding before them.

Meanwhile, the employees of The Creo Room couldn't quite believe their luck. They were astonished to see *Bugs Morganfield*, premiere bebop king, walking in unannounced with his horn.

Luther, the head of security who had supervised Walter's tussle with Oak Tree out in the back alley, hurried over to Bugs with a balding, heavyset man. He held out his hand, grinning from ear to ear. "Bugs Morganfield?! What a fine surprise! What brings you to our elusive little hideaway, my brotha?"

Bugs smiled back but hoped to downplay their excitement. He wasn't really in the mood for any attention, but he knew how to play the game. "Well, my brotha, I've heard some really great things about this place and wanted to get a taste of the old Delta. And I hear I don't have to worry about my cabaret card here if I wanna go onstage with Louise and sit in for a couple of tunes." He winked at Luther. He knew the issue with getting his cabaret card revoked was a valid one.

If humanly possible, Luther's grin grew even larger. "Yes, sir! You certainly don't have to worry about that here." He moved to show Bugs to the VIP section. "Right this way…." He turned and walked right into his coworker who, still starstruck, hadn't gotten out of his way fast enough. "Take that dizzy look off your face and go get the man a drink!" Luther yelled at him.

To Bugs, the grin etched on his face again, he said, "What would you like to drink, brotha?"

Outside in the alley where Walter's last visit to The Creo Room had been unceremoniously terminated, he crept along the lonely side street, trying not to attract any attention. He peered down into the same window as before and again saw Laszlo, this time alone. He was seated in front of a mirror talking on the telephone while straightening his tie. Walter made his way over to the back door and crouched down awkwardly behind the lone dumpster and overflowing garbage cans, biding his time.

Bugs was now seated at the VIP section with two women on either side. Scatman had noticed when Luther had escorted him to a booth. So once Cab took the microphone and started singing, Scatman made his way offstage and over to the saxophone player. They shook hands, making small talk.

"Would you like to play a tune or two?" Scatman asked.

"Oh, I'd love to," Bugs replied. "I haven't seen Cab since Hartford, when I broke up that knife fight he and Dizzy got into. Hope he's still not mad at me."

"Nawww, of course not," Scatman assured him. "Tempers were just flaring, you know how it is. C'mon up."

"Okay. Lemme just use the john first and drain the vein." Bugs put his hand up to attract the attention of a club worker, and before it was even all the way up, Luther was there. He offered to escort Bugs to the washroom, but he waved him off and had him point out the way.

"I need you to do me a huge favor, my brotha." He stared at Luther, who was all ears. "See that?" Bugs pointed to the horn case next to his feet. "I don't want you to take your eyes off her, not even for a second." Luther nodded and smiled, but Bugs didn't reciprocate, keeping his stare cold and focused.

"She was loaned to me by a man at the crossroads, and I gotsta give it back to him on my day of judgment. So if *anything* were to happen to that horn, anything at *all*, it wouldn't be just me they'd have to answer to. You dig?" The color had all but drained away from Luther's face as he stared down at the black, beat-up horn case. "Don't let me down. Look after my girl, Louise."

Luther nodded at Bugs, shifting his attention right back to the instrument case.

"Thank you, my brotha."

Bugs glanced over at Scatman, who had been watching the short interaction from a few feet away. He winked at the singer when he got up and started on his journey to the bathroom. Scatman cracked up laughing, forced to put his fist to his mouth to contain it when he walked back toward the stage.

Luther was still staring intently down at the saxophone case when the employee who he'd previously yelled at came back with the table's drink orders. He tapped Luther on the shoulder so he could pass by and put the tray down. Luther swung around and screamed. "Damn! Don't you dare distract me, nigga! I got the most important thing in jazz right in front of me, and *you* wanna hand me a drink. Really, mothafucka?! *Really?!*"

Bugs made his way through the club with his brim down and head low, but still, enough onlookers noticed him that it took longer than usual to ease through the crowds, pausing every so often to greet the various clubgoers. He reached a dimly lit hallway and passed a scale for people to check their weight for three pennies that spit out fortunes on a card. Instead of turning into the men's bathroom, however, he walked by and entered the door at the end of the hall marked Private/Backstage.

He passed several doors before reaching the back of the club where he found the one that had EXIT painted on the back. He scanned the hall and opened the door. Walter saw the metal reinforced door swing out and made his move. He leapt up and slid inside the club, rushing around a corner in the opposite direction from where Bugs was headed.

The musician glanced over his shoulder to see if Walter had gotten in okay, and when he turned back around, he was startled by a large, portly gentleman who worked security.

A flash of uncertainty went by as the two sized each other up. Bugs tried to determine if the bouncer had seen what had happened. Bugs knew all the rumors, and it dawned on him how dangerous an establishment like this was.

The pause was longer than it needed to be, but the man grinned and blurted out, "Bugs Morganfield?" He pointed at the musician with a crooked finger. "Did you just sneak in our back entrance?"

Bugs laughed and exhaled a sigh of relief. "Ha! No, I was just lookin' for the john and took a wrong turn. Can you help me out?"

The heavyset man burst into loud laughter. "I was about to *say*. Haa! I heard the door shut and thought you snuck in, ha! Now that would have been funny! Haaah! Right this way, my brotha." They headed down the hall, the large man leading the way. "You couldn't imagine who we get coming through that door. All kinds of unsavory mothas. And I hope you brought your horn…"

Walter peered around the corner and watched as the man led Bugs down the hall and back out into the club. Once they were out of earshot, he tried to get his bearings. Stacked up all around him were the band's instrument cases and road gear along one wall, and against the other side were crates of food, alcohol, and soft drinks, all of which gave him a good amount of cover to hide and stay in the shadows. For the moment at least.

He saw several dressing room doors leading back toward the club, and two huge double doors which led to the kitchen. Finally he spotted an entryway that led downstairs to where he'd last seen Laszlo. He crept over and proceeded down the dimly lit staircase. The walls were lined with autographs and photos of the many musicians who had performed there. When he reached the bottom of the stairs, he cautiously peered around the corner.

He tiptoed down the aging concrete hallway. The ceiling was low, perhaps only eight feet high. The walls were cracked, and at points, the concrete had been broken away, exposing the brick and mortar behind. Although muffled, the band was quite audible, even down here. Walter heard a noise coming from within one of the rooms, and a door opened at the end of the hall. He ducked into a darkened area marked PRIVATE and waited until the person walked by. He carefully opened the door in time to see a man heading up the stairs. Whoever it was, it wasn't Laszlo.

Using the sliver of light from the doorway, Walter glanced back over his shoulder to see what was inside the room. Something in the shadows caught his eye. He grabbed his lighter from his pocket and flicked the hammer against the flint with his thumb, causing a spark and flame on the first try.

Against the far side of the room, around five feet away, was some kind of Haitian Hoodoo Voodoo shrine, and not a pretty one. It was atop an old, decrepit wooden half-table and covered with used red candles that had dripped veins of dried wax down onto the floor; it was adorned with feathers, trinkets, chicken bones, and other paraphernalia of the religious kind that Walter instantly recognized. He couldn't tell if those dried crusty veins that decorated the table down to the floor were actually made of dark red candle wax or thick dried-up blood. One could never really tell with this sort of thing.

He held the Zippo up to get more light on the shrine and saw a couple of wallet-sized, black-and-white, crumpled-up pictures of different people; some were taken outside from far away, others professionally done at a studio. Walt's eyes widened. They were barely identifiable in the darkness, but he could make out scribbled writing in red ink, and cigarette holes burnt into the chests, faces, and the eyes.

This all made Walter very uncomfortable. All of this kind of thing dealing with this did. "Whoops, definitely the wrong room." He emerged from the space and started back down the basement hallway.

He listened against another door and could just make out the muted voice of someone speaking German on the other side. He turned the knob and nudged open the door, which luckily didn't make a sound.

Laszlo Strozek was sitting at his dressing room table. He checked his watch and began to wrap up his phone conversation, unaware of Walter's entrance. He held a marijuana cigarette and put it to his mouth as he said goodbye to the person on the other end of the call. The detective stepped into the room just as the piano man hung up the receiver. Walt purposefully made a noise when he closed the door, locking it behind him.

Laszlo swung his head around and his jaw dropped.

"Remember me, friend?" Walter asked, more rhetorically than anything, with one hand on the doorknob and the other on his injured side.

"Mister Morris, what are you doing here?" Laszlo inquired, his entire body tense.

"Drop the routine, Strozek. Or *Herr* Strozek."

Laszlo lunged toward a desk drawer and clumsily attempted to open it. Walter's automatic was in his hand and pointed at Laszlo before the drawer was even half open. The piano man froze.

Walter shook his head. "Tsk, tsk! You make another move and I'll put a hole in you the size of a grapefruit."

The whites of Laszlo's eyes were visible and he looked like a statue. Walter walked over and gripped him by the collar.

"No! Please, don't!" Laszlo shrieked.

Walter put his index finger up to Laszlo's lips to quiet him. Laszlo gasped. Walt put his gun away and checked the drawer Laszlo was going for. He found a small .22 revolver. "Whose is this? Is this what you were going for? A woman's Gat?" Walter pistol-whipped Laszlo in the head and the piano man winced in pain. Walt stuck the .22 in his waistband and scanned the rest of the room. "Didn't think you'd see me again after that little soiree on Long Island, eh?"

Laszlo played dumb. "Wha…?"

"Thought that was pretty cute, huh? Now, where are they?"

Laszlo looked genuinely confused. "Who?"

"*Who*?" Walter pulled out the .22 and hit him again. Laszlo recoiled in pain. "Caldonia Jones for starters, your goddamn girlfriend! Where is she?"

Laszlo seemed truly flustered. His customary slicked-back hair was flopping in front of his face, and at the top of his head, near his hairline, there was a small trickle of blood from the beatings. He had dropped his Americanized accent and was now speaking with a heavy German pronunciation, one he usually tried so hard to hide. "Don't you hurt me. I know people…you can't lay a hand on me!"

Walter rolled his eyes. "Where's Hayden and the girl?"

He could tell Laszlo wasn't used to being in such a vulnerable position. The piano player was panicked.

"You can't hurt me!" Laszlo yelled. "I've got a deal with your men, the OSS!"

"OSS?"

Laszlo proudly blurted out, "The Office of Strategic Services—"

"—Services?" They both finished the final word in unison.

Laszlo had a huge smile on his face while flailing around to get loose of Walter, who still had him held by the collar. "That's right!"

Walter laughed. "Your agent friends Helms and the Mathers guy? The ones I saw you playing with. Is that who they work for? What, are you a spy?"

"Well, I never!" Laszlo screamed.

Walter put the revolver back into his belt, gripped him by the throat, and started to apply pressure. "Who the hell are you *really*, Laszlo?"

Laszlo strained to speak, all the blood rushing to his head. "The war is over, Mister Morris. Hitler is dead! Think outside of Harlem. It's a mass exodus!"

Right now there was only one thing Walter was concerned about. "Listen to me, you Kraut sonofabitch. I want to hear the chapter on Caldonia's kidnapping, and I want to hear it now."

He pulled out the .22 and held the muzzle against Laszlo's cheek. Sweat was beginning to pour down the man's face, and the eyeliner and powder he'd applied for his performance was smudged and starting to run. He clearly didn't want to talk, and with every second that went by, it was evident he was falling apart emotionally. The more Laszlo squirmed, the tighter Walter squeezed.

"I ca—I don't know. I can't…" Laszlo focused on the end of the barrel. His eyes were open so wide that tears began form in the corners.

Walter tried to employ a different tactic. He smiled and motioned to the weapon in his hand. "You know, I hear hitmen like to use .22s. You wanna know why?"

Laszlo stared at the detective but remained silent.

"Because one, they don't make a whole lotta noise, especially in a loud club like this. And two, they don't have enough power to exit the body once the bullet goes in." He tapped Laszlo's forehead with the muzzle of the gun. "Once the bullet gets in there, it bounces around just enough to do some real damage. Hell, I've even heard of cases where it doesn't kill ya." Walter rolled the barrel of the gun over Laszlo's face, letting it slide down toward his mouth. "I guess you'd be just confined to a chair, staring at a wall and drooling for the rest of your days. You can kiss the piano goodbye, that's for sure."

Laszlo couldn't take it anymore. As a performer, he'd appeared in front of thousands of people, in all types of situations. But this…this wasn't the kind of stress he was used to, or able to handle. The unnerving, raw anxiety from this direct confrontation was unbearable.

"I—I—" he cracked. "They've got them! They used me to get to her, to get to him. They have them both. They deceived everyone. Please! I just want out. I just want to go live my life in some small American town somewhere. Don't you understand? I don't deserve this—not all of this!"

"*Who's* got them, Strozek?" Walter hissed.

Laszlo scrabbled at Walt's lapels, and in response Walter jammed the .22 harder into the man's side. "V...Von...," He paused.

"Von Stroheim?"

Laszlo was visibly stunned. "How do you know that name?" he whispered.

"'Cause I'm pretty sure he just hosted a goddamn dissection class at The Claridge Hotel on Garland Crane's body *while* he was conscious!"

Laszlo paled. "Oh my God...."

Walter was truly losing his patience.

Since Long Island, his worry for Caldonia had steamrolled into a tightly wound knot of panic in his stomach. She was innocent in all of this, and quite possibly might not make it out alive. A poor teenager caught between two worlds crashing together, right here in his home turf of Harlem.

Walter pressed. "Talk to me, you son of a—"

Laszlo's mouth opened and it came pouring out. "Von Stroheim has them! They took her as leverage. Hayden refused them passageway south, so they took her, but that idiot Hayden was too thick to figure that out... he thought she ran away, and he hired you." He jabbed at Walter with his finger. "They have huge plans."

"Alright, turn the record, keep talking...."

Laszlo closed his eyes and mumbled something inaudible in German, shaking his head. "I—I can't tell you."

Walter let go of his collar and slapped him hard in the face with the back of his hand. "Talk!"

Laszlo winced in pain and held a hand up to his cheek. "They need one of Hayden's freighters to get them out of the country, down to Brazil and to South America. They're forcing him to get their cargo out of the city."

The detective frowned, his eyes narrowing as he digested the information. "You mean the stuff at the Pier, in Icehouse number Four? They're taking all that down to South America? Those bodies there?"

"I don't know what you mean."

Walter grabbed him by the collar again and pointed the gun at his face.

"I don't, I don't! I just know they have cargo to move. I don't know what it is!"

"So what, you're afraid that your OSS pals will put you away for good if they heard what you actually know?"

Laszlo stared at him questionably, as if the joke was on Walter.

"Then what?" Walter cocked his head to one side and asked, "You worried about your doctor friend? Oh, what do they call him…?"

Laszlo immediately stopped squirming. His eyes focused directly on Walter.

"Mengele. Was that his name?"

Laszlo's expression remained unchanged, but Walt saw something unsettling deep within. His pupils had dilated and his breathing was shallow. "What did you say?"

"I said, are you worried about your doctor friend, Mengele?"

Terror appeared to overtake Laszlo, and Walter saw a frightened little boy deep inside him.

"How do you know that name?" He was almost trembling now.

"Doctor Mengele, the man in white. The one hanging around down at that Icehouse on the water. It's where all the hip kids are meeting up these days. That ringing a bell for ya?"

A look of pure terror washed over Laszlo. He brought his voice down to a whisper, as if afraid that someone would hear them within the small, painted-over, brick-walled room. "He's here? He's in New York?"

Walter nodded.

The color quickly drained from his face. "Herr Doctor is here, in New York City? Now?" Laszlo exhaled deeply. "He wasn't supposed to come here; he was supposed to get out by way of Italy…."

"I should let your friends Helms and Mathers in on this little double cross you've got going on, how you're playing both sides. They'd put you and your Kraut friends on trial and away for the rest of your lives for what you've been up to."

"Ha! Trial! Who do you think backs me being here in New York, you idiot? *Your* government! You call *me* a spy? I work for Uncle Sam, you asshole." Laszlo threw his head back and laughed. "They recruited *me*. I am in this only because of them. I facilitate defections for your government, you imbecile!"

"What about—"

"Don't you see? Helms and Mathers want to get Von Stroheim to get to the Angel of Death. They want him to work for *your* government! There will be no trial. They want the knowledge of the Third Reich before another country gets it first. They want to know about the technology, both medically and mechanically, the rockets and the bombs...."

When Walter spoke it was through gritted teeth, spitting as the words escaped. "But you're playing both sides."

"I have to. I have to! But if what you say is true and he is *here*, just—just please keep me away from Herr Doctor!"

Walter swallowed before he asked his next question. "What's in the warehouse, Laszlo? What are those...things? The ones they've got in ice?"

There was a brief pause as both men locked eyes, silently assessing each other.

"They're in ice?"

Walter nodded. Laszlo uttered something barely audible in German before saying, "Then it's..."

"It's what, Laszlo?"

"The *totten core*," Laszlo whispered.

"English, mothafucka."

"The *death core*." Laszlo's eyes were wide, his voice only a whisper. He subconsciously reached out for Walter's jacket to hold onto for stability. He glanced away, dazed. "That means Von Stroheim was telling the truth when he said they walked with him here." He looked back at Walter. "He has brought the *totten waffe* to this soil, Mister Morris. Hell walks the Earth. Right here in New York City."

"What the fuck is the *death core?*"

There was a loud knock at the door. Both men jumped with fright, an unconscious reaction to the noise. From the other side of the door came the low husky voice of the club's program director. "You're up next, Laszlo."

The men remained quiet.

There was another knock at the door. "Laszlo, you're up. You alright?"

Walter leveled the .22 and pushed it into Laszlo's gut.

He hesitated, but said, "Give me a moment, Tyrone, I'll be right up."

"Go out there and play just one song," said Walter.

"What?" Laszlo frowned, confused.

"Go out there, play a song, then you and I are going for a little ride."

"I don't understa—"

"I want you to pull yourself together, walk out that door, and perform as if your life depended on it because believe me, Strozek, it does. 'Cause at this point, honestly, I don't even know *who* you can trust." Walt shrugged, bluffing him. "From what I've seen, you're on everyone's hit list."

Laszlo's beady eyes widened to twice their size.

"So after your performance, we're both walking out the stage door and leaving together. You're not going to say nothin' about our little talk, and if anyone makes a move, you're the first one who dies. Meaning, if you say *anything* to *anyone*, you will be the first one who gets it, and not with your little baby gat here. With the heater under my arm."

Laszlo's eyes darted around the room, as though he was weighing his options. "I can't do that. You're—you're mad! And why should I be worried?"

Walter smirked. "Oh you should be, believe me. You're on their hit list." The detective didn't really know that to be true but knew Laszlo couldn't confirm that. "So just shut up, go play your song, then meet me out in the hallway by the back door. Don't make small talk with anyone. And hopefully, Mister Strozek, I can help save your life, savvy?"

There was a brief pause before Laszlo's demeanor changed as he started to regain his composure. He pushed Walter's hands away and combed back his hair with his fingers. He powdered his face to disguise any new discoloration, fixed his collar, straightened his shirt and jacket, and shot a glare of pure hatred at Walter. "Come along, Mister Morris."

CHAPTER 23

SHOWTIME

The club was packed, with many standing in the aisles just waiting to get their chance on the dance floor. Up on the stage, Scatman was the master of ceremonies, warming up the crowds; his commanding presence on the microphone was electrifying. Everyone was smiling and laughing, and being the true showman he was, Scatman had the audience eating out of the palm of his hand.

"I mean we even got Bugs Morganfield hangin' out at the club tonight." He called down to a group of older women sitting at a table up front. "Can you *imagine* what Ingrid at bible study is gonna say about *that* when you see her tomorrow?" That crowd laughed and a huge smile spread across his face as he looked out around the room.

"So are you guys ready for the coolest, craziest, blackest-*white* cat you ever did see?" Loud applause erupted throughout the room. "Ladies and gentlemen, the man people say was standing right behind Robert Johnson the night he met the devil on the crossroads to sell his soul to play, the one and only... Mister Laszlo Strozek!"

There was a thunderous ovation and the spotlight immediately found Laszlo as he emerged from the shadows to take a bow. The applause continued for a few moments, and he raised a hand into the air in appreciation.

Scatman stepped back and gestured to the RCA Ribbon microphone, offering Laszlo a chance to do his accustomed introductory banter, but unusually the schmoozer ignored Scatman's offer and walked over to the piano instead. Scatman furrowed his brow, but like the adamant professional he was, he stepped back up to the microphone smiling. "Ladies and gentlemen, introducing the man from the Black Forest, Mister Laszlo Strozek!" He clapped along with the club and walked offstage.

Laszlo counted off and the band began playing a fast-paced, swinging version of "St. Louis Blues." The entire crowd seemed to rush to the dance floor at the same time in an attempt to secure a spot to get down. Others moved their heads and grooved along to the beat from their seats or from where they were standing. Laszlo's style was definitely different from what he played downtown. Here, there was less of the traditional swing and more of the pioneering sounds of what was becoming known in the community as Bebop.

Three large men walked in through the front entrance of the club. When they stepped under the harsh focus of the overhead lighting, their features were visible for the first time. The one up front was a tall, muscular blond named Maximillian, a huge scientifically engineered monster. The same one who lost its arm on top of the car in Long Island, but now had another in its place as if nothing had happened. It had gray, sickly looking skin and, like the others, wore black goggles that hid any glimpse of its eyes. Its collar was turned up and it wore a large Stetson hat that covered the rest of its face, successfully shielding it from any patrons in the club. The second was named Karl, another gray-skinned ghoul, but this one had dark-brown stubble on its head. It wore the same black goggles and was dressed the same way as its counterpart Maximillian.

The last one was Hans Von Stroheim, who didn't seem that tall compared to his companions but still stood a slender six foot four. He bordered on being gaunt and was even paler under the lights, giving him the eerie appearance of a demon that was trapped in the form of a man. Tonight his shorter jet-black hair was slicked back and matted down. He didn't bother to wear a hat but kept the collar of his long leather trench coat up high.

Stroheim surveyed the club and quickly spotted Laszlo performing on stage. He didn't need to say anything to his companions, who followed his every move like two Frankenstein-like shadows on either side. They began to make their way through the large crowd, toward the stage.

Walter discreetly peered out at Laszlo from the wings backstage, staying hidden in the shadows. The audience danced, cheered, and moved to the music. Many of the crowd, Bugs Morganfield included, were mesmerized with Laszlo's skill and speed while playing. They watched his intense concentration and incredible momentum, leading the tempo into a faster and faster rhythm. For those present who were musically inclined, his virtuosity made people's jaws drop. The people fed off his energy, reacting with greater and greater intensity to his performance.

People witnessing tonight's fevered show would remember it for the rest of their lives because of the groundbreaking and uncharted waters Laszlo was leading the band into musically, years ahead of its time.

As he began his solo, Laszlo glanced up and locked eyes with Stroheim, who was already over by the bar. Laszlo started to sweat, his playing becoming even more intense. He looked away, trying to keep his concentration and continue his fever-dreamed solo.

Stroheim and his companions were venturing through the crowds toward the club's basement when he paused mid-step. Eyebrows raised, he turned to look at the stage, sensing something was wrong.

Laszlo's solo began to increase in speed, as if the music was echoing his emotional state. He glanced around and spotted Walter watching from backstage and sweat trickled down the side of his temple. Stroheim was certain now that something was amiss.

"Karl. Maximillian." He dispatched his two monsters to flank the stage from either direction. The music turned, hitting the bridge, quickly building toward a crescendo. The two giants on either side of the club stood taller than anyone as they edged closer to the stage, sticking out like two killer whales in an ocean of seals. Stroheim stared at Laszlo coldly, curious about his strange behavior.

Walter had also noticed the change in Laszlo's demeanor. He seemed to be cracking under the pressure. He watched while he peered out several times, at something or someone offstage. The detective scanned the club to see what was captivating the piano player's attention. He stopped when he spotted Maximillian on the other side of the dance floor, and Stroheim, further back by the bar.

"Oh ssshit." Walter melted back into the shadows.

The crowd was hypnotized by the music, swinging and dancing, even in the aisles. Laszlo made eye contact with Walter. Stroheim saw their exchange and realized someone was offstage in the wings. He whistled, a very high-pitched sound that immediately got the attention of his companions. He motioned to Karl and pointed; the large ghoul diverted its course and headed toward the stage door leading to where Walter was hidden.

As Laszlo stared at Karl's change of direction, alarm bells went off in Walter's head. If one of Stroheim's monsters was on the other side of the dance floor approaching the stage from that side, then what prevented another from being on his side of the room? He swung around just in time to see Karl come crashing through the door. Its mouth gaped unnaturally wide, exposing sharpened fangs and a dry, decaying mouth, and let out a banshee-like shriek that raised the hairs on the back of Walter's neck. And much like a gorilla charging its prey, Karl rushed the private detective in the same fashion.

Walter's right jacket pocket exploded as he emptied Laszlo's .22 at point blank range, the sounds successfully muffled from being so close to the band on stage. The bullets hit Karl center mass but had little to no effect. Walter kicked it backward and drew Jacob's Colt .45 1911, only to have the gun snatched out of his hand. Karl broke the slide off and ripped the barrel apart. Jacob was gonna be pissed.

There was barely any room to maneuver backstage and before Walt could run toward the only conceivable exit, Karl leapt forward and seized him by his jacket, throwing the detective in the opposite direction.

Meanwhile, out front the song ended to a loud and thunderous applause. Laszlo immediately stood.

Walter took a few cleansing breaths and tried to keep his wits about him. He was trapped in a corner, and Karl was just a few inches from within reach. From the floor he spotted a large sandbag the size of a punching bag being used as a counterweight; it was hanging from a rope high above Karl's head. Walter's eyes darted up and over to see where the rope led. It came down along the wall and was attached to a large wooden board that held other ropes as well. They were all tied to different handles and secured the cyclorama in place that hung behind the stage. Walter jumped out of Karl's reach and ran over to the wooden board. He pulled his switchblade from his trouser pocket and grinned gleefully as he cut the line. But nothing happened. He cut the other ropes…still nothing.

"Oh, c'mon!" Walter yelled to God above.

Karl lunged at him. Walter fought back and stabbed him right through the goggles, into his left eye. Stunned, it moved back, taking the knife with it. The detective looked around in a panic and saw a heavy lead pipe laying in the corner next to some workman's tools. Karl staggered back and yanked the switchblade out from its eye socket. As it straightened up and turned back around, Walter grabbed the pipe and pummeled it hard against the side of its head. Walt landed another hit, then another, the force clearly breaking Karl's neck and knocking its head almost completely to one side.

Walter was stunned to see it still standing, trying to regain its balance. He swung the pipe with all his might, coming straight down onto Karl's head, knocking it to the floor.

Out on stage, Laszlo looked back and saw Karl on the ground struggling to get up, no longer able to support the weight of its own head.

Laszlo was horrified. "the *Totten core*…."

He bolted off the stage in the opposite direction and hurried toward the back exit. Walter followed close behind. From within the crowd, Maximillian saw the detective chasing after Laszlo and, in one smooth motion, leapt amazingly about ten feet into the air and landed onstage, sending some of the band members flying back off of their folding chairs. In the crowd, people were startled, and a few women screamed.

Luther, who was out in the audience, signaled to his biggest and most loyal employee, the one Walter called Oak Tree, to follow after them.

Laszlo darted out into the alley and sprinted over to where his little MG Coupe was covered and parked. He ripped off the cover and jumped in. Walter was right behind him and tried to open the passenger side door but it was locked.

He banged on the side of the car. "Open the damn door, Strozek!"

Laszlo hit the gas just as Walter stepped onto the sideboard. They screeched around the corner. Right ahead of them, Maximilian was running down the alley in their direction. As the coupe bore down, Walter crouched low and it was all he could do to hold on. At the point of collision, Maximillian jumped up high, stepped onto the hood, then over them, coming down on the trunk, feet back on the ground within seconds.

"*Holy shit!*" Walter yelled.

Oak Tree appeared from out of the backstage door. He didn't look before he walked into the alley and unfortunately, Walter turned just in time to see the MG hit him. His body flew up and bounced onto the right side of the car, knocking Walter off. Laszlo attempted to regain control, but the right side of the coupe was totaled, and the front end wasn't responding. The car jutted left and slammed forcefully into the side of the alley wall, coming to a complete halt and incapacitating the MG.

There was an eerie silence as the sounds of the city came gradually back into focus. Walter rubbed his side and picked his head up off the ground. The car sat smoking at the mouth of the alley, and about ten feet away from him was Oak Tree. He was dead. A tangled mess of broken bones.

The club's back door banged noisily open and out came Von Stroheim, followed by a severely injured Karl, who was bleeding from the ears, nose, and mouth. There was a gaping hole in the left eye socket, and it was somehow using its hands to keep the head upright. Despite this, Karl still followed Stroheim as they walked up to Maximillian.

Von Stroheim spoke to Karl in German. "Go fetch Laszlo and get back to the car before you bleed out." He turned to Maximillian and barked out another command in German. "Go and retrieve our new friend."

Maximillian took a few steps but Von Stroheim stopped it, this time speaking in English. "Alive, Maximillian. He is useful to us."

Maximillian walked over to Walter. He tried to crawl away but was picked up by the throat. The hand began to squeeze, and after a few moments the ambient sounds began to fade away, and the detective blacked out.

CHAPTER 23.5

ALBERT FISH

The jail itself was beyond ancient. It reminded Walter of the old medieval castles he'd seen in the picture shows and read about in dime-store novels. Except this was real, right here in the middle of Manhattan. Young and nervous, Walter Morris made his way up a steep cement staircase, following behind an elderly guard. They made their way through the various waiting rooms, past the many checkpoints and multiple guard stations of the stone prison.

The deeper into the facility they went, the more isolated Walter felt. He was nervous but didn't let it show. He needed to do this, and since some of the police officials understood why he'd made the request, they hadn't made too much of a fuss once they'd known his mind was made up.

He was escorted down a long hallway and told to wait on one side of a holding cell. He was left alone for several moments, but soon the cold steel-riveted door opened on the other side and two guards brought Walter in. The child killer Albert Fish walked into the room handcuffed and shackled. It took a couple of minutes for his chaperones to secure his chains, attaching him to the concrete table and to the bolts on the floor. They sat him down opposite where a young Walter was seated. One guard exited the room while the other stayed to monitor the visit.

Albert Fish, an elderly, gaunt, and feeble-looking man was covered in a five-o'clock shadow and a thick mustache. He surveyed his surroundings. After examining his leg irons, chains, and handcuffs with interest, he settled his cold and calculating gaze upon his visitor, the young Walter Morris.

"You really look like him," Fish said in all seriousness.

Walter didn't respond; he wasn't really sure what to say to that.

"So you've come to find out what I did to your baby brother?"

Walter wanted to leap over the table and rip his goddamn heart out. He wanted to take the pencil in his pocket that he'd gotten from his job running numbers for Amos Rattler and ram it into Fish's lifeless eyes. After that, he'd stick it down his throat, or maybe in one of his ears. But, his throat dry, all Walter could do was nod, his words lost somewhere deep within him.

Fish adjusted in his seat, unconsciously acknowledging his pain from all the various self-inflicted metallic pins, rods and nails he'd inserted into himself over the years that still resided inside him. After shifting to a less painful position, he clasped his hands together and looked Walter directly in the eyes, methodically and expertly reciting his firsthand account.

"In 1894 a friend of mine shipped as a deck hand on the steamer *Tacoma*, Captain John Davis. They sailed from San Francisco to Hong Kong, China. On arriving, he and two others went ashore and became intoxicated. When they returned, their boat was gone."

Every muscle in Walter's body was tense as he sat and listened to the story.

"At that time there was great famine in China. Meat of any kind was sold for around one dollar to three dollars a pound. So great was the suffering among the poor that children under the age of twelve were being bartered for food in order to keep others from starving."

Walter's eyes locked with Fish's, caught in his cold, hard stare.

"Children under the age of fourteen were not safe to walk the streets. You could go into a shop and ask for meat, and part of a child's naked body would be brought out for you to choose what kind of cut you wanted. A boy or girl's behind…," he grinned, "…is the sweetest part of the body."

Walter began to gradually become cognizant of another world. The space around him went from darkness to light as a voice invaded his thoughts, bringing him away from the terrifying stone prison of his childhood, gradually back to consciousness. The voice intensified, becoming more predominant, getting louder and louder.

CHAPTER 24

THE PIANO ROOM

Walter's head was draped over to one side, the angle straining his neck and shoulder. In the distance a voice badgered him, calling him back from his unconsciousness. After several minutes of prodding, he started to come around, his eyelids fluttered, and he eventually opened his eyes. It took some time, but he became coherent enough to realize he was no longer outside The Creo Room.

He felt groggy, as though he was still asleep and this was all just a bad dream. Disorientated, he squeezed his eyes closed and took a deep breath, trying hard to distinguish reality. His head was throbbing with pain, far worse than any hangover he'd ever suffered from. He must have banged it in the car accident.

The voice from his head came gradually into focus, and Walter recognized Laszlo Strozek's German accent. "Yes, yes! Wake up, you fool! Hurry. Wake up!" Both men were restrained, their arms bound and ankles tied to their chair.

Walter was having problems distinguishing the thoughts inside his head from what was going on around him. Even though he was awake, he still periodically saw and heard Albert Fish just as clear as Laszlo next to him.

A bone-chilling scream ripped through the room from outside the door. It knocked away any remaining cobwebs in Walter's thoughts and vision. His eyes were wide open. He looked around. This definitely wasn't The Creo Room. They were in a large, dark, Victorian-style ballroom. It had a small dance floor off to one side and on the other side was a luxurious grand piano. Past that, French doors led out to a veranda. One wall was covered entirely in mirrors, from floor to ceiling, giving the illusion that the space was double its actual size. It was possible they were in some sort of music room or recital hall. It was lit by a single lamp that was situated next to where they sat, making parts of the darkened room fade away into the shadows.

Laszlo was still trying to get Walter to focus when the terrifyingly loud screaming started again. From the sounds of it, someone was being violently tortured. The noise was muffled, which led him to believe the victim was in another part of the house.

Walter wasn't sure if he had suffered a concussion, but when he heard Albert Fish's voice again, it disturbed him.

"*John stayed in the Far East for so long that he acquired a taste for human flesh. On his return to New York he stole two boys, ages seven and eleven. Took them to his home and stripped them naked. Tied them up in a closet and burned everything they had on. Day and night he spanked them—tortured them—to make their meat nice and tender.*"

"Wha…What did you just say to me, Laszlo?" Walter asked, trying to steady his breathing.

"At last! I said wake up, you imbecile."

"Did you not just hear that voice?"

"Of course I heard it, you fool, the screaming is what awakened me!" Laszlo shot back.

"No, I meant the…the other voice."

"What? Pull yourself together, man." Laszlo used his head to gesture to the shut double doors several feet away. "Do you hear that? *That* is what's real!"

As if on cue, more gut-wrenching screams came from beyond the door. Outside, lightning brightened up the sky, occasionally illuminating the walls and areas of the wooden dance floor.

"You need to wake up!" Laszlo yelled.

"Yeah…." Walter turned to look at Laszlo. The piano player was covered in sweat, as though he'd just dunked his entire head into a bucket of water.

"I have to get out of here. You did this to me! You have to help me! Explain it to them, tell them I have nothing to do with you, that I told you nothing."

"What are you on about?" Walter tried to move his arms. "What the hell is going on?"

"Listen to me, you fool!" Another flash of lightning exploded from outside and Laszlo paused. He continued talking in a deliberately calmer tone. "You have to help me, or we are both dead." He peered up at the ceiling, an expression of terror on his face. "They're here. The *totten core* are here…." He stared at Walter, who had stopped struggling due to the level of intensity coming from Laszlo. "They are in this *very* house."

"Who?" Walter asked quietly.

"The *dead core, death core*. I didn't believe the rumors until tonight."

Walter felt nauseous. The room was spinning and he could hear Albert Fish's voice again, as he had many years before.

"*John killed the eleven-year-old boy first because he had the most meat on him. Every part of his body was eaten…except for the head, bones, and guts. He roasted him in the oven—or fried him. The little boy was next, he went the same way. At the time, I was living at 409 East One Hundredth Street, and he would frequently tell me how good human flesh tasted, so I made up my mind to try it.*"

Walter forced his eyes to completely open to help decipher his reality. His side was on fire and he was pretty sure he had a concussion by how his head was feeling. Plus he still couldn't shake this dream he was having, even though he was wide awake.

The screaming continued from somewhere inside the house.

"Where the hell are we?" he asked.

"At the Hayden Estate, I suspect. Jesus, man, get to your senses…*shnell!*"

Walter shook his head, hoping to somehow clear his mind. "Um…" He exhaled slowly and deliberately. "Where's…where's Hayden?"

Laszlo motioned to the barbaric screaming coming from outside the room. "Well, that's what woke me up."

"What's going on here, Laszlo? These guys don't die when you put them down."

Laszlo narrowed his eyes and stared coldly at Walter. "You're so goddamn naive. Haven't you listened to anything I have said?"

The screaming abruptly stopped. For a moment there was an uncomfortable silence, all except for the distant thunder and the raindrops that had started to beat against the glass.

Walter heard Albert Fish so clearly he could have been standing in the same room.

"*On Sunday, June the third, 1927, I called on your building—408 East Sixteenth Street. I was painting a vacant flat. That's when I saw him…your brother. He sat on my lap and we shared a coke. I decided right there and then to eat him.*"

He gulped and looked around. Laszlo wasn't hearing his delusions, or even looking at him.

"What about Caldonia? Where is she, Laszlo?"

"I—"

They heard footsteps, then a key being inserted into the lock of the large double doors. They opened and Hans Von Stroheim entered the room, followed by Maximillian. He looked the two prisoners over and approached Laszlo, whom he started questioning in German. Whatever he was asking, Laszlo strongly denied. After a few moments of a very heated discussion, Stroheim stepped back with a look of pure disgust on his face. Laszlo began to plead with him.

"Quiet!" Stroheim yelled. "Your actions have made you worse than a Jew…a Bolshevik Jew at that! You are not to speak until you are spoken to." Laszlo looked absolutely horrified, his body slumping in defeat.

Stroheim turned his attention to Walter. "Well, sir… Haven't you been a clever little mouse?" Von Stroheim smiled at the detective.

Walter spat blood onto the floor. "It wasn't very hard. If you read Chester Gould you could probably figure it out." He looked up at Stroheim, who hadn't gotten the reference. "You used Laszlo there to help you kidnap Caldonia, to get leverage on Hayden, right? You wanna borrow some money from him, is that it?"

That got an even bigger grin from Von Stroheim, on a face that didn't look like it smiled very often. "You Americans make me laugh. You wear your ignorance as if it were a badge to be proud of. So unaffected by the outside world." He smirked. "You do know that the world is at war? Or does your American naiveté make you oblivious to that as well? Does being a Yank hinder your intelligence?"

Walter smiled politely. "Well, Stroheim…that's your name, right? What actually even brings you to the Big Apple? The pizza? 'Cause an hour north of here, New Haven has the best pizza. Or are you part of the Operation Overcast thing?"

Von Stroheim's eye twitched, the smile fading from his face. His eyes hardened. He bent down at the waist, his tall, thin frame like a crooked tree. "You smug little insect," Stroheim hissed. "You all live your sheltered and pathetic little lives here in this utopia, which you've been brainwashed into believing really exists," he said with a level of disgust and contempt. "You haven't seen a war on your homeland in almost one hundred years; your land hasn't been invaded or plundered by a foreign army in almost double that time!"

He straightened up and glared down at Walter, tied to the chair. "How your people forget the *horrors* of this world. You think you are so tough… ha!" He pointed at him. "You wouldn't have lasted two days in the KZ. All of this American 'bravado;' men like you would have been broken in a day."

Stroheim raised his hand, and using his thumb and index finger, he mimicked the shape of a handgun, pointing it at Walter's temple. "I have personally killed *thousands* of men like you." He let that sink in. "Men who lived in a fantasy world filled with such delusions. Men, women, children…understand?" He lowered his hand and held them both behind his back. "So do not think your attitude gives you the upper hand or in some way intimidates me." He exhaled loudly. "Ah," he said while shaking his head, "the KZ would have taken away all the disillusionment you possess!"

He closed his eyes and calmed his temper and chuckled to himself. "If you'd have even made it past the 'selection' process." Stroheim opened his eyes back up and glared into the darkness at the far corner of the room.

"What do you think, Herr Doctor? Would he have passed your selection?"

A figure could be seen standing in the far corner, his outline barely visible. As if on cue, there was a crash of thunder from outside and with the delayed flash of lighting, the figure's silhouette became much more predominant. Along with the realization that this person had been in the room with them this entire time, even prior to Stroheim's arrival, observing and listening to everything they were saying.

"Well, Herr Oberscharführer, he might have indeed gone to the left." The man took his first steps out of the shadows, moving toward the other side of the room.

As he crossed the shiny dance floor, another flash of lightning made the man visible again. He had dark-brown hair and was dressed entirely in white, with the exception of a green hospital-style apron that was covered in coagulated blood. His gloves matched the apron, also bloodstained. On his forehead he wore a small head mirror, something surgeons would use to reflect light. He had both hands clasped together in front of him while he watched the scene with a look of pure fascination.

Laszlo's worst fears were confirmed when he saw the man's face and recognized Doctor Josef Mengele. He unconsciously let out a gasp and started to weep.

As the doctor approached, he unclasped his hands and there was a terrible ripping sound as the sticky blood on either glove tore apart like two pieces of tape. He continued over to the double doors and knocked lightly over his shoulder. They opened simultaneously and a solemn-looking male nurse entered the room, rolling a small medical cart with two square cases positioned on the top shelf. On the bottom shelf was a large bowl of steaming hot water and a stack of neatly folded white towels.

Mengele removed his blood-stained gloves and threw them onto the floor, then lifted up his arms for the nurse to untie his apron and remove it.

An older man, who was bald and had a slight limp, entered next. He was carrying a briefcase and was dressed in a white medical gown. He was followed closely behind by Karl, who was heavily bandaged about the face and neck. It wore a thick metal brace to support its head and a new pair of goggles to cover its eyes. Finally, three young men hurried in, all dressed in matching gray trench coats and dark gray hats. They each carried grease guns and wore black bandannas that covered the lower half of their face. Two placed themselves by the double doors and the third moved over to the French doors that led outside.

Von Stroheim's stare hadn't deviated, he continued looking right into the eyes of Walter and Laszlo to gauge their reactions.

"Because of our timetable, Mister Morris," he said, "I must introduce you to my colleague who will be able to maximize our time here with you…Doctor Josef Mengele."

The two conversed in German as the doctor nodded and motioned to his assistant, the bald man. The assistant opened the first case on the cart. Several knives of various sizes were on the top rack, and under that, an assortment of tools and horrendous-looking medical apparatus. The second case concealed a small black device. On one side was a silver crank and next to that, a tiny silver button. Connected to the other side were five long wires that each had pads at the end. And at the edge of those pads were tiny metal claws.

The meticulous unpacking had Walter and Laszlo's utmost attention. The piano player's eves dropping got him even more despondent.

Von Stroheim finished his discussion with Mengele, who was nodding. "I understand," he replied in English.

"I am sorry, Herr Doctor, we do have a strict schedule to keep."

Laszlo's body trembled in fear, but he looked up with determination as he cleared his throat and spoke calmly, "Herr Von Stroheim—"

"Your fate, Herr Strozek, was sealed the moment you tried to barter with the OSS," Von Stroheim barked. "Do you think your location exonerates you from your duty to the Fatherland and to the cause?"

Laszlo persisted, keeping his tone non-confrontational. "But Herr Von Strohei—"

"What did you think, that they would just hide you away with no questions asked? No, Herr Strozek! You would have to give them something that's as valuable as your freedom." He exaggerated his movements as he raised his arms in front of Laszlo. "And what is the only thing you could possibly offer them?"

"I never thought they wou—"

"Why, nothing but the locations of our fleeing brothers from the Fatherland, of course. The ones they don't possess in their Operation Overcast dossier. It's so popular even our Negro brother here knows about it."

"But—"

Von Stroheim's voice started to become much louder, a volume that didn't seem possible was coming from within the slender man, a noise level perfected from the many years of screaming over gunfire and artillery out on the battlefield, or more recently from speaking over loud and agitated crowds.

"You are *filth*, Herr Strozek! And because of your sins against the Reich, you shall die."

Laszlo shook his head and began weeping uncontrollably, mucus and spittle running down his face. "No no no no no no nonono—pleeease, Herr Von Stroheim. Please, no. Herr Oberscharführer…"

Von Stroheim curled his lip and sneered at Laszlo, scrutinizing him for the last time with a look of pure disgust. He turned to Walter. "It is time to bid you farewell, Herr—ah, excuse me, *Mister* Morris. I feel like I should pity you for what will be *your* last few moments of life."

Walter looked up at Stroheim. "Herr Oberscharführer, is it?"

Their eyes locked momentarily and Walter did the only thing an American could do in the situation.

"Screw."

Von Stroheim responded with a smile but the grin dropped, and he viciously backslapped Walter hard in the face. "You will not speak unless you are spoken to, *American*." He paused, looking for a reaction. "You are a nobody, Mister Morris. Just one of the masses. You won't be remembered after your death by anyone but the local barman who will miss your coin. You are nothing! Just an ant. An ant who picked the wrong boot to walk under."

Von Stroheim took few deep breaths to calm down, his face now visibly relaxing. "Herr Doctor, please get as much information as you can from him before he dies. We have appointments to keep."

Doctor Mengele nodded.

"Give no quarter. We have a schedule to keep with the outside talent; they will get Maximillian and Hans down into the room."

"You are still going through with it, tonight? Are you sure?"

"Of course, there is no reason not to. It will help us get away. We must stick to the plan." Stroheim pointed to Walter. "He will tell you if our operation is compromised. If we do not hear from you, tonight is still a go."

It looked as though Mengele was going to speak, but instead he gave a polite nod.

"You have your work cut out for you, Herr Doctor. Heil Hitler," Von Stroheim said proudly.

"Heil Hitler."

Von Stroheim took his eyes off Walter and turned his attention to the doctor. He changed his footing and, in complete willingness to the cause, he replied back, a little more forcefully, "*Heil* Hitler."

Mengele straightened, expanded his chest and saluted. "*Heil Hitler.*"

Von Stroheim smiled and quickly barked out an order to the men in the trench coats before leaving the room with Maximillian and the sentry who had been standing on the far side of the room.

The large, wooden double doors locked behind them.

CHAPTER 25

DOCTOR JOSEF MENGELE

" *First I stripped him naked. How he did kick, bite, and scratch."* Albert Fish grinned at that remark, as if he were embarrassed. *"I choked him to death, then cut him in small pieces so I could take my meat to my room."*

The room grew quiet after Von Stroheim's departure. The doctor's assistants busied themselves with prepping their equipment, and the only thing audible aside from the downpour outside was Laszlo's sniffling. Walter heard the faint sound of car doors shutting and vehicles speeding off into the night.

Doctor Mengele stood with his arms crossed, looking down at the two captives, deep in thought, observing. His pleasant and friendly demeanor never left him, nor either the polite smile on his face.

Karl was standing in the center of the room as if it had been temporarily "turned off" and was waiting for instructions.

Walter still couldn't get his eyes to focus properly and didn't want it known that he was having a hard time deciphering his dream from reality. He felt like a freight train had derailed in his head.

He looked over at the dance floor and saw Albert Fish as clear as day, sitting in handcuffs at that same prison table from 1930. Fish had been caught and convicted of murder, but he wasn't sentenced for all the victims he admitted to killing, or for the crimes he'd implicated himself in. One of those crimes was for the murder of Walter's younger brother Stevland, who was deaf and dumb and under Walt's care the day he went missing. And because his body was never found, Walter was allowed to speak to the man himself before he was executed, and Fish was more than happy to tell all about his past exploits to anyone who would listen.

The problem now, though, was that he could see Fish sitting across the room on the dance floor and he seemed as real as Laszlo or the crazy doctor. Walter couldn't actually tell the difference. It was only after studying everyone else in the room that he came to the conclusion he was the only one seeing the "Brooklyn Vampire." Fish had gone to the chair at Sing Sing back in '36. So this had to all be in his head, of course. It was probably from the concussion, or maybe it was a side effect from Gray Matter's pills. But it was like someone had started a movie reel and Walter couldn't get the projectionist to shut it off.

Fish started talking again, but only Walter could hear.

"On the pretense of taking your brother to a party, I took him to an empty house in Westchester that I had already picked out. When we got there, I told him to remain outside. He picked wildflowers. So sweet. I went upstairs and removed all of my clothes. I knew if I didn't, I would get his blood all over them."

"What do you think?"

Startled, Walter turned, and Mengele was looking down at them.

"Gott mit uns, ja?" He stared at them both for a moment, deep in thought. "So it was you who almost destroyed one of my prototypes? We nearly had to thaw another in his place. Our Uber-soldiers. They are the future of warfare."

Mengele caught sight of a phonograph player on the other side of the room and walked over to it. He turned it on and put the needle to wax. The Pied Pipers' version of "A Journey to a Star" began to play.

Walter shook his head in an attempt to focus, then spit out a little more blood.

"Herr Doctor," Laszlo said in a soft and respectful tone, "Pleeease…I will pay you whatever price you ask. Please."

The doctor didn't respond. He listened to the angelic and dreamy melody of the Pied Pipers with his back turned to his guests.

Walter perked up. "Is that guy one of those *totten core* fellas?"

Mengele strolled over to Karl. The ghoul had not moved since he entered the room. He unbuttoned Karl's shirt and exposed its oversized bare chest. Numerous fresh .22 caliber wounds decorated its cadaver-like frame where Walter had emptied into it. They were filled with dark, coagulated blood and covered up multiple older injuries. Its chest had large, aging medical incisions, the kind commonly seen on a body after a post-mortem had been performed. There was something rectangular implanted underneath the gray skin, stretching the length of the torso, with smooth and metallic steel corners that penetrated the skin from underneath, breaking through areas of its chest and creating an unnatural purple at the edges. The swelling appeared to have healed long ago.

"See, Herr Morris…there's a plate of steel behind the flesh for added protection. The whole chassis is reinforced to take up to a .50 caliber round in the chest. And the binary pistons I fused to the muscles with electrodes, they give them the strength of ten men."

Mengele stepped back and held his arms out wide.

"Behold… The most bloodthirsty SS division there is." He turned to face Walter and Laszlo. "Even surpassing the Occultists and the Fanatics." He paused for effect. "I have perfected *the* ultimate soldier. One who wouldn't need to be fed, who wouldn't complain or be bogged down with human emotion, especially *fear*. One who could endure the brutally cold winters of the Russian Front and just as easily traverse the scolding hot dunes of North Africa. or the wetlands in the Pacific."

He turned back to Karl. "This is the future of warfare." Exuding pride in his words, he began to take a victory walk around his creation. "The most infamous brigade in the Third Reich, a name you already seem to know. The *Totten core…the dead core*." He casually regarded Walter. "You may be the first American to have the name cross your lips."

Laszlo stole a quick glance at Walter while Mengele smiled up at Karl with satisfaction. "Made from the remains of dead soldiers, murderers, sadists, and even the insane. These prototypes were bodies donated by the most pristine specimens in the entire Reich. True full-blooded Aryans with the willingness to sacrifice their bodies, *themselves*, to the movement. Now they have been brought back, not dead but not alive. Horrific beings actually."

He walked over and picked up a long, sleek scalpel from his set of instruments on the tray. Laszlo gasped, but Mengele headed back toward Karl and buried it deep into one of its gunshot wounds.

"They were transported to the battlefields and let loose." While a metal scratching was audible as he dug deep into Karl's flesh, it remained lifeless, the expression unchanged. A .22 projectile fragment fell out of its wound and hit the hardwood floor, rolling in a small circle.

He cleaned his scalpel on a cloth and turned back to Walter and Laszlo. "But then unforeseeable issues arose. They couldn't be controlled by the commanding officers on the frontlines. They started behaving unpredictably, and there were a few instances where they even attacked their own comrades. It was the pure bloodlust you see." Mengele regarded Karl thoughtfully. "German troops did not like sharing the battlefields with them and their commanders agreed. So they were withdrawn for further study. We were all then sent out on submarines into the North Atlantic before our ports were closed and lost, to await orders that never came. Berlin by then had fallen. We have maybe a half dozen or more of these submarines navigating the dark depths of the Atlantic, perhaps as deep as two thousand fathoms, waiting for instructions that will never come. They only have coding equipment set to receive, not transmit. Once the humans perish waiting for those orders, the *totten core* can man the U-boats until the subs run out of fuel. But they will still be alive down there…waiting, always waiting. Luckily Herr Oberscharführer Stroheim managed to secure us sanctuary here, in New York City. The last place anyone would think to look." Mengele chuckled. "And here we are, in your Westchester. It's very lovely."

A thought began to form in Walter's mind.

"The only shortfall?" Mengele continued. "Their source of power. Blood. They need blood transfusions for optimum performance, much like cleaning the oil in your motor car. That is why humans were sent along in the U-boats. And where would one come by such vast amounts of blood here in New York City?"

Walter's eyes were wide as he put the pieces together. "You're the New York Ripper."

Mengele smiled at the moniker. "No one that will be missed. Though Oberscharführer Stroheim kept the blood as pure as he could in honor of the *Fatherland*." The doctor laughed a little. "Personally, I wouldn't care if he ran on pure Aryan blood or the blood of a Jew or a Negro like yourself. On the battlefield, blood is blood. It is all for the bigger cause, don't you see? There are sacrifices for this," he gestured to Karl. "Years and years of study and medical research."

He moved over to his bags and laid out a sterile cloth. He started to carefully remove unpleasant-looking medical tools, placing them delicately onto the fabric.

Laszlo took the lull in conversation to again plead his case. "Herr Doctor. Please, I am begging you. I will pay you whatever amount you desire. Anything…. Please, I'll leave the city, this country even! Please, Herr Hauptsturmführer."

Mengele went into another bag. "You should be proud, Herr Strozek. You are dying for the *Reich*," he said almost mockingly. "For our cause." He pulled a needle and a small bottle out of the bag.

Laszlo's eyes focused on the needle. "I don't give a damn about the Reich. Hitler is dead! The beautiful Fatherland has been forever disgraced. Jesus Christ, I beg you. Please…"

Mengele drew a small amount of liquid from the bottle up into the needle, knocking out any air that was left inside. Despite Laszlo thrashing his head from side to side, he managed to plunge the needle into the left side of Laszlo's throat, between his jugular and larynx, then methodically did the same to the right side.

Laszlo screamed and howled, not only at the pain caused by the needle, but because of the hopeless situation he knew he was in.

"I share some of your sentiments, Herr Strozek," Mengele said. "And though you ask me to grant you liberty, I am afraid I cannot."

Laszlo's voice began to break, his vocal cords becoming unconsciously relaxed. He tried to scream, but it came out as a whisper, and in a matter of seconds he was no longer able to talk, the only noise being the panicked sound of him exhaling and inhaling.

Ignoring Laszlo, Mengele turned to Walter. "Did you know, Mister Morris, we were able to advance medical research by twenty years at the KZ in just a mere twenty-six-month period? We made unprecedented progress in the medical field."

"The KZ?" Walter asked, feeling like the doctor was prompting him to do so.

Laszlo began to shake in his chair, a panicked and frantic response to not being able to deal with the paralysis of his own throat.

Mengele removed a large surgical knife from one of the trays. Walter's eyes bulged at the blade in the doctor's hand. Meanwhile, the nurse casually unbuttoned Laszlo's shirt, exposing the piano player's bare chest before stepping back.

"I guess you wouldn't know what the KZ is over here? So some truth does exist in the Oberscharführer's statements, then?"

Mengele stepped in, and while still speaking to Walter in a kind and pleasant manner, he carefully made a deep lateral incision into Laszlo's chest.

Walter's head shot back. "Hey-Hey-Hey-Hey!"

The piano player started to violently shake but was held down by his restraints. Mengele ignored him and continued on. Walter couldn't believe what he was seeing; he started to feel dizzy. On the dance floor, Albert Fish continued his story from more than a decade ago.

"When I was ready, I called him from the window. Then I hid in a closet until he was in the room. When he saw me naked, he began to cry and tried to run down the stairs. I held him by his little throat...."

Laszlo was in agony. Saliva flowed from his mouth as he tried to scream, but the only thing that would come out was either wheezing or heavy breathing.

"Stop, stop, stop! Please stop this...stop!" Walter tried to break out of his restraints, utilizing all the reserve strength he could muster, but it was to no avail.

Mengele calmly carried on, as though he were simply having a conversation while making dinner. "Work sets you free...I think the term is.
That probably describes your entire life, your entire *being*, eh? A detective
for hire?"

He retraced his incision three times, the blade going deeper with every
cut. "As you may know, after the great war, Germany was beaten. The
Treaty of Versailles destroyed us as a country. We fell into great poverty,
and the German people began to see a common enemy who were surviving
through it all, thriving off it. It was the Jew. We developed an enormous
amount of hatred toward them because of what they helped do to us and
how they continued to profit from our people's plight. And don't think
this view that developed is strange or alien; it's not isolated to Germany
alone. Look at your country. Need I point out how the Negro is treated in
society, especially the laws regarding your people in the Southern states,
that's eighty years after your kind was freed?"

Mengele handed his knife to the nurse. His bald assistant held the
doctor's next tool, a separator which was connected to a scissor-type
device. Walter continued to scream at him to stop, but it was as though his
pleading was going completely unnoticed. Mengele positioned the separator in the twelve-inch-long incision and began to open up the area, then
using another small scalpel in his other hand, he cut away the inner-lining
subcutaneous tissue that connected to the fat, muscle, and bone. Laszlo
entered into a state of deep shock, his whole body convulsed, and he soon
passed out.

Mengele carried on talking to Walter as if he were giving him a college
lecture on his favorite subject, even getting passionate.

"The sub-humans were our enemy, you see. We told them to leave
our cities and society behind, but they refused. So, we attempted forced
migration." He shrugged casually. "But they still wouldn't go. They
obsessed over their material possessions and were too stubborn to leave
their land. They were too arrogant, too proud.... They just wouldn't leave.
Couldn't. As a culture, it wasn't in their nature. And no one wanted them."
Mengele pointed at Walter and counted on his fingers. "Europe, South
America, this country of yours...yes, your great land of the free, *no one*

would take them. Hell, before Hitler invaded France, they were openly giving us their Jews as a sign of good faith, hoping that the Reich would leave them alone."

The nurse broke open the smelling salts and waved them under Laszlo's nose. He started to come around.

"So, the government was forced to remove them from society and place them into the ghettos, away from the public. But then what, Herr Morris? We were now at war with all of Europe. How do we realistically take care of such a vast amount of people? An entire population? Numbers that were growing exponentially every day due to the new territories we conquered across Europe. How do you feed millions upon millions of people while feeding an entire army who are fighting two fronts and, at the same time, take care of the citizens at home?" He looked at Walter like he was expecting an answer. "We could not waste vital supplies on such parasites. Something had to be done."

Walter's mouth was parted as he tried to focus on breathing normally. His eyes were wide open, an expression of shock and disbelief on his face as he struggled to watch what was being done to Laszlo. The doctor had fully exposed the middle of his thorax, from his sternum up to his diaphragm.

"We started a mass deportation and sent them to the concentration and work camps we set up in Dachau, in the hills of Mauthausen, and Buchenwald. This is where the industrialization of mass extermination was perfected, on such a scale it would make the fathers of the Industrial Revolution proud."

Walter was so confused, he felt he was losing his mind "Wha…what are you talking about?"

"Extermination, Herr Morris!"

The doctor sliced away at the surrounding membranes and the layers that were connected directly to Laszlo's breastbone. "We started out by simply putting a bullet in them."

Walter glanced nervously at Laszlo. He swallowed back waves of nausea and quickly looked away again.

"But that was a waste of a much-needed bullet, and realistically…," he clutched Walter's chin and forcibly turned his head to look at him, "…

one cannot have a young soldier executing women and children for fourteen hours a day. It just wasn't good for morale, you understand." Mengele nodded and let go of his chin. "So they were driven around in trucks with the tailpipe going into the compartment. We'd burn the bodies, and it was all very effective, but it took thirty minutes and only killed maybe sixty people at a time." Mengele chuckled. "I must say, I *am* enjoying our little conversation, Herr Morris."

Walter stared vacantly at Laszlo's impromptu surgery.

"Work sets you free."

Walter didn't know what to do. "You need to stop. Please…you need to stop. Stop," but the Doctor wasn't listening, and Walter was finding it hard to comprehend the unimaginable cruelty being committed in front of him. His eyes were glued in horror on Mengele, watching while he worked, and simultaneously he heard everything the man said.

"But…" Mengele held the detective's chin again, turning him until they made eye contact. "You want to know what the KZ is, eh? Or was."

Walter blurted out, "Please stop now…please!"

Laszlo passed out for a second time. The doctor stepped back while the male nurse swooped back in with smelling salts. The nurse slapped Laszlo in the face and he started to regain consciousness.

"Vast buildings were developed. They each held chambers and were connected to a crematorium. We told them they needed to be disinfected after their long journey, so that lice or fleas wouldn't enter the camp." Mengele grinned. "A band of their own people played parlor music while they waited to enter the buildings. We handed them a cake of soap and gave them a hook for their clothes, and even told them to remember the number so they could retrieve their belongings."

Walter teared up, unable to cope with what was being said. At the same time Laszlo started to twitch again, and he awoke, convulsing in agony.

Mengele carried on speaking to Walter without breaking his concentration. "We'd lock them in and gas them with Zyklon B. It's an industrial disinfectant. There's no Zyklon A, only B. The bodies would be cremated in the furnaces. We could average three hundred at a time." He finished his incisions and glanced back to make sure he held eye contact with Walter. "I think our best day was nine thousand out of a single furnace."

He handed an instrument to his assistant and the nurse immediately stepped in to control the bleeding, applying gauze to the surrounding tissue of the wound.

"In forty-two, I was promoted to *Hauptsturmführer*—eh, captain. I was transferred to Auschwitz, outside of Birkenau. Have you heard of that place yet?"

Walter shook his head.

"They called the extermination camp at Auschwitz the *Konzentrationslager*, KZ for short. That is the place Herr Von Stroheim spoke of."

Once the nurse was finished, Mengele moved back in and continued his improvised surgery. "You must understand, we are not mad, Herr Morris. We even kept a good amount of the population for labor. But a 'selection' had to be made. And as the head doctor of the KZ, I oversaw every aspect of those selections."

He tilted his head back, and the perspiration on his brow and forehead were automatically wiped by the older assistant.

"The deportees arrived by train in groups of six hundred or so, from all across Europe. When they finally reached us, some of our work was already done. Ten percent of them didn't survive the journey, stacked so close together they couldn't sit down or even move." He locked eyes with Walter, hoping to signify the grandeur of his next comment. "So a plan had to be formulated, a method of eliminating this problem."

Mengele raised his arms outward in the air to about the height of his shoulders, with his palms facing Walter, like a cross. "I would stand on the platform and they would line up." He raised his left arm and made a nonchalant gesture with his hand. "To the left, the old, the sick, the crippled, the women with young children, the ones who wouldn't separate.... To the right, well, those we deemed fit were forced to work hard labor in support of the war effort. Or they were given to external companies, like Bayer, Siemens, and Mercedes, to work in their factories. The others..."

His smile widened, as though recalling a fond memory. "I can remember some of the small *kinder*…excuse me, *children*. They would be so scared, I would hold their hands and turn their last walk into a game. It was called On the Way to the Chimney."

Walter exhaled deeply, clenching his fists to remain calm as rage seared through him.

The assistant handed the doctor a pair of large shears, ones exactly like a gardener would use.

Walt's mind was playing tricks on him again. He was seeing Albert Fish, with his gaunt frame and sunken eyes, but this time he was standing in front of him, right next to Mengele. With that deadly ice-cold stare.

"I cooked and ate him. How sweet and tender, he was roasted in the oven. It took me nine days to eat his entire body."

Fish, a man who had been executed long ago now, stared into Walter's terrified face like he was about to whisper a secret, just as he really did when they spoke all those years before.

"I did not fuck him, though. I could have had I wished. He died a virgin…."

"Nooooo!" Walter yelled, his glare frantically finding its way back to the doctor.

Mengele looked at him, frowning slightly, and in that instant Walter felt sure the doctor had seen Fish too, but only for a moment. He soon came to his senses again when he saw what was happening to Laszlo. Walt prayed silently for him to stop.

Mengele continued to address Walter while putting one leg on Laszlo's shoulder; the nurse put an arm around his neck and held him down. "And those chimneys glowed on the Birkenau horizon for three whole years, Mister Morris." He held three blood-soaked fingers in front of Walter's face. "Twenty-four hours a day, seven days a week. Sometimes we'd get up to a dozen transports a day." Mengele chuckled. "Some of the older prisoners said the smell in the air would change depending on what part of Europe a new transport was from. But the average prisoner would only last twelve weeks."

Mengele stuck the shears into Laszlo's thorax and carefully cracked it open, trying hard not to damage any of his surrounding organs. "I didn't want such an opportunity to go to waste, so I was able to take my pick of the selection, various specimens to help me in my research. Help with my experiments. The Reich was obsessed with eliminating inferior races and replenishing the land with Aryan natives, perfect people. So it was me who would have to research this."

Laszlo was panting loudly, hyperventilating. His body shook uncontrollably before he went limp, his head rolled back, and he stared blankly up at the ceiling.

"My thesis was selective breeding, Herr Morris. If we have young Aryan mothers producing twins, at the very least, we could repopulate the region exponentially and wipe out undesirable tendencies. So the secret was *zwillinge*…I would collect twins, mostly children under the age of sixteen, and subjects with other oddities, such as dwarfism, and I'd use them in my experiments."

Mengele finished using the shears, stepped back, and handed them over to his nurse. His older assistant approached and placed a clamp on either side of Laszlo's wound, then began to crank open the breastbone to expose his heart.

Nausea clawed at Walter Morris's throat and he had to repeatedly swallow to force down bile.

"I would make sure they were fed, clothed, and taken care of. You see, I needed to dissect them. And I put it to you, Mister Morris, when does one ever see a set of twins expiring at exactly the same moment? Every millimeter of each body was examined, searching for the slightest of variations developed at birth, thus hopefully bringing us closer to learning why it occurs at a biological level, so we can someday replicate it."

The nurse applied gauze and towels to the area bleeding, just like in a normal operating environment. The heart was visible now, frantically beating away. Laszlo was deathly silent, in a state of deep shock.

Walter let out an anguished scream.

The doctor ignored the detective's cries and removed another syringe from out of his bag, along with another small bottle.

Walt violently shook his head. "No, no, please, no!"

Mengele was careful to tap out any air bubbles after he withdrew from the vial. He leaned in close to Walter, mere inches from his face. "And to kill the children instantly, at the exact same time," he gave him a genuinely warm smile, "I personally liked to use a shot of chloroform, right to the aortic chamber."

He turned, and with a calming precision, stuck the needle directly into Laszlo's heart. His body immediately started to convulse, and Mengele watched with an intense curiosity, getting lost in Laszlo's facial expressions, studying his reaction with a great wonderment.

After a few moments, Laszlo Strozek took his last breath.

"Ah, Jesus, no! Jesus! You're a coward! You didn't even give him a fighting chance. You bastard, you fucking *bastard!*" Tears flowed down Walter's face.

Mengele turned away from Laszlo and put his arms behind his back. "*That* was the KZ."

Albert Fish was gone, the memories of the past faded. But Walter Morris could no longer distinguish between the monster from so long ago and the one standing just a foot away from him blatantly showing off, excited to talk so openly and honestly about his "work."

"But the real question here…is *why*? Why you didn't know what the KZ was. Would you like the real ugly truth *why* people here in America have not heard about the KZ or our other camps yet? Because your wonderful government chose to ignore it; they decided to do nothing. Luckily for us, the entire world did *nothing*. They all just let it happen. All that death." The doctor grinned.

"No, you're a liar!" Walter screamed. "That's—that's why we're fighting a war over there!"

"Am I a liar? Is it too incredible to fathom? You don't think your allies had aerial reconnaissance of every inch of Europe?" Mengele pointed a gloved finger at Walter. "We even encountered systematic bombing outside of Auschwitz but never inside. We know your government had conclusive proof because two of our prisoners escaped in forty-three."

He was so close to Walter's face that their noses briefly touched. "Understand? They could have even used the bright flames from our crematoria chimneys as targets to take the camp out. Three years they burned."

Walter shook his head vigorously, trying to somehow make sense of what the doctor was saying to him, denying to the core what he was being told. "They probably didn't want to hurt the prisoners, you—"

Mengele shook his head. "Tsk tsk. The barracks were far enough away to be able to successfully destroy the chambers and ovens. Not only could hundreds of thousands of Jews have been saved, but the casualties to them would have been negligible." He raised an eyebrow. "And, even if they were worried about casualties, why weren't the railway lines ever targeted to stop the constant flow of insects into the web? Eh, Herr Morris?"

Walter was horrified. All this information, it was just too much. But what Mengele was saying made sense. That was what scared him. Why did what he was saying make so much sense?

The record ended, and the repetitive scratching of the needle in the center of the wax disc echoed throughout the space. Walter stared blankly out into the dark room, a mixture of sweat, tears, and spit running down his face. The fogginess of his concussion and the fading memories of Albert Fish had left him altogether, along with whatever naiveté he still had. This senseless barbarity had cleared his mind.

The doctor finished with his observations of Laszlo's body and barked out a command in German. One of the sentries next to the double doors left the room. Mengele handed the empty syringe he was holding to his assistant.

Walter Morris slouched in defeat. His body and mind felt numb, numb to everything, like he'd just downed an entire bottle of bourbon. He was consumed by his own thoughts, the evil, humanity's naiveté, his mind even second-guessing all he'd been taught to know and love. It seemed wrong, even with the war which had been going on for four years now.

When the sentry came back into the room, he was leading a blindfolded female by the hand. It was Caldonia Jones. Mengele removed the blindfold, and she opened her eyes. Her pupils were an unnatural ocean blue.

"Our insurance policy," he told Walter. "I was told she needed to be kept alive, so I gave her a bilateral transorbital lobotomy." He indicated with his pinky finger at the top of her ocular sockets. "I entered the brain via the orbital cavities here and here, with…well, in layman's terms I would call it an ice pick. So it would keep her nice and docile while she holidayed with us." He pointed to her pupils. "And here, methylene injections to make her a true Aryan. Ha! Hitler used to love that."

Walter glanced at Caldonia, who was in a catatonic state. "My God… My dear God, no!" He broke down sobbing.

"I did my research. I looked you up. The child murderer Albert Fish killed your brother when he was ten, yes? Ate him too? You confronted him in jail. He believed he was saving innocent souls from Hell on Earth." Mengele leaned in like he was speaking for only Walter to hear. "Did you see the evil in his eyes as you see in mine?" Mengele whispered. "Do you think your brother was saved?"

Teary-eyed, Morris looked over at Caldonia. She was standing opposite Karl, staring out into empty space.

"No response? Well, let us get on with it, then."

It was at that precise moment that Walter Eugene Morris broke. A big piece of Walter died away. Morris stared out into space, contemplating what he'd just witnessed and learned. And all he could do was react like any man would when they break.

Just quietly sob.

Mengele smiled at him. He gave another command in German to his assistants. The nurse rolled the cart with the large black box over to the detective and, without resistance, started hooking up various wires to his fingers on the right hand. Meanwhile, the older assistant loaded a Luger and chambered a round, then handed the pistol to Mengele, who placed it in his waistband.

Seeing the butt of the weapon woke Morris from his stupor, and his eyes traveled up the doctor's frame, taking in every little detail until he reached his face, where he found Mengele staring right back at him. All at once, the blood rushed to Morris's head as anger flooded through his veins.

Mengele calmly nodded at him, one learned man to the other. The detective appeared to have garnered the doctor's respect, so being straight with him was the only decent thing to do. "I'm not going to shoot you, Herr Morris. No, none of that, unfortunately. We are on the dark side of the moon. We are too deep into the black forest for that. We must take our time here. And for the sake of full disclosure, I would like you to know that this experience and you have made me completely reevaluate my preconceived perceptions of the Negro. Because of that, I will be entirely honest with you. You have knowledge that we want, and as one professional to another…," he motioned to the large ghoul standing motionless in the middle of the room, "…I would really like to repay you for what you did to Karl."

The nurse walked over to the record player, flipped the 78 over, and put the needle down. The Pied Pipers' song "Dream" began to play. Mengele closed his eyes and his head swayed to the dreamy melody. "Beautiful, just beautiful." He opened his eyes and nodded, a smug smile remaining on his face. "American music."

He moved close to examine the wires connected to Morris, making sure everything was perfectly in order, then stood tall with his arms clasped behind his back.

"I will now ask you some questions, Herr Morris. It is in your best interest to be honest with me. Every time you do not answer a question correctly, you will be electrocuted. From there, I will start to remove a phalanges bone for every incorrect answer. After the fifty-six bones that make up the joints of your fingers and toes are gone, I will place electrodes on your temples and your scrotum. For every false answer you give me, a current will be passed throughout your body that will send you into epileptic convulsions." Mengele didn't skip a beat. "I will resuscitate you of course, and for every false answer you give me after that, a small pin will be inserted into your eyeball, after three pins, leads will be added, and you will be electrocuted through those. By that time, when your eyeballs reach boiling point and are turning into liquid, you will be begging for me to end your life." He chuckled. "Let us hope by that point I am still feeling this optimistic."

Using the silver crank on the machine's side, the nurse wound up the black box until it could twist no further. Morris stared at the wires connecting his fingers to the box.

"This is the Black Mariah."

Morris whipped his head up to the doctor.

"Mister Hayden hired you to find his daughter."

"No, Mister Hayden hired me to find his maid's daughter." Morris glanced up at Mengele.

The doctor smiled. "Come now, why else would he care about some Negro maid's child?" Mengele waited for an answer that never came. "What have you uncovered?"

Morris remained silent.

"*Nein.*"

The nurse pressed the silver button next to the crank. An unimaginable pain coursed through Morris's body, making him convulse in agony. It was much more painful than he'd imagined it would be, and he involuntarily let out a loud wail. He didn't even realize he was screaming until he heard his own voice. A moment later the assistant turned the box off. His body went limp and he slumped against the restraints.

Mengele motioned at the black box. "Packs a powerful punch. Not even trained British agents from the Secret Service Bureau can withstand the Black Mariah for long." He yelled over his shoulder. "Karl!"

Karl's head straightened up and it pushed its shoulders back, like a large machine being turned back on. It took two steps toward them. The doctor calmly issued a command in German and Karl grabbed Morris's left pointer finger. The detective tried to pull away, but his restraints kept him in place. Karl's grip was firm but cold, like the wrinkly touch of someone whose hands had been underwater for too long.

"Tell me, what have you uncovered? What have you been told about Grand Central Terminal? How familiar are you with Herr Oberscharführer Stroheim's plans for tonight?" The doctor paused. "Trust me when I say he will not just break that finger, he will tear it off."

"Grand Central?" Morris physically trembled. "You can't...I don't know what—you...I—I don't know. Please, I really don't know!"

Out of nowhere, the lock section of the double doors exploded in a spray of metal and kindling from the force of a shotgun blast. The door was kicked open and Agents Helms and Mathers rushed in, followed by Howard Crothers and some of Hayden's estate staff.

Caldonia remained in the center of the room, motionless.

Helms discharged the second barrel point-blank into Karl's head as the beast charged toward them. Its head exploded and the body continued to stumble around blindly. Seeing this, one of the sentries ripped open his trench coat to expose a grease gun. He unloaded half a clip that accidentally tore through Mengele's older assistant as it hit Mathers.

Mengele caught two pellets in his shoulder from the shotgun blast but quickly disappeared out of the room. Morris was still strapped to the chair, so he could do nothing when he saw him leave.

Helms pulled out a .45 and dropped his shotgun. He killed the sentry with the grease gun and unloaded the rest of his ammo into the nurse, who then released his hold on the Black Mariah. The gunfire ceased and Helms hurried over to untie Morris.

"See to him," Helms said, motioning toward Mathers, who lay wounded on the ground. "I'm going after Mengele."

After he freed Morris, Helms bolted out of the room, and the detective joined Howard, who was already seeing to Mathers. The special agent was on the dance floor, bleeding profusely.

"Kick that chopper from that motha's hands!" Morris shouted to Howard, who frowned and looked over to where Morris was pointing at.

One of the estate staff hurried over to the dead sentry and violently kicked the machine gun away from the corpse's hands, then kicked him repeatedly in the face several more times, making sure the man was dead. Apparently really dead, dead.

Morris peered back down at Mathers. "Just hang in there, ya sonofabitch," he said in a sarcastic tone to hopefully make the Special Agent laugh, but it didn't work. From down the hall, they heard machine gun fire erupt between Agent Helms and the fleeing intruders. Sporadic bursts were exchanged, followed closely by handgun fire.

The detective shot a glance over to Howard and the two butlers near the door who were keeping a close watch. "My man," he said, "go find something in here to put over his gunshot wounds. We need to help stem the bleeding." Howard stumbled over toward the other side of the dance floor where a waiter station had linen table clothes stored underneath.

Blood dribbled down Mathers' chin and he was in a great deal of pain when he spoke. "You have to stop them."

Morris propped his head up with his forearm. "How'd you find me here?"

"We...tailing you at The Creo Room...lost them when they left the city. When we got up here, the house staff directed us."

"He asked me about Grand Central. What's that?"

Mathers narrowed his eyes, but didn't hesitate to respond, "We... think they're gonna blow the whole thing up...."

"Blow it up?" Morris exclaimed. "I thought it was just gonna be a robbery?"

Mathers winced as he nodded. "They stole the blueprints. Classified blueprints. At the Empire State Building. They parachuted off—"

"Oh my God."

"No one knew at first, they covered their tracks...bought themselves time. Made it look like they were robbing a vault designing company instead."

"Grisham Vault Company. I saw Laszlo giving the Irishman Rory Caven those specs."

Mathers nodded. "Yeah, they probably made money or roped them into the scheme somehow by giving him those diagrams."

"Luring the Caven mob in to help them with Grand Central."

"They didn't shop it to the Italian or Jewish mobs; they stayed low-key and lured the Caven crew in...." Mathers coughed up blood and appeared to be getting weaker. "We need to tell the G-Men."

"What are they gonna blow up? A train? Is the president coming to town or something?"

The agent appeared to be relaxing in his arms and his breathing became shallow. He began to whisper and Morris had to lean in to hear him clearly. Mathers hesitated at first because of the sensitivity of the information, but the situation invalidated any classification it might have.

"About eight stories or so under Grand Central Terminal are two massive AC/DC turbine generators. They power the entire eastern portion of…of the New York Central Railroad…." Mathers coughed, and dark red blood caught in between his white teeth. "Everything from Boston to Philadelphia. She grinds out power for all of that winding rail, *plus* for every building that sits atop the Grand Central railyard."

Morris frowned. "So what do they want?"

Mathers's lips curled and he spoke through gritted teeth, accenting every other syllable with a mixture of spit and blood. "Think about it! With the war going on…every infantryman, sailor, Marine, and pilot who leaves to fight from New York by boat arrives first on a train in Grand Central."

Morris looked at the situation around him while processing what Mathers was saying. Caldonia was still standing in the middle of the room where she had been left. She was covered with splatters of blood but miraculously had not been shot. Her treacherous dead boyfriend Laszlo was several feet away from her, tied to a chair and surrounded by a pool of his own blood. Karl's headless body was still attempting to keep on walking, even though the walls were holding it back. Every other second, blood would shoot up into the air from its carotid artery, coming down onto the chassis and the floor around it.

"Hey!" Mathers yelled, which snapped Morris out of his thoughts and back to the man in his arms. "If something were to happen to those generators, you'd knock out the power supply to the railroad…"

"And virtually stop all the troop movements on the Eastern Seaboard," Morris finished.

Mathers nodded before coughing up a dark, phlegmy mixture of blood. "The Army has been guarding that thing around the clock for the past three years."

"Then it's all going down tonight, and they're using Rory Caven and his Irish mob as a type of Trojan horse, and they probably don't even know it." He glanced down and saw Mathers was slipping. "Shit *no*, okay, okay.

Stay calm...." Morris realized the effects of his concussion or whatever it was were now gone, leaving him with an incredible headache. At least he wasn't hallucinating anymore.

Mathers was fading fast. "Take it easy now," he said with concern.

Mathers grabbed his suit jacket at the biceps, as if he were trying to use the leverage to climb up toward Morris's face. "Go find Hayden! We... we didn't have time to search the mansion...but...but they got Hayden... you got too close...forced him to help them get awa...y..." That was about all the energy that Mathers had left. He collapsed down to the floor. "Ain't much time left."

"Hey!" Morris said to one of the staff. "Go look after her!" He pointed to a lifeless Caldonia and a kitchen worker ran over and placed his jacket over her shoulders. Her facial expression didn't change to acknowledge the person helping her.

Agent Mathers was now staring behind him and up at the ceiling. He exhaled one last shallow breath and died in Morris's arms. The detective held onto him for a short time before letting out a deep sigh. He laid Mathers down, then got to his feet.

Howard came back over with the linen and covered up Mathers's body. He followed Morris as they both hesitantly approached Caldonia. The man who was tending to her briefly made eye contact, and the detective instantly knew by his solemn expression that something was terribly wrong. Caldonia stared blankly out into space. Any hope that Morris had left within him dissipated. He waved a hand in front of her bright blue eyes. She continued to stare. She was long gone.

The detective wanted to shed a tear but wouldn't; he was still on the job. "Please, I need you to look after her and round up everyone else who works here," he said to Howard. "Get them to a safe place away from the mansion and wait for the police to arrive. Okay? And make sure they've been called."

Howard nodded in compliance. "Will do, sir."

Morris picked up one of the loaded machine guns from the floor and came back to the elderly man. "Take this grease gun and keep your head low. And please, be careful."

CHAPTER 26

CUTHBERT HAYDEN'S LOT

Morris stepped out with Agent Mather's .45 automatic and made his way down the hall. His head was throbbing every time he moved, but at least his side was completely numb. He checked his pockets and still had the Pervitin tablets Gray Matter had given to him, so he took double the amount to try and take the edge off. But the horror show he'd just witnessed firsthand had knocked out any of the lingering fogginess remaining in his head.

He rounded the corner and stumbled upon Agent Helms, lying dead on the floor. He was on his back, his limbs in unnatural positions, sprawled out. The top of his head from above the nose on, looked like a broken gumball machine. Various sized chunks resembling shards of an exotic watermelon with hair, smeared outward in an explosion across wall and cream carpet, already pooling up and soaking in.

Morris continued onward and saw a large door that was slightly ajar. He crept over and kicked it open. It was an enormous library filled with bookcases on every wall, each as high as the room's vaulted twenty-foot ceilings, the kind with ladders on tracks in order to access the higher shelves. Taking up the entire east wall was an enormous stone fireplace big enough to park an entire car. A small flame still flickered within and was throwing off a warm orange glow around the room.

Past a pair of black leather couches and a colossal free-standing globe was a large desk in front of huge cathedral-style windows. And on top of that desk was Cuthbert Hayden, lying on his back in repose. A floor lamp was next to the desk, shining down harshly on the body like a spotlight. As Morris made his way over to Hayden, the brutality of what they had done to him became apparent. Hayden's limbs had been skinned, along with his stomach and torso.

"Jesus Christ." The detective's stomach churned.

In the center of Hayden's chest was a mechanical implant, half exposed and half imbedded in his skin. It looked to have been implanted a long time ago, perhaps even dating back to the original car accident that crippled him. To Morris, it was clearly another one of Von Stroheim and Mengele's devices, much like Howard Crothers's leg. Next to his implant were two extremely disgusting-looking input holes that could each fit a quarter-inch cord, presumably for an external power supply. They had been filled with what appeared to be petroleum jelly.

Hayden's face had been severely beaten, both his eyes were completely swollen shut and a pool of dark coagulated blood surrounded the back of his enlarged head, flowing down to form a large stain on the floor.

Morris listened to his chest. He was still breathing, but barely. The machine sounded pained in its function. "Shit! You're one of *them*, those scientifically engineered...." Morris couldn't even begin to fathom the implications. "Hayden...Hayden, can you hear me?"

Hayden inhaled loudly, like he was taking a lifesaving breath deep into his body, straining the mechanical pump even more. "Aahhhhhhhhhh..." He opened his eyes as much as he could and found Morris gazing worriedly back at him. It was a few moments before he could place the detective, and it took all his energy to look down at the apparatus in his chest.

"You know my secret...I would have never survived my accident without them." His eyes closed, he was starting to remember again. "Stroheim..."

"Yes, Stroheim and Mengele, they both got away."

"He took my Caldonia away...my little girl."

"I know, Hayden." Morris sighed, suddenly faced with the sad reality of the girl's condition. But now wasn't the time to be the bearer of bad news. "We found her. She...she's alive. Don't you worry."

Hayden began to cry. His speech was slow and tired. "They took her because she's the only thing I care about anymore."

"Where are they going?" Morris pressed on before he lost him. "How are they getting out of the city?"

"I saw her…they brought her to me. I saw what he did to her. They took my Caldonia away from me. My baby…."

Morris paused; he was becoming frustrated and needed answers. "How are they getting out of here, Cuthbert? Please tell me, you must remember."

There was no response. Hayden's eyes started to roll back into his head and his machine made loud suction noises.

"Hayden!"

Hayden's eyes flew open. "…a boat."

"A boat, as in a freighter?"

"Yes, my boat. The *Demeter*…."

"That's its name?"

"Yes, they need it to…to get their plunder out."

Morris' brows furrowed. "Plunder? What plunder?" Hayden was beginning to drift off again and he needed to keep him talking. "Hayden! Come on, stay with me. What plunder?"

Hayden opened his eyes "…the fortunes they looted…all from the millions of Jews and Poles that they gassed and murdered. It's all here."

Morris gasped. He thought back to the icehouse and what he'd found in that one crate. Gold fillings, bridge work, and other precious metals. Beyond the frozen bodies in ice, he could only begin to imagine what else could be hidden in the hundreds of other crates of various sizes that he saw in the warehouse.

Hayden sniffled. "My baby girl…my poor baby…I'm sorry…I'm sorr…"

The machine in Hayden's chest stopped working and he went into cardiac arrest. Morris attempted to save him, but with his injuries and implant, he didn't know where to begin. He banged on his apparatus to see if it would start to function again, but nothing happened. Hayden Cuthbert was dead.

Morris made the sign of the cross and gently closed Hayden's eyes.

CHAPTER 27

THE CHASE

Morris hurried out of the Hayden mansion, and no quicker than his feet had hit the gravel of the horseshoe driveway was he met with gunfire. He slid across the ground and kept low while glass, mortar, and brick exploded behind him. He leapt forward and took cover behind an extended four-door Lincoln Continental. There were two men in dark gray trench coats, dressed exactly like the other sentries, both carrying Thompson submachine guns and hiding behind a 1940 Ford Coupe some yards away.

"You've got to be kidding me." He couldn't catch a break.

The pair unloaded a burst of fire. The bullets ricocheted and landed in the front fender and hood area of the large sedan. Morris drew the .45 he'd stowed in his waistband and returned fire, something they hadn't counted on. When both their drums were empty, he opened the passenger side door and crawled in, his foot hit something heavy on the floor.

He felt around and discovered a Browning automatic rifle. He checked the breach and ejected the magazine; it was full. It must have been Mengele's ride and was left by the dead henchmen inside the house. Morris crawled over and checked the ignition, which luckily still had the keys in place. He started the engine and the Lincoln purred. Morris quickly put it into gear and dropped the pedal to the floor, careening down the long and winding driveway that led down to the guardhouse and onto street below.

The men fired off a round before jumping into their Ford Coupe and screeching off after the detective. The sentry in the passenger seat opened his door and positioned a foot on the running board. He stood ready to fire at Morris's car whenever it came into view.

Morris had gained some distance between himself and his pursuers. Also because of the curves in the road and the heavy tree line that sheltered the driveway, the gap was so great that the other car didn't even have his Lincoln within sight. His vehicle gained momentum as it descended down the road, and it took all of his might to hold the wheel and keep it on track at the current speed he was driving.

When he turned the final corner on the home stretch, he spotted a mid-thirties Chevrolet pickup truck being moved out to block the exit. Morris slammed on the brakes, stuck his .45 out the driver's side window, and while the car skidded, he unloaded the gun at the driver of the pickup, putting five or so projectiles into the cabin area and killing the man instantly. The sedan came to a screeching halt, just ahead of the pickup.

His eyes quickly darted to the rearview mirror. Around the inclined bend he saw the woods light up from the impending Ford Coupe's headlights. He grabbed the BAR from the passenger seat and exited the Lincoln. He cocked back the bolt and made sure it was set on "full auto." The car rounded the corner and Morris leveled his rifle and squeezed the trigger, unloading the full mag of thirty-aught-six rounds at the engine and front tires. Both tires exploded and the driver cut hard to keep control of the vehicle, forcing the Ford to flip over. Because of its speed, it continued to roll, becoming a projectile. The passenger was instantly crushed and thrown off the running board into a tree.

Morris's eyes widened as it became apparent the tumbling Ford was headed straight toward him. He ran for shelter behind a large tree a few feet away, right as the car was upon him. The coupe toppled sideways and came to an unexpected halt when its roof slammed violently around the tree that was shielding Morris from the impact. Panicked, he checked his body thoroughly to make sure everything was still intact, and not quite believing his own luck, took a step away from his hiding place to survey the damage to the Ford.

Morris pulled himself together and rushed over to the Chevrolet. He threw the dead guy out, jumped in, and moved the truck away from the gate. Once the exit was clear, he got into his Lincoln and put the car into gear. He flew out of the compound, took a left, and traveled down the road as fast as his Continental would allow on the dark back roads of Westchester. Morris put the pedal to the floor and the Lincoln hit its top speed once he reached the highway. The car even began to shake because of the high rate of velocity. He came over a hill around Yonkers and made a little air. As the Lincoln crashed down onto the asphalt, the undercarriage sparked on the road and a hubcap flew off, spinning into the night.

The bright lights from the towering skyscrapers of New York City came into view in the far distance.

Morris cracked his neck and checked his watch. His side was still numb, and he figured Gray Matter's painkillers were thankfully doing their job. He reached for a cigarette in his front breast pocket and was reminded of the pain in his hand from being shocked. When he found his cigarettes, half were either broken or ripped. He went through them and managed to find a crooked, but nonetheless whole one. Now he just had to find a light....

CHAPTER 28

GRAND CENTRAL TERMINAL

At top speed, it only took Morris about twenty-five minutes to drive into Midtown Manhattan from lower Westchester. He'd lost the left front fender of the Lincoln trying to get past a double-parked delivery truck on Forty-Second and Tenth as he sped across town from the West Side. He drove along Forty-Second, dodging in and out of traffic as fast as the congestion would allow, and arrived at Grand Central Terminal. He swung left onto Vanderbilt Avenue which bordered the station on the west side. Morris quickly pulled the beat-up sedan into the covered pick-up and drop-off area under Park Avenue.

The jalopy came to a halt up on the curb next to a few parked checkered cabs. The cabbies who were standing around chatting jumped back, startled by the vehicle. Morris threw the car into park and shut her off. The engine started to steam and continued to make a noise while it powered down. He jumped out of the vehicle and nodded at the hacks, adjusting the .45 he had stowed in his waistband, fixed his collar and tie, then headed inside.

The detective entered by the top of the grand staircase on the west side of the terminal. He immediately saw a suspicious-looking gentleman standing by the railing on the first landing of the stairs, overlooking the station. He was wearing a dark trench coat and dark cap. The pointer finger on his right hand was wrapped with white boxing tape and in his left hand he was holding something large in position under his trench coat. Morris quickly walked down the steps, looking at the departure boards so not to draw attention.

As he descended the stairs, Morris scanned his beautiful surroundings. In the center of the floor was the infamous circular information booth with the opal clock on top. Between that and the stairs was a brand-new German Tiger tank apprehended fresh off the battlefields of Europe and shipped back to the States. It was on display with an "Uncle Sam" exhibit next to it that read: *This is what our boys are up against...BUY WAR BONDS!!*

Morris passed the questionable-looking man on the landing and zeroed in on the Irish gangster, Rory Caven, and four other guys all waiting by the clock carrying large suitcases. Timing-wise, it was almost as though they were waiting for Morris to enter the station so they could begin their little performance because once the detective clocked them, two of the men broke away from the group and walked in opposite directions. They were also dressed in identical trench coats. The two men positioned themselves at either side of the large concourse, one by the platforms and the other in the large waiting area in front of the Forty-Second Street entrance.

At the bottom of the staircase, Morris turned the corner and headed out of the mammoth commuter hall with all the other passengers rushing to a departing train. He passed the baggage room, making a beeline for the phone booths at the end of the corridor. The first booth he tried had a sleeping wino lying low within, so he slipped into the next one and toggled the cradle until he heard the soothing voice of a female operator.

"Operator? Sergeant Ambrosio at the Thirty-First Precinct, please. Tell him it's Walter Morris. As fast as you can. Thank you." Morris waited. After taking longer than it needed, he heard life on the other end of the line.

"Ambrosio? It's Walt. Listen because I only have time to say all this once. Get some men together and get your asses down to Grand Central, 'cause it's all going down right here, now. Next, get on the line to your local G-Men office and tell them Agents Mathers and Helms from the OSS are dead." Morris winced. "Mathers and Helms. Stop asking questions, just listen to me—a stooge named Laszlo Strozek, a German piano player, set it all up but he was a front to a Fifth Column—", Morris shifted his weight from his bad leg.

He turned and barked into the receiver. "Ambrose, it's on the level—yes, a bona fide Fifth Column…. Bigger than your wildest dreams, hiding behind a piano player who was the key to New York's working class—who didn't even know himself how deep he was in, the poor bastard. He hid 'em, Nazis for Christ's, on the run from Europe, he hid them in the shadows, up in the jazz clubs in Harlem, and blackmailed Cuthbert Hayden for finance and transportation. And Rory Caven's mob now is being used as muscle. But his crew is being set up in the biggest confidence scheme I've ever seen. The idiots think there's a bank vault in Grand Central's basement…." He paused to let Ambrosio get a word in. "Yes, I know there's no bank vault. But everyone, including the guy who set it up, the piano player, seems to think it's a robbery."

This was taking a lot more time than necessary. Morris needed the cavalry down here and fast.

"Look, just trust me on this. Get your ass down here, to Grand Central, and pronto. They think it's a vault robbery, but I'm pretty damn positive they're unwittingly sneaking a Nazi bomb down there. Yes! That's what I said, Ambrose. Nazi. Hell, it's Nazi Frankensteins. Yes, I know how that sounds. Christ, just please hurry!"

He slammed down the receiver and shot out of the booth, heading back toward the main concourse. When he arrived in the massive hall, he recognized a man walking in the front entrance as one of the German men who had left with Von Stroheim. It wasn't the Oberscharführer himself, but behind him was a towering giant of man, Morris's old friend Maximillian. It was carrying a brown backpack and wearing the customary dark black goggles that shielded its eyes from view. They crossed the main terminal floor and approached Caven and the other men waiting under the clock. Hans, the German guard, nodded politely at the men.

Morris tried to edge a little closer, ducking behind passing commuters so not to be noticed.

Almost on cue, a Grand Central employee walked over to Rory and the mob. He was a black man with a matching pair of nasty scars that spread outward from his mouth. He was the same man from the bar when Morris first visited The Creo Room. Without even looking at them, the man unlocked the door to the information booth and hurried away as though nothing ever happened.

The small crew automatically pulled up their jacket collars, a few of them putting on gloves. The German tied a red handkerchief over his mouth and nose, and the Irish mob removed Cagney, Robinson, Bogart, and George Raft masks from out of their pockets, the very same masks worn by Von Stroheim's crew back at the Empire State Building robbery. Once everyone was sorted, Rory put on a Paul Muni mask.

Robinson opened the information booth door and walked inside, where he immediately stuck a gun into the side of a railroad employee who had his back to the action. The man froze. Robinson whispered something, the worker listened then nodded. A moment later Bogart came in, and as instructed, the employee opened up an inner door in the middle of the booth which led to a spiral staircase concealed inside.

Except for the man in the George Raft mask, who stayed in the booth with the railroad employee, the crew proceeded to follow Cagney down the cylinder steps. Maximillian was at the rear without a mask.

Morris watched it all unfold. "Shit!" He glanced around, quickly trying to formulate a plan. "C'mon, Morris...think."

He saw another Grand Central employee, an elderly baggage man, coming out of a staff door on the far side of the concourse. He tried to look as nonchalant as possible while he scurried over to the gentleman.

"Hey there, excuse me." Morris took out his wallet, flashed it open, then swiftly closed it again. "Police."

The employee was only just getting to look down at the wallet before it was halfway back into Morris' pocket.

"Uh, what do you want, officer?"

Morris looked from side to side and lowered his voice so no one else could hear. "I need you to get me downstairs, to the basement."

The man gestured to the two staircases on either side of the grand space that both descended to the lower level. "The stairs are over there and the—"

"No," Morris said matter-of-factly, while still keeping an eye on the remaining men lingering in and around the station, "I mean to the sub-basement, where it goes down to the basements below. You know, my brotha." Morris winked.

That employee stared back at the detective, his mouth wide open in shock. "What? No one can go down there, not even me. Hey, what's all this about?"

Morris sighed, he didn't have time to convince the old man. He looked around, then quickly flashed the butt of his holstered firearm. "Buddy, I'm so sorry for this, but I'm in a real rush, and at this precise moment, I gotta go save the world, you with me?" The man's eyes widened in horror. "Don't get nervous, pal. Trust me, I'm the good guy. But we gotta go, and now."

The old man unconsciously nodded in agreement and turned toward where the information booth was, but Morris stopped him and placed his hand on the man's forearm.

"Naw, not that one. That's where all the trouble is. There's got to be another one, let's use that."

The worker glanced around, thinking of other options. "Oh, yeah, of course, there's another one down off platform twenty-five, by where the Twentieth Century Limited is arriving tonight."

"Great, sounds like a plan." Morris formed the biggest and brightest smile he could muster. "Let's move."

CHAPTER 29

THE M42 BASEMENT, SUBSTATION IT AND IL

Rory Caven and his masked crew continued down the narrow, winding staircase. Heading up the rear were the German and Maximillian, which stuck out like the proverbial sore thumb due to its towering stature.

Morris followed the elderly baggage handler down to track twenty-five, walking along the luxurious red carpet that ran the length of the platform, put down in preparation for the arrival of the Twentieth Century Limited from Chicago. They continued past an enormous Art Deco-stylized diesel locomotive that idled on neighboring track twenty-six but shared the same platform. As they walked by the man's fellow porters, conductors, and other baggage handlers who were busy preparing for the Limited's arrival into New York, the men took notice of their coworker walking with Morris, and all stared inquisitively at the pair who were heading toward the darkened tunnel and underground railyard.

The robber with the Cagney mask cautiously peered out behind the door at the bottom of the spiral staircase. It opened up to a large vestibule area not accessible to the public. There were many other doors, all leading to different areas of the basement. About thirty feet away, a military guard was sitting on a wooden stool reading a newspaper, right in front of a single freight elevator door labeled M42. Cagney methodically brought his .22 High Standard Model B pistol out through the small gap in the door, and with one eye, aimed his weapon, which had a sound suppressor attached. He fired one muffled shot, no louder than a mechanical function of the action of the pistol, and a hole simultaneously appeared in the guard's newspaper, blood splattering on the inside half. The guard fell to the ground and Cagney rushed over to put a second round into his temple at close range. Cagney rifled through the keys attached to the guard's belt while the others blocked the doors so no other railroad personnel could accidentally interrupt them.

Hans hurried over and regarded Cagney with disdain. "He will not have keys to the lift on him, that is why we need you men," he said through a thick accent.

He motioned for their safecracker, the man behind the Edward G. Robinson mask. Edward G. stepped over them, removed a few tools from his work bag, and began to unscrew the large electronic lock and keypad that controlled this elevator.

As they got closer to the end of the platform, the baggage handler was starting to show signs of nervousness due to Morris being in such a hurry and also not talking.

"Hey, listen, mack, I don't know what your play is here, but you *really* can't go down there. You could be shot, they have guards."

"I'm hoping for that, my friend."

When they reached the end of the platform, they both walked off and into the underground railyard.

The robbery crew waited patiently while their specialist, Eddie G., toiled with the electronics of the lock, stripping down the right wires and twisting them together. It caused a sudden spark which shorted out the box and the elevator doors flew open. They all packed into the large metallic freight elevator and Eddie G. began to unscrew the panel inside, gaining quick access to the electronics that controlled the lift's buttons which, like the doors, usually required a key in tandem with a six-digit code. He hot-wired the box and within seconds the panel was illuminated. He hit the basement button and the elevator began to descend.

They dropped eight floors, and when the elevator doors opened, there was another vestibule where a military guard was stationed. The doors weren't even fully open when a shot rang out from a pistol and the guard was killed. The masked crew exited the lift and headed through an archway that led down a short flight of stairs to the sub-basement. They reached the bottom step and opened the door.

Two military police were positioned at the end of a corridor, both sitting beside a steel desk in deep conversation. One was eating a sandwich while the other was flicking through a late edition of the local newspaper.

Two of the gang looked at a masked Rory, who nodded. Their hands disappeared into their jackets and each came back out holding revolvers.

Hans raised his hand and the Irish gangsters stopped to look at him. "May I make a suggestion?"

Maximillian entered the hallway and in an instant was upon the two like a shadow. The first guard turned his head just in time to see Max snap the neck of his colleague who was eating. He dropped his newspaper and opened his mouth to scream. Like a bolt of lightning, Max's arm shot out and a second later retracted with the man's larynx. The MP tried to speak but the only thing that came out was gargling. Max shoved the palm of its other hand hard into the man's face, splitting his nose like a banana, instantly stunning him. The giant then forced the head down and with the other hand struck the base of the skull with the force of a sledge hammer. The guard's lifeless body dropped to the floor.

The men were speechless as they walked into the hallway. A little warily they passed Max, who stood silently near the dead men. They continued to the end of the long, narrow corridor and opened another door which led to yet more stairs.

"All right, Kraut," Rory said to the German, "take Liam and Tom here," he motioned to the men in the Edward G. Robinson and Humphrey Bogart masks, "with you and your pal Frankenstein to the bottom. Liam can crack open whatever vault they got down there. When you fill your bags, have your friend there bring 'em back up. Me and Oli here," he pointed to the man wearing the Cagney mask, "will stay and watch the door."

Hans nodded, and made a noise with his mouth that sounded somewhere between a whistle and *psst*. Maximillian automatically sprang to life.

The small group began their descent down the flight of stairs. They started to notice a thunderous humming sound, getting louder as they continued. When they reached the bottom, the noise was almost unbearable.

They turned a corner and saw a guard walking in the opposite direction on a vast metallic walkway. It snaked in and around nine titanic rotary turbines that were nearly thirty feet high and weighing fifteen tons each. The entire room was enormous. Blasted out of solid rock, it was a twenty-two-thousand-square-foot space with a forty-foot-high ceiling buried far below the busy train terminal, unbeknownst to the average commuter and New Yorker. Against the wall was a twenty-foot-high machine helping to run and monitor the eleven thousand volts of alternating current, being converted into direct current by the nine deafening turbines. They were needed not only to power all of the trains above, but also two thousand miles of track throughout the Northeast.

The power station moved back in 1913 so developers could build skyscrapers on the surrounding land along Park Avenue. Its location became a godsend thirty years later, hidden from saboteurs once the war began. That was, until now.

Bogart crouched low and ran down the metallic walkway, pulled out a large ice pick, and got the drop on the guard. He put one hand around his forehead and pushed the ice pick into the base of the man's skull with the other. The guard dropped to the floor, convulsing. Another guard rounded the corner, coming into view from behind one of the enormous AC/DC turbines at the opposite end. Max drew a pistol and shot the guard dead from the other side of the huge room.

Hans and Edward G. began to look around for the vault. As they continued, their attention was increasingly drawn to the massive turbines in front of them, running with a near-deafening sound.

"Christ, they must generate enough energy hidden away down here to power the entire railroad. So then, where's the vault, mate?" Edward G. asked.

Morris and the elderly railroad employee arrived in front of a door. The worker paused and looked back at the detective.

"What's on the other side of this door?" Morris asked, motioning with his hand.

"What you're looking for."

"Okay, you get outta here before the shooting starts and go wait for the cops. They're on the way."

The employee shot him a puzzled look.

"Believe it or not," Morris said, "I'm actually trying to prevent something very bad from happening."

The rail worker didn't look convinced. "Whatever you say, brotha, just please don't hurt me, I got a family."

Morris rolled his eyes and yelled. "C'mon, I said screw!"

The man scuttled off. Morris turned to open the door, but it seemed like it was jammed. It wasn't locked, but something was definitely preventing it from opening. He tried harder and really put his back into it. He eventually forced it open and peered into the vestibule, where he saw a dead military guard laying on the floor. The detective looked around and saw the open freight elevator. He quickly ran across the hall and got in, descending to the lowest level. He stepped out of the lift and instantly saw the other military officer also dead on the floor, behind him the doorway that led down to the sub-basement staircase.

Down in the colossal generator room, the large turbines hummed away at a deafening decibel. Maximillian stood and surveyed the entire room with its black-goggle-covered eyes, taking in all of its dimensions.

Morris hit the bottom of the stairwell and cracked open the door just enough to peek in. He carefully repositioned himself so he could see the other end of the hallway. He spotted Cagney and the masked Rory guarding the door behind a desk; the two MPs were dead on the floor.

The Irishman with the Bogart mask hurried back around after jogging the entire length of the walkway which encircled the huge machines. He rushed over to Hans.

"Where the fuck is the vault?"

He ignored Bogart's question and instead, turned his head and said something to Max in German. The ghoul dropped to one knee, removed its backpack, and began to rummage through it.

Edward G. hurried around from the other direction, after himself doing a once-over of the room. He ran up to Bogart and looked from the German to Maximillian and back again.

"Hey, ya big gowl, for fucks sake, man! Where's this safe I'm supposed to break into?"

He approached Max, and as he got closer, Maximillian backhanded him, sending him sliding painfully across the metal catwalk. Bogart raised his Thompson in the confusion. Hans was quick to pull out one of the Colt .45s modified to full auto and let off a burst of rounds. Bogart crouched down but was caught in the shoulder, causing him to drop the machine gun.

Edward G. jumped onto Max's back and tried to fight it with a large switchblade. "Rory, it's a setup!" he screamed up the stairs as loud as he could.

The German swung around and tried to get a clear shot, but a quick burst from Bogart's Thompson, right into his back, ended Hans's life. Bogart used the machine as a crutch and managed to get to his feet.

Still on Max, stabbing away furiously in its back and shoulder blades with his switchblade, Edward G. yelled to Bogart, "It's a setup, Tom! Get outta here and tell Rory! Hurry, lad!"

Bogart dropped the gun and made a break for the way they came in, passing Edward G. and Maximillian tussling.

Upstairs, Rory and Cagney could hear the gunfire.

"Shit!" Rory said to his companion. "They're shooting down there!"

In response to the shooting, Morris peeped his head out with the .45 in hand.

Clutching his bloody shoulder, Bogart raced out of the generator room and ran up the steps. He saw his boss at the top of the stairs.

"It's a setup, Rory!" Bogart yelled as he stumbled coming up. "It's a trick!"

Rory stiffened and turned to Cagney. "He said it's a trap! We gotta get outta here."

Morris stepped out from behind the doorway and made his move. "It's all over, Caven. The Germans set you up. Throw down them rods and—"

Cagney swung around with his Thompson in hand, spitting hot lead at Morris. The detective leapt back into the doorway to take cover from the ricocheting metal. Luckily the whole place was made out of concrete and the projectiles from the machine gun that splintered the wooden door embedded themselves into the stairwell steps. But Morris was getting tired of yelling out orders like he was a cop.

He stepped farther back against the wall because of the ricocheting bullets. "Jesus…," he uttered.

Down in the generator room, Maximillian had Eddie G. by the head, holding him up in the air and slowly crushing his skull. He screamed out, in horrendous pain. Bone and cartilage began to crack, and blood started to ooze out of the eye and breathing holes in the mask.

Bogart got to the top of the stairs and helped to lay down fire at the doorway where Morris was hiding, while Cagney reloaded his machine gun. Rory weighed his options and motioned to another door on the other side of the guard's desk, labeled STAIRWAY EAST. He remembered from the blueprints they'd gotten from Laszlo that this exit led to a long staircase that went up to the terminal.

Rory pointed over to the doorway. "We gotta make a run for it, lads!"

Cagney finished reloading and clicked back the slide, then charged at Morris's doorway, gun blazing. Behind him Rory and Bogart followed. Morris swung his door shut; luckily there was metal on his side, so it blocked most of the machine gun fire. The three made it to the exit but the door was locked. Bogart and Rory shot out the lock and Rory kicked it open, while Cagney finished unloading his magazine at Morris's door. The gun clicked empty, and Morris, who had been waiting for the machine gun to stop firing, swung the door open, stuck his arm out, and squeezed off a few rounds, hitting the already-wounded Bogart. He fell to the ground while Rory and Cagney exited the hall and ran up the long flight of stairs, back toward the terminal.

Morris crept out. Bogart was on his back. He rolled over and with a small revolver in his right hand, squeezed off a round that went wild. The detective ducked to a knee and fired back, killing Tom, the man in the Bogart mask. He got up and cautiously crossed the hallway, surveying the situation around him. He contemplated going after Rory, but the door that led to the generator room was calling him.

"Shit…," Morris said, cursing himself for making the decision to head down to the "super-secret" basement and make sure they didn't leave anything down there.

He took out his tablets and popped a few more pills, noticing that he was almost out. Once they were gone, he'd come back down to Earth quickly and would no doubt need immediate medical attention because of his injuries, including the probable internal bleeding he theorized he was currently suffering from. So he needed these to last.

Morris descended the stairs, heading down toward the turbines. When he got to the bottom he looked out carefully, not knowing what to expect. The body of Edward G. lay lifeless on the ground, a dark pool of blood surrounding the crushed mask, with what looked like the remains of a squashed watermelon where his head used to be.

Maximillian was busy placing the last of the explosive charges from its bag onto one of the turbines. They were strategically located around every massive machine, and each device connected to a large wire that ran along the floor to the center of the room; for now that wire was temporarily coiled up.

Sergeant Ambrosio and Davies, along with several other officers, screeched to a halt in marked and unmarked Plymouth RMPs outside the main entrance to Grand Central Terminal on Forty-Second Street. They jumped out of their patrol cars and raced into the station. They reached the main concourse right when Rory and Cagney stumbled out of the cramped information booth after emerging from the spiral staircase and coming back up the way they knew how.

Their lookout in the George Raft mask was dumbfounded when he saw the expression on Rory's face, and due to his panicked state, Rory didn't see the law storming in, guns drawn.

"Quick, it's a bloody trap, mate!" he screamed at Raft. "Every man for himself!"

George Raft, who still had the barrel of his revolver aimed in the employee's ribs, turned back just in time to spot the police almost on top of them. He pushed the station worker to the ground and, without hesitation, began firing at the policemen. The information booth's glass shattered from the projectiles.

Hysterical late-night travelers ran for their lives, screaming. A porter dropped the luggage he was carrying and slumped to the floor as his chest exploded. The woman behind him had the back of her head burst wide open, splattering her crimson blood, and her tall heels left the Tennessee pink marble floor when the bullet carried her slender frame back an entire five feet.

The robber who was positioned by the ticket windows watched the police hurry by. Once they passed, he put a Rags Ragland mask over his face, opened his coat, and revealed a sawed-off pump-action shotgun. He got one blast of a buckshot off, which embedded in the back of a uniformed officer, sending him flying in the air.

The man who had been standing up on the landing of the stairs by the Vanderbilt entrance slid a Barton MacLane mask down and whipped out a Thompson submachine. As he opened fire on those below, the people on the crowded floor looked like roaches scattering when the lights came on, panic propelling the commuters in every direction, running to get out of the open space and find cover.

After the man behind them discharged his shotgun, Ambrosio dropped to a knee, spun around, and emptied his .38 revolver. Rags Ragland tumbled into a nearby timetable stand before falling dead to the floor.

The gunfight was on as everyone exchanged rounds.

Morris kept low while he scanned the carnage in the generator room. Maximillian was on a knee, removing from the bag a large silver box which appeared to be a detonator. Max carefully set the device on the floor, taking the wires that laid coiled together and attaching them systematically to the box.

A guard appeared on the other side of the room, coming in from an entrance over by the control room. He saw the dead bodies and the wiring going from the explosives to the large detonator that Max was kneeling over. The guard's hand traveled down to the holster on his belt. He fumbled to get his small revolver out, his hands trembling as he unloaded the tiny firearm at Maximillian. The giant turned with a level of extreme irritation after the slugs landed in its back and shoulders. Max walked over to the guard when his pistol had emptied.

This was Morris's chance. He hurried out from the stairs and over to the detonator.

Max smacked the weapon out of the guard's hand and picked him up by the throat. His eyes became bloodshot as all the air was squeezed out of him and his neck was crushed. The old man's cranium flopped unnaturally to one side.

Morris rushed to untie the wires on the detonator. Max swung around and saw him...actually recognizing who the detective was. It dropped the guard's lifeless body and was vocal for the first time, screaming like a demon seeing its only exit out of Hell.

Morris froze, the color quickly draining from his face as Maximillian charged at him. The detective raised the .45 in his hand and emptied it. The projectiles hit center mass, with the last round striking the left side of Max's face, removing the meat of the cheek, the ear, and the cheekbone itself. It astounded Morris to see the ghoul completely unfazed by all the injuries.

Maximillian grabbed him by the collar and lifted him up into the air. Morris attempted in vain to whack it in the head with the butt of his empty gun; every hit that landed made a hollow and heinous sound. Finally Max had decided it had had enough, and hurled Morris far across the room into a concrete wall.

Morris landed on the floor, the wind knocked out of him. Max sprinted over, howling like a banshee, terrifying the detective. It kicked him hard in his side and Morris screamed out in pain, certain that last impact had reopened the stitches down his side. It grabbed Morris again, throwing him into another wall on the far side of the room. His damaged body came to rest on an electronic operating console that was on top of a wooden table. Morris lay there momentarily before falling onto the floor.

Max walked over to the detonator to reattach the wires.

Morris flopped over onto his back and stared groggily up at the ceiling, trying to regain his bearings and block out the ear-piercing noise. If he didn't have the protective wrap around his torso and the glue holding his wound together, he figured his insides would have been spread all over this metal walkway.

At the end of the huge room, another Grand Central security officer burst out of a doorway on an overhead catwalk that snaked around the room, giving sight and access to the very tops of the large turbines. The young guard wasn't seen by Max due to the noise, and perhaps the damage to the left side of its face, which serendipitously obscured the movements high above. The guard hurried down a metal staircase and caught the detective's eye. Morris realized that he didn't have a gun, only a flashlight and a long, old-fashioned lead pipe.

He was off the stairs in a flash, racing over with his arm held high in the air, and as hard as he could, he smacked Maximillian forcefully over the back of the head. A large crack appeared from the severity of the blow, exposing metal and bone. Its cranium began to instantaneously bleed, the color of the blood so dark it almost looked black. Max turned back toward the guard, revealing not only its horrendously bloody face, but the entire left side that was missing. The man recoiled in shock, accidentally dropping the pipe from his hand. He made a run for the exit, hoping to get reinforcements. Max picked up the lead pipe and threw it through the air like an axe, eventually spearing the fleeing man through his chest. He stumbled along, his own momentum keeping him going, but soon collapsed on the walkway like a discarded ragdoll.

Morris managed to stand up and was leaning against the wooden work table in the corner by the wall. He was on the verge of losing consciousness due to the extreme pain in most of his body. He took the second-to-last tablet of his precious Pervitin, putting it into his mouth and chewing. That would delay the pain long enough and give him the energy to leave the wooden table currently supporting him.

He glanced around for something to use and saw a toolbox under the table. Next to it was a can of oil or some other type of high-end-looking lubricant. It didn't matter what it was, only that Morris's eyes lit up once he saw the flame decal on the side of the metal tin, as well as the large red words reading: DANGER! HIGHLY FLAMMABLE…. He snatched it up, delighted to find the can was practically full. He delved into his pockets, digging so hard he thought he might actually rip through his trousers, but soon found what he was looking for. With the oil can in his hand, he gradually made his way over to confront Maximillian, right as the giant turned to face him.

Morris tore off the lid and threw dark liquid into Max's face. That blinded it long enough to give Morris the time to finish dumping the entire contents onto Max's head and shoulders. He flicked back the top of his Zippo and his thumb came crashing down on the flint wheel; it sparked the very first time and the wick lit. He'd never been quite so happy to see those beautiful blue and orange dancing flames.

"Suck on this!" Morris heard himself say before realizing the words had left his mouth. With a careful grace, he lobbed the Zippo right at Max's face.

The whole upper part of its body erupted into a colorful blaze of dark blue and golden yellow. Maximillian screamed, its hands and arms trying desperately to put out the fire. Its features began to disappear as the flames engulfed the body, spiraling upward in a fiery dance. It attempted to frantically grab hold of Morris but was unsuccessful.

Morris felt a renewed sense of life. He pawed at the detonator, not bothering to detach any of the wires, just yanking them all out at once. He summoned all the energy he had left within him and ran toward the door.

Max continued to scream, its arms thrashing around, furiously searching for the detective, giving Morris an idea.

"Hey, Maximillian! C'mon, you gruesome son of a bitch! Follow me!" He began to make a lot of noise, clapping his hands.

It worked. Morris fled up the stairs with Max giving chase. For a guy whose head and upper body were on fire, it kept up pretty damn well.

Ambrosio and the G-Men, who had all arrived by now, had finally started to get the upper hand in the gunfight, along with the other police officers. Barton McLane, the man on the landing, had been shot dead, tumbled headfirst over the marble railing, and fallen twenty feet onto the stairs below. George Raft and Cagney had also been killed, pieces of their flesh and blood now sprayed all over the information booth window and marble floors.

Rory Caven, still wearing the Paul Muni mask, ran across the station toward the train platforms, to where his last shooter was positioned. He almost made it to the large doorways where the track number boards were but was gunned down by law enforcement. Rory stumbled forward as he ran, tripping over. He fell, sliding and coming to a rest within a few feet of his masked gunman.

This last robber, wearing a Peter Lorre mask, threw down his shotgun and put his hands in the air. Ambrosio and his men took that as a cue to advance with their guns raised, screaming for him to get to his knees and keep his hands up. The last torpedo quickly followed their commands and sunk to his knees, cowering at the head of the luxurious red carpet of the Twentieth Century Limited. The uniformed officers hurried over, ripping off his mask once he was secured and cuffed.

All the shooting had now ceased in the main concourse. And through the haze of gunpowder lingering in the air, there was a moment of peace and silence blanketing the room. Spectators who were huddled in corners and hiding behind baggage carts started to move again, uncovering their eyes and ears, breathing a sigh of relief. Officers attended to the wounded and made sure everyone was okay, amazed at the gunfight they had all been a part of. Davies tore the Paul Muni mask off of the dead body lying on the floor near him, discovering what they had already known: it was Irish mob boss, Hell's Kitchen's own, Rory Caven.

All of a sudden, there was a loud noise from a train's air horn, startling people. It was the Twentieth Century Limited coming out of the tunnel and decelerating as it approached the plush platform. Everyone breathed an enormous sigh of relief when they saw it was just the famous train arriving. But the horn continued to blow, with a deep and frantic urgency, drawing the attention of those on or near the platform. They all turned back to get a clear view of the locomotive pulling in.

It was one of the brand-new Art Deco engines that looked to be in perpetual motion. It had a front end which jutted downward at a forty-five-degree angle as it neared the bottom, becoming the traditional "cow catcher" and shielding the front wheels from obstructions. Its chimney produced a thick gray smoke that shot up almost fifteen feet, and the train itself was like one long, chrome, metal snake with the engine blending seamlessly into the rest of the other fourteen cars it pulled.

It was about this time a figure appeared from out of the darkness at the far end of the platform, someone running at full speed and carrying something. Once that figure cleared through the train's fog, a gray haze lingered around his limbs and torso. The police realized it was Private Detective Walter Morris. Those who were watching raised an eyebrow, a look of curiosity upon their faces. Ambrosio took a couple more steps toward the platform, bewildered by what he was seeing.

A glow appeared behind the locomotive's smoke, moving at a rapid speed. The shape of a large figure came into focus, the bright glow becoming a burning flame. Maximillian emerged from within the darkness. It was in full-speed pursuit of Morris, the upper body still ablaze. The fire was burning so bright now it rivaled the intensity of the incoming loco-motive's headlamp.

The train was slowing at a greater rate than normal, Morris passed it as he ran and the porters, baggage men, and conductors who were waiting on the red carpet jumped out of the way to make room for the detective and the flaming demon on his tail.

The police were flabbergasted at the scene they were witnessing. When Morris got closer to them, he started shouting.

"Ambrosio! Ambrosio! Ambrosio!"

Frowning, the sergeant stepped closer. "Walter?"

Morris saw Ambrosio was at the head end of the platform and screamed as loud as he could. "Chopper, Chopper! Get me a Thompson!"

He had almost reached them, but Max was right behind. It had just passed the train, screaming and smoking like a road flare. The train engineer was so shocked he didn't even notice the cigarette drop from his mouth or the hot cherry explode, red hot embers falling down the front of his dirty overalls. He poked his head out of the window to keep the incredible scene in his view as the train continued to decrease speed.

"Thompson!" Morris kept shouting. "Thompson!"

Without taking his eyes off the situation, an older uniformed officer who was standing next to Ambrosio remarked in a slight Irish brogue to the sergeant, "I think he's asking for a Tommy gun, sir."

Ambrosio nodded at the cop then looked over at another officer who had a machine gun. "Is that loaded?"

"Yes, sir. A full cli—"

Ambrosio grabbed it from him before the young man could finish getting his sentence out.

"Thompson!" Morris screamed again as he got toward the end of the platform. He turned to the older Irish cop and shouted, "Catch!" and threw him the detonator, which miraculously the policeman caught.

Ambrosio simultaneously tossed the machine gun toward Morris. The detective caught it and quickly cocked back the bolt, swung around, and slid onto his back, unloading the machine gun at the flaming goon behind him.

Maximillian was close enough that the landing projectiles made a violent impact. Morris kept the Chicago Typewriter in control and didn't relent as the bullets shot downrange and into Max. It caused the ghoul to stumble and lose its footing as it ran, widening the distance from Morris. As the last rounds hit the legs, it tripped and fell off the platform, down onto the tracks and into the path of the oncoming train.

The engineer laid on the horn and recoiled in horror as the locomotive ran over Maximillian on the final yards of track before finally coming to a stop at the head of the platform.

Police officers helped a war-weary and bloody Morris to his feet. He waved the empty machine gun in air while he shouted over to the train engineer, "Hey! Don't you worry. That was a bad guy. It's okay! Bad guy."

The train engineer grimaced awkwardly and waved his hand, unsure of what to do but hoping that what he had just been told was correct.

Morris limped over to Ambrosio and handed him the empty Thompson, placing it in both of his arms. Before the sergeant could say anything, Morris bent over, putting his hands on his thighs. He took slow, even breaths. "I gotta catch my breath…oh my God…wow." He was exhausted and looked at Ambrosio and Davies with a pained expression. "You might wanna take a few guys with rods and go make sure that mutha's D-E-D, dead."

Nobody responded at first.

"Are you serious?" Ambrosio asked him honestly.

In between his slow and pained breathing, Morris nodded. "Serious as a heart attack, old buddy." Morris put a hand to his own chest. "Which I feel like I'm having right now…"

Ambrosio motioned to the uniformed officers, who took out their revolvers and with their shotguns in hand, headed over to take a look.

"Yeah, Flash Gordon's got nothing on him." He kept an eye on the officers as they stopped the train from disembarking while the undercarriage of the locomotive was being searched.

Morris looked the stunned passengers waiting to get off. "Let's hope Ingrid Bergman isn't on the *Limited* tonight." He smiled between Ambrosio and Davies. "Okay, so there's one piece here…but I need a head start to get the drop on them, and then *hopefully* have you guys come in like the cavalry. I gotta stop this heel before he's able to escape. He's behind this whole horror show."

Ambrosio nodded, blinking slowly. "How much time are you gonna need? 'Cause this isn't a fucking picture show. We can't just delay our end because of you."

"Please trust me," Morris said. "These guys are fucking Nazis, the real deal. Straight outta Germany, I kid you not. I gotta get there first and kick them in the swastika, make sure they can't get away, and then you guys can swoop in and get them."

Ambrosio shook his head, at a loss for words. He glanced over at Davies, and his partner simply shrugged. "So what does this entail exactly?"

Morris gestured for them to follow him as he headed into Grand Central's enormous main hall. "First and foremost, I'm gonna need a rod, preferably an automatic. If I could maybe borrow one, that and a rifle or a shotgun if possible." Morris hurried across the hall, passing the various onlookers trying to get a good view of the bodies next to the clock. He looped around them and headed toward the front entrance.

"Jesus, Walt. Okay, then what?" Ambrosio begrudgingly asked.

Morris was hesitant to ask his next question but knew there was no getting around it. "And…I'm gonna need to borrow one of your patrol cars."

Davies laughed. "And what are we gonna do, sit back and let you take it out to Jones Beach? I've heard it's nice out there this time of year. Hey, Ambrosio, I hear Guy Lombardo puts on one heckuva show at their—"

Ambrosio jumped in, cutting his partner off. "Cut to the chase, Walt. Why would we ever let you have one of our vehicles?"

Morris made his way through the passenger waiting area. "I don't need the entire New York City Police Department accompanying me, it'll spook them, and I'm telling you, this guy will cut out of here so fast we may never see him again." He headed toward the front doors. "I want to get a head start and get into position so that when you and General Patton arrive, they'll be disabled and have no place to go. If we don't do it this way, then they will slip through our fingers."

The two police officers stayed on his tail. "And then what?"

"Then...." Morris stepped out onto Forty-Second Street, to where all of the police cars had been abandoned when the cavalry arrived. "Then when I get to where they're going, which is in the city, by the way, I'll call you on one of those fancy two-way radios you've got in some of your cars now." He gestured toward all the black-and-white coupes and sedans. "Just give me one with a radio."

Davies was grinning, as though Morris was completely crazy. But the sergeant had furrowed brows. He was standing with his arms crossed, staring intently at the detective.

"C'mon, Ambrose, you know me. You know you can trust me. Time's a-wasting. Let's get these guys."

CHAPTER 30

PIER 72, ICEHOUSE #4

Morris was given their latest Ford sedan with the new two-way "Walkie-Talkie" radio system that was being tested in the Radio Motor Patrols, or RMPs. She was brand new and raring to go, looking almost as beautiful as his baby, which after all this was over, he still had to go out and retrieve from Long Island. Morris slammed the door shut and placed two automatics, a Browning and a Smith & Wesson pistol, onto the passenger seat. They even let him borrow a Thompson and several mags, which he threw onto the passenger floor. He hit the gas without even saying goodbye, not giving Ambrosio the time to renege on this little deal they had made. Morris couldn't have the whole Army descending on the docks; he just needed a head start to guarantee those sons of bitches couldn't go anywhere once the police were on the way.

He turned on the party hat and sped down Forty-Second Street, heading out toward the West Side. Once he got there, he'd radio in with his location, hopefully giving him enough time to sabotage their plans before the cavalry arrived to save the day. He had a straight shot with the sirens blaring, and in a fancy new black-and-white patrol car, people got the hell out of his way. His body was about to quit on him, and he had no idea how he was still even functioning. Whatever these pills were, they did the trick. He took out his last Pervitin tablet and tossed it into his mouth.

Morris got down to the West Side Docks in record time. He turned off the sirens on the highway and tried to be as inconspicuous as possible when he got off the exit. When he pulled onto the street along the waterfront, he turned off all the lights so as not to attract any unnecessary attention. He focused his attention on the numbers, looking for Pier 72. He turned into an unguarded Pier 70 and parked the cruiser behind a warehouse, out of the view of spying eyes. He holstered one of the automatics and crept along the side of the warehouse wall heading toward Pier 71, hoping to sneak over to Pier 72 and Icehouse #4. When he got to the fence he knelt down low, surveying the situation.

At the docks of Pier 72 a large, weathered freighter named the *Demeter* was docked next to Icehouse #4. Huge spotlights were trained on the massive vessel, where it looked like a small army was in the middle of frantically loading the ship's belly. It seemed like every available dock worker in New York City was on hand, completely oblivious to what they were actually loading, and for whom. How could they ever know they were busy moving the Nazis' stolen booty from their bloody conquests in Europe, as well as the future of warfare, the undead herculean ghouls surgically altered to be panzer tanks? Morris laughed at how insane it all sounded, even now.

High above the *Demeter*, two tower harbor cranes with long horizontal arms worked in tandem, each taking turns lifting the heavy payloads down into the ship's cargo hold.

He did his best to creep out onto Pier 70's dock to get a clear view of the *Demeter* as she was being hastily loaded. He spotted Von Stroheim up on the flying bridge deck, which was right outside the boat's control room, where he was supervising the ship's cargo. He had his jacket collar turned up to shield his face, but Morris recognized his figure and hat. The detective counted almost a hundred men, all working together in a synchronized dance to get everything on board, and it was looking to be maybe halfway done. From what he could tell, most of the dock workers were normal hardworking longshoremen, doing the most efficient job possible in order to get the freighter to depart.

Another man walked out of the control room and onto the flying bridge, then wandered over to speak with Von Stroheim. The man's glasses reflected in the harsh light, and Morris would recognize that slicked-back hair anywhere. It was Mengele. Apparently the whole party was here. Stroheim raised his hand and barked out an order, and everyone's rate of loading went into overdrive.

"Shit...," Morris said. "How in the hell am I gonna cripple a steamer that size from being able to..." he trailed off, trying to figure out an answer to his own question.

Morris hurried back to the patrol car. As promised, he sent out a radio call for reinforcements, letting the powers that be know where it was all going down. Then he suited up; he placed the other .45 automatic in his belt, putting the extra mags into all of his available pockets, and headed out with the machine gun in hand.

The freighter was nearly loaded and most of the workers were winding down dockside. Only four more bundles of boxes remained, wrapped up in cargo nets and waiting to be hoisted onboard.

On the dock's edge, on either end of the freighter, were the two enormous cranes situated on rails. The nearest crane to Pier 70 was also the farthest from all the action. The small control booth for the crane sat above the tower, behind the long arm that extended out high above the *Demeter*. The operator sat inside at the controls, lethargically loading the heavy cargo onboard. He lifted up an oversized palette that had two large and heavy touring cars secured upon it: a Mercedes-Benz 770 and the ultra-rare 1939 Bugatti Type 57c.

The cab door opened and Morris climbed inside. The crane operator looked over and did a quick double take upon the realization that it wasn't an actual employee. His first inclination was to question Morris, but he quickly noticed the submachine in his hand, the two handguns in his waistband, and the numerous ammo magazines bulging out of his pockets.

"Huh...you my relief?" he said with a healthy level of skepticism.

Morris tried to keep as nonchalant as the situation would allow. "Yeah. Go and get a fresh cup of joe."

The crane operator's eyes darted to the Thompson in Morris's hand and nodded at the detective's suggestion. "Yeah, a cup of coffee would certainly do a fella a bit of good right now." He had already unbelted and was halfway out of the seat. "I'll be right back."

"Hey, while I have you here, if one needed a tiny refresher on how all of this worked, could you help a brotha out?" Morris gave the man his warmest and most sincere smile, plus a slight nudge with the machine gun.

Von Stroheim was now standing on the bow overseeing the loading process with another one of Mengele's undead army, a newly restored Heinrich, who Tatum and Morris had plowed into and driven over out on Long Island.

Toward the rear of the ship, past two large open hatches that led down to the hold area, was a huge structure that enclosed the crew quarters and had the ship's bridge at the top. Stroheim continued to bark out orders at the dock workers, yelling at them to hurry up. His attention became diverted when the large crane by the stern lifting the two cars unexpectedly stopped moving. Stroheim yelled in German at a ship loading supervisor who was the intermediator between the freighter's crew and the dock workers, asking what had happened. But the crane began to move again, lifting the heavy load into the air. Satisfied, Stroheim diverted his attention to another issue at hand.

Once the goods were over the cargo hold, the loading supervisor signaled for the crane to stop and begin its descent down into the belly of the ship. Instead, ignoring the supervisor's commands, it continued past the hold and kept going, pivoting to the right until it was directly over the bridge of the *Demeter*. The crane jerked to a stop, causing the cargo to sway lazily back and forth in a dangerous fashion. Von Stroheim saw the commotion and joined in with the chorus of men yelling up at the crane's control booth. Men outside on the flying bridge jumped up at the dangling guide lines, trying desperately to get a hand on the ropes to gain control of the swaying pallet.

A hush fell over the workers as more and more people turned to see what was happening, their mouths open wide in shock.

The cargo dropped, sending the men below running from the ship's enclosed bridge. The pallet holding the two huge cars came crashing down on to the wooden and metal structure, destroying the main bridge area and the many antennas atop. The line that held the heavy load took its time getting taut again but once the slack was taken back, the pallet was raised haphazardly for a second time. The Mercedes-Benz 770 completely broke free from its position and rolled off headfirst, hurtling down into a head-on collision with the foredeck below. It balanced there momentarily until its weight tumbled it forward and it disappeared with a tremendous crash deep in the ship's cargo hold.

The pallet was now leaning precariously to one side above the wrecked bridge, unbalanced by the 1939 Bugatti. It was raised again and then dropped, completely destroying the bridge and radio room next door. Small sparks and explosions erupted from the collapsed structure, steam flew up in the air, and the twisted wreck that was once the rare Bugatti burst into flames.

Stroheim screamed in anguish, the stark realization hitting him that his vessel was mortally wounded. Heinrich's head snapped to readiness and looked over to its commander, like a dog when his master was upset. Von Stroheim looked up at the crane's cab just in time to see Morris exit the small door to get a better look at his handiwork. Mengele came back onto the deck to see all the commotion. Von Stroheim howled a vicious shriek, a battle cry that within it had the decades of service to his Fatherland. He shouted out an order to Heinrich, pointing up at Morris on top of the crane. Heinrich tilted its head and zeroed in on the detective. It sprang into action at an unnatural speed, and in a maneuver that no normal human could ever accomplish, leapt off the forecastle at the bow, jumping down to the main deck below, where it scurried for the gangplank that led off the ship.

Sirens echoed from the surrounding streets, wailing down the road from every direction. It looked like every squad car in the five boroughs was on its way. Armies of police cars, trucks, vans, and motorbikes. Von Stroheim yelled loudly, and everyone onboard the ship started to panic while the dock workers on the waterfront were confused, some even taking their gloves off and putting their hands up, not wanting any trouble.

Morris stood halfway in the doorway of the cab, watching down in triumph at the disaster and chaos he had caused. He smiled at the onslaught of police descending, feeling ecstatic and overjoyed at the situation below. Out of nowhere a bullet ricocheted off a piece of metal and shattered the cab's front window. Morris immediately came back down to Earth, ducking for cover. Another projectile bounced off the metal control panel.

From down on the forecastle, Von Stroheim fired an M1 rifle up at Morris on top of the crane. The en bloc ammo clip sprang out with the last shell casing, the rifle now empty. With rapid speed, he reloaded another en bloc clip and continued firing up at Morris's position.

Morris ducked again and laughed, giving Von Stroheim the finger. "Go USA, you Kraut bastards!"

Fixated on Morris, Heinrich ascended the ladder inside the crane's tower at an incredibly fast rate. Its teeth were exposed as it panted, showing more emotion than Maximillian or Karl ever had.

Von Stroheim fired off another round at Morris, screaming up at the detective with a fury. "C'mon! Pay attention to me, you dumb son of a bitch!"

Morris was ecstatic, laughing at Von Stroheim below while watching the police swarm the docks and round up the confused longshoremen. Had the detective been looking around and not just focusing on the *Demeter*, he would have seen the monstrous figure that rose up behind him.

A gorilla-sized hand grabbed Morris's ankle from below, causing him to fall hard on the metal floor. Heinrich's head appeared through a hole in the grating standing at the top of the ladder. It pulled out one of the mini-automatic machine guns, but Morris quickly kicked it out of the ghoul's hand, and the gun spun away and fell into the crane cab.

Morris recognized the ghoul instantly. "Oh, for fuck's sake!"

He kicked Heinrich in the face several times with his other foot, giving him an opportunity to look for an escape route. Morris first reached into the cab and grabbed his forever partner, his Thompson.

Von Stroheim used this opportunity to sprint past the commotion, deck side, wanting to personally even the score with the private detective who had caused all his problems. He headed for the gangplank, M1 in hand.

Up above, Morris clicked back the bolt and pulled the trigger, right as the ghoul stood up onto the metal grating. Heinrich was no more than six feet away when it took the entire magazine of thirty .45-caliber rounds that were instantly embedded into its face and chest. Morris was only vaguely able to see the damage he inflicted from the illumination of the muzzle blast. Once the gun clicked back empty, he weighed his options, knowing the only way down was the ladder his opponent was blocking.

Back down on the ship, Von Stroheim sped through the crowd and over the gangplank like a bulldozer, unloading his carbine rifle at a police officer in his way, a direct assault. The dead officer fell down into the water and another ducked for cover. He laid down heavy fire as he crossed and everyone scattered, giving Von Stroheim a straight shot to the crane ladder.

Ambrosio and Davies ducked behind their squad cars, overwhelmed like everyone else by Von Stroheim's firepower. Cops and longshoremen alike ran for cover. They returned fire but Stroheim disappeared behind a stack of crates and into the shadows. The police turned their focus back to the freighter. They charged the gangplank and came aboard firing, screaming for people to throw up their hands.

The surge of law enforcement convincingly overwhelmed those onboard and they threw down their weapons almost in tandem, shocked and crestfallen that the war was over. Mengele merely smiled and ducked into a doorway out of sight, vanishing into the bowels of the ship.

Far above the action, Morris found his current location eerily quiet, except for the steady howl of the wind and the occasional echo of gunfire that found its way up, distracting him from the one task he had to concentrate on, which was keeping a careful track on where he stepped in the darkness. Morris ventured further out onto the massive scaffolding, creating some much-needed distance between himself and Heinrich.

He still held the empty machine gun in his free hand as he continued out onto the crane's horizontal arm. Morris realized from his tight grip on the weapon just how nervous he was being so high up; he needed to be *extremely* careful where he stepped. With his free hand, he precariously held on to the cylindrical beams above for support, spreading his legs wide and almost having to leap forward to continue on the metal superstructure. The wind was beginning to pick up and the crane's movement in the breeze was visibly apparent, making Morris queasy. He wasn't a fan of heights so he tried to focus on where he was stepping and not on the ground below.

The detective slipped and momentarily lost his footing, but he was saved by his secure grip on the construction above. He froze. The experience had severely shaken him, and his first impulse was to remain there and never move again, but he made sure to quickly regain his balance, knowing that he needed to put some distance between him and the ghoul.

Von Stroheim threw his empty rifle down and started climbing the tower ladder.

Morris decided to check on his companion here in the heavens. He glanced over his shoulder to see the fate of Heinrich.

The undead ghoul's face was entirely gone; the goggles still obscured its eyes, but its forehead, jaw, and cheeks were down to the bone. The nose and other distinguishable features were no longer visible; a thick, black crimson oozed out of the bare skull. The chest was a hideous mess; chunky pieces of bullet-ridden flesh did very little to hide the exposed metal shielding that had been surgically implanted. But still the bleeding mess continued to move, and Heinrich's bare teeth opened and shut, sucking in air. It started after Morris, making a hissing and moaning sound as it continued toward him.

Along the docks numerous police boats sailed over to pick up any stragglers who'd jumped ship. Boats were being directed by officers on the pier to shine their spotlights up to the top of the cranes. Another large spotlight from a police truck was switched on and the blinding beam of intense light shined high up to the crane's arm. The many streams of bright light found Morris, and everyone below gradually stopped what they were doing to watch.

Now the blackout had been lifted, there was a dark crimson warning light at the end of the crane's arm, systematically blinking every few seconds and enveloping Morris and the surrounding area with a hellish red glow.

Heinrich was performing a balancing act, climbing further out and getting closer with every methodical step. Morris, however, who was running out of crane to crawl on, was holding on for dear life. The further he ventured out, the windier it was getting. He finally reached the end when the arm became too narrow to crawl any further.

If he dropped the machine gun he could probably reach one of the exterior rigging cables that ran above him and along the length of the arm, but what then? It would be a heavy upward climb, but he could possibly crawl up the pendant line to the boom hoist rope and follow the wire back to the tower peak where the two riggings met. From there he could get down to where he started out, to the area where the crane's booth was...but it was impossible. Barnum and Bailey didn't employ a high-wire walker that could successfully traverse that rigging. This was the end of the line, where Morris would have to make a final stand against the real-life monster slowly gaining on him.

Morris focused in on the impending danger, Heinrich.

On the ground the other officers were keeping tabs on Morris's situation like it was some kind of ball game. Davies grabbed a group of beat cops and headed toward the base of the crane. Ambrosio was setting up a row of motorcycle cops, all armed with Thompsons, like they were civil war soldiers out on the front lines, three squatted on a knee and three were standing tall behind. He held them at the ready.

Morris was crouched down, wedged into the upper rigging of the jib arm. He ejected the empty Thompson magazine and it clanged against the scaffolding below him, swallowed up by the night. He dug into his pockets and found a brand new mag, but during the process he accidentally knocked loose the only other one he had, and that, too, vanished into the darkness below. Cursing, he reloaded his rifle.

He pulled back the bolt and looked up at Heinrich. The monstrosity was almost three-quarters of the way across, seemingly having no problem navigating the jungle-gym-style scaffolding. Its face was truly that of a skeleton now from the force of the strong breeze. The white bone was a stark contrast to the mutilated pieces of muscle and flesh blowing precariously from the sides of its head and the blood oozing down its damaged chest and tattered clothing. Heinrich's mouth opened unnaturally wide and it bared its sharp teeth. It screamed a gargled high-pitched noise at the detective and then snapped its jaws shut.

Morris took a few steady breaths to calm his nerves, then squeezed the trigger. He unloaded at the ghoul's face, before aiming at the feet, hoping to throw off its balance. Heinrich stumbled, but kept its grip and regained its footing.

Ambrosio pointed up at the jib. "Okay, boys, see the big guy in the middle of the crane's arm? Light him up. Just be careful not to hit our man on the end."

They directed and unloaded their entire drum barrels up at the target, their projectiles completely savaging Heinrich and the surrounding scaffolding, shredding its clothes and what was left of its skin. It held on tight to the bars above, trying to help stabilize its body as the projectiles hit. The machine guns clicked back empty, and the police officers reloaded.

Morris fired the last of his own rounds and his gun emptied. He climbed over the bars and began bashing the butt of the Thompson into Heinrich's face. After several hits, it ripped Morris's gun from out of his hands and threw it off into the night. The men on the ground were unable to get a clear line of fire because the two above were so close together.

Morris clung to the cylindrical poles above for leverage and begin kicking Heinrich's wounded body as hard as he could. Heinrich stumbled. Its foot slipped and the giant fell through the bars but caught itself with one hand and dangled there. Morris pounced, crushing its fingers with the heel of his shoe. When he stepped back to catch his breath, Heinrich took another barrage of rounds from the police below, but unbelievably started to climb back up onto the bars, using its elbows to lift itself up. The machine gunners below stopped shooting for fear of catching Morris in the crossfire.

Morris grabbed the .45-caliber automatic from his waistband and chambered a round. He moved toward Heinrich and leveled the weapon less than an inch from the giant's head. Heinrich had both arms locked, holding on to the bars and about to swing a leg up. It was defenseless from any attack. Morris unloaded the magazine of seven .45-caliber bullets into the monster's head as fast as the weapon would mechanically allow. What was left of the face was eviscerated by the projectiles, even breaking the black goggles covering its eyes.

When the mag was empty, Morris could see underneath the shattered goggles for the very first time. He gasped in horror at the evil he saw, and instinctively smashed the gun at its face, breaking off the jaw and knocking out some of those pointed teeth. Morris held on to the bars above and with everything he could muster, kicked both legs hard into Heinrich's horrific face.

It finally lost its grip and fell backwards, smacking its head on the crane and unable to latch on again. Heinrich fell in a tangled mess down through the grating, its arms clanking loudly, the last fleeting sounds from the ghoul. It fell down into the darkness, the spotlights silhouetting the flailing figure as it descended down into Icehouse #4. Heinrich's body crashed through the warehouse roof, shattering the many blocks of ice inside, before crashing down through the wooden planks of the floor and plunging into the water below.

Morris very carefully climbed across the long arm of the crane, eventually making the long distance back to the tower section. He dropped down onto the catwalk and hauled his battered body into the cab. The detective was just about to look for a radio when he was shot in the side of his back. He collapsed to the floor.

Morris turned his head to the side and looked over to the tower access ladder. Von Stroheim was on the last rung with a small automatic in his hand. He fired another shot and it nicked Morris in the shoulder.

"You destroyed everything!" Stroheim roared with fury. He discharged another round as he climbed over but it missed and ricocheted off the metal skeleton of the crane.

Morris turned his body around and propped himself up so he could see the German. He felt up and down his broken torso, making sure the trauma hadn't fogged his memory enough not to recall the odd gun that might be stowed in his trousers. There was none.

"Ha..." Morris laughed. He was pretty numb to it all at this point. This is what happens when you lose your mind, and he found the whole darn thing quite funny. He had to, otherwise the sadness would hollow out whatever was left within him. So it really didn't matter whatever happened next.

Von Stroheim cleared a jam in the slide mechanism of his automatic, checked his magazine which he slid back into his gun, and chambered a round. He then pointed it directly at Morris's head. "You bastard, your ticket is punched!"

Morris stopped laughing, exhaled, and closed his eyes.

A loud shot rang out that made Morris flinch, but he didn't feel a new wound.

He opened his eyes and saw an exit wound on the top left side of Von Stroheim's forehead. Morris looked down through the floor grating. Davies was maybe ten or so feet below on the ladder with his gun raised. He'd gotten a clean shot upward.

A brief sign of confusion flashed across Von Stroheim's face. He tried to speak but couldn't. The gun dropped from his hand as he struggled to regain control. After a slight delayed reaction, blood began pouring from out of the large exit wound in his upper forehead. Stroheim twisted his body to glance down at Davies. He turned back around and attempted one last time to go after Morris, but shock had set in and his motor functions began to fail him. He tried once again to speak, but staggered forward and collapsed onto the grate, facing the detective.

Von Stroheim looked directly into Morris's face, his eyes darting around showing signs of life. His hands lethargically tried to make the journey to grab Morris.

"And fuck you too!" was all Morris could muster.

He pulled his leg back and gave Von Stroheim a heavy kick to the face. It was strong enough to knock his body off the edge of the crane's catwalk. He plummeted through the air, crashing onto a squad car below and crushing the hood and fender.

It took a few moments for the detective to realize the danger was finally over.

Davies holstered his weapon and stepped up onto the crane, cautiously making his way toward Morris. "Jesus, I'm sorry, Walt. It might take a minute, but I just really, really hate heights. I'll be right over."

Morris grinned, closed his eyes, and let the darkness claim him.

CHAPTER 31

BACK IN THE TOMBS

Morris looked across the table at Special Agent Graham, deep inside the New York City Tombs. He spat out another mouthful of blood and saliva onto the floor. He was still handcuffed and raised his wrists as high as they would go to take a final drag of his cigarette. He stubbed it out into a metal ashtray that was next to an empty milkshake glass, containing the remnants of his chocolate float.

"Well, you've done a man's job, sir, haven't you?" Agent Graham said with an air of learned appreciation. He took a minute and put his lighter and pack of cigarettes back into his breast pocket. He closed the notepad that he had in front of him.

"That's it? We're done here, then?" Morris remarked coldly.

"Just about," Graham replied, not making eye contact, instead taking the time to make sure his pen caught the inside of the breast pocket when he slid it in. "Anything else you want to say?"

Morris sat back and took a moment to think. He tried to shift his weight but realized very quickly that the move caused a great deal of pain. He stared at Agent Graham. "What I've learned these past couple of days...the things I've heard and seen...it changes a man." Morris thought about his statement, comparing it to when he had first been told that his little brother Stevland was not just another missing person's case, but the victim of a child killer. What made this realization, this truth he'd been exposed to, any different? "I don't think I will ever be able to go back to where I was a just over a week ago."

Graham pursed his lips and stood, finally making eye contact with Morris. "Tell that to our boys when they get back. Question is, what now for ya?" He turned to leave.

"What now? What now. Good question." Morris surprised himself by even asking.

"Learn to forget. And live. Simply, and truly live." Graham had a polite smile that was supposed to exude professional confidence.

"Be sure and take care Mr. Morris. An ambulance will be in route to take you to get patched up."

He knocked on the large cell door and a moment later it opened. He gave Morris a quick nod and walked out. It slammed shut behind him.

CHAPTER 32

VICTORY DAY

Morris examined his bruised face, prodding it with a light touch. The tenderness of the area answered back with a dull throb and his reflection winced in pain. The Pervitin that Gray had given him was now long gone, taking the masking of his pain with it. His battered body creaked and bore the scars of his trauma. Both physically and mentally, he was realizing with every passing day, it was all so different now.

The radio was on and he was listening to a program about a man who'd gone around the Delta and Mississippi, recording farmhands and sharecroppers performing all kinds of ingenious songs for the Library of Congress. At the moment, an ex-con named Leadbelly was performing a tune called "Where Did You Sleep Last Night?"

Morris' mind wandered while staring into the little four-by-six-inch vanity mirror attached to the small cabinet above the compact sink in his office. He traced the edges of the large bandage attached to the left side of his forehead, his fingers subconsciously moving down to the other deep stitched cuts on his cheek and chin.

He thought about his unique and singular practice that he shared with his partner and founder of the agency, North England's own Jacob Roland. A black and a white, an American and a Brit, two men who met working on a transatlantic ocean liner and decided to go into business for themselves in a city where they could make it rich by being able to fit in and blend in with anyone. Yet Morris was numb to all that now. His eyes had been opened to what horrors men were truly capable of, men like Josef Mengele, Hans Von Stroheim, and Albert Fish. There was no difference between any of them—except for their methods. Each one believed deep in their heart that what they were doing was right. They thought God was on their side, that He understood and condoned it.

Morris felt like running, running like he'd done before. But he was too old now. And where would he run to? Back to the bowels of a steamship or the bottom of some hellish coal-lung mine? Not a lot of opportunities for a man of his age, his disposition, and his skill set. No, he knew this time he had to absorb it, do the best he could where he was to close part of himself off to this horribly damned world.

He broke his own stare and finished cleaning his hands. He found himself incessantly washing them these days and didn't know why. He'd also drift in thought and at times just felt like he wanted to cry. He couldn't figure it. After drying them, he closed the cabinet door above the sink and walked over to the radio. When Leadbelly was over, he turned off the wireless so to not engage his attention with another tutorial and performance.

Morris did something he rarely did anymore; he went into his wallet and took out the picture of his little brother. It was a photo of the brothers together; his mother had it taken at a studio out on Coney Island one Sunday afternoon. It seemed like several lifetimes ago now. He stared down at the image and only when his eyes began to water did he cross over to his desk and insert the little memory in the top right drawer underneath his copy of *The Negro Motorist Green Book*, given to him by the publisher himself, Victor H. Green. He made sure the photo was secure and wasn't creased, then eased shut the drawer.

Tatum came around the desk in the waiting room and entered his inner office. Morris had meanwhile seated himself behind his desk.

"How are you doing?" she asked him

He shrugged, trying to look busy.

"What will happen to Caldonia?"

"Hayden's estate is gonna finance her extended stay in Creedmoor. There's nothing upstairs anymore. She's got long days in a white room to look forward to."

"That's so sad."

They were both silent for a while before Tatum spoke again.

"What about the doctor?"

"I'm going to hope the OSS got him."

She walked over and hugged him. "Why don't you take some time off?"

Morris didn't respond. There was another long pause and an emotion flashed over his face, and as quick as it was visible it was gone again. His demeanor changed and he smiled warmly at Tatum. "Hey, so what do you do during the day now?"

Tatum smiled. "Well, if Zallerilla gets dumped or left on a planet by Johnny Flash next season, I might be spending my time just loafing."

"You wanna answer the phone and call people for us here at the agency?" Morris winked.

She laughed. "A secretary, you mean?"

He smiled lovingly at her. "If that's what they're calling it nowadays."

She moved closer. "Why do you think I hang out with you? I knew you'd eventually start giving me money."

They both laughed and continued to gaze at each other. Morris had just placed his hand on her shoulder when the door opened.

Jacob Roland entered, carrying a suitcase and an overnight bag. They looked over to him as he set his bags down.

"Looks like I found the party. Geeze, Walt, don't tell me you've been sitting here the entire time! You got to be kidding me. You find a secretary at least?"

Morris nodded and the smiles faded from his and Tatum's faces as they stared blankly over at Roland.

"What?" Roland asked. "What have I missed? I'm sorry I was gone for almost a week, but I got one helluva case to tell you about!"

CHAPTER 33

TOMORROW

It was well after midnight as the fog crept in on the lonely stretch of New Jersey motorway. Tall forests of pine populated either side of the road. In the distance the mountain ranges were silhouetted against the moon's illuminated shine. The low hum of an engine rose and drifted across the evening air.

A Kenworth needle nose tandem-axle semi-tractor-trailer truck crossed the top of a hill towing a huge trailer, followed closely behind by two other rigs. The three trucks continued down the long, quiet road. The convoy began to decrease in speed when they saw a patrol officer standing in the middle of the highway, flashlight in hand, flagging them down. The patrolman and his partner had positioned themselves about a mile before the New Jersey/Pennsylvania border.

When the rigs were close enough, the officers could see that all three trucks belonged to the Army, green with white stars and stripes on both the rigs and their trailers.

The first Kenworth crawled to a halt directly in front of the two New Jersey State patrolmen. The two officers crossed from their vehicle and greeted the driver.

Three men in Army fatigues sat on the bench seat of the cab. A flash-light's beam traveled across their faces. The driver and middle man smiled down at the officers. The last man had his cap resting over his face and his head laying against the passenger window. His mouth was visible under the brim, half open, and his arms were tightly locked across his chest which rose and fell like he was in a deep sleep.

"Evening, fellas," the first officer said. "Can I see your manifest?"

The young driver flashed a look of awkwardness, then grabbed the clipboard, handing it carefully out of the window and down to the officer who examined it. The driver lit a cigarette.

The police officer thumbed through the manifest's pages and spoke without looking up. "What ya carrying?"

The driver took another puff. "Artifacts from Albany, bound for the Smithsonian in DC."

That piqued the patrolman's interest. "Wow. Really?"

The driver smiled, getting animated as he spoke, "Yeah, we're not supposed to say anything, but since you guys are brothers in blue...," he stuck his head out and glanced back at the two tractor trailers behind them, "...those trucks got mummies and other shit from Egypt that our boys rescued after we drove a Sherman up Rommel's ass in Africa. From what I've heard, all this stuff only just made it back stateside."

The Army officer in the middle chimed in. "I guess it wasn't Patton's top priority." He chuckled.

The driver laughed too and turned back to the officers below. "Scary stuff, from what I've heard."

"Really?" the second cop said, eyes wide with interest.

The Army guy in the middle nodded. "They ship 'em in ice nowadays to keep them from drying out."

"Wow...that's exciting. I was with Patton in the Thirty-Fourth Infantry Division in North Africa and then Italy," the officer told them. "Got injured at Monte Cassino and they shipped me back. Spent a year in the hospital recovering."

The driver kept his smile, staring down at the patrolman. The officer in the middle nodded, silently watching the officer's body language.

"Well, everything seems to be in order." He handed the manifest back up to the driver. "Take care, guys, and drive safely, okay?"

"Thank you." The Army driver took back the clipboard "You too. 'Night."

The second officer backed their patrol car out of the way. The truck driver shifted the rig into first gear and the machine growled to life and pulled away. The cops waved the other two trucks on. The tractor trailers blew their horns in gratitude.

They cruised away and the lead truck driver handed the ID back to the man seated in the middle, who pulled out the automatic handgun he'd hidden behind his back. He clicked the hammer down into place and put the weapon back behind himself.

"He didn't even look at it," the driver said, referring to the identification. The man in the middle replaced it back into his breast pocket.

The third man who was sleeping lifted his cap and straightened it, slyly watching the patrol officers in the rearview mirror get smaller. It was Josef Mengele, clean-shaven, with a fresh, short military-style haircut. He took his round glasses from out of his pocket and put them on.

"I am glad we didn't lose all of you English-speaking commandos in the Bulge," Mengele said in his native German.

The driver answered back in German, an air of pride in his voice. "Thank you, Herr Doctor…*Heil Hitler.*"

Mengele nodded.

The convoy crossed into Pennsylvania and continued down the lonely highway into the night.

EPILOGUE

*D*octor Josef Mengele went on to live a quiet life in Paraguay. The world's most notorious war criminal passed away while swimming in a cove in 1979. His remains were later dug up in 1985 and through dental records, the White Angel of Auschwitz's identity was finally confirmed.

THE END

APPENDIX

Prologue – Edward R. Murrow was embedded with the troops in Europe and was the first reporter on scene of the liberation of the Buchenwald concentration camp. Surprisingly, most of the American public had been unaware of the horrors the Nazis had perpetrated against the people of Europe, and Murrow was one of the first one to officially bring it to the public psyche.

Chapter 1 – The Office of Strategic Service, or the O.S.S., was the precursor to the modern C.I.A.

Chapter 2 – There were monumental measures taken in the United States and New York City specifically to aid in the war effort, including but not limited to many restrictions of things such as meat, rubber, and metals, which were being used to help make supplies for our boys overseas fighting the war. Since New York City was considered a premium target for our enemies at the time (with reports we learned only after the war that German U-boats were on the outskirts of New York Harbor and even dropping people off on the tip of eastern Long Island), all lights from buildings, theater marquees, streetlights, and even vehicles were extinguished at night for fear of being targets of aerial attacks. Lorraine B Diehl's 2010 book, ***Over Here: New York City During World War II,*** and ***World War II: Film and History*** by John Whiteclay Chambers II and David Culbert in general were invaluable resources for this knowledge.

Built into the design of the Empire State Building, the spire was intended to be a mooring station at the very top, for zeppelins; in 1929 when the building was devised, dirigibles were thought to be the future of air transportation. The height of the building was increased by more than 222 feet so a mooring mast could be installed. Alfred E. Smith, the leader of a group of investors who were financing the Empire State Building's construction, explained passengers were to disembark via a gangplank to the building while the almost 800-foot-long blimps could swing in the breeze, and within seven minutes visitors could be down at street level, ready to set out into Manhattan. Only once, in 1931—the year of the building's opening—did a privately owned zeppelin dock for three minutes, in 40-miles-per-hour wind. It immediately became apparent how impractical it would be. The Goodyear Blimp, the *Columbia* later that year delivered a stack of *Evening Journals* by lowering a 100-foot-line. NBC began broadcasting from the tower by year's end.

Chapter 4 – The *RMS Olympic* was the first of the Olympic Class Fleet of White Star Line ocean liners, of which the legendary *RMS Titanic* was a part. It was the only ship that did not sink like its sisters the aforementioned *Titanic*, and the later *HMHS Britannic*. The *RMS Olympic* had a 24-year career of service, including as a troopship during World War One. It was decommissioned in 1935.

Chapter 5 – Father Divine was an iconic African American Spiritual leader who was active from 1907 to his death in 1965. He was hugely influential on many levels, and also claimed to be God.

Chapter 7.5 – Albert Fish was a real life serial killer, child rapist, and cannibal. He had many aliases, such as the "Moon Maniac," the "Brooklyn Vampire," and "The Boogey Man." He boasted that the number of his victims was in the hundreds. He was finally apprehended in December of 1934, and executed by electric chair at age 65 in January of 1936.

Chapter 11 – Operation Paperclip (Overcast) was a top-secret program which ran between 1945 to roughly 1959 where German engineers, scientists, and the like, many of whom were former Nazi Party members, were secretly brought from Europe to America after the war because of the building tension between the Soviet Union and the United States, for the purpose that the West would have the strategic and military advantage in development of post-war tech. Doing this gave the United States unprecedented advantages in the medical, aeronautics, and weapon making fields. Probably the most famous benefactor of this program was Wernher von Braun. It was first called Operation Overcast, until the name was changed to Paperclip in July of 1945, (perhaps because of this story?)

Chapter 12 - M1911A1 .45 pistol full auto conversion, known as the "Swartz Conversion", named after a Colt Industries engineer. This was an experimental weapon that Colt developed themselves in the 1930s. The notorious gangster John Dillinger had himself one made, and it was able to fire up to 700 rounds per minute, using a huge, 25-round magazine. The United States tested prototypes in 1940, but found them impratical because of control, the speed with which the weapon would empty, and potential jamming issues the mechanism encountered. But something as compact as this was *literally* the stuff of fantasy and shocking to behold, back when most other machine guns were the size of long rifles and weighed ten pounds unloaded.

Chapter 16 - The Kent Automatic Garages existed from the late 1920s to the early 1960s. There were several locations around Manhattan, along with other cities such as Chicago, Cincinnati and Philadelphia, known as a "Hotel for Autos". With the boom of automobiles in dense cities after the First World War, architects were attempting all kinds of ways to store them while not in use. These skyscraper garages had electric automatic parkers, using the same principle and tech that modern car wash carousels use. Some locations could hold up to one thousand cars. A vehicle could be brought up via an elevator to an assigned spot, and then brought back down, without even starting the automobile's engine. After World War II and increase in size of newer cars, their large size cut the capacity of the Kent garages by half. And the onslaught of large-scale underground garage along with the ballooning size of sedans spelled the death knell for these Kent garages. The Manhattan locations went out of business and the buildings were rehabbed into office and condo buildings, but the super-structures are still visible if you know the addresses.

Chapter 19 – Pervitin were tablets the Germans supplied to their soldiers, particularly their pilots, which basically was an early version of crystal meth.

Chapter 22 – By 1943, New York's cabaret laws on the books made it so all musicians had to carry "cabaret cards" to be allowed to perform in bars, halls and nightclubs. These licenses could be pulled or revoked at the slightest perceived "offense", which basically blacklisted a musician from performing in New York City.

Chapter 23.5, 24 & 25 – The confession serial killer Albert Fish delivers is the word for word confession the fiend sent in a letter to the mother of Grace Budd, a ten-year-old child he murdered and ate. If it can be believed, the most heinous of the details of his letter were omitted because of the sheer horror. The physical letter was the piece of evidence which led to Fish's arrest, by tracking the letterhead on the paper to a boarding house that the killer had recently lived.

The method by which Josef Mengele murders Laszlo Strozek was the way he would euthanize the twins he would experiment on; by stopping their hearts at the same virtual moment, so he could then dissect the bodies and analyze the differences in the physiology of the twins. His goal was to figure out how to genetically engineer twins, specifically Aryans, so they could then impregnate a woman so to guarantee they would have twins, and then grow their population by double or perhaps triple within only a generation or so.

The grisly facts, points and stats Mengele discusses in this chapter sadly are all factual and correct, despite how unpleasant and disturbing they might be. Books like ***Auschwitz: A Doctor's Eyewitness Account*** by Miklos Nyiszli; ***Devil's Doctors: Medical Experiments on Human Subjects in the Concentration Camps*** by Christian Bernadac; ***Mengele: The Complete Story*** by Gerald Posner and John Ware; and finally ***Darkness Visible: Memoir of a World War II Combat Photographer*** by Charles Eugene Sumners, among many others, were invaluable for his dialogue to be historically accurate to the letter.

Chapter 28 – The M42 basement, known as the substation 1T & 1L, was in fact a top-secret sublevel far below Grand Central Terminal, considered the deepest in all of New York City. It houses the AC-to-DC converters that provided electricity to the terminal, the surrounding buildings that stood above the underground railyard, and the power to the track's third rails. This area was a wartime target as German spies hoped to stop troop movement around the Northeast by knocking out the converter turbines by throwing something as simple as sand into the machinery. For that reason, it was kept a secret and placed under twenty-four guard during the war years, and persons risked being shot onsite-no questions asked-if caught trespassing.

Epilogue – Josef Mengele, among many other Nazi war criminals, were able to escape Europe during the final days of the war simply due to the chaos that was ensuing, and the overwhelming number of civilians who were displaced during the conflict. Many Nazis simply blended in with the refuges. Mengele used his real name first but went unnoticed because the list of war criminals was still being compiled, and because serendipitously he did not have the usual SS blood group tattoo that almost all Waffen-SS Nazi members had under their arm. This tattoo denoted their blood type, which became an undisguisable war marker post-war, as identification of Waffen-SS. He obtained false papers and eventually escaped Germany in 1949, managing to obtain a passport from the International Committee of the Red Cross under another alias, which allowed him to South America, where he lived in obscurity as allied forces believed him already deceased. His family eventually joined him, and he lived comfortably until his death in 1979. Exhumation of his body and dental records confirmed the identity in 1985, and DNA testing again confirmed beyond a shadow of a doubt in 1992. His remains are now stored at the São Paulo Institute for Forensic Medicine.

ACKNOWLEDGMENTS

I promise not to make this nearly as long as my 2018 book's acknowledgment section was. That novel's backstory was a tale to tell.

This project was another in the cycle that was first written as a screenplay starting as far back as 2002. It was the alternate to *Blood in the Streets*; which meant that when I wasn't working on one *or* if I was stumped, I'd jump to the other and put the current one on the backburner so it could percolate, and once it came back to a boil in a month or so, and I was hitting the wall with the current project, I'd switch the pots. I pushed myself to work on one or the other incessantly.

But as with my other screenplay, *Blood in the Streets*, once completed, it was impossible to get anyone interested or frankly even to talk to anyone in the industry without an agent. To complicate matters, the only connections at my day job, Fox News, were to people who almost completely dealt exclusively with nonfictional, current-event, mostly political *literary* content—far from the material I was pumping out: historical fiction thrillers like *Morris PI* or a 1970s police genre pastiche, *Blood in the Streets*. (I go into the journey of how and why the script for *Blood* was turned into a book in the acknowledgments of that 2018 novel.) So, in 2019, *Morris PI* became the second to be adapted into a novel.

The original screenplay was set out to be a love letter to the world of the serials found within the movies and radio shows of the 1930s, '40s and '50s; to the private detective literary genre of the '20s, '30s, '40s and '50s and the legendary authors of that era; and to the subgenre of films of *my* childhood that took those ingredients and sprinkled a small element of the fantastical to make them all really cook with gas. Stuff like the *Indiana*

Jones Trilogy, *The Rocketeer, Dick Tracy* (1990), *Batman* (1989), and *Who Framed Roger Rabbit*. But I didn't want to satirize the content like an *Indy* or *Roger Rabbit* may do, but instead treat it with all the seriousness of a *The Boys From Brazil, Angel Heart, The Untouchables, Chinatown* or even a *Blade Runner*.

Another huge particular influence on this story was the series of gangster/thriller films made by Warner Brothers and other the Hollywood studios in the late 1930s and 1940s that seemed to always use that amazing summer-stock of actors playing the heavies. Men like Peter Lorre, Conrad Veidt, Sidney Greenstreet, Lionel Atwill, Rondo Hatton, Barton MacLane—heck, we can even throw Vincent Price in there for good measure due to his sheer villainy, among maybe a dozen other character actors of the era that have today sadly fallen into obscurity. From these geniuses we now have those classic archetypes they articulated and established from the source material, which went on to become the standard tropes of a genre, and almost become clichés of those very same genres because of the sheer over-frequency of use. Things that the hands of time have made us (as audience members) all but forget- where these particular "character types," "styles," and /or "devices" used within stories even originated from. The blueprints that were laid down by these master thespians that have been followed and evolved for almost a century now, I can only hope can be seen within this story here. And I hope, an educated eye may even guesstimate without a doubt, where those iconic actors above would be cast and who they would be playing within this story here.

Also, I have to mention a writer I discovered almost two decades ago that influenced subsequent rewrites of the original spec script drafts of *Morris PI*, a man named Chester Himes. I discovered him while doing deep dives into the pulp/private detective/crime/cop/police procedurals literature of the era, following the gradual evolution in those subgenres. I serendipitously stumbled onto his incredible and groundbreaking *Harlem Cycle* and his iconic detectives Coffin Ed and Gravedigger Jones, which were game changers. As influential as writers like Hammett, Biggers, Gardner, Chandler, and Spillane were for me- the unbelievable perspective and simplicity that Himes brought to the detective genre (for me, a guy writing a story that was *also* set within the world of Harlem roughly within the same era) was incalculable.

Now right off the bat, I have to thank the one who this book is dedicated to: my wife, Helen Grace. She had to read my early drafts and decipher the complication of what I can only gather is a self-diagnosed dyslexia. So, she'd give me a piece of her mind while pouring over it all my incoherent scribes, but she was there to get through it before it left the house. Thank you, my darling.

Next, I have to thank again the writer, producer, director, and professor, my friend, Robert J. Siegel. Bob was my professor while I was in film school. Upon graduation my idea was to write myself into the movie industry with a script (or two), and Bob was kind enough to volunteer his time to read revisions of this and the *Blood in the Streets* script. Those brainstorming sessions early on were clutch for me because in those days, he was the *only* outside person taking the time or even who cared to read my content and the subsequent revisions, and give me feedback. So once again, my hats off to Bob for being such an amazing person and friend.

I'd like to thank my parents Pat and Clare for their support as always, as well as my beloved sister Nicole, who continues to inspire me every day.

I'd like to also give a shout-out to my old film school friends, Aaron Lenchner, and my podcasting cohort in crime, J. Blake Fichera. The whole catalyst for the idea of writing a story like this—the original concept of a period private detective with a fantastical element injected in—was from my long talks with Aaron. It came from our mutual love for the detective genre both in film and in print, and particularly those crossover stories that added a dose of science fiction to the old tried-and-true formula. *Those* conversations were the original spark that got the little light on in my head that started to grow in intensity, and got me wanting to try my hand at a pulp detective yarn. (Though Aaron was pitching me aliens, and that was a little too crazy, even for me! Ha.) And Blake was there in the early days as I sounded out the plot, to bounce ideas off of, and was kind enough to read a draft in screenplay form, and his notes were spot on.

I'd also like to thank all my other friends, old and new, including a shout-out again to Kevin Pickney, who also read this back when it was still a screenplay and gave me notes. He then was also a sounding board for when I converted it from script to novel, always showing an interest in the story's progress. Along with all the rest of my friends, I'd like to thank you for *all* your support and reassurance.

Thank you to Anthony Ziccardi and his crew at Post Hill and Permuted Press. His help, support, and advice between books and getting this novel written and to market was fantastic. Thank you also to Heather King and her team. I'd like to thank everyone at Dupree Miller—Lacy Lynch and Dabney Rice. Thank you again to Felicia A. Sullivan for her help in the editing process. Also, a huge thank you to Clayton Ferrell for all his *detailed* help in the final stages. And a BIG thank you to Joe Rombi for all the last-minute help too. Thank you all.

This project was the second in a long, winding journey that also took nearly twenty years to come to light, and another which lived within my head for so long that it's still mind-boggling to me that this would *ever* be read past a few of my close friends, if any. Thank you everyone who helped make it all possible, and here's to one day getting this and its older brother *Blood in the Streets* turned *back* into screenplays and up onto the now-defunct silver screen!

ABOUT THE AUTHOR

Dion Baia was born in New Haven, Connecticut, where he grew up before moving to its suburb, Hamden. He graduated from SUNY Purchase College's Conservatory of Film in 2001, and immediately began working in the industry—specifically, behind the camera in television at Fox News, doing in-studio audio on shows like *Your World with Neil Cavuto, Hannity & Colmes, The Kelly File with Megyn Kelly, Hannity, The Story with Martha MacCallum, The Greg Gutfeld Show,* and *Kennedy,* among others.

It was during this time at his day job that he first wrote his 2018 book *Blood in the Streets,* as well as *Morris PI: The Men from Ice House Four,* both as screenplays, in an effort to break out from behind the camera and transcend beyond a technical capacity into cinema. After having no luck getting eyes on these works, and now two others—an inner-city gothic horror script and a revenge western screenplay—he decided in 2012 to translate *Blood in the Streets* and *Morris PI* into novel form.

In 2011, Mr. Cavuto began using Dion in front of the camera on his show, where Dion acted as a kind of comic relief in order to help promote the new channel the Fox Business Network. He periodically appeared, performing small, self-written comedic vignettes and encouraging viewers to call their television providers to "Demand It" ("It" being FBN).

That same year, he also began his podcasting career, and in 2014 cofounded the *Saturday Night Movie Sleepovers*, a nostalgic deep-dive into the films that helped shaped his life. He also graduated to contributing weekly to panel segments on *Your World*, which he still continues to do to this day.

In 2018 he published his first novel, *Blood in the Streets*, with Post Hill Press. In 2020, Dion costarred in the John Schneider comedic car chase adventure film, *Stand On It!* and will return in the 2021 sequel, *Poker Run*.

He currently lives in Westchester, New York, with his wife Helen-Grace; their son Babe, an opinionated Yorkshire Terrier; and their cat Tofu Roberta.